AIRBORNE ALL THE WAY

Here I am wearing a parachute! How the hell did I get into this situation?

"I swore I'd never jump out of a plane again," he muttered.

"We're jumping out of a boat, not a plane." Commander Lawrence fitted his own breathing mask over his face. "So technically, you're keeping your oath." He turned and muttered quickly to his three remaining men, using mostly hand signals that Kiernan could neither see nor concentrate on in his dark and panicking state of mind. "All right, we go in five! Four! Three! Two! One . . ."

Kiernan twisted the dial.

The device at his chest began to thrum.

He closed his eyes, gripped the switch with two fingers, and flicked it up.

Heavy pressure. Like being crushed in a trash compactor. His body turning to lead, dense as a star . . .

Then Switzerland vanished, and he was abruptly in a copper-green sky, falling like a meteor.

The dimensional shift never failed to startle him. The calm terrestrial night air was replaced by a stinging crosswind, nipping at his exposed cheeks and hands. He was plummeting—not into the calm waters of Lake Lucerne—but to a sprawling canyon of greenish stone. Freakish geological formations like mammoth tusks rose toward the sky.

BAEN BOOKS
by SEAN PATRICK HAZLETT

Weird World War III
Weird World War IV (forthcoming)

WEIRD
WORLD WAR
III

edited by
Sean Patrick Hazlett

BAEN

WEIRD WORLD WAR III

Copyright © 2020 by Sean Patrick Hazlett

A Baen Books Original

Baen Publishing Enterprises
P.O. Box 1403
Riverdale, NY 10471
www.baen.com

ISBN: 978-1-9821-2568-4

Cover art by Kurt Miller

First printing, October 2020
First mass market printing, October 2021

Distributed by Simon & Schuster
1230 Avenue of the Americas
New York, NY 10020

Library of Congress Control Number: 2020029382

Printed in the United States of America

10 9 8 7 6 5 4 3 2 1

✪ Dedication ✪

This volume is dedicated to my brother-in-arms, Captain Ralph J. Harting III (1976–2005), who rode honorably with the Blackhorse Regiment in the sands of Mesopotamia. You sacrificed your life so that others could live. One day, I hope to share a pint with you at Fiddler's Green, where the souls of cavalrymen rest forever. Allons!

This anthology is also dedicated to Mike Resnick, who passed in 2020. A legend in the genre, Mike always made a point of giving back to the science fiction and fantasy community by taking new writers and editors under his wing. I consider myself one of his "writer children" as do several of the authors in this collection. I owe a great deal of my publishing success to his mentorship and support. It is with both great pride and profound sadness that I have the honor and privilege of sharing one of his last stories in this anthology, my first as an editor. Mike's advice and encouragement were instrumental in bringing this project to life. Without his guidance, this anthology would not have been possible. Fare thee well, old friend.

CONTENTS

CONTENTS

★

Acknowledgments

"The Price" © 2020 by David Drake; "Shadow Rook Red" © 2020 by Brian Trent; "The Third World War" © 2020 by Mike Resnick; "Where You Lead, I Will Follow: An Oral History of the Denver Incident" © 2020 by Erica L. Satifka; "All Quiet on the Phantom Front" © 2020 by Brad R. Torgersen; "Anastasia's Egg" © 2020 by Kevin Andrew Murphy; "Tap, Tap, Tapping in the Deep" © 2020 by Dr. Xander Lostetter and Marina J. Lostetter; "The Ouroboros Arrangement" © 2020 by Martin L. Shoemaker; "Last Chance" © 2020 by Sarah A. Hoyt; "Oderzhimost'" © 2020 by Deborah A. Wolf; "No Plan Survives First Contact" © 2020 by Stephen Lawson; "The Scholomance" © 2020 by Ville Meriläinen; "It's a Mud, Mud World" © 2020 by Peter J. Wacks and Bryan Thomas Schmidt; "A Thing Worth a Damn" © 2020 by Alex Shvartsman; "Evangeline" © 2020 by C.L. Kagmi; "Bleak Night at Bad Rock" © 2020 by Nick Mamatas; "Zip Ghost" © 2020 by T.C. McCarthy; "Deniability" © 2020 by Eric James Stone; "Second Front" © 2020 by John Langan.

WEIRD
WORLD WAR
III

PREFACE

★

Sean Patrick Hazlett

I grew up during the Cold War, when the threat of nuclear Armageddon loomed over the globe like a metaphorical Sword of Damocles. The world was a bipolar one then, in which leaders and pundits gauged every geopolitical turn from the perspective of whether it advantaged the United States or the Soviet Union. Hundreds of thousands of US troops were stationed with their NATO allies in West Germany, poised to protect the Free World should Red Army and Warsaw Pact tanks ever advance through the Fulda Gap. Tens of thousands of US soldiers hunkered down along the DMZ on the Korean peninsula, ready for an invasion by a North Korean Soviet client state. The CIA ran clandestine and covert operations to thwart its KGB nemesis in locales as varied as Cambodia, Cuba, Angola, Afghanistan, Iran, and many, many other global hotspots.

And then there was the stranger or weird side of the Cold War—secret projects on mind control, remote viewing, and the investigation of unidentified flying objects. The US government ran a slew of actual projects such as MKUltra, Sun Streak, Grill Flame, Stargate, and Blue Book that explored these strange phenomena as the arms race extended toward increasingly esoteric ways of waging war. This anthology explores those areas and much, much more. It is a love letter to a bygone era, when the world was simpler, but the stakes were existential— where one errant signal could unleash the dominos of mass destruction.

What if the United States had gone to war with the Soviet Union? What if they had fought on land, sea, air, and the astral plane? What if alien technology had fallen into the hands of one of these rival superpowers? What if the Soviets and Americans had struggled for dominion across parallel dimensions? What if they had summoned demons to gain decisive advantage? What if these two global adversaries could transcend both space and time? How would the world have changed? What wonders could have been unveiled? What terrors could have haunted mankind from those dark and dismal dimensions?

Come closer, peer through a glass darkly, and discover the horrifying visions of World War III from some of today's greatest minds in science fiction, fantasy, and horror.

THE PRICE

★

David Drake

For what shall it profit a man if he shall gain the whole world, and lose his own soul?—Mark 8:36

I was sitting in the kitchen when I heard a car pull into the drive. I opened the side door and saw a yellow taxi with a Fayetteville address on it. A very thin man in slacks and a checked sport shirt had gotten out and was paying off the driver. He picked up his blue gym bag and turned.

God he was thin!

"Jesse?" I said.

"All there is left of me, Ab," he said as he walked to the steps. He still had the grin I remembered from when we were kids. "Gonna invite me in?"

"Come on in," I said, holding the screen door open with my right arm. "The Army called and said you'd be released at eight A.M."—the voice had actually said, "Oh-eight hundred," but I'd translated it in my mind—"but that you'd be making your own way here."

Jesse turned on the mat and we both watched the cab

5

back up the driveway. I said, "I thought the Army'd send a car."

Jesse's smile seemed tired as he followed me into the kitchen. "They would've," he said, "but they'd held me for another month after I got to Fort Bragg. I decided I didn't want to spend any more time in Army Green than I had to. I picked up a cab right at the front gate and paid him for both directions."

He'd have stopped in the kitchen but I walked him through to the living room and gestured him to the easy chair in the corner in front of the bookcase. It was where Dad had always sat.

I'd kept things like they were when Dad was alive. I'd have liked to keep everything like it was when we were kids. The world doesn't work that way; but I could save a bit.

"Do you want a drink?" I said.

"Does a bear shit in the woods?" said Jesse.

I brought a bottle and two glasses from the kitchen cabinet. "Jim Beam all right?"

His smile again. "It always has been," he said. "Mostly what we got in-country was Suntory. Which did the job."

He took a big swallow from the glass I handed him. I put the bottle down on the end table and sat on the couch myself, turning to face Jesse. "Ah . . . ," I said. "I saw you were limping a little, but you seem generally in good shape?"

"Generally, yeah," Jesse said, raising his left arm and rotating it so that I could see the weal running from the edge of his hand and onward until it disappeared under his shirt sleeve. "It goes right on down to the heel of my foot. It's not bad, but I'm glad it's my left side and not my right."

"Lightning?" I said. I swallowed. He looked and sounded like my kid brother, but he'd been flattened and bleached out somehow. His skin was very tan, but the irises of his eyes were barely visible as pale gray rings around his pupils.

"Yeah, sorta," Jesse said, bending forward to refill his glass. There were more bottles in the kitchen if we needed them. "I don't think they were holding me so much because of the burn but because they were worried about my attitude."

He leaned back in his chair and added, "I was starting to wonder if we were really the good guys."

"They thought you were pro-Red?" I said, trying to keep my voice calm.

"I don't know what they thought!" Jesse said. "I just know that in the field it's not always the way it goes into the reports. Guys find it hard to hide their thoughts from an interrogator when you're toasting their fingers. Sometimes it's even better if you toast their little girl's fingers. I had a lot of downtime in hospitals and I did some thinking."

I took a sip of my bourbon; I hadn't drunk much, but my mouth was very dry. "Jesse," I said, "it's not just field expedients. Your own team brought the evidence back. What the Reds are playing with threatens not only our philosophy but life. *All* life. It threatens the world itself."

He chuckled and poured more bourbon. He wasn't meeting my eyes. Abruptly he looked up and said, "Ab, I know what we learned when we were tasked to check a

Red site in Cambodia. But what if we'd been put on a US site in Mexico? What would we have found there?"

"You wouldn't find that the US is working with demons," I said deliberately. As I spoke, I felt a shudder of doubt that I didn't let reach my face.

Jesse snorted, but he said, "Maybe we wouldn't've. That's above my pay grade anyhow."

He looked down at the glass again. Then he said, "Look, Ab, I wanna talk. You must have clearances up the wazoo or you wouldn't know about that last mission, so I guess I can talk to you."

"I've got clearances, yes," I said, "but I'm sure people would tell me that I don't have a need to know."

Jesse shrugged. "I don't much care about that," he said. "*I* got a need to tell. You and I are all the Cathcarts there are, Ab."

"I'll listen," I said. I finished my glass of bourbon. There didn't seem much reason I shouldn't get shitfaced drunk if it seemed like that'd help me today.

He settled back in the chair. If I squinted, I could imagine that Dad had come back. Jesse looked a lot like Dad, but in personality he was Mom to the life: bright and sparkly, no way to pin down. And talent like heat lightning when he was on, lighting the sky up but out of nowhere.

"You know I've been in a patrol team," Jesse said. "Mostly in Vietnam, but it's not like there's border posts in the regions where *we* operate. This last one was into Cambodia, and it was real different. We were really just transportation."

"What do you mean?"

"'There was a Red site in Cambodia that the suits wanted to know more about," Jesse said. "It was shielded like you wouldn't believe. It was supposed to be in a temple—that was from HUMINT, I suppose, though how you'd get a human asset close to anybody who knows anything about a project like this is beyond me. Well, like I say, it's above my pay grade."

"The Angkor Wat Incursion back in May," I said. I hadn't been part of the planning, but you hear things.

"Yeah, an Airborne brigade and God knows what all else," Jesse said as he took another drink. "Somebody knows, I ought to say—I'm pretty sure it's not God. There must've been fifty thousand troops when you counted in the Thais. They went over Angkor Wat stone by stone and they found fuck all. Whatever they were looking for, it wasn't there."

"Were you involved with that?" I said.

"*Hell* no, that's not what they use us for," Jesse said contemptuously. "I heard they were thinking about running an armored regiment in from the east, but they didn't need to. They had enough already to protect their seers, really top-level people. They'd had to get them *really* close to be sure they weren't being blocked by shielding."

He shook his head in disgust. "They left a lot of people behind, too. The extraction was worse than the insertion, which it generally is if you try to go back the same way you came in. If you're that far away from your base you don't have a lot of choice."

He lifted the Jim Beam but put it back down when he saw how little there was left in the bottle.

"Go ahead," I said, starting to get up for another bottle. I was sure I had Scotch; less sure about bourbon.

"Naw, not unless you want it for yourself," Jesse said. "I didn't need the docs to tell me I was hitting it pretty hard even before the last operation. I knew they was right."

I sat back down.

"Anyway, what the suits were looking for wasn't at Angkor Wat," Jesse said to his empty glass, "but they got a notion about a patch of Cambodian jungle that didn't show any damned thing. Not on satellite or from a U-2, and not from their best remote viewers. But some clerk had found a temple on a French survey from 1887. The fact it couldn't be found there anymore convinced the suits that the Reds were really shielding something. This time instead of sending a brigade, they sent us—like they should've done at the beginning. They didn't have good enough coordinates to do the job mob-handed again or I swear that's what they'd have done anyway."

Jesse was right about that, though I didn't say so. He knew I was doing something hush-hush. I knew he was doing long-range patrols. Neither of us had really understood how close the other was to the top of his particular pyramid, though.

"Anyway, they tasked us," Jesse said. "The Dai-Uy, that's Captain Howes, kept us on course, but for pathfinding we had Manford and his number two, Slick. Slick would be lead pathfinder in any other unit. To screen us from remote viewing we got Mitch and Elgy. And there's me to see threats. You remember that."

"I remember in a poker game you always knew where the dangerous cards were," I said. "I watched you do it all the years we were kids. Sometimes I'd get a flash of it myself so I knew how it worked, but I don't think another human being could be as good as you."

Jesse grinned. "Yeah, I remember them card games," he said. "It comes in real handy in the field too. I can't read minds, but there's a link there. I don't think it's exactly mental."

"I've studied it," I said. "I'm sure you're right, but nobody yet has figured out what the other factor is."

Actually, I'd spent my whole working life on the question and I probably understood it better than Jesse ever would. But what Jesse could do was beyond any kind of electronic enhancement.

"They set us down in a clearing about twenty klicks out," Jesse said. "That's a hell of a hump through the boonies, but they didn't want to spook the Reds. The real problem was Doc, the seer we were taking along. That's what I mean about us being transportation. If they inserted any closer they'd have to use a brigade again. We were just there to get Doc close to his target."

"How much were you told about your goal?" I asked.

"Jack shit," said Jesse. He grinned and added. "Which is par for the course."

He didn't sound bitter.

"Doc was a wispy guy I thought was fifty or so, but close up he might've been younger and just lived hard. He was dead game, I give him that, but he just didn't have the strength for the job; the Dai-Uy next thing to carried him. I don't know how he did it, but recon is the kinda job where you just go on till you drop. The six of us on the team hadn't dropped yet and we didn't now."

I thought about the man across from me, the man I'd grown up with. I'd never thought Jesse was stupid, but he didn't have the sort of mind I do and I suppose I always looked down on him. I was suddenly very ashamed.

"Once the Dai-Uy gave us our direction, he didn't have an every-minute job like the rest of us, of course. One of the pathfinders led, with me behind him. Manford and Slick traded off on point; the other one took drag. Once—"

He touched the empty bottle again and grimaced. I started to get up but he waved me down again and continued, "Once we detoured around a Red picket. I was really *on* that day and felt 'em in plenty of time. The other time it was a three-man post and it was at the only gap in a band of bamboo. Nobody goes through bamboo, not even tanks. Elgy and I took 'em out. I had a CAR-15 and Elgy uses a revolver he picked up from the Air Force, a .357."

"Wasn't that awfully loud?" I said.

"It's okay in the jungle," Jesse said. "Anyway, we didn't have a choice this time. They were Khmer, not Viets. A lot solider to look at.

"We mostly don't talk in the field, but the Doc started whispering in the Dai-Uy's ear and he signaled us to hold in place. I don't know how long we'd been humping, and we'd never really known where we were going, so I figured we must be close enough for the Doc to work. Or anyway, he thought so.

"Me, I was just doing my job. Keeping my eyes and ears open, but mainly keeping my mind open. I wasn't getting anything hostile unless you want to count—"

He chuckled.

"—a whole shitload of leeches off to the west maybe fifty yards where I guess there was a swale. That's what I mean about not reading minds. There's not a lot of mind in a leech to read.

"Mitch carried the Prick-25. The Dai-Uy took the handset from him and called base to arrange an extraction. Then Doc sat down and crossed his legs. He put his hands together just like he was praying. For a moment I watched from a corner of my eye, but then I got too busy for even that. I felt the Reds start swarming like hornets out of a hole in the ground. Whatever Doc was doing, the Reds heard it loud and clear.

"Doc jumped up and shouted, 'Straight to Hell! They'll let all the demons loose on Earth!'" Jesse shook his head. He had a rueful smile. "You gotta understand, Ab, you *don't* talk on patrol. It's like the President steps out at a news conference and takes a dump in front of the cameras. Looking back, I guess I can't blame Doc much— he wasn't one of us, after all—but right then I wanted to wring his neck like a chicken.

"I gave the signal to bug out, which we did. We weren't going to make it, though, not with Doc; and if Doc didn't make it back with his info, we may as well have stayed in Da Nang. I could feel them coming for us, and they must've known right where we were. Mitch and Elgy weren't any use at all. We'd gotten Doc close enough to get through the best screening the Reds had, and when they'd been blown anyway, they brought out the best pathfinders *they* had.

"I told the Dai-Uy and he called it in. Base gave us a

vector, but then they told us to hold in place. That was fucking crazy. The Reds were gonna be on top of us in half an hour. I figured the suits didn't know their ass from a hole in the ground, like usual. I'd have just kept on humping, but the Dai-Uy said sit and so we did. I knew it wouldn't make five minutes difference anyway."

Jesse got up and walked to the piano, just to be moving. He opened the keyboard and closed it again. Neither of us had ever learned to play. Dad didn't either, but he'd kept it around anyhow. Maybe he'd thought Mom was going to come back some day.

"There was the loudest goddam bang I ever hope to hear," Jesse said. "I was squatting, trying to keep track of the Reds, and it knocked me over on my side when the ground rippled. It was a fucking Daisy Cutter so they must've laid the mission on at least twenty-four hours back. Loading a fifteen-thousand-pound bomb on a C-130 isn't something you do without a lot of prep.

"The Dai-Uy stood up and pointed, then lifted Doc again with an arm over his shoulder. Slick was leading this time. I was back at the end with Manford, having a bitch of a time following the team while feeling the Reds closing in.

"We weren't going to make it. I couldn't see the sky but it was past time for the monsoon to hit today. We probably wouldn't gain anything from that, but it might make it a little harder for the Reds to shoot up the bird extracting us. It'd probably make life harder for the pilots too, but I figured they'd prefer the trade-off. Not that any of us were getting a choice; and it wouldn't matter to me regardless.

"I shouted to Manford, 'Go on! I'll hold 'em up!'" I dunno what he thought about it, but there was no time to argue.

"I put my back to one of the emergents, a big tree even for this place. There were twenty-three Reds strung out for a hundred yards—way too close together except they knew as well as we did that it was a race now. I figure they were getting orders, same as the Dai-Uy had. The Reds chasing us may not have even known what the Daisy Cutter had been, but they knew we were heading for it and that it can't have been good for them.

"I could feel them holding back just short of where I'd be able to see them—but in this jungle that was about as far as I could spit. I threw my CAR-15 down on the ground—I didn't want the Reds to shoot me.

"I couldn't hear the Reds' discussion but there must've been one. Two Khmers stood up. One kept his Kalashnikov aimed at me while the other stepped forward and turned his rifle for a butt-stroke. I stuck my right hand straight up like I was pointing at the sky somewhere above the tree canopy. Maybe the Reds thought I was gesturing to them. What I was doing was adding the storm clouds to the circuit that was me and the twenty-three Reds.

"I didn't feel the lightning bolt, just a pool of white light that I was falling into."

"That was how you got the burn?" I said, gesturing toward the scar running up his arm.

Jesse shrugged. "I guess," he said. "I hadn't had it that morning when I got up. The next thing I remember is an old guy—must've been about eighty—leaning over me and chanting. I couldn't hear the words—I couldn't hear anything. It was about three weeks before my ears really worked right. I couldn't raise my hands either or I'd probably have grabbed him.

"I hadn't been unconscious that I know about, it was just the white flash and me lying on my back watching this old guy chant or whatever. He was in some kinda camo fatigues. When they debriefed us, they figured the uniform was Russian but none of us were spending a lot of time looking.

"The old guy's face splattered. Manford carries a twelve-gauge Ithaca he got his daddy to send him. He and Elgy had come back for me. They were damn fools to do it, but I'd have done the same thing if it was one a them. They carried me through the jungle, one by each arm. By the time we got to the clearing I could just about move my feet again but I was still a dead weight. I hadn't paid much attention to my surroundings before they picked me up, but Manford tells me I was ten feet from the tree I'd been standing by. The lightning had blasted the undergrowth all to hell. He saw a half dozen bodies. I figure there must've been a lot more than that because nobody was shooting at us as we ran."

Jesse threw himself back onto the easy chair. "We'd landed on LZs cleared by Daisy Cutters before but we'd never had 'em blow an LZ to extract us. I hope to God I'm never that close to another one when it goes off. It's liquid explosive and it spreads out before they set it off. There's no crater to speak of, just all the vegetation cleared away. There on the near edge of the clearing was one of them mother-huge Navy Sikorskys instead of a

Huey like usual. I was surprised the bird had stuck around so long because Elgy and Manford weren't exactly setting speed records carrying me there."

He chuckled, a broken sound. "When they tossed me in the door, I saw the Dai-Uy was holding Doc but Mitch and Slick each had a gun against the back of a pilot's helmet. Turned out the pilots had had orders to lift as soon as the seer was aboard, fuck the rest of us. The team didn't see it that way."

Jesse was breathing hard and staring at the empty bottle. This time I didn't start to get up.

"Well, it was back to Da Nang for the first leg and right away onto a DC-8," Jesse went on after a moment. "I don't know if Doc was still with us or not. I don't know much of anything at all about the flight. I know we touched down a couple times. They had me in a compartment with a medic. A doctor stuck in his head sometimes, and I saw the rest of the team too. I guess they had me gorked on some kinda dope.

"We landed back in the World at Travis, then it was one hospital after another for me. Finally, they told me they were letting me out." Jesse gave me a smile. "They couldn't find anything wrong with me, but they weren't gonna let me go back in the field. By then I was ready to be shut of them too. I asked them to let me out at Fort Bragg, so here I am. I figure whatever they've had you doing, we're still brothers."

"We're still brothers," I said. I took a deep breath. "Look, I'm going to tell you what I've been doing, because you're a big part of it. Growing up with you and seeing you spot threats showed me what was possible."

Jesse frowned. "You could do it too, Ab," he said. "I've seen you do it."

"I had just enough talent to understand what you were doing, Jesse," I said. "And to know that I'd never be that good myself. But it seemed to me that with the proper electronics, I or somebody with even less talent—and pretty much everybody has *some*—could get a lot better. And that's been my working life."

"Can a machine do it?" Jesse said.

I shrugged. "Better with some operators than others," I said. "If you're amplifying something, it matters where you start. And nobody ever is as good as Jesse Cathcart all by his lonesome. But at ports of entry and interrogation centers the machines work very well, or they did until last year. That's what they've had me—well, my team— working on, figuring out how the Reds have started getting through the checks. It was your information that gave us the key."

"You mean this last mission?" Jesse said.

"Yes," I said. "We were assuming the infiltrators were human. We didn't think the Reds could work with demons even if they were willing to take the risk. When we learned they could, we started on a completely different direction."

"Did it work?" said Jesse, pursing his lips.

"This was the first real test," I said.

Ferraro opened the door from the porch which Dad had closed off for a study. He was my chief deputy and had manned the equipment while I was talking to Jesse. "Yes, beyond doubt," he said.

There were two men in the hallway to the bedrooms and three more coming from outside through the kitchen.

They wore uniforms with no patches or insignia. Jesse started to change but he was still in human form when the bullets tore him to shreds.

The submachine guns were silenced, but the bolts slamming back and forth into the barrels sounded like a bell chorus. A bullet casing bounced off my cheek. I shouted in fright, though I doubt if anyone noticed. The air was gray with propellant smoke.

I stumbled into the kitchen. The gunmen moved out of my way, but my shoulder bounced off the doorjamb.

I made it outside and down the three concrete steps to the yard before I fell to my knees and vomited. I retched several times until there was nothing more to come out.

When I finally raised my head and looked, at least a dozen cars had pulled into the yard or were parked on the asphalt out front. A couple were sheriff's department with their blue lights on. I didn't envy drivers who were going to have to turn around here. The ditch on my side is pretty shallow but anybody who goes off on the other side is going to be lucky if he doesn't need a wrecker.

Schumacher was standing beside me. I didn't know how long he'd been there. We don't report to him exactly, but he's our liaison with the political side.

"Are you all right?" he said. He didn't look down at me.

"I guess," I said. I stood up very carefully. "I will be."

"I thought it might be fitting if the former members of your brother's unit provided the support team," Schumacher said, "since after all he was dead if they were called on to act. Their leader Captain Howes said I shouldn't even mention the thought to the others, because some of them might not be as controlled as he was."

"I'm sure he's right," I said.

"But Jesse Cathcart was already *dead*," Schumacher said. "He died when a Siberian shaman replaced his soul with a demon!"

"He was all that was left of their friend, Jesse," I said. "All that was left of my brother."

Schumacher looked toward the ambulance. The red light was flashing, but it and the rest of the vehicles had arrived without sirens.

"Well," he said. "I'm very glad we didn't need that. You know I was against you taking this risk. You're far too valuable to the country to chance losing you."

I looked at him. I said, "You've lost me as sure as if something had chewed my head off. I'm done with you and I'm done with the project."

I wondered if I could find Captain Howes to share a bottle with. A lot of bottles.

SHADOW ROOK RED

✪

Brian Trent

His flight to Lucerne, Switzerland, had been a night hop from Heathrow, and he'd barely stepped from the private airfield when his local contact pulled up in an unmarked car. The man looked grim.

"There's been a development," his contact—and friend of twenty years—said. "We're going straight to the safe house."

Kiernan Rayfiel of the Central Intelligence Agency climbed into the car, laying his briefcase in his lap. The night was dark. The car pulled away from the airstrip and was suddenly barreling along deserted streets, hemmed in by quaint houses. "This war has been one endless series of developments," he muttered. "What's going on, Charlie?"

"Our asset failed to check in. He *never* fails to check in."

Kiernan looked at his watch in the gloom. "It's just past three thirty A.M. Maybe he's asleep. Isn't that what normal people do? Sleep?"

There was enough starlight that the worry lines on Charlie's forehead were visible, not so different from the topographical maps Kiernan had been studying on his flight over. "Hell if I know. I haven't gotten eight hours of sleep since '74. Since . . ."

"The paradrop," Kiernan finished for him. Not wanting to dwell on that six-year-old memory, he added quickly, "When's the last communication you had with the professor?"

"Thirty minutes ago. He radioed me from the yacht, said he was typing up his report. I left to get you, and was pulling into the airfield when the guys at the safe house called." He touched the car phone.

"And?"

"The professor's boat had revved up and was making its approach to the safe house when it just . . . stopped. Like it had gone dead in the water. It's sitting there now, on the lake. And the professor isn't answering our calls."

Kiernan felt a thrum of tension. Charlie steered the car down one twisting street after another, arriving at last at the pier of a lonely boathouse on Lake Lucerne. There, they stepped out into a crisp, star-bejeweled night. Kiernan felt his breath catch as he gazed at the lake and the snow-capped Alps beyond it. He'd never been to Switzerland before—the Swiss were adamant about preserving neutrality in the war between NATO and the Soviet Union. Consequently, they tolerated neither CIA nor KGB operatives working in-country, and they kept a watchful eye on their borders—both on Earth, and in the shadowy parallel world next door.

Nonetheless, Kiernan had always wanted to see the country. In a world at war, it seemed to epitomize a safe haven. An idyllic pocket-universe.

Charlie pointed across the lake to a large yacht. "That's where the professor lives."

"*On* the boat?" Kiernan asked, surprised.

"Remember how paranoid he was at CIA briefings? He's gotten worse. Comes ashore for supplies and to deliver his reports, but otherwise stays out there."

"But the safe house is right *here* . . ."

Charlie shrugged. "Says it isn't safe enough for him, even under the protection of the Shadow Rooks. To be honest, I can't blame him. You know there's been incidents elsewhere. Bombs being gated into offices. People disappearing. And he knows the world of Arali better than anyone . . . been studying it since the Montauk breakthrough in '64. He's made more trips there than anyone."

Kiernan considered the solitary boat. "So he stays on the boat to avoid a Soviet snatch-and-grab?"

"It makes sense. You're seeing a lake *here*, but this same location in Arali—"

"—is a three-thousand-foot chasm," Kiernan remembered suddenly, and clicked open his briefcase to consult his dimensional readout box. The device resembled a compact Tandy TRS 80, attached to a vinyl strap for easy carrying. Its oblong screen displayed green vector graphics peppered by varying sea-level altitude readings and topographical features of Lucerne. Kiernan flicked a silver switch, and the graphics flushed red, showing a wildly different landscape on the other side of the dimensional membrane: Instead of a tranquil lake, a massive chasm stretched like a mighty scar, running south through the middle of the country. He squinted at the numbers there. "Three thousand and sixteen feet, where the yacht is."

Charlie took a deep drag of his cigarette. "Exactly. It's not like the Soviets can just walk out there, toggle into his yacht, and toggle back with him as their prize."

They were quiet for a while, steeped in the night's deceptive tranquility. Kiernan's gaze returned to the mountains again—only this time, he imagined he was seeing through them to the Swiss-German border. The latest satellite images had shown Soviet divisions massing in West Germany. The Red Army had renewed its offensive in the hotly contested Fulda Gap, but the storied American Blackhorse Regiment continued to fight tenaciously in the most bitter and brutal theater of combat since Normandy.

Not so long ago, Kiernan thought, *nukes would have been brought to bear to halt the Soviets. But now? There was no way to know if target cities were even viable targets anymore; the Russians were believed to have shifted essential military resources to secret Arali bunkers. They could just as easily toggle their tanks and troops out of harm's way, too, the instant a launch was detected. If the West exhausted its nuclear coffers on improper target discrimination, the Soviets could pop back in and launch a more effective counterstrike.*

The door to the boathouse swung open. Kiernan watched a black raiding raft glide onto the lake, pulling alongside the pier. A six-man squad operated the craft.

They looked like Navy SEALs, he thought. Yet they seemed unusually loaded down with equipment, even for a SEAL . . .

"These are our local Rooks," Charlie explained. "They'll take you to the yacht."

Shadow Rooks. The best of the best. Handpicked from elite JSOC units like the Navy SEALS, Army Rangers, and Delta Force, they represented a fifth service that focused on interdimensional warfare outside the Army, Air Force, Navy, and Marine Corps's purview.

Kiernan approached the raft. It was a low-lying craft with an outboard motor. Looked as if it had been plucked straight from the Mekong Delta. "Who's in charge here?"

The men eyed him with hard stares. The stares of men who were steeling themselves for the worst. One of them, a large, bald fellow, said, "I'm Commander Lawrence, Shadow Rook Red."

"Mister Thompson. I'm with the agency," he responded, using his cover name.

The man said nothing, making no effort to hide his displeasure. Kiernan could appreciate that. The Shadow Rooks had trained together for a spectrum of scenarios and contingencies. Having a CIA spook aboard added an unknown factor. A weak link to their chain.

On the pier, Charlie flicked away his cigarette. "Commander, the CIA has operational jurisdiction here. And Kiernan is the agency's presiding expert on Arali. We need him to assess the situation."

"But—"

"He goes with you, commander."

The raft's outboard motor sounded like a muffled chainsaw in the water as the seven men bore down on the professor's yacht. The main cabin lights were on, visible through tiny portholes. Beyond the yacht, Lucerne was a sleepy Christmas village by starlight.

At a signal from the Rook commander, the raft cut engines and glided alongside the target vessel. Before Kiernan realized what was happening, the men deployed in a coordinated spread along the deck, carbines low and carried at the waist in anticipation of close combat. Kiernan waited on the raft for the all clear, anxiously clutching the briefcase in his lap.

After a minute, one of the Rooks signaled him. He stepped aboard and went straight to the main cabin.

Commander Lawrence was waiting for him inside.

"The boat's empty."

Kiernan glanced around. What did the floating office of the world's premiere interdimensional cartographer look like? It was a mess—consisting of a desk, keyboard, and dot-matrix printer, but the floppy drive was gone. A file cabinet had been opened and pilfered. The professor had a cassette player, too; the floor was strewn with cassettes of Stravinsky, Bach, Mozart, and—oddly enough—Neil Diamond.

The yacht's controls were installed in the bow-facing wall. The bulletproof circular windows looked out starboard and port.

"The door was locked from the inside," Commander Lawrence reported. "We had to break it down to gain entry."

Kiernan surveyed the room. There was a cup of coffee by the yacht controls, still hot to the touch. "He was *just here*. We couldn't have missed him by more than ten minutes."

"Then his abductors couldn't have gone far."

Kiernan set his briefcase down, pulled out the dimensional readout box. Its red display glowed bloodily in the cabin. "There's a chasm around us. Maybe his abductors used a helicopter—"

"Not a chance," the commander scoffed. "Due respect, have you ever been to Arali?"

Kiernan held the man's gaze, fighting the urge to say: *I've stepped through the dimensional membrane on three continents, thank you very much.* Instead, he said, "Many times."

"Then you know about the constant, gale-force winds over there. Helicopters can't navigate that for long. Sure as hell can't fly in from Arali parallels of Moscow or Berlin. Besides, the Swiss watch their borders on both worlds."

"So maybe they grabbed him by boat. On Earth."

"We were *watching* the boat!" the man snapped, and—seemingly more to himself than Kiernan—added softly, "*I* was watching it approach. No other vessel was out there. I saw the yacht turning about, start its approach, then bang . . . the engines cut."

Kiernan tasted bitter adrenaline in the back of his throat. There were some wounds that didn't heal, he thought. Ever since his violent wake-up call to the grim new realities of combat in '74, he was cursed by a constant anxiety. What people in another age would have called "jumping at shadows." Crazily, he wondered if the expression was still around, and if so, if it had the same dismissive meaning as before.

Professor Lumet had been in his yacht. Behind a sealed security door. Yet someone had popped in like a nightmarish jack-in-the-box, grabbed him, and whisked him away.

The world was far more terrifying than the public understood.

Shaking his head, Kiernan said, "His abductors came in from Arali, regardless of the chasm there. I don't know how they did it. Maybe they built a three-thousand-foot step ladder. What's important is that your team get him back before . . . before . . ."

He trailed off as a peculiar sound filled the cabin. It was a sudden, persistent rattling. Briefly, he wondered if it was just the vessel creaking in the water. But no . . . this was distinct and close-at-hand. Kiernan paced around the room, aware of the Rooks watching him dubiously.

What the hell is that sound? he wondered. *It's like the clicking of many small teeth.*

Then he looked to the floor.

To the compact cassettes strewn over the carpet.

They were trembling in place, their spools vibrating in response to some unknown tremor.

Kiernan seized an edge of the carpet and yanked it back, exposing a closed storage hatch. Quickly, he swung the hatch open and there, in the narrow space, was a round, silver device with a display showing bright Cyrillic characters . . . counting down.

"It's a toggle!" he screamed, jumping back to his feet. "Commander—"

The Rook commander reacted with astonishing speed—an operator's speed. He seized Kiernan's arm, yanked him out of the room, shoved him toward the raft. "Fall back!" the man screamed. "Everyone fall back *now*!"

The air was suddenly thick. As if molecules were condensing around them, like an invisible python tightening in a death squeeze. Kiernan recognized the sensation. He leapt over the yacht's rails to the raft. Commander Lawrence leapt aboard next, followed by one, two, three of his men. The remaining operators were further back, running full tilt, eyes wide in fear . . .

. . . and then the yacht vanished.

The screams of the men were snatched away as they were pulled through the dimensional membrane.

The night was quiet once more.

A toggle bomb.

The activation hadn't just taken the yacht, but some of the water, too, leaving a temporary hole in the lake. The raft was near enough that it tipped, as if at the edge of a waterfall, nearly pulled along with the disappearance. Then the membrane closed, and lake water sloshed into the hole where the yacht had been.

Kiernan clung to the raft, heart pounding. He couldn't stop thinking of the missing men. Their strained expressions. Their bulging eyes. Their screams right before the universe shut the door . . .

Those men are falling to their deaths right now, he thought. *Screaming the whole way down . . .*

That was the challenge in toggling to Earth's shadowy parallel neighbor: The terrain rarely lined up. You might leave Earth from sea level and end up buried in a mountain. You might depart from a hilltop and find yourself falling into an abyss.

Using Arali as a new theater of war, therefore,

depended on accurate surveys of where it corresponded—and where it didn't—with Earth. Intelligence suggested that the Soviets had so thoroughly mapped their country from Moscow to Vladivostok that they'd managed to build interdimensional offices that lined up room for room.

The space race had been tense enough—and that had just been the threat of a Communist moon. Now, the anxiety was of red shadows pooling across the world's dimensional backstage . . .

Someone seized him by the shirt, hauled him to his feet. Kiernan found himself staring into Commander Lawrence's face.

"I said suit up," the man said. "We're going in."

Kiernan couldn't seem to make his mind form coherent thoughts. "What?"

Dimly, he realized that in his horrified stupor, the surviving Rooks had been busy, climbing into harnesses, discarding some pieces of equipment, and gathering up others. Now, the commander signaled one of his operators, and Kiernan felt his arms being pulled through a body harness, a heavy device strapped secure to his chest. He glanced down, saw the scratched plastic casing of a toggle activation unit. Its central display was simple—simpler than many toys Kiernan had seen in mall display windows.

It consisted of a large dial flanked by a single metal switch.

Yet within the casing was the most advanced technology ever produced by mankind . . .

"We're going in after the asset," Commander Lawrence explained. "It's your idea, and I agree with it."

"But—"

"If we don't grab him now, we lose him forever." Another nod, and Kiernan's arms were again being pulled through straps—this time, a parachute harness. He felt his blood turn to cold slush.

"Wait a second! I can't—"

"You said you've been to Arali before." The commander slung a pair of goggles and a breathing mask over Kiernan's face, fitted them securely in place. "'Many times,' I believe were your exact words."

"Under controlled circumstances!" Kiernan protested, voice tinny behind the mask. "At CIA listening posts! On stable ground!"

"In other words, you've used a toggle before. So you know: Crank the dial, let it charge, and flick the switch."

"But—"

"I just lost three of my men, Mr. Thompson. Professor Lumet is being smuggled through an Arali canyon while we waste time here. Have you ever paradropped before?"

Kiernan numbly touched the parachute's ripcord. "Six years ago . . ."

The commander hesitated, seeming to do the math and realizing suddenly the grim reality behind it. "I see. You deployed at what—a thousand feet? Clear conditions? Well there's no such thing as clear conditions where we're going. When we go through, you count to three and pull that cord, understand?"

Kiernan felt himself nod, heart pounding. Crazily, he remembered the set of orders he'd received straight from JSOC just a few hours earlier: *Rendezvous with Lumet in Lucerne, and debrief him on his latest findings.* It was to be typical CIA business. Sitting in a comfortable

room. Poring over dry research papers. Comparing topographical surveys. Drinking coffee. Firm ground under
his feet.

*And yet here I am wearing a parachute! How the hell
did I get into this situation?*

"I swore I'd never jump out of a plane again," he
muttered.

"We're jumping out of a boat, not a plane."
Commander Lawrence fitted his own breathing mask
over his face. "So technically, you're keeping your oath."
He turned and muttered quickly to his three remaining
men, using mostly hand signals that Kiernan could neither
see nor concentrate on in his dark and panicking state of
mind. "All right, we go in five! Four! Three! Two! One..."

Kiernan twisted the dial.

The device at his chest began to thrum.

He closed his eyes, gripped the switch with two fingers,
and flicked it up.

Heavy pressure. Like being crushed in a trash
compactor. His body turning to lead, dense as a star...

Then Switzerland vanished, and he was abruptly in a
copper-green sky, falling like a meteor.

The dimensional shift never failed to startle him. The
calm terrestrial night air was replaced by a stinging
crosswind, nipping at his exposed cheeks and hands. He
was plummeting—not into the calm waters of Lake
Lucerne—but to a sprawling canyon of greenish stone.
Freakish geological formations like mammoth tusks thrust
out toward the sky. It was a surrealist landscape, reminding
Kiernan of some nightmarish *Omni* covers he'd seen.

He sucked crisp oxygen through his mask.

The blood pounded at his wrists. In his head.

And for a moment, he was back in 1974.

Back in the ill-fated paradrop on the outskirts of West Berlin.

The news had come down that East German forces had somehow bypassed the Berlin Wall and were in the streets, capturing the French, British, and American sectors. Like the Greeks suddenly—impossibly—behind the walls of Troy. NATO quickly approved a combat drop of several thousand US paratroopers to try retaking the city, and Kiernan—a private stationed in West Germany at the time—found himself in a C-130 with his fellow soldiers, flying low.

Most of the C-130s never made it through Soviet air defenses. Despite a heavy bomber escort, Kiernan watched in horror as Soviet surface-to-air missiles incinerated the aircraft carrying many of his fellow soldiers from the 82nd Airborne. Only a meager four hundred souls survived long enough to make the jump.

They jumped at a thousand feet. He deployed his parachute. Landed in an exposed German airfield. No one around . . . the mysterious invasion had not yet taken that corner of the city . . . but he could hear the chatter of gunfire. Kiernan had taken his first step toward the front . . .

. . . and then the enemy planes appeared.

As if by magic. The night was split by wave after wave of enemy planes.

Soviet planes.

As the American troops stood amazed, the planes dropped their payloads. In seconds, the entire drop was decimated. Four hundred soldiers reduced to a couple dozen survivors standing amid hellfire and sizzling corpses.

The planes vanished as easily as they'd appeared. Pop! Gone like a nightmare before dawn. But then enemy tanks and troops toggled in, cutting off their retreat. The op dissolved into chaos, Kiernan and Charlie and their fellow survivors were forced into a desperate escape while being pursued by hostiles at every turn. In two days, ninety percent of Germany was firmly under Soviet control, and six goddam years later Kiernan still woke up, heart pounding, tasting the adrenaline, thinking he was back in the city, being stalked by interdimensional soldiers . . .

Until that infamous episode, no one had known the Soviets had toggle technology. It had been pioneered by the US in the infamous Philadelphia Experiment of '43. Too unstable and dangerous at that time. In '64, the Office of Naval Research resumed its study. Success was achieved. The first, tenuous steps were taken into a realm the team nicknamed Arali after the shadowy underworld of Sumerian mythology.

But no technology stays secret for long. Soviet scientists—working behind the Iron Curtain—had figured it out for themselves. And in 1974, they showed their hand. Operation Red Shadow. A first strike against NATO. The opening salvo of a new age of war.

That disastrous intelligence failure had been the reason Kiernan had joined the CIA in the years that followed. Intelligence was of the essence in warfare, Sun Tzu had written two thousand years earlier, and Kiernan wanted to do his part to make certain the US was never surprised like that again.

Kiernan forcibly buried the memory. Falling, the rip cord in his hand, he focused on the now.

The stinging wind.

The acid-green sky above him.

Far below, he spied the shattered remains of the professor's yacht. Like an egg smashed open on an alien landscape.

At a thousand feet, Kiernan pulled the rip cord. The canvas snapped open, and he was immediately jerked eastward by the crosswind. Around him, the Shadow Rooks swept down like little spiders riding strands of silk.

Kiernan narrowly missed a rocky spire and landed hard, spilling over, the chute whipping out ahead of him. It dragged him a hundred meters before getting caught on a mushroom-shaped boulder. He cut it loose and stood, trembling, regarding his surroundings. Sand hissed around him, driven by the relentless wind.

Gloam Canyon.

On Earth, Switzerland was a country of mountains, but its parallel coordinates in Arali were a frightful landscape of empty canyons dividing high plateaus. The largest of those canyons, Gloam, ran south from Lucerne to northern Italy like a knife wound.

Kiernan noticed two figures dashing toward him through the sandstorm—Commander Lawrence, and one other Rook operator. They hunkered down with him by the boulder.

"We saw a van moving south," the commander said. "Looked like a local vehicle, but my guess is it's not driven by any Swiss citizen. The Russians must have their own safe house in-country. I think I understand how they captured the professor." He hesitated. "You okay?"

Kiernan squinted through his goggles. "Just three of us now? What happened to the kid who helped me into this getup?"

"Sergeant Kuprin. I ordered him to take the raft to Kapellbrücke—it's a bridge that runs over the River Reuss. More importantly, it parallels an Arali cliff south of us. While you, me, and Sergeant Scott here pursue the enemy van, Kuprin can provide supporting fire, cutting off their escape."

Kiernan glanced to the overcast sky. He saw only dark green clouds, but he pictured what was occurring on Earth right now: The operator named Kuprin was driving a raft directly over their heads.

He looked back to the commander. Beyond the man's shoulder, the yacht wreckage lay scattered. "I'm sorry about your men."

"We all know the risks," the commander said. "I'll retrieve their bodies when we complete the op. Follow me."

Kiernan trailed the Rooks west, where the cliffs hemmed them in like a massive wall.

"We're right below where the safe house is," he muttered, consulting his dimensional display, tied by its strap around his right arm. He squinted at the cliff wall, not really expecting to see the safe house.

It wasn't there, of course; all he saw were exotic, precipitous peaks. Yet he spotted a narrow trail zigzagging down the cliff wall.

Commander Lawrence followed his gaze. "That's how

we travel back and forth between the safe house and canyon."

"It's why the CIA purchased the house," Kiernan remembered, nodding. "A natural footpath, letting our people come down here without Swiss authorities knowing. I understand the professor used it plenty of times to conduct his research down here. We . . ."

His words died as he saw the Rooks do a remarkable thing. The two men had gathered around what *seemed* to be just another boulder in the canyon. To his amazement, the "boulder" was revealed as a camouflaging tarp; the men tore it away to reveal an FAV—a Fast Attack Vehicle.

"Hop in," Commander Lawrence said, taking the wheel. As Kiernan rode shotgun, Sergeant Scott climbed into the back to helm a mounted fifty-caliber machine gun.

Then they drove off, turning south along the canyon in pursuit of their quarry. Driving at the head of the alien storm.

"Don't suppose you can tell me what the professor likes to do down here," the commander said as he navigated the FAV around several enormous boulders.

Kiernan adjusted his breathing mask. "You've accompanied him, right?"

"We have, yes. Each time he heads down, we act as chaperones. He sets up equipment, takes rock samples, scurries into caves like a rabbit. Never tells us what he's doing."

"And you've never asked?"

The commander jerked the wheel around a particularly massive boulder. Sergeant Scott clung to the mounted machine gun in the back, scanning for signs of their quarry ahead. "Sure, I've asked him. Told me it was classified."

Kiernan nodded. "And his answer stands, sorry."

"Don't mind if I speculate, do you?"

"Go ahead."

The commander drove around one natural obstacle after another with the skill of a professional stunt driver, and then floored the vehicle as they reached an open stretch. "I think he's looking for oil. That's the real goal here, right? The professor is tight-lipped, but he mentioned that Arali used to have oceans. No surprise: You can see the rocks here look like dead coral. So I'm guessing that whatever alien plants were here might have turned into oil. Vast, untapped reservoirs deep underground. That would have a big impact on the global stage."

Kiernan said nothing for a moment. "Interesting theory. But I have a question for *you*, commander: How the hell did the Russians grab the professor? You said you had an idea..."

"The van we're following? It must be Russian, outfitted with a toggle. Somewhere in south Lucerne, they would have gated in ... wherever the terrain let them access the canyon. They could have driven until they were directly beneath the yacht. Then a few of their *Spetsnaz* commandos exited the van and toggled to Earth. Still under the yacht, but now underwater. Swam up to the boat. Probably hopped onto the roof and toggled through it—like ghosts. Grabbed the professor. Toggled back the way we did—parachuting down with him in tandem to..." He broke off, leaning toward the windshield. "Contact dead ahead!"

Kiernan saw it. A gap in the sandstorm had opened; a dark van was revealed. It was bumping and jostling along the canyon floor at high speed. Only a thousand yards ahead of them.

Commander Lawrence floored the accelerator, closing the distance. "Tires!" he shouted to the sergeant.

At the mounted gun, Sergeant Scott opened up with the fifty cal. The van's rear right tire was shredded. The van swerved, its driver fighting for control.

"Remember that the professor is in there," Kiernan warned.

The back doors of the van flung open. A man leaned out, hefting something like a rocket launcher. Commander Lawrence cursed, veering aside as the man fired.

It wasn't a rocket launcher.

Twisting around in his seat, Kiernan saw a hole appear in the sandstorm where they had just been. It looked, for all the world, like a vortex of muddy water circling a drain. A sudden hole in reality.

"It's a toggle launcher!" he cried.

The FAV wove around a jutting spire of rock. Sergeant Scott squeezed off another controlled burst and the van's front right tire disintegrated.

"We got 'em!" the sergeant cried joyfully. "We—"

And suddenly he was gone

Kiernan was watching him when it happened. The enemy with the toggle launcher must have fired another round, because Sergeant Scott—along with the mounted machine gun, a fuel bladder, and a rear chunk of the FAV—was messily torn away. As if an invisible monster had clamped its teeth down and . . . and . . .

Jesus Christ, Kiernan thought, staring.

The sergeant's torso-less waist slumped forward, spurting blood into the FAV's two front seats.

The toggle effect had snatched the rest of him, pulling with enough force to rip him away above the waist.

His body has just burst into the River Reuss. It might wash up somewhere, and people will wonder where it came from . . . this legless corpse and portions of a vehicle and gun . . .

Somehow, Commander Lawrence kept control of the FAV. Kiernan saw the enemy van swerving wildly on its rims. It spun out, sideswiped a boulder, and flipped over.

The commander slammed the brakes and leapt out. Using a low boulder as cover, he aimed his carbine at the van. Kiernan followed him out into the storm, drawing his own sidearm.

The van lay like a downed animal. Sand skittered against it, blowing out like plumes of jet exhaust.

The back doors reopened. A man emerged—the bastard with the toggle launcher. He staggered into the wind. He froze as he saw the FAV. Raised the launcher.

A shot rang out. The van's windows were painted red as the man's skull blew open. He collapsed in place.

It took Kiernan a moment to realize that *he* had been the one to pull the trigger.

Another shape stumbled from the van; Kiernan almost reflexively fired again, and it was Commander Lawrence who stayed him. The shape emerged—*two* shapes, actually, one holding the other at gunpoint and using him as a human shield.

One was Professor Lumet. He wore a breathing mask

and goggles, and the same winter coat and gloves Kiernan had seen him wear in Arali expedition footage. The man resembled some out-of-place Arctic explorer.

The second man wore a full-body black toggle suit, complete with headgear that reminded Kiernan of World War I gas masks. It had a snout and two inset eye lenses. The man pressed a pistol to the professor's head.

"Put down your weapon!" Kiernan shouted, and switched to Russian: *"Opustite oruzhie!"*

The crack of a sniper rifle rang out from the cliffs above the canyon. Commander Lawrence grunted in pain and slumped to the ground.

Kiernan instantly dropped beside him, pulled him to the cover of a boulder. "Shit!" he cried, seeing the spreading patch of blood from the commander's shoulder.

The commander blinked behind his goggles. "There's another goddam Russian out here. Shot came from above."

Kiernan consulted the dimensional display box tied around his arm, flicked its screen to green. "We're almost directly below the Kapellbrücke. I'd say they had the same idea as you: They posted someone at the bridge to provide supporting fire."

Commander Lawrence pressed two hands against his wound, staunching the blood. "Then they've got us pinned down here."

Steeling himself, Kiernan risked peeking out from behind the boulder. It was just a glance; he pulled quickly back as a bullet thumped the ground where he'd been. But he'd seen enough: the gunman with the professor as hostage, slowly retreating up a natural ridge to higher ground. Trying to get above the waterline.

And then?

Then he'd toggle back to Earth with the professor.

They'll smuggle him out of the country. Maybe at the Swiss-Italian border. Maybe through some Arali fissure, cave, or pass the Swiss don't know about or don't have the manpower to guard. Hell, no one has the manpower to guard national borders on two goddam worlds. Strategy now involved multidimensional thinking...

Kiernan stiffened. He had an idea.

"Wait here," he muttered.

Commander Lawrence frowned. "Where are *you* going?"

"To get the professor. I'll come back for you."

And with that, he cranked the dial on his chest, flicked the switch, and—

—was underwater.

Beneath the River Reuss.

Cold water slammed him, knocking him about. Kiernan struggled to orient himself in the currents. He twisted, kicked off toward where he'd seen the ridge... where back in Arali, the Russian was making a slow retreat with his hostage.

The water was dark around him. His only light, in fact, came from his dimensional display box, glowing like a flare from where he'd tied it. Kiernan swam, lining himself up with coordinates just above his target's trajectory. He oriented himself again, hanging in the cold darkness. Then he cranked the dial on his chest, flicked the switch again.

He snapped back into Arali.

Three meters above the ground, as it happened.

Kiernan managed to land on his feet despite the height and a rush of river water appearing with him. The Russian spun around with his hostage, nearly losing his balance in the torrent of water swirling around his ankles.

Thinking fast, Kiernan untangled his dimensional box, wound back, and swung it like a medieval flail. The Russian was fighting to regain his footing when the blow caught him in the side of his head. He was knocked out cold, crumpling like a discarded doll.

Professor Lumet turned in wonder to his savior. Eyes wide behind his facemask, he cried, "Kiernan? Is that you? How—"

Kiernan threw the harness back over his shoulders, cranked the dial again, flicked the switch. Wrapping the professor in a bear hug, he was suddenly—

—back in the river.

The professor still in his arms.

Professor Lumet, to his credit, didn't panic in the water. Together, they kicked for the surface and breached. The Kapellbrücke spanned the river overhead. They pulled themselves onto the ancient wooden bridge. It was deserted at the early hour. The snowy peaks of the Alps were aglow with sunrise blushing in the east, painting the river and surrounding city in autumn hues.

Panting, shivering, Kiernan looked across the river and spied a raft out there, only fifteen yards away. The raiding raft! He could see that Sergeant Kuprin was aboard, too; the man appeared to be asleep, sprawled out, as if staring at the sky.

Shit, Kiernan thought. In the dawning light, he saw the hole in the man's chest, center of mass.

"There's a sniper nearby," he whispered to the professor. "We have to get you to the safe house before he reappears."

The professor gave an anxious nod. Together, the men ran along the bridge. At the end of its length they stepped onto the road there.

And froze in place.

A man had appeared across from them. Arriving like a magician's trick, in a swirl of greenish sand. He wore a full-body toggle suit like his comrades in Arali. A sniper rifle was cradled in both hands.

Kiernan stood, dripping and cold and afraid. The Russian raised his rifle. Squinted through the scope. Lined up his crosshairs.

In a burst of sound and movement, the FAV appeared and plowed into the sniper at high speed. The man was flung across the street, rifle skittering away. He flopped over once, and didn't move again.

Kiernan and the professor stared as the vehicle circled around and braked. Commander Lawrence sat in the driver's seat, looking pale and pained, but a little proud, too.

"Figured I'd come back for *you*," he said, and waved them over.

By 1900 hours, Kiernan was on a return flight to Heathrow. He'd barely had a chance to glimpse his idyllic Switzerland from the safe house windows. In a quiet corner office, he'd debriefed the professor, reviewed the man's latest Arali findings, and was then being driven by Charlie to the airfield for a hasty jaunt out of the country . . . all while local news percolated with stories of a hit-and-run in Lucerne, the body of an unidentified gunman, and shots fired near the River Reuss.

Kiernan leaned back in his window seat, a coffee clutched in both hands.

He wasn't thinking of the local news, though. Wasn't thinking of Switzerland, either. To his surprise, he wasn't even thinking of the infamous paradrop of '74—a memory never far from reach—when Operation Red Shadow had first unfurled its terrible claws.

Rather, he sipped his coffee and reread the professor's report. It lay opened before him, printed out in dot-matrix text on a spool of white-and-green paper. Kiernan trembled as he read, and reread, the opening lines:

My explorations of the cave system beneath the canyon have now yielded the proof I've long suspected, and which the attached photographs and documentation will attest. What the United States, and indeed the rest of the world, will do with this I can only wonder. But here's the situation:

Arali is *not* a dead world.

There are things slumbering beneath it.

And they're beginning to wake up.

THE THIRD WORLD WAR

✪

Mike Resnick

Nobody saw it coming.

After all, why would they? We're not talking about Russia here, or China. Think smaller. *Much* smaller.

Or, better still, let's start at the beginning, which most historians agree was on June 20, 2031, when Bangladesh refused to allow a United States fighter jet the opportunity to land and refuel.

Then, on August 17, Cambodia uttered a strict warning to the effect that the United States was forbidden the use of its air space.

Ghana followed suit, and even little Burkina Faso got into the act, demanding that the United States close its embassy there.

"This is ridiculous!" said Secretary of State McTavish.

"I agree," chimed in Secretary of Defense Willoughby. "It's like walking barefoot over a series of anthills and being nibbled to death."

President Cavin sighed deeply. "We'll protest at the United Nations and elsewhere, but we'll honor their

47

requests, at least until we can find out what's behind them." He stared around the room at his assembled cabinet. "Find out what you can."

Surprisingly, it didn't take that long.

"Well?" said President Cavin when he had assembled his cabinet again six days later.

"It strains credulity," said his secretary of state, "but there is a new coalition in the world."

"A new power?" asked the President.

"I wouldn't go that far," was the answer.

"Well, who's in it and what do they want?"

"Let me begin by assuring you that I am telling the truth, sir," said the secretary. "That this is not a joke."

"Go ahead."

"The power—and I use the word advisedly—confronting us wishes to be known, formally, as the Twice-Named Coalition."

"Twice-named?" repeated the President, frowning.

The secretary of state withdrew a paper from his vest pocket, unfolded it, and glanced at it.

"It seems to be a coalition of countries that have had their names changed in the past century or two."

The President frowned. "Explain."

"The member states are Burkina Faso, which was Upper Volta; Botswana, which was Bechuanaland; Cambodia, which was Kampuchea; Ghana, which was the Gold Coast; Malawi, which was Nyasaland; Zimbabwe, which was Southern Rhodesia; Zambia, which was Northern Rhodesia; Bangladesh, which was East Pakistan; Benin, which was Dahomey; Ethiopia, which was

Abyssinia; Sri Lanka, which was Ceylon; and Iraq, which was Mesopotamia."

"What the hell do these countries have in common, besides the name changes?" asked the President.

"They're all as poor as church mice," replied the secretary of the treasury. "Not a day goes by in which two or three of them aren't begging for money, which of course they have no intention of ever paying back."

"So they're threatening war if we don't finance them?"

"It seems like that, sir," answered the secretary of defense.

"Okay," said the President with a deep sigh. "What'll it take to win a war?"

"I'll need some time at the computer," answered the secretary of the treasury.

"Go," said the President. "This meeting is suspended until you come back with some figures."

It took just under forty-one hours.

"I have the numbers, sir," said the secretary of the treasury.

"Well?"

"If we go to war, I think we could conquer every member of the coalition for just under eight billion dollars—and that's assuming they put up a fight, which I am not at all convinced they would."

"Okay," said the President. "Let's get on to the operative question. We agree to go to war. We conquer all of them in three or four calendar months, which seems rather lengthy, but we'll use it for the sake of argument. Now, once we're in control, how much is it going to cost us to maintain this new—and obviously impoverished— empire?"

"I anticipated your question, sir, and have already conferred with state and defense on it."

"And?" said the President.

"Approximately four trillion dollars a year, sir."

"And as things stand now, what are we spending with no war and no dependent states?"

"One point two trillion a year."

"Interesting," said the President.

"So have we an answer to the Twice-Named Coalition?"

"We do," said the President. Suddenly he smiled. "And I don't think they're going to like it."

On November 2, 2031, the United States of America surrendered and acknowledged defeat at the hands of the Twice-Named Coalition.

The history books still refer to it as World War 2.001.

WHERE YOU LEAD, I WILL FOLLOW: AN ORAL HISTORY OF THE DENVER INCIDENT

✪

Erica L. Satifka

Victor Delaney, high school teacher:
Oh, I certainly do miss Follow the Leader. It wasn't your typical cell phone game. Instead, it was what NewzBuzz.com called an "augmented-reality" app, meaning that the elements of the game were incorporated within the real world. You'd look through your phone and see all kinds of things that didn't exist. The trees would be dripping with colorful candies, and there were little creatures you could trap with this pixie you walked around on a leash. Oh, surely you remember what it was like. I know I do.

In addition to shaking trees and collecting creatures, there were Instructions. These were a later addition to the game, but they really enhanced the experience. A golden envelope would slide onto the screen—it usually did that

51

about two, three times a day—and assign you a task. All of these Instructions earned you points if you chose to take them on, and most of the time people did. There were regional leaderboards for people who carried out the most Instructions in a week. Usually the game would ask you to do things like snap a picture, or give a stranger a compliment, or take the long way to work. It always seemed to know when we did these things. I guess it tracked us from satellites or some such thing.

The principal tried to ban Follow the Leader from school grounds when it was at its height of popularity. She called it a distraction, which was true. But it was a distraction that roughly four fifths of the country engaged in. You just can't ban something with that kind of reach.

And of course, everyone on staff played it too. We're only human, right? Hell, if they hadn't shut down the server that hosted it, we'd all *still* be playing Follow the Leader, even after the big kablooey.

Sorry, that was insensitive of me. I should never refer to the Denver Incident that way. Can you cut this part out, please?

Follow the Leader was a real good thing for the kids, socially speaking. It forced students to work together to complete Instructions, so that a whole class could get their names up on the leaderboard. Somehow the Russkies managed to drill cooperation into their heads better than the American school system.

Sometimes I think that it's still helping us. Rebuilding is going well, ahead of schedule in fact. Almost like older people learned a little something about working together from the game too.

Russia may have beaten us, but they haven't *beaten* us if you know what I mean. You know what I mean?

Abigail Foster, retiree:
The first time I saw the game? We were at a park, this pioneer-themed historical recreation down near Lakewood, Colorado. I'd taken my daughter-in-law Dakota and my grandson Isaiah out on what I thought would be a fun, educational day trip. Isaiah didn't look up from his phone the whole time.

Dakota snapped at him, but I asked him what he was looking at. You can't just snap at children. Have to get down to their level. I'd braced myself for something scandalous, something a teen boy with too many hormones and not enough sense would have on his phone. Surprisingly, he showed me his screen. He said it was a new game called Follow the Leader and explained the mechanics of the game. He said his mom played it too. That *everyone* did.

Well, I didn't play it. But I wasn't about to pass up an opportunity to interact with my grandbaby, even if it was through a game. After the park—which wasn't all that fun and barely educational—I immediately bought a new, better phone and downloaded the game.

I created my character—oh, she was a cutie pie, with blue hair and a lion's tail—and added Isaiah as a friend. He was *so* happy that I played the game too. Who says there's a generation gap?

For the two years that Follow the Leader ran, Isaiah and I got up to all kinds of shenanigans. We even formed a battle party at the local playground with other grandmas and their grandkids. Those were some epic days. Isaiah says that word a lot, "epic."

Isaiah doesn't play games on his phone anymore. He's just so listless ever since his mother ran off to play Good Samaritan in Virginia. I wish he'd lighten up. It's not like *we* lost anyone in the Incident, for goodness' sake.

Julianne Kowalski,
Airman (dishonorably discharged):
I hope you don't mind my attorney being here. Even though my part in this Russian plot is small—barely significant, really, when you think about it—we don't want to take any chances.

So, where do I begin? Life on a military base during peacetime is boring, so to pass the time we'd play games. And the game that everyone was playing at the time was that "augmented-reality" cell phone game, Follow the Leader. What else were we gonna do cooped up on a military base?

Why do they call it the Denver Incident, anyway? Warren Air Force Base is nowhere near Denver. It's in Wyoming. If I had to guess, it's probably 'cause the missile was launched from a 90th Missile Wing silo in Northern Colorado.

The game shouldn't have even been playable on the base. Follow the Leader was built around publicly available maps found online, and this is a classified site. Maybe a drone mapped it out, or maybe someone smuggled in surveying equipment. There were never as many candies and creatures on base as there were in the civilian world, so the only way we could get on the leaderboard was by completing Instructions. Hundreds and hundreds of Instructions.

Even though we *definitely* weren't doing anything wrong, we still hid our gaming from the colonel. He found out anyway, of course—because he played it himself! We caught him in the mess hall performing an Instruction: swapping the position of the knives and forks. He couldn't very well ban the game after that, unless he wanted to quit playing himself. And since the colonel was ranked fifth in the state of Wyoming, *that* wasn't going to happen.

There wasn't any one Instruction that led to the so-called "incident." Sure, I'm the one who pressed the button, which is why I get to be on all those lovely news websites with the ever-increasing death toll on a ticker below my picture. Seriously, I should sue them for libel. It's not like I knew it was *the* button.

No, I don't feel any guilt. Never did. I know some others didn't take it so well, even if their place in the overall scheme of things was much smaller than mine. One in every ten military personnel stationed on this base has committed suicide. I guess some of us are just made of stronger stuff, huh?

If there's any blame here, then it goes to all of us. But it's not just us. Everyone played Follow the Leader, literally everyone. Even all the people who died in Washington. So isn't it logical to think that some of the guilt even falls on them? That's just the way I see it.

I'm not in the Air Force anymore, but I still live near the base and I'm not planning to leave any time soon. Everyone knows me here, both the airmen and the townies, and they know I'm not a mass murderer. They all know I was just following Instructions.

Reverend Caleb Jefferson, Presbyterian minister:
"God moves in mysterious ways." That phrase is a cliché at this point, and it's not even from the Bible. Some English poet wrote that. It's true in a tautological sense, of course: No human truly knows the will of the Lord.

Here in West Virginia, we're near the edge of the fallout zone, so we've had some losses. For a while, there was a funeral damn near every day. That's leveled off, though. I spend most days here at the refugee camp, trying to heal the broken spirits of those who've suffered so much in the past month.

The government says the Russians made this game. Some other men and women of God claim it was the Devil working through those programmers who then in turn worked through us to achieve his own brutal ends. Me, I believe it doesn't matter. Four million people are dead, and another million will die before the year is out. Russians, Satan, God . . . who cares?

I guess you could say I've lost my faith, and you wouldn't be wrong. But I'll still be showing up at that hospital tomorrow, and the next day, and the next. My parishioners need me, but not as much as I need them.

Olaf Andersson, programmer:
Follow the Leader wasn't a pretty game.

It wasn't entirely our team's fault. PlayMore—that was the name of our start-up—had already released four mobile games by then. While they weren't nearly as complex as Follow the Leader turned out to be, each was a small work of art. The glowing reviews bore this out.

The problem was, the games weren't selling. Despite superior graphics and animation, the five of us in PlayMore hadn't made back any of our initial investment, and we were nowhere close to being able to draw a salary. We almost broke up the company. My father would certainly have liked that; PlayMore took up the entire first floor of his house.

And then, a miracle happened, or at least it seemed like a miracle at the time. Dagmar had been sketching out ideas for a game that used the world itself as its playing field, immersing the player in a sort of augmented reality. She'd saved it in the cloud, which was encrypted and password protected. Somehow the storage was breached and Dagmar's preliminary coding was discovered by someone who wasn't one of the five PlayMore employees.

The email was brief. The person who wrote it, who never signed their emails for the entire time we were in contact with them, offered to invest in our "quality-type game" in exchange for partial control of the coding. What they offered . . . well, I won't go into specifics, but it would have been enough money to make me, Hakim, and Dagmar very rich indeed.

Dagmar didn't want to do it, even after seeing how much they planned to pay us. This was *her* game idea, *her* baby, and she didn't want to give some stranger creative control. I'm ashamed to say that the rest of us in the company voted her down. We couldn't pass up the kind of money the angel investor was offering, and he or she or they had already deposited half of our payment into the PlayMore PayPal account.

Dagmar's original concept had been a horror-themed game which superimposed zombies and ghouls over a real-world environment. You'd pick them off with a crossbow. Our benefactor had a different vision. The zombies became colorful trees that you'd shake to receive rewards, and the crossbow became a leashed pixie who generated the dust you needed to defeat the "bad guys," a gang of wood sprites who were less scary than ladybugs. Dagmar quit the moment she saw her edited sketches. She wasn't interested in "kid stuff."

But the rest of PlayMore—me and Hakim in Stockholm, and our two contract employees in Melbourne and Taipei—we carried on. It was just *so much money*, you know? We dutifully sketched out the game our investor wanted on Dagmar's augmented-reality code. Then he or she or they said the game needed to be ready in five weeks.

So, we cut corners. Fewer varieties of trees, the pixie was noncustomizable, and we didn't bother to edit the "Instructions." They were seeded into the game exactly as the investor had written them, which is why the grammar is so bad.

We were all ready to release a new patch when the Incident happened. Were less than twelve hours from doing so, in fact. I wonder if it would have changed anything if we would have been able to push it through. I probably shouldn't wonder about that, though, unless I want to wind up like Hakim. He slit his wrists a week ago.

Dagmar works for Nintendo now. I heard she's developing a zombie game. Good for her.

Isaiah Foster, student:
For a while, I really liked going to Gramma's house. Between me, her, her friends, and their grandkids we could do a lot of fighting. Our battle party even made the state leaderboard a couple of times.

Gramma watched me all the time back then. Mom was out a lot, since she had a waitress job in the morning and another job as a janitor at night. Sometimes I didn't even see Mom for a week, but I know she was just providing for me.

Mom doesn't live here anymore, and she never calls or writes. Gramma said that she moved to the area around D.C. to help with the rebuilding. I like that I have a mom who'd do something like that.

Diana Zhong, reporter (on indefinite sabbatical):
Out of our whole newsroom, I was the only one who survived. Most of the time, I wish I hadn't.

I'd been working for NewzBuzz.com for three years before the Denver Incident. I telecommuted at first, writing quizzes. Two of my biggest hits were "Which *How I Met Your Mother* Character Are You?" and "We'll Tell You How Old You Are from Your Soda Preferences." The second one in particular got quite an audience, lots of engagement on Facebook and other social media platforms. That's what NewzBuzz really wanted, quizzes that would be interesting enough to post to your feed so they could sell you ads geared to your interests as revealed through your answers to the quiz. It wasn't what I expected to do with my journalism degree, but at least it paid enough to cover my student loans.

Then, Follow the Leader hit the scene, and it was such an instant hit that NewzBuzz decided that they'd put a reporter solely on the augmented-reality beat, with a hefty pay bump. You're looking at her.

I flew from Sacramento to D.C., and rented a postage stamp of an apartment in Takoma Park with three other women. NewzBuzz said they needed me in the main office, and well, they were certainly paying me enough to live there.

For the next year and a half, I buried myself in the world of Follow the Leader. In addition to my work at NewzBuzz, where I wrote gripping articles like "How to Pick Up That Hottie You Saw While Completing Instructions" or "How to Adjust Your Display Based on Your Astrological Sign," I also made a little bit of side money writing about Follow the Leader for video-game blogs. I was churning out at least three pieces a day, although I could pad them out with gifs. What did reporters ever do before gifs?

I was addicted to the game, of course, what with it being my job and all. Some days I'd clock a good fifteen hours on the game map, completing every Instruction I received. It was an Instruction that saved me that day.

While the missile was streaking its way across the Appalachians, I was in my cubicle banging out a listicle about the five best trees to shake to boost your pixie dust. The familiar yellow envelope slid onto my phone screen. Whereas before Instructions had led me to new undiscovered features in the game world—things I found a few hours before everyone else, almost like the game wanted *me* to write about them first—this one told me to head to a broom closet in the basement. It emphasized that I should come alone. The word "alone" was in magenta and was underlined three times so I'd *know* it was important to follow that part of the Instruction.

So that's why I wasn't with the others when the NewzBuzz building fell along with everything else in D.C. The pocket of air inside the closet was just large enough to sustain me until the emergency crews came in with their equipment and combed the area for survivors. The last thing I saw on my phone before they whisked me away to surgery was a digital trophy made out to "one of our largest friends." A fucking trophy, Jesus Christ.

I don't play games anymore. These hook hands aren't great at manipulating menus and direction pads for one thing, and for another I just feel kind of paranoid. Why did the game save *me*? Am I its "largest friend" because I wrote articles about it, articles that were highly shareable and, therefore, exposed millions to the game? Does this mean I'm responsible for the Denver Incident in some small way?

I go outside and walk the streets of Sacramento when I can. I try to do it when there aren't many people around. Sometimes you just don't want those looks of pity.

General David Alvarez, United States Army:
I signed that order, yes I did. The order that turned over the United States government to General Dashkova and her allies. It simply had to be done, you realize. We had

no idea what insane Rube Goldberg situation the Russians planned to set off next. They'd already vaporized D.C. and nearly every official in our government, including Congress and the President and Vice President. The only surviving cabinet member, poor old Secretary of the Interior Skip Hawkins, died of a heart attack when he saw the footage. He was ninety-one, probably never played a cell phone game in his life.

Oh, there's no doubt in my mind that the Russkies are behind it, especially once we discovered that the ISP address of the emails sent to those Swedish programmers led straight back to Moscow. Can't trust a Slav. Follow the Leader was all a sick long game designed to trick US Air Force personnel into launching a nuclear missile right at the Capitol building while Congress was in session, without even knowing what they were doing. Not all that surprising though the zoomies have always been less disciplined than the other services.

This isn't over, no matter what that surrender document says. The Russkies haven't licked us yet. It's only a matter of time before America stands tall once more with a new elected government that can lead us from tyranny. Our remaining nukes may be decommissioned, but our *spirits* are still online.

Dakota Foster, aid worker:

I'll never pay back what I did. Never. But I guess this is a start, a drop in the bucket. It doesn't mean much—it doesn't mean anything—but I'm here anyway. I couldn't *not* come.

The ironic thing is, I didn't even play Follow the

Leader that often, and I tended to let my Instructions pile up. The way they work is that you have a set amount of time to complete each one, which is different for every Instruction. After that, the Instruction fizzles, and your avatar loses a little bit of its life force. Maybe you'll even drop a level. Some people took the game really seriously; my mother-in-law, Abigail, for instance.

But me? Nah. Just checked it when I happened to think of it, which wasn't often. Only did the Instructions that seemed easy enough and wouldn't take up much of my time.

The day of the Incident, I'd just gotten to Warren Air Force Base from my other job at the diner. Thank goodness Abigail was around to watch Isaiah. I could never have gotten through the horrible year after Ted's passing without her.

Of course, then I wouldn't have had any time to play stupid video games on my phone, either. So perhaps that was a mixed blessing.

My role was slight, the attorneys tell me. They pinned most of the blame on that Kowalski woman, but even she didn't face any punishment. Nothing they did to her would have brought back four million people. It's despicable to think that anything could.

Airman Kowalski pushed the button. But she also had good reason to think that it was disabled. There's a long, long list of checks and balances that goes into a nuclear facility, hundreds of fail-safes, layers upon layers of protection. You don't just press a button and launch a nuke. That's not how it works. There were dozens of smaller Instructions that brought the button Kowalski pushed to life, and a number of others that pointed that nuke straight at the Capitol. And one of them was mine.

I was just heading back from break when an Instruction popped onto my screen, one of those canary-yellow envelope icons. I opened it. It was a time-restricted Instruction, one set to erase itself within thirty seconds, and it came with a million-point bounty. That score would have jumped me about twenty levels, to the very top of the Wyoming leaderboard. Maybe I would have even made the national one.

Go into the next room, it said, *and delete the last line of code from the computer closest to the door.*

The smart thing would have been to ignore it, or maybe alert the colonel in charge of the base. To me, this seemed *way* outside the bounds of what a normal Instruction should be. I'd gotten a couple of these weird, invasive Instructions lately, always when I was on the base. I didn't get them in town. That should have told me something.

But the airmen here did this kind of shit *all the time*. I'd seen them move shredded papers from one bin to another, snap pictures in restricted zones, and read off serial numbers and coordinates into their phones. At least, I think they were serial numbers and coordinates.

How do you blow a whistle when you're not sure anyone's actually doing anything wrong? You don't, at least not if you have two jobs, a kid, and a mountain of debt. I couldn't lose this job. So I let all these weird little adjustments slide, especially after I saw the colonel doing them too.

I followed that Instruction. I deleted that code. In my defense, I also left the man who worked there a note telling him what I did and why I did it, but the investigators never found that. Maybe a different person got the Instruction to destroy my note, or the programmer himself sabotaged his own code even deeper in yet another Instruction. I'll never know. Even having the code up on the screen was a violation. Likely, the programmer had gotten his own Instruction to leave it. We'll never know for sure, since he killed himself afterward along with so many others at the base.

Anyway, that was the code that angled the nuke toward Washington, D.C.

I'm stationed at a refugee camp in Beckley, West Virginia, which is just outside of the contamination zone. We try to make things here as nice as they can be. I help out in the medical ward, mostly, tending to children from Alexandria who've suffered radiation burns from the fallout, and Baltimoreans who got in car crashes because they were distracted by the mushroom cloud blossoming over the Potomac River. D.C. itself is a total loss, aside from a few stragglers who managed to hole themselves up in basements at just the right time. One of the women from D.C. who came through here said Follow the Leader told her where to hide. She'd just lost both her hands, though, so she was probably delusional.

I tell everyone I meet here what part I played. I figure it's the right thing to do, because maybe they wouldn't want to be treated by a person who had a small but significant role in blowing them up with a nuclear bomb. But so far, nobody cares. I swear that some of them are more concerned about losing Follow the Leader than they are about the bomb.

I don't use a cell phone anymore. Trust issues, you understand. Isaiah and Abigail know where to send letters. If you head back to Wyoming after this, please give them my love.

General Valentina Dashkova, interim head of Russian Holdings in North America (as told to translator):

The last thing I ever expected was the surrender of your country. That fat *mudak*, General Alvarez, barged onto the beach with a handwritten paper, begging me to sign. I was still in my bikini. Talk about sloppy.

I wasn't even here on official business; I was vacationing in Hawaii with my brother and his kids. But I was the only high-ranking general in the Russian Armed Forces in the United States at that time, so it fell to me to sign the document. I did so, barely aware of what I was signing, and then there were all these news cameras in my face, telling me that Russia had dropped a bomb on Washington, D.C. Then, after it was revealed that the bomb came from *within* the United States and that some cell phone app was involved, they reported that we created *that*.

In truth, we are not responsible, as much as you would like us to be. We didn't contact any Swedish programmers. Yes, what little trail they happened to find did lead back to Russian ISP addresses, but that doesn't mean anything. Don't you have trolls here who could fake that kind of thing? Maybe your own trolls did this, and blamed it on us. That would be just like your country.

Games don't work how they said Follow the Leader

worked. They *can't*. If Follow the Leader responded to the environment in the way your news media claims it does, the game would have had to be acting on its own. No coder could ever plan these Instructions so carefully; it would require a level of sophistication beyond even what we Russians are capable of.

You're asking me if the game is alive? Oh, you Americans. Perhaps it is for the best that we are here, to protect you from yourselves. You blew up your own capital because a game told you to. Does that sound like the action of a sane country to you?

I never played Follow the Leader, as it was never translated, and now that it's been pulled from the market it won't ever be. We do have a similar "augmented-reality" game in Russia—I believe it's called Shipwrecked. I'll show it to you. It's new, just hit the market a few months ago. You walk on this deserted tropical island, read signs that tell you where to go, and fun things you can do for points.

No, it is absolutely nothing like Follow the Leader. And even if it's similar, the outcome won't be the same. We Russians are not all dumb *mudaks* like you are. Now, please, you must excuse me. I have a meeting to attend. I can't very well spend all day playing Shipwrecked like some spoiled American!

Oh, can you please step aside? There's a treasure chest right behind you. There, I've got it.

ALL QUIET ON THE PHANTOM FRONT

★

Brad R. Torgersen

Tendrils of sulfurous vapor curled up from the pentagram's blood-soaked lines on the concrete bunker floor. Everyone in attendance blinked, as purple spots slowly cleared from their vision. Where once there had been two American Army Rangers and one British Royal Marine, there were now only damp footprints—the only trace remaining of the men who'd tracked in moisture from the dew-laden grass at the edge of the bunker's box-step entrance.

"What happened?" barked British Brigadier Campbell, who was among the hastily assembled congregation of senior NATO officers observing the ritual.

"I'm . . . not particularly sure, sir," admitted British Army Captain Davies. He stared at his counterpart on the other side of the pentagram, a United States Army captain by the name of Brown, who was rubbing two grimy fists at his otherwise sunken eyes. When he opened those eyes, he too stared at the pentagram in shock.

69

The incantation had been intended to summon people, not make them disappear.

Brown picked up his lime-green hardback notebook from where he'd dropped it on the dirt-crusted cement, and began to hastily flip pages. He felt his heart sinking as he realized something must have gone wrong during translation. Though he knew a bit of Lithuanian, his command of the language was nowhere near fluent. The village's old woman—dubbed a witch by the locals—had been barely intelligible. In either her own tongue, or in English.

"God forgive us," said United States Army Chaplain Mayfort, who'd voiced his disapproval before the summoning commenced, and now glared at the whole room with scarcely concealed condemnation. "I've been saying for six months we can't fight fire with fire. And no matter how many souls we lose to this diablerie, you people keep finding ways to lose more!"

"That's enough," said Major General Featherstone, quieting the chaplain. As the ranking NATO man in the room it had been his ultimate decision to go through with the summoning. But the sharpness of his glaring eyes spoke of barely restrained anger. Because Chaplain Mayfort was right. They were losing too many people to the black art. And at an alarming rate to boot.

"Uhhhh," Captain Brown said, still flipping pages, "I don't understand what could have gone wrong. We used blood, like the old woman instructed."

"But what *kind* of blood?" Featherstone demanded.

"Sir?" Brown said, looking up from what he'd written hastily three hours earlier.

"Pig's blood? Cow's blood? Something else? What did she *say* when you and Captain Davies interrogated her?"

"She didn't specify, sir," Brown replied.

"And you didn't think to *ask* her, Captain?"

Brown swallowed hard.

"Nossir," he said.

Major General Featherstone placed a gritty hand to his face and slowly ran his fingers over the four days of stubble on his cheeks and chin. Like all of them, his otherwise impeccable hygiene had slipped. Not that it mattered for practical purposes. Almost nobody had a pro-mask strapped to his thigh anymore. If the first days of the war had been marked by certain terror that nuclear and biological weapons were going to be thrown over the Russian border, nobody much feared that possibility now. Something much more sinister had been deployed. And Moscow was being devilishly peculiar in its methods.

"My great-grandmother was Creole, from New Orleans," Featherstone said. "She'd either laugh or cringe at how amateurish our attempts have been. And now the brigadier and I have to explain the loss of three more men. On top of whole companies that have gone missing before them. Dead."

"We still don't know that," Brigadier Campbell protested.

"Those three were going to help us find out, Brigadier, because they were the last men who interacted with Lieutenant Batesworth's platoon before the lot evaporated. And the old woman in the village said you had to have at least three people who'd had contact with the subject you're trying to retrieve from oblivion."

"Or what might be worse than oblivion," Chaplain Mayfort said dourly.

Again Featherstone ran a hand over his face.

"So . . . what kind of blood was it?" he finally asked, looking at Brown.

"A chicken's," Captain Davies said.

Featherstone swiveled his head to regard the British officer.

"I suggest you two go back to the village and ask our elderly mystic what kind of blood for sure. And tell her we lost three more people today. There will *not* be any more."

Brown eyed his counterpart, and nodded.

Davies merely said, "Right," and went to where his body armor, helmet, and weapon were perched on a battered folding chair. His British-issue equipment's camouflage pattern wasn't terrifically different from that adopted by the United States Army in Afghanistan, and which covered Brown's helmet and armor. Not that temporal concealment would do either of them much good against an enemy which could seemingly snatch whole groups of people from the face of the Earth. Without a trace. No bombs, no bullets, no rocket cannisters of fatal gas. Across a thousand miles of distance. The victims merely . . . ceased to exist.

Purcell Brown had studied political science during ROTC, and gone into military intelligence upon commissioning. When the Russians sent tanks over the border into Ukraine, Brown and thousands of other American men like him had been activated to fill the countless empty seats in both combat brigades and the joint task forces which had been hastily hurled into Eastern Europe and the Pacific alike. The Global War on Terror took a back seat to this newest, greatest war, with China bulldozing Hong Kong prior to commencing a naval siege on Taiwan, and Moscow eager to reclaim the land between it and the Black Sea—as well as its former Warsaw Pact satellites to its west.

US forces in Poland had rapidly advanced into the teeth of things, while everyone quietly worried about the unthinkable—the prospect that the war might escalate to the point of nuclear annihilation.

But something much more troubling had occurred.

"Bloody superstitious guesswork," Davies said grimly as he walked at Brown's side. The two men had been working together constantly for the past three weeks. Nothing in their training had ever prepared them to deal with a supernatural threat.

"You ever go to church when you were a kid?" Captain Brown asked.

"I'd have set the chapel on fire," Davies said, allowing himself a grin. "Never much cared for the vicar. Nor any of the rest of what he was pushing."

"Chaplain Mayfort seems as puzzled and fearful as the rest of us," Brown observed.

"Your chaplain is grappling with the realization that his God cannot help him," Davies said, his grin dropping to a frown.

"My mother used to tell me that even if you stop believing in the Lord, the Lord never stops believing in you," Brown said.

Davies made a scoffing sound as they climbed into the American-issue HMMWV where a driver, his truck commander, and their hatch gunner waited. The young enlisted personnel acknowledged both captains respectively, then the driver started the vehicle's diesel engine. It was half an hour back to the village, which lay to the rear of the command site Brown and Davies had recently departed.

Brown buckled himself in, and grimaced as the vehicle punished his kidneys by rapidly pulling out onto the bumpy, muddy yard surrounding the Joint Task Force's motor pool. Then they headed for the gravel road which would take them five kilometers to the nearest hardball highway.

Along the route they cleared two armed checkpoints—one NATO, the other native Lithuanian—the guards looking every bit as tired as Brown and his British counterpart felt.

The vanishings were disturbing enough. But the night terrors were an insult to injury. The latter had begun almost immediately in the wake of the former. Visions so horrifying that grown men would wake up screaming. The same dream, each and every time: being taken to hell. A very literal, garish, flame-engulfed underworld. Replete with cloven-hooved, forked-tongued, horned demons. Wielding pitchforks. Who inflicted eternal torment on the bodies of the damned.

Which sounded silly as described to an Army psychologist. Except for the fact that that same psychologist had been having the exact same dreams too, and her hand shook as she tried to write down Brown's description.

Eventually Brown stopped going to sick call. The morning line at the tent had gotten much too long, and what was the use when the same thing was happening to all of them anyway? You could look your neighbor in the eyes across the table at the chow trailer and know that he had been woken from sleep in exactly the same awful manner as you, night after night. To the point that many people were deliberately trying to keep themselves awake for as long as possible. Until exhaustion ultimately swept them away. To be tormented all over again.

Brown looked at the young men sitting in the seats in front of him. Were they still safe to drive? Were *any* of them in any shape to handle a weapon? Sleep deprivation took a toll no matter how tough a soldier might be.

When they reached the village, both Brown and Davies struggled to remember precisely where the old woman lived. After several dead ends, they finally asked one of the locals for directions, and were immediately warned— as they had been the first time—that the witch was bad news.

"She's the only one who seems to have any idea what can be done about all of this," Brown said to the young man in civilian clothes who looked as tired as any American trooper. The nightmares had not been visiting soldiers alone. As in the last world war, this new mass weapon did not discriminate between military and civilian targets.

"Danute. The crazy. She's got the devil in her head," the teenager replied, with remarkably good English.

But he still corrected their reckoning, and soon the humvee was idling in front of a mortared cobble cottage, which looked like it dated to the nineteenth century. There were no windows, save for the two wood-shuttered squares—which permitted no visibility. And a constant finger of white smoke twisted off the top of the stubby chimney crowning the cottage's steep roof.

"Think she'll make us into meat pies this time?" Captain Davies quipped as he wrestled himself out of the back seat.

"'The worst pies in Lithuaniaaaaa!'" Brown sang half-mocking, remembering the expensive Broadway production he'd taken his wife to the year before.

"Should we keep 'er running, sir?" the sergeant in the right seat asked.

"Nah," Brown said. "The Russians are a long way from here. And I doubt we'll need to make a quick getaway."

"Looks just as creepy as before, sir," said the young private in the cupola, manning the .50-caliber machine gun.

"You're so right," said Davies.

The two officers tentatively approached the door while a tentacle of unease snaked its way up Captain Brown's back. The place really *did* look like something out of a Grimm fairytale. And when the old woman cracked her front door—following several loud knocks from Davies's fist—her appearance hadn't altered one bit. A messy bun of nearly white hair was knotted inexpertly on the top of her head, while her skeletal neck looked barely strong enough to support the weight of her skull. The color of her eyes had washed out to a translucent gray, and she squinted, holding up her hand to block the sunlight diffused by the autumn clouds.

"Not good, you," she said in thickly accented English.

"No, not good at all," Davies said. "Three blokes are gone, and it's our fault—and your fault too."

"You have the words," she said, irritated. "In book."

"And we said the words, and three soldiers just like us vanished—as if it were the two of us who've been making all the others disappear."

"Gone?" she asked, her eyes suddenly going wide.

"Gone," Brown said.

"What kind blood you use?"

Davies replied, "Chicken's blood."

"You used chicken?" she said, her manner suddenly going much more erect. If before she had stooped in her doorway, now she lifted herself up to her full height—which was still a good head below either the American or his British counterpart.

"What the bloody hell else *would* we have used?" Davies said, irritated. "You didn't tell us *not* to use a chicken. And where else does a chap get fresh blood that doesn't come out of his mate's arm?"

She shook her head.

"Come inside."

The two men removed their helmets—but not their armor vests—and entered the cottage. Several bare bulbs dangled from sockets suspended by exposed wire, which had been strung up in the ceiling with bent nails. A tiny fire flickered in the old hearth, which sported an ancient iron kettle spit which could be levered in and out of the fire for cooking. Books of various ages and descriptions were shoved onto several wooden bookshelves—some of which appeared to block the spots where the windows might have been—and half-melted stumps of hundreds of candles appeared to decorate just about every other horizontal surface.

The only clear space was on a central parlor table. A luxurious pine-green velvet cloth was draped over the tabletop, with a collection of what appeared to be crystals at one end, and the skull of what had been an adolescent deer resting on the cloth at the other. The woman moved two wooden chairs up for the men to sit, then she herself took a chair opposite them—resting her left hand on the deer skull, and her right hand on the little collection of crystals.

Doubtless the chaplain would have curled his lip at this pagan presentation.

Brown himself would have found it comical, if he'd not spent night after night witnessing literal hell in his sleep. The empty eye sockets of the deer skull seemed to stare at him.

"Lamb's blood," she said, after chewing on a thumb for several seconds. "Use lamb's blood."

"Why didn't you tell us before??" Brown demanded.

"Sorry," she said. "Forgot."

"More to the point, Danute, where did our three men go? What's *happened* to them, and all the rest who're gone?" Davies pressed, leaning over the velvet cloth and staring hard at her face. The tension in the British officer's posture was palpable. If he'd tried to maintain a sense of humor upon their arrival, that mood had left him. He was all business now, and for good reason.

"I don't see it," she said.

"See what?" Brown asked.

"The place. Hidden from my eyes."

"So they've not been slotted," Davies said. "Are you sure?"

Danute looked to Brown, her face making a questioning expression.

"He means, they've not been killed. Is that right?"

"Killing would be mercy. This is . . . much worse."

"*Worse* than killing them?" Davies asked, growing even more tense. He was half out of his seat now, crouching low across the table.

"The chaplain did have a hunch," Brown said, putting an arm on Davies's shoulder, and gently urging the man to return to his chair. The Brit slowly sat, but his eyes were drilling holes in the old woman's face.

"I don't think any of us would believe what's happening if it weren't for the identical nightmares," Brown said. "The two are connected. The disappeared people, and our dreams. One came right after the other started."

"You scared?" she asked, looking directly into Brown's eyes.

The American paused for a moment, feeling a tremor run through him, then he swallowed and said, "Yes, more scared than I think I've ever been in my life. You can teach a man to work past the threat of a bullet, or a bomb. But this . . . is on a level no American soldier has ever had to deal with. We don't believe what's happening to us. Yet, events *force* us to believe. Which means we have to understand. So that we can fight it."

"No way to fight," she said firmly.

"Bollocks," Davies said. "If it's a weapon—and it must be, whether physical or psychological, or both—then there's a defense. Or at least a counter-weapon. We offered you money the first time. We can offer more, if that's what's needed to get the information we want."

Danute inhaled slowly, then sighed. Her hands slowly moved from off the skull and crystals, finally resting in front of her on the velvet, fingers laced thoughtfully together.

"They call me the witch," she said, this time with much less accent and far better English grammar than had ever come out of her mouth before. "And in another time and place, I'd be executed for the crime. But do you know *why* the villagers don't come for me?"

Both Brown and Davies straightened in their seats.

"It's because they're terrified of what I can do. They know the rumors. So, I lay low and let them think the worst of me, without revealing or letting on too much."

"Would you care to elaborate?" Captain Brown said, intrigued.

"I was in the KGB's paranormal research lab," she said, "back when there still was a KGB. They liked to harvest us from the smaller countries. We were a team, all women, and all sensitive to . . . the *other side* as it were. Lithuania, Latvia, Belarus. There were even some Polish women. Most of us could tell the same stories. About the dreams we'd had since we were old enough to talk. And seeing things that were never real to other people. But they *were* real to us."

"What things?" Brown asked, leaning forward slightly.

"Good things and bad," she said. "Sometimes, *very* bad. The *other side* is a place constantly brushing up against the real world, but never fully interfacing with it.

A few people are sensitive to that. Most are deaf as well as blind. And these days almost nobody wants to admit the *other side* exists at all. Having cracked the atom and put men on the moon, the science of men has displaced almost all of the old knowledge. Only the churches touch the truth now, and even they seldom have the stomach to tell the whole of it."

"If only a few people are sensitive," Brown asked, "how come we're all suffering from the same awful dreams?"

"Captain Davies is correct," she said, "that specific phenomenon *is* a weapon. All of us working the *other side* for the KGB knew about it. But our chief problem was we never found a powerful enough projector."

"I don't know what that means," Davies said.

"Think of it like a normal rifle. The more powerful the cartridge, the farther a projectile can go, and the more damage it can potentially do when it gets there. Myself and the other girls could successfully *project* visions onto other people, but only individual to individual, and at close range. What's happening now is that the Kremlin has somehow discovered a way to project visions broadly, and at great distance. I shudder to think how or why this has suddenly become possible. It's not an earthly thing."

"So . . . you've been having the nightmares too?" Davies intuited.

"Of course," she said. "I can't block them out, any more than one of you can block them out."

"And what about the disappearances?" Brown pressed.

"Teleportation and telekinesis were also things the KGB had the women's group working on."

"Only females?" Davies asked. "Why not males?"

"There was supposedly a male program too, but the KGB never let us talk to or interact with them. Attraction between and mixing of the sexes was viewed as a potentially destructive distraction."

"So the Russians have been . . . teleporting our troops." Brown said, testing the word on his tongue. It sounded absurd. But in his agitated and sleep-needy state, the far-fetched no longer sounded quite so. Three men had literally vanished from right in front of him earlier that day. If he'd harbored doubts about what might be going on, such doubts had left him. All that remained was to discover the truth, and seek a solution.

"Why not just murder us in our bunks?" Davies said. "If they can 'project' like you're claiming, what's to stop them from interfering with the function of the brain or the heart? Give the whole of the Joint Task Force and all of its downtrace units a collective myocardial infarction."

"The KGB tried to explore that option too, with very limited results. What you have to understand is that in terms of the *other side*, all life in our world has a kind of force to it. Or current. Or maybe *charge* is the best English word? This *charge* resists the kind of on-and-off 'switching' from the *other side* which is necessary to kill in our world. It *can* be done. But again, at very limited range, and only individual to individual."

"How do you know?" Davies asked. "Did you see it done?"

"Yes."

"On a person?"

"Yes."

"But it doesn't work as a mass-effect weapon?"

"No. And it also tends to cripple the killer. I lost a few friends that way. There is a backlash effect. None of us kills without cost. Though I don't tell the locals this. It's better for them to fear me."

Captain Brown gradually sat back in his chair, and ran a thumb along his chin. What she had said chilled him to the bone.

"Why tell us—two foreigners—different?" he asked.

"Because you want what I want. You want the Russians driven back to their own country, and you want to end the new paranormal threat which nobody in NATO understands. I may have been a tool of the KGB, but when the Soviet Union collapsed, I escaped to come home. Many of the others were not as lucky. They got bullets in their skulls. I managed to break out, and come back to a country which was finally its own nation again."

"Fair enough," Brown said. "But you said teleportation doesn't have the same *backlash* as trying to kill a man outright."

"No."

"Why?"

"To move something or someone from our world, to somewhere else in our world, you simply have to open a coherent doorway to the *other side*. Which then forms the conduit. I've managed it with pots and pans. And once, with a cat. But the cat stayed gone for three days, and when I got her back, she was so wild-eyed and fearful, she hissed at and bit everyone who came near her. She wouldn't eat, and wouldn't stop shrieking like she was in mortal pain. She was eventually put down. Out of mercy. I still miss that cat. She was my pet."

"Is that what's been done to NATO personnel?" Brown asked. "They've been transported through this . . . this place you keep referring to. The *other side*. And now they're somewhere else, perhaps permanently damaged?"

"I suspect it," she said. "Though, as I said earlier, I suspect there is a level of power working here which is far beyond anything I could imagine. To move that many full-grown people in large batches . . . none of us on the KGB paranormal project could have ever hoped to manage it. At best, we might have sent two or three adults in a single event."

"So, what was the ritual you gave us intended to do?" Davies asked. "Wouldn't it require your specific presence to work?"

"The *other side* is not linear science in the way a chemist or engineer might approach a problem. You asked me to help you find out where your missing platoon had possibly gone. I suspected I knew what was happening, and gave you the language, and instructed you to use tools which would open a very brief doorway. The lamb's blood—the life of the lamb itself, the *charge* I spoke of— would be fuel for the opening. Not that you'd have been thrilled by what you saw on the *other side*. It might have driven you insane. Remember my cat?"

"And you didn't *warn* us?" Brown said, rising out of his chair and slamming a fist on the velvet.

She didn't blink.

"Would you have believed me if I'd warned you?" she asked.

Brown merely stared at her.

"Did you even believe me when I sent you away—instructions in hand—the first time?"

Again, Brown merely stared at her.

"No, I have to admit that I didn't," he said coldly.

"Nor you, Captain?" she said to Davies, who had turned an angry pink.

"It sounded crazy," he said.

"But you had to return with *something* to show your general, correct?"

"That's right," Brown said. "And when three men disappeared in front of the whole command cell—right there in the middle of the bunker—I knew we weren't dealing with anything any of us understood. Which is why our boss ordered us to come back and confront *you.*"

"I am sorry if you feel I've deceived you," she said. "I meant it when I said I want the same thing you want."

"So if a chicken is wrong—not powerful enough—how come our three men got snatched anyway?" Davies asked.

"Like flies getting caught in a web. You caused a tremor, then your men disappeared, to be immediately funneled somewhere else on Earth. Or are suspended within the *other side* itself—as I fear happened to my pet."

"We have to find out for sure," Brown said, rapping his knuckles firmly on the wood beneath the velvet. "So, what can we try now?"

"You and Captain Davies were the last two people to interact with the newly missing men?"

"Yes," Brown said.

"We'll need a third. Did anyone else talk to them immediately before their departure?"

"Yes, actually," Davies said. "The chaplain shook their hands and said a short prayer."

"He's your third," she said.

"He will never, ever consent to a ritual like that again," Brown said firmly. "Not after he saw what happened."

"And what if *I* talk to the man?" she asked.

Brown and Davies both turned to look at each other, eyebrows raised.

Cramming three people into the back of the humvee—with the turret gunner still in the top hatch—had been a real chore. But they'd managed it. And driven extra slow back to the Joint Task Force's forward headquarters, so as not to make the ride too uncomfortable for their new guest. And while the soldiers at the Lithuanian checkpoint waved them through, the American checkpoint had a real problem with an uncredentialed foreign national being allowed inside the perimeter without the proper memoranda bearing Major General Featherstone's signature. The two captains argued with the checkpoint NCO for ten minutes, unsuccessfully, until Featherstone himself appeared—riding in the back of another humvee.

"You gents care to tell me who the hell this is?" he said gruffly, looking the old woman up and down as they stood—under armed guard, with the military police holding their loaded M4s at the low ready—next to the checkpoint's cross-beam roadblock, which had to be raised and lowered for each passing vehicle.

"Sir," Captain Brown said, "this is the Lithuanian woman we approached a few days ago, and who gave us the instructions for that pentagram ritual."

"And who's fault is that disaster?" Featherstone demanded.

"Mine," Danute said, in unison with both captains.

Featherstone stared at the three of them.

"And why the hell should I allow her into my bunker? In violation of half a dozen different security protocols, which will get my Top-Secret clearance yanked, and possibly subject me and you, Captain Brown, to court-martial?"

"We don't have to go anywhere near your headquarters, General," Danute said, "the ritual can be performed here at the checkpoint, for all that it matters. What's required is the specific participation of these two officers, and your chaplain—who had final contact with the missing men. Plus a sacrifice."

When Featherstone visibly bristled at her final word, Brown jumped in and added, "Sheep, sir. We need the blood of a sheep."

"Lamb, specifically," Danute clarified. "There is a reason why prophets of old used to sacrifice lambs on altars. The blood of a lamb is especially potent. Unless you want to shed a man's life and get *real* power. The priests of Central America knew it."

Brown was sweating beneath his uniform and armor. If he had intended to delicately introduce the woman to his boss, she was making a rude splash. And if circumstances had not evolved so extraordinarily, he was half-sure he'd have walked away himself. Except, she still seemed to be the only person with a handle on what was truly happening in this war. And knew what could potentially be done about it.

"Mayfort!" the general shouted back at his humvee. A second American emerged from the back seat. The chaplain was scowling as he slowly walked up to the general's side.

"Tell him what you just told me," the general ordered Danute. If she minded being given instructions by the man—despite not being obligated to any chain of command—she didn't show it. She merely repeated herself, and the corners of her mouth curled up slightly as the blood drained from the chaplain's face.

"It's an offense against God," he said gravely. "All of this is. We're screwing around with Satan's Tinkertoys, and you want me to directly participate!?"

"It's our best shot," Brown said emphatically. "I'm not sure I like it any better than you do, but with so much on the line, I think we have to be willing to take some risks. Even crazy or potentially blasphemous ones."

The chaplain simply stared.

Then he reluctantly said, "We'll have to get the G8 to cut us some local funds—to buy the lamb."

It was nightfall by the time arrangements were in place. With a lamb secured—the little creature bleating within its cage on the back of a humvee—an area of gravel had been cleared next to the checkpoint's guard shack. Danute would not set so much as a foot inside the perimeter, but proceedings would take place well within sight of armed backup. In the form of the MPs. Who watched the preparations with expressions of anticipation mixed with dread. Nobody was thrilled about what was to be done to the lamb. But all of them were tired and desperate and ready to try anything that might offer a way out from under the shadow of the nightmares and the disappearances.

Danute would conduct, while the chaplain and two captains took their assigned places at different points on the pentagram, marked with chalk on the gravel—and which would soon be coated in lamb's blood after the animal had been sacrificed.

"Gonna be one mother of an after-action report," Major General Featherstone muttered as he personally oversaw preparations through the afternoon. A sentiment Captain Brown understood all too well. This was so far beyond anything any of them had ever prepared for— prior to the war's outbreak—they were truly in uncharted territory. Nobody back at the Pentagon understood what was happening in Europe. Even after reviewing the details of the missing personnel and units. What would they say when word of *this* particular exercise reached their ears? Would necromancy be added as an additional skill identifier for their military occupation specialties?

Brown shook his head, and joined the small group of officers who'd been selected to draw straws—to see who'd get to do the little lamb in.

When Brown came back with the shortest straw, he closed his eyes and crumpled it up in a fist.

"Fine," he said, and went to get his M9 pistol from the MOLLE holster attached to the front of his armor. The weapon's modest parabellum cartridge was not especially powerful in comparison to the midsize cartridge used in the M4 rifle. But he only needed to put the creature out of its mortal misery. Not inflict man-killer damage.

Captain Davies led the little sheep out of its cage by a

rope, and the tiny creature looked around for a few seconds—bathed in the light of multiple humvee headlamps, aimed inward from a large circle of surrounding vehicles—before dipping its head to the ground and nibbling experimentally at a tuft of grass poking up through the gravel.

Captain Brown aimed his pistol about where he thought he should—it had been at least two generations since anyone in his family had worked on a farm—then flipped the M9's safety off, exhaled slowly, and pulled the trigger.

The lamb's body dropped limply.

"Now, quickly, the throat," Danute ordered.

Brown—feeling somewhat breathless—willed himself to take the razor-sharp folding blade from Captain Davies's hands, then knelt by the creature and inexpertly cut the creature's neck.

As blood flowed freely, Danute lifted the limp lamb by its hind legs and quickly walked the five-pointed-star shape of the required pentagram.

"Please be thorough," Brown said, feeling a bit sick with himself, "I'd just as soon not have to do that over again."

She traced her steps twice—careful not to disturb the lines of splashed blood with her shoes—until most of the carcass had been emptied. At which point she took it back to its former cage in the bed of the humvee, and reverently placed it inside.

"To your posts," she ordered.

The chaplain, along with Davies and Brown, took up their stations. If Brown felt a bit odd about what had just happened, the chaplain looked positively aghast. But, being a soldier, he had the discipline to carry out his part of the plan. With himself standing at one point, and the two captains standing at points opposite his, he looked to Danute and said, "God save us and carry us through this wicked trial."

If this had been meant as an insult, Danute seemed to ignore it. She merely held out her hands—brightly illuminated by the humvee light—and began to speak the words of the incantation. They weren't words in English, nor Danute's own language. Rather, they were phonetic sounds hearkening back to some much younger, much more visceral tongue the likes of which modern men seldom heard. The noise was much harder on Captain Brown's ears than when he himself had tried to speak them. Which may have also been part of the problem. Inexpertly drawing down the *other side* in such a way, may have doomed the two Rangers and the Royal Marine before they ever had had a chance.

When Danute was finished speaking, she clapped her hands together once. Very loudly. And for a moment, it sounded as if an echo of thunder had reverberated across the checkpoint. All of the personnel present—Americans and British alike—glanced at each other worriedly. There had been no storms reported for the night. In fact, the sky had cleared of clouds, and the stars above were fairly bright this far from modern civilization.

Brown dared to glance up at them, and watched in horrified fascination as they gradually turned red, and began to smear across the heavens like the trail of blood left from the wound in the dead lamb's neck.

"Good Lord, they're gone!" Captain Davies yelled.

Brown brought his attention down from the sky, and observed that both the humvees and the other personnel present, had all disappeared. The landscape itself seemed to remain intact, as did the pentagram—which no longer appeared as splashed blood, but as a pulsating, practically thrumming geometry of pink-white lines. Brighter than the brightest neon sign back in the States. So bright, it was hard for Brown to look at them for more than a moment.

"*She's* not," the chaplain said, aiming a finger across the pentagram, at the cloak-wrapped silhouette of Danute.

"Of course I'm not," she said. "I'm your way back."

"Back from where, exactly?" the chaplain asked.

"This is the *other side*," she said matter-of-factly.

"It looks like the checkpoint, except no man-made features and no other people are here," Captain Davies said.

"It will only hold this form for a moment," she said. "Soon the reflective picture of our world will fall away, and you will all see what I have seen—at various times— throughout my life."

Brown's stomach suddenly leapt into his throat as the gravel under his boots melted and washed away like hot wax. It was replaced with a fog-like ether the depth of which was impossible to gauge. He almost fell over, clutching meaninglessly at nothing, only to realize he was still perched on the particular point of the pentagram where he'd been standing for the last minute.

Davies and the chaplain had similar reactions.

"How are we supposed to find our missing men in *this?*" Brown demanded, trying very hard not to think about the formless cloud of vapor that drifted under his feet.

"You don't travel to them," Danute said, "you reach out *for* them. In your heart. You especially, Chaplain Mayfort. You blessed these three men before they were taken. That may form a string of connectivity. And we do have to act fast. Unlike when a person's life is spent, the life of a spent lamb cannot keep the doorway open for too long."

The chaplain bowed his chin to his chest and spoke softly, as if no one else could hear him.

Brown himself merely thought of the three missing men—none of whom he'd known personally—just as he thought of Lieutenant Batesworth. Somewhere in all of this . . . emptiness, or *through* it, was the answer. The key. A way to stop or alter what was happening. And make a difference.

As an intelligence officer, Captain Brown had never expected to do anything dramatic in the field. His job was to ensure the boss had accurate information and advice, with which to make a plan and give orders. But now, suddenly, he was deployed to another kind of field entirely. One so far beyond his experience, he wasn't sure he hadn't taken leave of his rational mind altogether. How would he even know? The sensation of standing on firm Earth—or formerly firm Earth—didn't match with the swirling vapor of nothingness which surrounded them all.

Suddenly, the vapor blew back all at once, and the ground beneath the pentagram seemed to race at an absurd speed. Like time-lapse motion photography. The whole continent shifted and moved while the pentagram remained the sole fixed object in their universe. Until

Brown, Davies, and Chaplain Mayfort were standing—with Danute off to the side—in a huge brick-walled courtyard. The light there was monochrome and redshifted, so that true colors eluded their eyes.

There were men in the courtyard. Hundreds of them. Huddled in groups. Their faces turned downward, and their shoulders hunched. They wore the uniforms of NATO men, mostly American and British, but with a handful of other countries too. The walls of the courtyard were over two stories high, and topped with spirals of concertina wire, occasionally punctuated by the enclosed glass boxes where guards kept watch.

If anyone noticed the pentagram, or the presence of the four people seemingly attached to it, they didn't show it. Rather, the ground seemed to shift again of its own accord as Chaplain Mayfort's speaking quickened in pace and volume.

Eventually the pentagram came to rest next to a group of about a dozen men who'd taken seats on the dirt, conversing among themselves. None of the people on the pentagram could hear the words.

"Where is this?" Brown asked out loud.

"Not a clue, mate," Davies responded, looking around, astonished.

"I know where it is," Danute said coldly. She stared at the walls of the courtyard like one stared at the bars of a former prison.

Suddenly one of the men in the circle stood up and pointed, shouting, "Holy shit, where did they come from?"

Two other men—one of them recognizable as the Royal Marine, and the other being the second of the two

Army Rangers—also stood up. They stared in disbelief at the glowing strands of the pentagram, which continued to pulsate, without giving off any sound, nor heat.

"Can you see or hear me?" Captain Brown yelled at them.

"I can!" shouted the first Ranger.

"So can I," said the Royal Marine, his Cockney accent very apparent.

"That's the chaplain!" shouted the second Ranger. "He shook our hands and said a prayer for us."

Mayfort looked up, his face covered in perspiration, and said with a husky voice, "Christ our Lord in heaven, it really worked!"

Brown observed that nobody else from the circle of men seemed to notice or care that the Royal Marine and two Rangers had departed for the pentagram, which hovered perhaps a centimeter off the dirt. The entire scene still maintained its monochrome, redshifted appearance, but the three men themselves—who now seemingly realized they were in a bubble of altered space that surrounded the pentagram—had taken on much sharper, clearer definition. They were unarmed, and dressed only in the basic uniforms they'd been wearing earlier in the day just prior to their disappearance.

"There are two free points on the pentagram," Danute said, pointing her finger. "One man for each."

The Rangers and the Royal Marine exchanged a guilty glance, then the Royal Marine said, "Go ahead, mates," and motioned for the other men to take their places.

"Wait," Captain Brown said. "Our mission was to get them *all* back."

"If we get your Rangers back to the checkpoint fast enough," Danute said, "there may be time to return for the third."

Just then, a horrendous belch of quaking laughter peeled out of the sky. So low on the bass register as to almost not be recognizable for what it was.

"I know that voice," Danute hissed, her face twisting into a mask of hate.

"HELLO, YOUNG LADY," the intruder's voice blasted—felt, as much as heard.

"The Evil One cometh!" shouted the chaplain.

"OH NO, MY FRIEND," the intruder replied, his words making the lines of the pentagram grow fuzzy and fluctuate. "YOU WOULD BE FORTUNATE IF ALL YOU HAD TO FACE WAS THE MORNINGSTAR'S BRUTAL AFFECTION. I AM AFRAID YOU'VE DISTURBED A DIFFERENT GOD ENTIRELY!"

One of the walls of the courtyard began to distort and shift, like soft clay, until a man's face had formed—huge, and menacing. The face had no hair, but the eyes glared with a palpable malice which Captain Brown found almost choking in its intensity.

"Comrade Sokolov," Danute said, turning to stare at the horrid face towering two stories over her.

"VERY GOOD, MY DEAR. I AM SO GLAD YOU REMEMBER ME. I KNEW IT WAS ONLY A MATTER OF TIME BEFORE WE'D BE SEEING EACH OTHER AGAIN. MOST OF THE REST OF YOUR GROUP ARE DEAD, OR HAVE BEEN ABSORBED BY ME. BUT YOU? I COULD FEEL YOU WERE STILL OUT THERE, SOMEWHERE. WAITING."

"Who—or what—is this person?" Captain Brown managed to ask, through a throat which was rapidly closing up.

"Sokolov was the KGB administrator put in charge of the women's research group dedicated to the *other side*," Danute said. "He was an old man, then. It is not possible that he's still alive now."

"DEATH IS NO LONGER ANY OBSTACLE FOR ME, DANUTE. OR DO YOU BELIEVE YOUR EYES LIE TO YOU? COME, DON'T TROUBLE YOURSELF WITH THESE MERE MORTALS. IT'S TIME FOR US TO BE TOGETHER AGAIN. THIS TIME, FOR ETERNITY!"

The shape of the moist-clay face seemed to ripple and distort briefly, as if a thousand other faces suddenly manifested in its skin—each of them a mask of pain and torment, crying for release.

Then, just as suddenly, the giant face's skin became smooth once more.

"Hateful abomination!" Chaplain Mayfort shouted at the face.

"You have no idea," Danute said.

"What's happened?" Captain Brown demanded. "What's he done?"

"I think I am beginning to understand," she said, turning to look at Brown with tears streaming down her face. "He didn't die when the Soviet Union fell! He deliberately crossed into the *other side* and transfigured himself by absorbing the bodies and souls of others. Their *charge* became his *charge*. And he's kept on consuming whenever he needs to replenish himself. That's why the

Russians haven't launched their warheads. Sokolov needs your troops alive. Like mice trapped in the wild, then kept caged. For when the snake is hungry."

"YOU ALWAYS WERE QUICK-WITTED, DANUTE. YOU UNDERSTAND INTUITIVELY IN A SINGLE BREATH WHAT IT TAKES OTHERS YEARS TO GRASP. I LOOK FORWARD TO HAVING YOU AS PART OF MYSELF. NOW THAT MOSCOW IS ONCE AGAIN FINDING USE FOR MY ABILITIES AND TALENTS, YOUR ABILITIES AND TALENTS SHALL SERVE MOSCOW TOO."

The glowing lines of the pentagram began to strobe erratically.

"I think we're losing it," Captain Davies said. "Are we all stuck here because of that thing, or can we still get back to the checkpoint?"

"We can get back," Danute said. "But only if we go now."

"But we can't leave a man behind!" Brown shouted.

"Somebody has to step off the pentagram," Danute said.

The five men glanced at each other across the flashing, quivering lines which threatened to burst into a thousand motes of light at any moment.

"I'll do it," said one of the Army Rangers.

"No, *I* will do it," said Chaplain Mayfort.

"You'll be stuck with the hundreds of others," Danute warned. "We won't be able to quickly come back and get you. Not now that *he* is aware of what we're doing."

"Doesn't matter," the chaplain said. "Somebody's gotta let those brothers and sisters know—the ones who are still left!—that there's hope. And a plan!"

"Chaplain, I think—" Brown began to say, but he was cut off.

"Tell the general what's happening here!" Mayfort said, taking two deliberate steps backward. His shape grew fuzzy and less distinct, the moment he made his move.

"Come on!" Danute shouted, motioning for the Royal Marine. "Now or never!"

The man blurred into action, almost throwing himself on the empty point of the pentagram.

More booming, hideous laughter filled the air, but then everything blurred like a time-delay movie. The failing pentagram was whisked violently—without sound—across the landscape of war-torn Europe, until it snapped into place back at the checkpoint.

Captain Brown collapsed through the light shed by the headlamps of the humvees. A sulfur-stench vapor boiled from where the lamb's blood stained the pea gravel. And strong hands gently pulled him to his feet, while also pulling Danute, the Rangers, the Royal Marine, and Captain Davies to their feet as well.

"Son of a bitch," Major General Featherstone's voice said. "They're actually alive. And they brought our Rangers and Royal Marine home!"

A cheer rose up from the men of the Joint Task Force, as their three lost comrades were boisterously welcomed back to the fold.

"But where's the chaplain?" Featherstone asked.

"Sir," Captain Brown said, "I think we need an emergency sit-down back at the bunker. There's a whole new front in the war. And we're right in the middle of it now. If we want to get Chaplain Mayfort—and any of the rest of them—back, there's no time to lose."

The major general looked at Danute, and she nodded. Still sniffling at the tears running down her face.

"No time indeed," she said.

ANASTASIA'S EGG

★

Kevin Andrew Murphy

Yevgeny Dmitriov was not his true name, but it served well enough. Most of the analysts in the Kremlin's esoteric-artifacts division simply referred to him as *the old man*, or *that guy who's been here forever*, or more rudely, *that creepy old bastard—isn't he ever going to die?*

The last came closer to his true name than any had in a while.

Yevgeny had been old for almost all of his very long life. But he never got tired of living, and while he hadn't been around quite forever, he had been around a very long time.

He savored his vodka and surveyed the scene about him. Silly young Muscovites, drunk on capitalism and easy rubles, venerating the West, the whole bar styled to look like a Wild West saloon, at least as imagined by the set designers from a Spaghetti Western. For all that, it was spitting distance from Red Square. One young blond man twirled in circles on a mechanical bull, whooping wildly and waving a cowboy hat, while his comrades cheered him on.

No, not comrades. That term had fallen out of fashion along with communism. And *friends* did not apply either, since they were in as much competition as appreciation.

But young men had always been such. Young women too. Human nature didn't change, no matter how much or how often it restyled itself. Cowboy hats were in, Cossack hats and *kokoshniks* were out, but the games were still the same.

Of course, once it would have been real bulls and real death, or even more amusing divertissements to while away the long winter nights until spring's return. Bear baiting had been pleasant enough, as such things went, and always funnier when the bear escaped and ate some idiot. Throwing a fox into a cage of hounds to hear it scream was likewise the old style or throwing a fool from a sleigh to let him be eaten by wolves. Winter idylls were always such delights, painting the snows as red as poppies. So many ways to die, each more amusing than the last.

Yevgeny savored the pepper in his vodka and sighed. He'd become something of a connoisseur of death, having tasted it many times himself, but never quite swallowing. He'd had other agents attempt to assassinate him over the years, both foreign and national, using everything from polonium-laced teapots to ricin-tipped umbrellas, and even before he'd come to the agency, he'd been stabbed, shot, beaten, poisoned, and thrown in a frozen river to drown, and still he'd survived.

That was just the previous century. Before that? Many other brushes with Death, both lesser and greater. Yevgeny had been locked in a cell for years, starved, with nothing to drink, but still he had not died. He had been betrayed by an ugly old hag and by a beautiful young woman, hoping she would be his bride. He should never have trusted either. He'd even been struck with an arrow that should have killed him, for it was tipped with his death, and he'd been left for dead . . . yet still he lived.

Some in the agency swore that the old man had nine lives, like a cat, which only made him laugh.

The truth was, Yevgeny had been born the same as any man, with one life and one death. The life he savored. The death? That he had locked away long ago, safely and securely . . . or so he had thought.

The young yahoos finished with their clockwork-bull ride and came to the bar, loudly calling for vodka and ordering American delicacies with silly names like Buffalo wings and turducken sliders.

"You ever hear of such a thing, old man?" gabbled the drunken lout beside Yevgeny, looking like many young idiots over the years. "They put a duck inside a chicken inside a turkey, then roast the whole thing! The Americans are crazy!"

"I've heard of similar things," Yevgeny allowed. "I have been around."

"My people did it first," declared a finely dressed young Arab, reeking of privilege and power.

Yevgeny curled his lip in distaste, but discreetly, hiding the expression with a sip of vodka. The Arab was a prince, obviously, wearing an ostentatiously gaudy gold signet ring on his left index finger. It was set with a ruby the size of a plover's egg and looked worth the proverbial king's ransom. Princes had never been good for him, and the more insipid and idiotic, the more dangerous.

But the Arabians had so many princes it hardly seemed cause to brag. "For wedding feasts, we stuff three chickens with eggs, then place them in a goat, inside a sheep, inside a camel, then roast the whole thing!"

The youngsters laughed, clinking glasses, tossing back vodka, and noshing on turducken sliders. Then a lovely young Russian woman, a classic beauty with a face straight from a storybook, mentioned diplomatically, "Your custom is ancient indeed, my prince, but on this point, we Russians hold the bragging rights. We did it first . . . at least if you believe the legends. Long, long ago, so long ago that the dates have been lost to fairy tales, the sorcerer Koschei the Deathless hid his death, placing it on the tip of a needle, which he hid inside an egg inside a duck inside a hare inside a boar inside a dragoness!"

Everyone laughed except Yevgeny, who would have spewed his vodka if he hadn't already swallowed it. He set his shot glass on the bar top abruptly, staring at the young beauty.

She smiled back, her teeth white as pearls and even more beautiful, but not a word was spoken between them until the prince and his entourage had left the bar and gone back to the mechanical bull. "Vasilisa," Yevgeny pronounced at last. "Do you prefer 'the Wise' or 'the Beautiful'? I could never get that straight."

"I prefer neither, for it's been a long while since I've been known by that name." She'd replaced her royal *kokoshnik* with a modern blonde bob, and her flowered gown was now a western girl's flour-sack print patterned with waterlilies. But her face and form were still Russian to the core. "If you must call me something, call me V."

"Very well, then, V," Yevgeny told her, "but I will point out you were rude enough to name me first."

She waved a pretty hand with a fashionable acrylic manicure, her nails green to match her dress. "I merely alluded to old folklore, which anyone can find in books in the tourist shops." She took a sip of vodka and cocked her head. "What are you calling yourself these days? Grigori Rasputin?"

"That was a hundred years ago," Yevgeny spat. "I am now just Yevgeny Dmitriov, Russian intelligence analyst."

"One would have thought he'd have died by now." Vasilisa's perfect lips made a perfect moue, and she sipped her vodka as daintily as if it were a demitasse of the finest espresso. "You've been him longer than you *ever* were the mad monk."

"Rasputin was higher profile," Yevgeny informed her.

"True," she admitted. "He even has a song. Have you heard it?"

"Not since Eurovision before the Wall fell."

Vasilisa laughed. "Then it's fortunate I requested it." She signaled to the DJ across the room.

The cowboy music, some insipid nonsense about an achy-breaky heart, stopped abruptly as the DJ called out, "Now here's a little number requested by Miss V! Something popular in the American goth clubs she says—Boney M.'s 'Rasputin'!"

Not only did the music start up, but so did the video, a German-Jamaican group of African ancestry, like ABBA with Afros, wearing capes and leotards and dancing to the beat of seventies disco.

"Like it?" Vasilisa inquired.

The dancers on the floor broke the straight ranks of the American country line and curved themselves into the familiar patterns of a Russian circle dance, one young man crossing his arms, kicking high while squatting low, in the manner of the Cossacks.

"It has its charms," Yevgeny pronounced at last, "but it's not at all accurate to what transpired, as well you should know." He'd never slept with Empress Aleksandra, no matter what the song said.

"Those were not my designs," Vasilisa stated plainly. "I only sought to protect my descendants from you, not have them enslave you."

"And yet they did," Yevgeny told her. "You have only yourself to blame for what happened. It was not *my* doing. At least not directly . . ."

It had been quite simple, actually. A whisper in one ear. A suggestion in another. An anonymous mailing of some books by the German writers Marx and Engels to a third, and no magic beyond a bit of tea-leaf reading that went unnoticed beside the palace samovar. Tsar Nicholas and his family's extravagance had done the rest. . . .

"The children were innocent!" Vasilisa hissed. "Surely you'll admit that!?"

"Why don't you ask Baba Yaga?" Yevgeny smiled as he had not smiled since he was known as Koschei the Deathless. "She always kept impeccable standards for the innocence of children." He grinned wider. "Not a one of the Romanov spawn would have survived her tests, least of all the little bleeding brat!"

He seethed at the memory. He had reinvented himself as Grigori Rasputin, monk and mystic, a perfectly reputable cover identity for an ancient sorcerer, so he hadn't thought much of being summoned to the presence of the tsar and his wife, despite the history of their family.

Lost in mists of legend was their ancestry, how they descended from Vasilisa the Beautiful, whose children had always been destined to rule, and the equally pretty simpleton Prince Ivan, whose idiocy had cursed the dynasty more than once.

If Vasilisa had just accepted Koschei's marriage proposal, it would have all been so neat and easy. Their heirs might be ruling to the present day, with her beauty and wisdom, and his cleverness and power.

But no, bad blood and bad breeding all around. The Romanov boy had been cursed with the bleeding sickness, an illness incurable by the science of the day.

The magic? Well, miraculous healings were for saints, and Koschei the Deathless was no saint. He was a prince among sorcerers, a wizard, and a necromancer of great note, and he had gouged his death out of himself with the tip of a needle, like an unwanted splinter. He had then hidden the death-tipped needle inside an egg, for, as Baba Yaga had taught him many years ago, the egg is the ultimate symbol of life, so it was the perfect repository for death—especially if you didn't want it to be detected and fall into the wrong hands. Hence the gambit of hiding the needle in the egg in the duck in the hare in the boar in the dragoness, all of them nested like the matryoshka dolls Baba Yaga had shown him to illustrate the theory. The same dolls she no doubt showed to Vasilisa before outright telling her beau Ivan where she'd surmised Koschei had hidden his death.

Of course, the popular legends were not always accurate. The stories said that Prince Ivan, on recovering the needle, tied it to the tip of an arrow and used it to pierce Koschei through the heart. The fairy tales failed to mention that the wound was not quite fatal, the fell needle snagging on Koschei's robes while the rest of the shaft went in, only giving him the faintest prick and the taste of his death. The stories also neglected to note what became of the deadly needle after that.

"I meant it as a mercy," Vasilisa told him. "There had been too much cruelty between us, and I just wanted it to end. A simple request—to let the world think you were dead, to let Ivan be famed as the man who killed Koschei the Deathless, and to never trouble us or our children or our children's children ever again."

"And I took it as that," Koschei told her. "I never troubled you, V, nor any your children, or their children, for all of the generations—though I was sorely tempted more than once. Peter the Great's grandson Peter was a particular ninny, taking after your Ivan in mind if not looks. If that clever German princess hadn't done away with him, I don't know what I might have done."

"I can see where you would favor Catherine," Vasilisa allowed.

"And I did, though not until she'd done away with him herself. Vows are vows. But Catherine the Great wasn't your blood, and I always had the knack for taking the form of a horse. But that is another story." Koschei steeled himself with more vodka. "However, the Romanovs were your blood, and so I kept my word when they summoned me. I had thought it would be something trivial they might want, a tea-leaf reading or a horoscope, but a healing for a doomed child? I was never a healer. A shapeshifter and master transmogrifier? Yes. A necromancer? Proudly. A mesmerist of some note, so I could make the boy forget his pain, and I even took a taste of his death into myself, for his doom was not mine. But I could not save him, and he was as much a dunce at sorcery as your Ivan, so he couldn't save himself either.

"So imagine my surprise when his mother Tsarina Aleksandra decided to show me a bauble her darling husband Nicholas had given her, an Easter present she said, a dainty golden egg festooned with jewels, fashioned by Fabergé, the imperial jeweler—a tedious if harmless bit of extravagance I dutifully praised—and then, with pride and malice on her pretty face, she activated a cunning mechanism to reveal a tiny coach driven by an even tinier Cupid, who sat with arrow nocked, but instead of a golden dart, he held one of blue steel, an ancient needle with my death still there at the tip."

"That wasn't my design," Vasilisa pled.

"No? You give your descendants a weapon to protect them from Koschei the Deathless, prince among sorcerers and necromancer nonpareil, how soon will they realize that they have a weapon they can use to enslave Koschei the Deathless?" Yevgeny gave a glance to the room, noticing the Arab prince whooping and twirling on the mechanical bull, then made the smallest and slightest of gestures, a side-eyed glance to the control knob coupled with a twist of his shot glass, the most simplistic of sympathetic magic powered by the barest drop of spite.

The prince began whooping even more wildly as the

bull spun at high speed, then flew off, landing with a loud but not sickening crunch, more was the pity.

"That was petty," Vasilisa chided, making her pretty moue again.

"When you get to be my age, my dear, you take your pleasures where you can."

She raised an immaculate eyebrow. "I'm almost as old as you, you know."

"Not hardly, V. I had lived for centuries before you were born. Besides which, eternal age is a different experience from eternal youth. You know more about being a frog than you ever will of being an old woman." He smiled then. "Now that was pettiness, I'll admit. But if I hadn't cursed you into the form of a frog to punish you for refusing my proposal, you never would have met your Ivan. A miscalculation on my part, truth to tell. But transformation and necromancy were always my strong suit, not divination, and I'd not thought you'd find another prince willing to kiss you and break the spell." Koschei leaned closer and leered. "But tell me, for I've always been curious—did Ivan kiss you on a bet or was he just into frogs?"

Vasilisa had always looked even prettier when she was hurt. "Ivan was as kind as he was handsome, and I loved him for it. . . ."

"Ah yes, the blessed idiot, always making friends. Pity he never learned the trick of making himself immortal."

"No, he never did," Vasilisa admitted, then looked up at him and added, with just a taste of a frog's poison, "but Anastasia did—and she has your egg."

"Anastasia!?" Koschei sucked in his breath with a hiss.

"That slip of a girl!? Who taught her, and how? And my egg?"

Another drop of frog-princess poison: "As clever as you claim to be, Koschei, you should be able to work it out yourself...."

Koschei did. Unlike the rest of the Romanov daughters, Princess Anastasia had always been a kind and quiet girl. Koschei had taken her to be a simpleton in the mold of her ancestor Ivan, but Anastasia obviously had more than a bit of Vasilisa in her too, listening to conversations considered above her and taking mental notes.

Koschei had had other concerns. He'd tried to teach her doomed brother Alexei sorcery, but the brat had never had any talent, too wrapped up in his pain and his playthings and the foolish idea that a prince could just order people to give him anything he wanted, even immortality.

Magic seldom worked that way. Unless you had the services of incredibly powerful spirits—demons and the like—it took cleverness and talent as much as knowledge and willpower to get anything of worth. And dealing with demons was so devilishly dangerous, you might as well be dealing with Death himself, who Koschei avoided as well.

Anastasia was certainly young when he'd last seen her. What was she, seventeen? More than a girl, but not quite a woman. But if faced with a choice between certain death and possible immortality? Entirely possible, especially since Yevgeny remembered, in his guise as Grigori Rasputin, that she *did* do exquisite needlework, and a needle was the instrument he'd used as Koschei to extract his death.

He'd also heard that Anastasia and all the girls had

sewn jewels into their girdles. Jewel magic was ancient magic, so it was likely not hyperbole that the first bullets had bounced off Anastasia and the rest of her sisters, since the best and most loyal stones would crack to preserve their owner from a fatal blow.

But the greatest jewels were the Fabergé eggs, and Tsarina Aleksandra had gone to almost ludicrous lengths to keep a literal shell game going, one day having the deadly needle as the dart in Cupid's bow, the next day as the second hand of the empress's wristwatch, the next as the actual needle in a lady's necessity kit housed in the golden shell of yet another exquisite gold egg.

"The *Nécessaire*," he breathed at last, pronouncing the French name for the jewel, one of the ones still lost since the Revolution, "the little *étui* that Anastasia always coveted." He remembered it well, another one of Fabergé's frivolous confections, the shell positively studded with brilliants, rubies, emeralds, and sapphires. "She was always begging her mother to borrow it, and I know a needle case was among its treasures because Aleksandra, once I told her I couldn't save her son, took my death out of it, and she asked me to try harder, all the while using it to embroider handkerchiefs. Needless to say, I took her point. So that *was* the last egg Aleksandra used to hide the needle . . ." Koschei looked up then, to the lovely face with the frog-green eyes. "It all makes sense. What doesn't make sense is why you're revealing this to me now. What is in this for you, V?"

She gestured with her pretty manicure, indicating the bar. "Isn't it obvious?"

Yevgeny Dmitriov took it all in, the frivolous falsity and

fantasy of the West's golden age, with cowgirls in Stetson hats prancing about in tooled leather boots, while a video of an extravagantly wigged and bosomed songstress wailed for "Jolene" to spare her man.

He had not heard of Jolene before, but she sounded like a formidable woman, as implacable and insatiable as . . . "Baba Yaga," he snapped in realization. "Last I heard of her she was trying to get the lance of Longinus to make Hitler unable to lose in battle. So, what game is the old crone up to now? Plotting World War III?"

Vasilisa demurred. "I think you know."

"She plays a very long game," Koschei mused. "When first we met, she was as in the fairy tales, with her iron teeth, her fence of skulls and children's bones, her flying mortar and pestle, and her chicken-legged hut, equal parts nightmarish and absurd. When last we crossed paths, she'd restyled herself as Helena Blavatsky, mystic and spiritualist, creating her Theosophical Society." He nodded, remembering recognizing Baba Yaga behind her charms and glamours, seeing no profit in exposing her as anything other than another mortal mystic. "I saw nothing of her fence of skulls and bones until Blavatsky's work inspired the Thule Society, who in turn inspired Hitler, creating a great many fences and many, many more bones for her to grind in her mortar and make porridge for her and her sisters to consume, continuing their witchly immortality. But, of course, you knew all that, didn't you, V? Long ago, she gave you one of her flame-eyed skulls to burn your stepmother and stepsisters to ash, so when you saw Hitler use the *Totenkopf* as his badge, you knew exactly what *that* signified."

"I took no part in it," Vasilisa said defensively.

"Oh, no, I'm certain you never dirtied your dainty hands with anything so unpleasant." Koschei sneered. "Vasilisa of the fairy tales was always too good and kind for any of that. But she was also beholden to her hag of a godmother for freeing her from bondage, first to her stepmother, next to myself. So, Vasilisa couldn't say a word against Baba Yaga. In fact, I suspect you swore an oath to that effect, for even now most of what you're saying is questions and riddles." Koschei laughed nastily. "You're complicit, Vasilisa. Not only did you put me in a position where I had no choice but to start Russia's Revolution, causing all those necessary and unnecessary deaths in the process, but you knew about the Holocaust *and did nothing to stop it.*"

Vasilisa burst into tears, hiding her face in her hands in shame. She was always prettier when she cried.

Koschei signaled to the bartender, telling him, "Leave the bottle. And bring me a plate of those turducken sliders. I'm feeling peckish. . . ."

Koschei poured himself another vodka, then some for Vasilisa. "So," he inquired, savoring a bite of mixed poultry spiced with Cajun seasoning, "I need to guess the rest of the old biddy's game, don't I? Well, since you mentioned Anastasia, I suspect that, since Baba Yaga always had chores for lost girls, your many times great granddaughter is working for her still, with the golden egg in her possession, with my death inside of it. But since the Holocaust should have provided enough bones to feed the hag and all her sisters many times over, what exactly could she and her sisters be playing at?" Koschei mused, remembering what he could of the secretive coven.

"There's Baba Yaga, of course, and Baba Roga. Baba Korizma and Baba Jezi . . ." He chuckled darkly. "For all I know there might be Baba Ghanoush and Baba O'Reilly! That crone has reinvented herself so many times and taken on so many guises, it's dizzying to keep them all straight. Was that gingerbread house in Germany her hut on fowl's legs with new siding or was it the dwelling of one of her sisters? Frau Trude, perhaps? Trude had a magic oven, as I heard tell, instead of a magic mortar and pestle, so I suspect she's the second one of the Baba sisters. It's all very Cold War, isn't it? But the Cold War is over, especially now that we've got Global Warming. . . ."

Vasilisa had stopped crying, her green eyes still brimming with froggy tears, looking not hopeful but hinting. She was not allowed to tell Koschei, not with the pacts and protections and fairy magics the witches worked with. But she could tip him off as to when he was getting warm, and he was very warm indeed, the pepper vodka burning in his throat.

Koschei laughed. "Oh, it's the oldest tale in the books . . . Three sisters, three witches, and each of them got a gift from their father's house. Baba Yaga got her mortar and pestle. Trude got her magic oven to bake brats into gingerbread. But there was a third treasure for the third sister, a simple food mill from the Dead Man's Hall, one that could grind anything you wanted when you turned the handle: bread, grain, gold, sweet porridge and salty herrings, everything but bacon, the sweet salty forbidden flesh the dead craved above all else and traded the mill for in one of the tales. But while bacon was forbidden, the Sampo could still grind the saltiest treasure of all, salt. . . ."

Koschei was boggled and awed by the complexity and perfidy of it all. "It's true then, isn't it, Vasilisa? Baba Yaga is the daughter of my old enemy, Death himself. So's Trude. And so's Louhi, the third sister, the sorceress of the Kalevala, who long ago stole the sun and plunged the world into winter."

Koschei sifted through the later stories and rumors, but they were scant. "But then Louhi somehow dropped off the map and into retirement when she lost her magic mill. Last anyone had seen her Sampo, it had sunk in the North Sea, still grinding salt, forever. That's why the sea is salt . . . and that's why the polar icecaps are melting now."

Koschei gave a bitter laugh. "And to think I'd once proposed to you! Death's daughter's god-daughter!"

"A magic mill?" said a voice. "What, you mean like a coffee grinder?"

Koschei turned, seeing the Arab prince who'd quietly taken up a seat on the barstool behind him. He had a black eye from his bout with the mechanical bull, but to his credit, he had taken his licks without complaint and eavesdropped as stealthily as Anastasia or Vasilisa before her.

"Oh, it could grind coffee," Koschei allowed, "or cocoa, or all the tea in China if you wanted. Whatever trade good or worldly wealth you desire. Everything but bacon. But right now, it's set on salt, as it has been for centuries. While I'd dismissed this as foolishness, a powerful witch letting her most precious treasure be stolen, I see now it's just another of Louhi's plots to doom the world. If you can't steal the sun and plunge the world into eternal winter, then you salt the seas and melt the ice until half the world drowns while the other half burns. Louhi's Sampo is at the bottom of the North Sea, exactly where she wants it, slowly grinding out doom until all the world is in the Dead Man's Hall with her father, Death."

The prince laughed. "The little frog gave me wise counsel then." He gestured to Vasilisa, his ring flashing red and gold. "She told me that she couldn't tell me what I needed to know, but her old suitor could. And you have."

"And who might you be?" Koschei inquired.

"I won't give you my true name, if that's what you're asking," the prince told him, "but as I've made pilgrimage to Mecca, you may call me Hadji. Or perhaps not, since some in the West use that holy name as a slur." He smiled, musing. "Call me *Suleiman* then if you must have a name. I'm just a prince who found a talking frog begging for a royal kiss to release her from an ancient curse. Your curse. V turned back into a frog the moment her Ivan died. But I'd read enough of the fairy tales to know of a princess who found a similar frog and tasked him with retrieving her golden ball from the palace well." The prince grinned. "In Arabia, our most famous tales tell of the djinn, commanded by Suleiman the Magnificent, by the power of his magic ring which, at the end of his life, he cast into the Zemzem, the sacred well at the corner of the Kaaba." The prince's ring flashed, and Koschei took note of Solomon's Seal carved into the ruby as the prince twisted the ring thrice round his finger.

A djinn appeared, taking the form of an immaculately dressed but hulking royal bodyguard. "O djinn, for my third wish, I wish for you to bring me the magic mill, the Sampo, that this man has just described, but instead of salt, make it grind turducken sliders and vodka shots so all here may share its bounty!"

"As you wish," pronounced the djinn, evaporating into air and smoke.

Prince Suleiman smiled, polishing Solomon's ring, and a moment later, the djinn reappeared, bearing a massive hand mill, the whirling crank forged from gilded iron, the bowl from barnacle-bedecked brass, the drawer below open, spewing enough salt to rim a thousand and one margaritas. "Grind, O Sampo, as my master has commanded!" The djinn clouted the mill on the side, the bowl ringing like a brazen bell. "Cease thy incessant saltiness and bring forth turducken sliders and vodka shots!" The Sampo gave a last cough of salt and seawater, and the crank stilled, then it started up again, spinning faster and faster, and turducken sliders began to shoot across the bar, alternating with shot glasses filled with vodka.

"My service to you is now at an end," the djinn told Prince Suleiman. "Call me again at your peril. . . ."

The djinn evaporated into smoke and fire, but Prince Suleiman just grinned at the wondering revelers, proclaiming, "And this is how Arabia has stopped Global Warming and saved the world!"

Of course, it is never that simple, for if Prince Suleiman had lived in the time of fairy tales—or even read the surprisingly accurate warnings still recorded in Asbjørnsen and Moe—he would have known that the curse of the Sampo was that its last owner had never learned the words to command it to turn *off*, a fault which readily became apparent as the mill began to crank into overdrive, shooting forth turducken sliders and vodka shots with the speed and accuracy of a surrealist's tennis-ball cannon. Koschei winced as one shot glass then another struck him in the shoulder with bone-shattering force. But he had suffered much worse . . .

Muscovites screamed and ran, but the mill was a physical object, easily puppeted by sympathetic magic, and Koschei twisted the shot glass in his hand, watching as the Sampo spun around, bringing its dispenser chute to bear on Prince Suleiman. A turducken slider hurtled into his open mouth, then a shot glass of vodka beaned him in the forehead with enough force to stun him, causing him to turn just so such that the second and the third thick-bottomed glasses struck him in the fragile bone of the temple.

Vasilisa cried out, but her pretty protest swiftly became a froggy croak as she dwindled into a tiny green frog still perched prettily atop her barstool, her prince *du jour* now dead.

Koschei turned the Sampo to pelt the wall with sliders and shot glasses, then leaned down and retrieved Solomon's ring from the late prince's finger. He knew it had all manner of useful powers if you wore it on different fingers, from flight to strength to invisibility, but calling the djinn, while perilous, was still the most necessary.

He placed it on his own left index finger and twisted it once. The djinn appeared in a flash of fire.

"No need for grandiloquent introductions," Koschei told the spirit. "My first wish is to know and memorize all the words and phrases to command the Sampo there, including and most especially the command to turn it *off*."

"As you wish, O master," the djinn intoned, prostrating himself in a grand salaam.

It came into Koschei's head all at once, like an epiphany, elegant in its simplicity, but devilishly hard to guess. "Rest, little Sampo," he intoned, "rest like the dead. We've all but the bacon and plenty of bread. . . ."

The Sampo shot a final slider and final shot glass to spatter against the wall, then stuttered and shuddered to a stop, resting for the first time since the age of legends.

Koschei turned to the djinn. "For my second wish, I wish to possess Anastasia's egg, the *Nécessaire*, the lost Fabergé egg made as an *étui*, with all its tools and ornaments safe inside of it, including and most especially the case with the needle with my death on its tip shut safely inside of that case, without anyone the wiser about it, including Anastasia, Baba Yaga, or any of her other sisters, comrades, compatriots, or servants."

"It is done," said the djinn, producing the jewel-encrusted egg with a magician's pass and placing it in Koschei's hands. "And for your third wish, O master?"

In place of a third wish, Koschei removed the Ring of Solomon from his index finger and placed it on his middle finger, the one that conveyed invulnerability. He let the djinn see his upraised middle finger as the spirit evaporated, since Koschei knew that the djinn of Solomon's ring was none other than the demon Samael who lived to tempt owners with a fourth wish for the price of one's soul.

Koschei then, in one motion, pocketed Anastasia's egg with his left hand and with his right caught the frog Vasilisa before she could leap away in search of a new prince.

Bringing her up before his eyes, Koschei smiled. "So, Vasilisa," he said brightly, "I am still a prince among sorcerers, and I think you've had quite enough time to consider my proposal. . . ."

TAP, TAP, TAPPING IN THE DEEP

✪

Dr. Xander Lostetter and Marina J. Lostetter

**November 29, 1979—Sea of Okhotsk,
Off the Coast of Siberia**

Serenely, she glided through the cold dark depths of the ocean waters, hovering mere meters above the murky seabed, creeping along at a deliberate one and a half knots.

Hunting.

Silent.

A sleek monster of iron and steel.

Over one hundred meters in length and displacing five thousand tons, her massive twin electric turbines delivered up to 7,300 horsepower via a Westinghouse S3W nuclear reactor. The only designators on her hull were the numbers 5-8-7 painted in white block lettering across the base of the conning tower.

Everything else about her screamed *oddity*. A massive bulge forward of the conning tower gave her the appearance of a snake that had swallowed an ostrich egg. A broad, shark-like mouth opened into a twenty-six-foot-wide hatch at her bow. And on her aft dorsal spine she carried a cylindrical pod that protruded up from the aft torpedo bay like an oxygen tank on a scuba diver. The craft was the only one of her kind in the entirety of the US Navy Submarine Force, and her name was the USS *Halibut*.

What had once been the wide forward-looking bay to hold and launch Regulus II nuclear-tipped cruise missiles, now housed what the crew affectionately referred to as the Batcave—the central nervous system of the most sophisticated espionage vessel in America's arsenal. The Batcave was home to the UNIVAC 1224 supercomputer mainframe, clusters of specialized electronics and sensor equipment, a pair of twelve-foot two-ton first-of-their-kind "Fish" submersibles, a darkroom for developing film, and a handful of CIA mission specialists—spooks—to analyze the data.

The *Halibut* was a Cold War luxury for the United States. But now, after the outbreak of hostilities and the initial limited tactical nuclear exchange along the East-West German border, the sub had become a Hot War necessity. Information was the lifeblood of combat—missions succeeded or sank on the quality of their intel, soldiers died or came home based on recon and analysis. Decrypted enemy communications were worth their weight in plutonium, and the crew of the USS *Halibut* was the United States Navy's information-gathering elite.

A lone spotlight splintered the murky darkness of the waters as the *Halibut* searched the seabed. Slowly. Patiently. Endlessly. The Fish submersible had been reeled out on an umbilical, its cameras snapping photos, its video sending real-time feeds down the lines to the spooks in the Batcave. The submarine scattered schools of deep-water fish, propelled through clouds of luminescent plankton glowing an eerie fluorescent green, and passed thousands of tiny blue jellyfish dancing like ballerinas. And still she skulked along the bottom.

Within the cylindrical pressurized chamber welded to the aft backbone of the *Halibut*, Chief Petty Officer Marie O'Reilly, Diver First Class, sat stiffly on one of two bunks welded to the wall of the inner lock, thumbing through an outdated issue of *Time* magazine. Despite its elite status, everything on this boat was outdated, from the creased, torn magazines (most of which were secondhand *Playboy* and *Penthouse*), to the twenty-year-old nuclear reactor housed deep in the sub's belly, to the very name itself.

Halibut.

Now there was a name chosen to strike fear into the soul of your enemy. If it had been her choice, she would've baptized the sub something menacing like *Seawolf*, or *Swordfish*, or *Hammerhead*. Or USS *Megalodon*. But nope. The sub was named after a behemoth bottom-dwelling fish with two eyes on one side of its head that did nothing but sit in the mud gobbling up everything that happened to wander past it.

She mused for a moment. *Perhaps we are aptly named after all*.

Marie marked her place in the issue of *Time* as she always did, with an old picture of herself at boot camp, shaking Donna Tobias's hand. Tobias was the first ever female US Navy diver and why Marie had gotten into the gig in the first place. The picture was less of a placeholder and more of a reminder—just as the magazine was. The bolded *WWIII* stenciled over the toxic-orange, fiery mushroom cloud on its glossy cover pulled gruesome images from the late-night news to the fore of her mind. Bile pushed up her throat as she recalled the clipped screams. The cover always made Marie sick to her stomach, but that was precisely why she carried it around. The inconceivable future they had all imagined could never be, was here. Now. Ghastly and real.

And she had a job to do.

They had a job to do.

Twenty-five-year-old Petty Officer Robert Hart, Diver Second Class, paced a small square in the center of the cramped space, shoulders slumped, hands clasped behind his back, head bowed with a pair of headphones on. Slim orange discs of foam covered his ears. The tape deck was the newest gadget he'd picked up while they were stopped in Yokosuka for resupply, along with all of three cassettes. *You mark my words*, he'd sworn, *the Sony Walkman is gonna be all the rage back in the States by next year*.

"Hart, will you quit pacing? You're getting on my nerves."

His head continued to bob, his feet continued to cut a pattern into the swirls of burnt-orange and puke-green carpet. She noticed small droplets of sweat gathering at his temples.

"Hart!" she tried again.

His shuffling stopped. He lifted one side of the headphones, and the tinny music of the Eagles' "Hotel California" blared out, Don Felder and Joe Walsh deep in the throes of their guitar solo. "What, Chief?"

"Stop pacing, *please*."

Hart shivered all over, shook a leg. Now that he'd stopped circling, the pent-up energy had to find a new outlet. "I can't help it." He reached down and pressed the STOP button on the tape deck attached to his belt. "It's keeping me calm."

She understood. She did. He'd been on, what, a dozen dives of this caliber? "It's a cable line from Petropavlovsk," she tried to reassure him. "Job's in and out." They needed to remove a previously placed wiretap and drop a new one. Easy.

Hart bounced one leg, rolled his shoulders. "Yeah, a cable line coming from a Russki naval base beneath four hundred feet of water. In these fucking waters. Visibility's—what?—ten feet directly under the Fish's lights—at best? Who knows what they've got cooking down there? Right? I mean, there are rumors—"

She cut him off. "Submariners like to talk. You scared of the Kraken, too?"

That brought a small smile to his lips. "There's plenty to worry about down there without the Kraken. This might be easy for you, Chief, you've got hundreds of dives. But some of us still get the shakes." He pointed at his bobbing leg in good humor.

She parted her lips to say, "What, you think I don't get nervous before every dive? You think I don't spook myself in the shadows down there? Think I've never dropped a cable line because a sea turtle snuck up on me? Think I don't have nightmares about kinked airlines and total blackouts?"

But then she thought better of it. Maybe he needed

to think she wasn't nervous. Needed his chief to be ready and reserved. They hadn't been in this tin can together long enough for her to know what he needed her to say.

He motioned at the PLAY button. A question. She waved him on, and the music screeched out again.

What did he need her to say?

Marie leaned back into her bunk with a sigh. In truth, it wasn't only her uncertain communication with Hart she was worried about.

She played with her finger, the wedding band absent, the bareness disconcerting to her. She couldn't dive with jewelry, and she felt naked without it. Instead, the ring hung on a gold chain next to her bunk. Below the ring, she'd taped a Polaroid from last year. It was already beginning to fade—evidence of its placement near her favorite window back home, recently liberated and sent to her by her husband. She'd received it last time she'd been topside.

In it, she and Garrett stood squeezed between Mickey and Donald, the spires of Disney Castle rising in the background. The vacation had been last minute—a surprise treat back before the nukes killed surprise treats. Before she'd been promoted into classified work. Back when she could still tell him where she was and what she was doing.

Back when she let him know her.

She ran the pad of her finger over Garrett's smile, and it melted her heart like always.

Below the photograph, a single piece of pink stationary was pinned to the wall, half curling in on itself like a dead beetle. It was supposed to be a letter. It could have been something simple, just thanking him for sending the picture. But she couldn't write it. Every time she tried, she felt like an impostor.

Since the opening salvos of the war, guilt had gnawed at her insides, chewed away at her like tiny little barracuda nibbling away her humanity. And for that guilt, the stationary remained blank on the wall, unpenned, empty, nothing to say and no way to say it. She rolled out from the bunk every day trying to figure it out. And she rolled back into the bunk every night, exhausted, with no answers. Her life was about communication, information. And yet those same things were ironically roadblocks set between the Garrett who told her everything, and the Marie who gave him nothing.

What does an impostor wife write to her husband?

Secrets were everywhere in the water. Only a handful of men and women in the world knew what she truly did for a living. Even the majority of the *Halibut* crew only knew *of* the Batcave, not what went on inside. After all, there be where spooks live.

The intercom buzzed.

She leaned over and flipped a switch. "O'Reilly."

"Chief, we've located the tap," said CIA mission specialist Cooper. "Ready to suit up?"

Marie checked her watch. "Running my calculations now."

Standard diving became realistically useless after one hundred feet. Oxygen toxicity, nitrogen narcosis, and decompression sickness were all very real dangers at depths beyond a hundred feet. At one hundred and thirty feet, divers were allowed no more than ten minutes before being required to return to the surface.

Nothing real could be accomplished by working divers with only ten minutes at operational depth.

And so the US Navy had developed saturation diving. Specialized pressure chambers purged nitrogen from the air, replacing it with inert helium gas. Under high pressure, the low-molecular-weight helium was absorbed by the diver's blood and tissue to the point of complete saturation, reaching equilibrium with ambient water pressure. This allowed divers to live and work at pressure for days and weeks at a time, without having to surface or decompress, and without suffering the incapacitating effects of nitrogen absorption.

It made the divers sound like they were the newest members of Alvin and the Chipmunks, but you got used to it after a while.

Marie double- and triple-checked her calculations: the atmospheric readings, the environment in the pressurized chamber, the water and tidal conditions. "Affirmative. We're good to go."

"All right, Chief—Hart—good luck."

Hart's leg began to twitch once more. Rhythmically, slowly, like a drum.

Tap. Tap. Tap.

Here they went . . . tapping in the deep. Waiting to crack open the line and reveal all the enemy's secrets oozing through the deep.

Several hours of preamble—final prep of the Tap equipment, one last mission review, and the suit up in

Westinghouse MK-14 rebreathers and Kirby-Norman recirculatory helmets—preceded their exit through the lockout chamber.

Despite the circulating 140-degree water—pumped between their suit layers via one of the life-giving tubes on their long, twisted umbilical—the sea felt cold as it slipped over Marie. The ocean temperature was a balmy 27 degrees Fahrenheit, the ocean salinity being the only thing keeping the entire Sea of Okhotsk from freezing into a thick block of ice off the Siberian coast.

The water always felt both like an old friend and an adversary. It accepted her into itself with ease. Enveloping. It caressed her just as easily as it could squeeze her. Drown her. Keep her forever.

She glanced at Hart. The harsh beams from the Fish cast strange shadows beneath his faceplate. She gave him the thumbs-up and he returned it.

Between them they carried the newest and most recently improved Tap: a massive nine-foot-long, cylindrical electronics marvel developed especially for these missions by the NSA. It held a recorder, data reels, an immense induction coil that wrapped around the Soviet undersea communications cable to tease out the transmitted electronic data, and a radioisotope TEG nuclear battery that could supply power to the unit for years on end.

Overall, visibility was low and the going slow. The water pushed heavily on them from all sides, and their feet kicked up muck and silt along the bottom, adding a cloudiness to the dark. The Fish's bright floodlights put them literally under a spotlight, and all beyond was the deep black of the unknown. Shadows roiled here—*there*—here again. Shifts in the water itself, or sea creatures lurking just beyond?

They trudged on and a giant crab scuttled into their ring of light—all harsh joints and long legs, like boney fingers clawing at the sand—before dashing out again.

Out of the depths a three-foot-long form darted right at them, bubbles rolling off its slimy, pale-gray back, along its side. Marie startled but swallowed her shout. The thing's head was half the size of its body, and unlike the crab, it did not go past, but rushed at her face. Eyeball to eyeball with her, it investigated—long teeth in its frowning mouth. There was an intelligence in there somewhere, behind the eye. She tried to ignore it, hoping the spooky thing wouldn't attempt a taste.

Eventually it skulked back off into the murky darkness, becoming a shadow, and then fading out of sight all together.

"How you doing up there, Hart?"

He was in the lead, carrying the head end of the Tap's cylindrical casing. Even at ten feet away, he was a gloomy figure shrouded in plumes of silt.

"I'm good, Chief."

After an agonizing slog, they reached the Soviet communications cable. It was no more than a bundle of lines sheathed together, about the diameter of her fist, running along the seabed between the Soviet nuclear-missile submarine base at Petropavlovsk to the Soviet Pacific Fleet headquarters in Vladivostok.

Finding it and tapping it had been an intelligence coup for the United States. Information equaled lives saved and resources protected. It meant soldiers got to go home to their kids. It meant some wives, somewhere, got to tell their husbands about their days. Got to forge connections. Didn't have to lie by omission.

The previous Tap's induction clamp was wrapped tightly about the cable. Somewhere within the casing, data reels were recording at that very moment, deciphering electromagnetic signals, and phone calls, and data transmissions. Capturing ship movements and SLBM targets.

"Let's prep the active Tap for shutdown."

"Aye, Chief."

They went to work dismantling the old beast, she at one end, he at the other. Their spotlight was just barely wide enough to encapsulate them both.

"Chief, can you look at this?" Hart asked, only minutes in.

She stepped back to gaze over toward her diving partner. "What is it?"

"Uhh . . . this doesn't look right," Hart said. "Uhh . . ."

Something wriggled in the sediment near Hart. Long, thin. Black, but shiny. At first, she thought it was another fish—or perhaps an eel or a seaworm—but then it coiled up, the tip of it sliding upward through the water. Long. Too long. "Hart—" She leapt toward him, to push him away from it. But the pressure made her movements muddled, slow. She stumbled in the thick muddy silt. Clouds of sediment plumed up.

He turned. The thing was lost in the curling grime.

"Was that—" she started. "What did you see?" She remembered her joke: *Kraken*. But this wasn't a thick tentacle. It was . . . Shivers trembled down her spine and into the pit of her stomach.

"Ack! *What the fuck was that?*" he shouted.

"I'm coming!" She leapt over the line, pulling herself along the Tap to his side.

Just as she grasped his hand, he yelped.

"Hart? You OK?" Marie asked.

Cooper's voice came in from the Batcave. "Chief. We've lost both video feeds."

"Hart?"

"I told you!" he said, voice edging into panic. "The rumors. I told you we don't know what's—" He wriggled his leg. A ghostly mockery of his nervous bobbing from before. He was trying to dislodge something.

He took her other hand in desperation. She held him firmly. She could just make out his shocked expression in the harsh play of light and shadows under his mask.

"Chief, it's got—"

A swift, sudden *yank* swept her off her feet. Took Hart right out of her hands.

He screamed, his terrified face seared suddenly—like a sunspot—into her vision even after he was gone. Gone into the dark. Into the deep.

Taken.

"*Hart!*"

"O'Reilly," Cooper called out from the sub. "What's happening?"

The water enveloped her like thick molasses. She wanted to will herself into the dark after him, but what could she—?

The deep-sea flood lights flickered momentarily, strobing.

There, she caught sight of him. Barely a silhouette, but there. She cried out for him again, and he came forward.

But not of his own accord. Pushed, propelled. His head lolling, body limp.

The flickering spotlight caught him. He bent, his entire body shifting like a puppet on strings, limbs were yanked out at impossible angles.

He thrashed.

The lights flickered out, and the seafloor plunged into oily darkness, like tar pitch. She heard Hart's screams rip through the communications line. His screeching howls were inhuman, a wild animal being filleted alive.

"*Robert!*" Marie yelled, lunging forward into the inky blackness.

"O'Reilly!" the mission specialist called out again.

Hart's screams ceased abruptly. Everything went dead silent, except the hissing echoes of her rebreather. No electronic static. No Batcave. No nothing. All communications lost.

She was alone.

In utter darkness.

Her heart pounded wildly in her chest. Her arms and legs were immobilized by a surge of fear. "Hart?" she asked hesitantly, quietly, into the dead mic.

She sensed movement in the cold black water. Though she could see none of it.

After an eternity, a soft dim glow.

A sickly fluorescent green radiance from the Soviet wire.

The light grew a little brighter. Only feet away, Hart's body twisted slowly in the water, as if adrift, twirling, spinning—a mangled pirouette. Thin, shadowy tendrils snaked over and around him in the dimness.

A massive electronic squelch blasted Marie's ears as the *Halibut's* searchlight snapped back to life, flooding the cold dark void. Voices streamed in from the Batcave, exasperated, demanding answers from the divers.

But Marie couldn't hear them. There was no sound, only this sight. This terror.

She was face to face with it. Thick, metallic arms had punctured Hart's diving suit, invaded his body, dug into his flesh and muscle. Tiny plumes of blood spilled into the ocean waters. Beneath the skin of his face, thousands of spindly tendrils squirmed and pulsed and breathed, emitting that radioactive-green fluorescent light as they dug through the tissue of his body. His mouth was locked wide open in the final agonizing throes of what had been a deathly scream.

He was gone. And now this *thing* possessed him.

The tendrils squirmed in the waters like grotesque worms, their metallic sheen suggesting they were mechanical in nature. They emitted an awful screeching sound that traveled through the dense waters and enveloped her with immobilizing fear.

Her eyes fell back on the Soviet communications cable. It had been severed.

And the multitudes of writhing, living metallic tentacles stretched out from *within* that severed cable. Impossibly thick, and far too many. But true. Dozens of them. Twisting and writhing like Medusa's snakes, all wrapped around Hart. His arms, his legs, his torso, his neck. Squeezing. Digging. Eating.

But there were also plenty of tendrils free in the water, searching outward from the severed cable.

They were coming for *her*.

"Hart's dead," she muttered. Shocked. "Pull me in." Her voice was so weak, the Batcave couldn't hear her over the calls of their own voices.

Hart was right. Hart had been right and she'd made a joke. The Soviets had—what *the fuck* did they have?

A tentacle corkscrewed through the water—sharp and determined.

"Emergency! Emergency!" she screamed, suddenly alive. "Pull me in! *Now* goddammit!" She scrabbled backward in a panic. "It's a fucking ambush!"

The safety line within the umbilical pulled taut as her crewmates began to reel her in. And to her horror, they were reeling in Hart as well.

A new voice came in over the comms. "Chief O'Reilly, this is the Captain. What the hell's going on out there?"

She tried not to panic, working with the safety line instead of against it, trying to use it to move quicker back toward the hatch. The tentacles snaked through the mud and silt after her.

"Captain, it's alive. The Russkies' communications cable is alive! It got Hart. They killed him."

"O'Reilly, can you repeat that? Are you saying Petty Officer Hart was killed by a live wire? Was it a power surge of some kind?"

"That's not likely," countered Cooper. "The Soviet cable does not contain any high voltage or high current lines. A severed live wire couldn't kill him."

She realized there was no possible way to explain any of this. How the Soviets had developed this kind of technology, she had no notion. But one thing was for certain: Whatever the hell this weapon was, she could not allow it onto the boat.

She unsheathed her diving knife, reaching out for Hart's umbilical lines. She took in his limp form one last time. He'd had so much to give, so much life ahead of him. And this damn war had taken it. These goddamned Soviet wires had *taken* it.

Anger started to override the fear. She sawed away with fury guiding her hand, keeping her blade steady. The line snapped. Hart drifted away, left behind, the wires still feasting on his flesh.

A dozen of the long tentacles suddenly dislodged themselves, squirming free of the captured body to seek out a new form, uninterested in indulging on the easy meal. Swiftly, they gave chase, wriggling through the mud and silt across the seafloor—giving off those horrid sonic waves that grated up her spine, causing her jaw muscles to clamp down.

"Pick up the pace! Reel faster, they've almost got me!"

"Chief can you repeat?" asked Cooper. "Is someone else down there?"

Her body boiled with frustration. "Affirmative! The Soviets laid an ambush. Aren't you picking up those acoustics? That *sound*? *That's* the Soviet weapon. It killed Hart. And if we don't move faster, I'm next!" She took a breath.

"Copy," he responded.

Her speed marginally increased.

But it wasn't fast enough.

She wasn't going to make it.

The closest tendril snapped out, wrapping itself around

her ankle, snaking up to her knee. "Fuck me," she whispered as the thing constricted. Two more were right behind it. The hulk of the submarine was above her now. Another fifty feet to the diver's hatch. It seemed so close . . . yet so far.

Even in the buoyancy of the water, her diving knife was heavy in her hand. A small comfort, but one nonetheless. She made a decision. Garrett's heart-melting smile flooded her mind—the smell of him on the morning sheets after he'd already gotten up to get in the shower—a laughing baby that was never to be—atomic bombs and millions dead.

Would anyone even tell Garrett the truth about what happened to her?

"Cooper, listen to me carefully," she said. "You tell the captain to get the sub out of here. We can't let these things on board. I'm cutting loose."

"That's a negative, O'Reilly," the captain cut in. "You get your ass back in here double time, that's a direct order. Do you understand?"

She held the knife edge against her umbilical. Ready. Determined.

And then the thing *struck*.

The viper head of the tendril on her leg reared back and attacked, biting into the muscles of her thigh. Immediate and intense agony as a wave of nausea washed over and through her. She could hear herself screaming, but it seemed someone else in another place and another time. She willed her knife arm to move, some tiny part of her mind desperate to remain connected to reality, to live, to fight off her attacker.

She felt the alien tendrils invade her body, reaching. Hunting. Searching. Taking control of her nervous system and tapping into her mind. Sifting through thirty years of memories. Assaulting the very core of her being. The glowing orange coals of the hot wood stove on Christmas morning as she and her brother opened brightly wrapped presents. The thick smell of wood smoke. The feel of hard leather beneath her hands as she heaved the Western saddle onto the back of her favorite, a chocolate-brown quarter horse she had named Milky Way. Brian, her first kiss in the parking lot of a McDonald's. Nothing but a mistake served with a side of mustard and onions. They dug deeper and deeper, probing for information, for the secrets that she had sworn her life to protect—for secrets she could not even share with her own husband.

The thing latched onto the image of Garrett. The memory of the Polaroid camera flashing. The spires of Disney Castle reaching up toward the sky, carefree. The memories were jumbled, but the thing had them by the neck, choking the life from them. Threatening to rip them all away if she did not give it what it wanted.

"Let's do it!" Garrett said excitedly, his beautiful eyes turning dark and menacing as they bore into her. The bright Florida sun sank behind dark purple and black storm clouds. Lightning splintered the sky over the Disney spires. "Let's have a baby," he said, his voice sluggish and deep and slurring, like a record player turned down two speeds too slow. "It's the perfect time to have a baby. You're safe. Everyone is safe. You can tell me now." His arm gradually snaked outward and grabbed her by the neck and shoulder, squeezing, pinching. Hurting her.

A distortion.

A fabrication.

Or so she hoped. She could not be sure. It was a mess of images in her mind.

If you tell me everything, we can be happy. Our love will be real, then. Tell me. Tell me.

"Teeeeeell meeeeeeeee . . ." the words dragged out of his mouth in grotesque slow motion as the reflection of a mushroom cloud glinted from the pupils of his stormy, violent eyes.

"No . . ." she whimpered.

"The secrets, the secrets, the secrets," a hissing voice whispered from the dark corners of her mind. It was not a Russian voice in her head, she realized. It wasn't even a *human* voice.

What was it? What is it? "What *are* you?" She drilled it for information, turning its own tendrils upon itself.

Deep, deep, deep, so deep and dark and cold. Home.

Cataclysm. Acid currents. Oceans burning. A threat to us all. From above. To the very waters of our existence.

A mission. Discovery. Hunt. Search.

Tap tap tap tap tap tap them for information.

It was enough of a distraction—this strange knowledge—to give her a brief moment, to feel the weight of the knife. To will the completion of a single action.

She came to in a massive gasp for air. Two divers hauled her out of the water and into the dive chamber. Extreme pain radiated outward from her left thigh. She looked down to see a foot-long mechanical tendril still clamped into her upper leg. But the rest of it had been hacked away. Hundreds of tiny, wormlike vines hung limply from the end of the hacked away cable, dead.

"Captain, we got her," one of the divers announced into the intercom.

Immediately, she felt the *Halibut* rumble to life as the electric turbines kicked in.

Chief Petty Officer Marie O'Reilly, Diver First Class, sat on the floor, leaning back against her bunk, staring at the empty bunk across from her. The issue of *Time* lay there, right where she'd left it, the toxic orange of the nuclear blast staring her in the face.

Hart should still be here, she thought. War takes things it shouldn't. And what is this war, now?

They'd lost the Tap, but they had new information. Perhaps the most valuable information in the world.

And still, she could not tell Garrett.

Making up her mind, she plucked the pink stationary from the wall, then scooped up the Walkman from where Hart had left it.

Maybe it was okay that she couldn't tell Garrett things. After all, the things she needed to know, needed to keep close, kept him safe. Their love wasn't any less real because she couldn't share these secrets. He understood what she had to do, that these secrets were part of her life, and loved her anyway. All she had to do was give back. Communicate what she could, how she felt.

Carefully, she placed Hart's headphones over her ears, and began to write.

Dear Garrett,
  The truth is, I love you . . .

THE OUROBOROS ARRANGEMENT

✪

Martin L. Shoemaker

Curtis Cole glanced briefly at the beer menu, wishing it was dinner time and not lunch so he could sample some. It had already been a long day at work, and if this lunch with Leonard ran long, that would lead to a very late night. He didn't see Beth and the kids often enough as it was.

But it was too early for beer. Besides, Curtis noticed the man sitting at the bar near the clock, who chose that moment to turn and glance in Curtis's direction. It was Captain Wainwright, the spook. Military intelligence, like Curtis, only this guy was still in the service. He was assigned to Defense LogiCom as security liaison for the government. It was his job to check up on DLC security, including Curtis, DLC's top security officer. A slight nod from Wainwright said: *Greetings, Mr. Cole, I'm watching you.*

Curtis was used to such surveillance, so it didn't faze him anymore. He made an equally slight return nod. Wainwright turned back to the bar.

The man would want to know what this meeting was

about, and Curtis would be expected to write up a complete report. That was just routine. The Pentagon was always wary of possible Soviet contacts, and Curtis had friends (like Leonard) who traveled to international conferences all the time. Curtis would've filed the report, regardless; but now he figured he had better put some meat in it. He would have to know what Leonard had to say, regardless of how long lunch went.

Forsaking the beer, Curtis set the little plastic laminated card back on the Formica tabletop, and he smiled up at the young waitress—a college student, no doubt. "Just an iced tea, please."

The woman scratched a note on the pad in her hand and nodded, her ponytail bobbing. "And are you ready to order? Or..."

Curtis shook his head. "I'm waiting for my friend," he said. "He should be here soon."

"Okay, I'll look for him. And I'll get your tea right out." She flipped her pad closed and headed back to the kitchen. She had no trouble navigating the narrow spaces between the tables and chairs. It was too early for the lunch rush yet.

Curtis sat back against the booth's polished wooden slats, listening to the music on the jukebox. "Smoke on the Water" cut over to "Katmandu," always a popular song in the Detroit area. "Nights in White Satin" followed. When the song switched to "Ridin' the Storm Out" by some group Curtis couldn't place, he wondered how long it would take for Leonard to get there. He knew once they got talking, they could easily exceed his lunch hour. That's why Curtis had chosen The Lantern for their lunch spot.

The food wasn't great, and the atmosphere was drab. The joint had no windows and its sixties-era decor was getting pretty shabby a decade later. But the place was right across the street from DLC, just a short walk from work, so at least Curtis wouldn't waste any time in transit.

He sighed. Leonard was a lot more casual about time, always had been, even going back to their college days. He always said he'd be at a particular point at a particular time, even promise to be early, but he had never been. Not in the twelve years Curtis had known him.

Curtis was just wondering if he had time to read that new book everyone had been pushing on him—*Shockwave Rider*, by some RAF officer named Brunner—when he heard a squeal of tires, a bump, a crash of metal, and sounds of breaking glass. Instantly, reflexes he'd learned in Southeast Asia took over, sending him into action. Curtis had been one of the dumb ones in Vietnam, or maybe one of the lucky ones since he'd survived it: He was the sort who ran into trouble, not away from it. The Army had taught him a fair amount of field medicine the hard way, and somebody might be hurt.

So he dashed past the waitress, returning from the kitchen with a tray of drinks. He didn't even look back as she cursed creatively and glass shattered on the floor. So much for his tea. He bolted up to the door, reaching it just ahead of Wainwright. Then another combat reflex took over: He paused and peered out through a small gap between the door and the door frame. He had no reason to expect gunfire when the sounds were those of an auto accident; but he worked for a defense subcontractor, and their regular security drills kept his paranoia in tune.

Radicals had targeted researchers on campuses across the country, so why not here in Ann Arbor?

Wainwright peeked out as well, and then nodded. Curtis thrust the door outward and barreled through and across the dull gray parking lot. Habit made him sprint right, then seek cover behind a nearby dumpster so he could better assess the situation. Wainwright ran left, taking cover behind a bench on the edge of the parking lot.

It was easy to see where the trouble was: An old Pontiac had collided with an orange Pacer. That had been the source of the glass sounds, all those square yards of window on the Pacer. DLC and The Lantern were nearly a mile off campus, yet a crowd of students still gathered around the wreckage. For once, Curtis didn't notice the hippies' shoddy dress and grooming. He was too busy looking for trouble.

And trouble was easy to spot: There were two knots of spectators around the cars, while a third clustered around the pavement to the north. Wainwright scrambled to the cars, where the drivers were slowly pulling themselves out. Curtis ran up to the third group, squeezing his way through the crowd.

Leonard lay curled up on the pavement, and Curtis feared the worst for his friend; but immediately, Leonard reached out a hand, feeling around. "Where are my glasses?"

Curtis knelt down. "Here you go, Len." He found Leonard's horn-rimmed spectacles and handed them to the man. "Are you all right?"

"Curtis? I'm . . ." Leonard half sat, wincing as he did. "I'm okay. I think. As long as—my briefcase!"

A tall, thin man in a light-green jacket stepped forward from the crowd. From his bearing and his haircut, Curtis guessed ROTC, but not in uniform so as not to draw the ire of the students. The man held out a battered gray valise that Curtis had first seen a decade and a half back. "Here it is," he said. "Are you sure you're all right, sir?"

"I'm—"

Curtis held up a hand. "Let me take a look, Len. Here." He took the briefcase and set it behind Leonard. "Use this as a pillow."

"It's a little hard for that."

Curtis grinned. If Leonard could complain, he was probably all right. But still, better to not take chances. "Just relax. Does anything hurt?"

"No."

Curtis looked and saw no obvious contusions, though Len's jacket was scraped pretty good. "Did they hit you?"

"No, I jumped out of the way. But I . . . slipped on something, oil in the road I guess, and lost my footing. So I took a tumble. Really, Curtis, I'm all right."

It was just a fall, and Leonard probably didn't break any bones. It was clear that Leonard's hands were working fine, no pain there. "Just in case," Curtis said, "wiggle your toes." Leonard waggled his wingtips, and his face showed no signs of discomfort. "All right, I don't think there's anything broken." Curtis turned to the tall student. "Could you help him into The Lantern? I need to help Captain Wainwright with the drivers."

"I'm all right," Leonard insisted as he started to rise to his feet.

"He looks all right, sir," the student said. "I should help you with the drivers, in case they're hurt."

Curtis looked at Leonard one more time, but his friend seemed to be standing steady. "All right," he said. "That's a good plan. Leonard, go in, sit down. I'll be in soon, I hope."

As soon as Curtis returned to the gloom of The Lantern, he saw the waitress. "I'm sorry," he said. "Let me pay for the glass and the tea."

She shook her head. "It was an emergency. I understand. The boss says it's covered. I already set another over by your friend."

"Thanks." Curtis wound his way between the tables back to the booths. In the time that he and the young recruit—Ted, his name was, Naval ROTC—had been attending to the drivers, the lunch crowd had arrived. Curtis counted fifteen, a lot for such a small hole in the wall. Seventeen counting him and Leonard.

Eighteen, Curtis noted, as Captain Wainwright snuck back in and found his seat by the clock.

Curtis got to the booth, and Leonard was sitting in his old spot, already two or three good gulps into a beer. Curtis tried not to resent his friend for indulging. The math department was a lot less stringent than were his bosses at DLC. So he sat on the other side, and he took a healthy swallow of the iced tea. "Leonard, you had me worried."

"I'm all right," his friend responded.

But Leonard didn't look all right. Physically, he was only mussed up; but emotionally, Curtis saw stress lines and wide eyes. It was a look of alertness verging on panic that Curtis had seen on many faces in the rice patties, but never on his quiet academic friend. With the life Leonard had led, that might have been his first close brush with death. The man had the perfect combination for deferment: a brilliant mathematical mind in a 4F body.

The two of them had bonded over tutoring, with Leonard helping Curtis to keep his math grades up so as not to get kicked out of ROTC. Leonard brushed it off whenever Curtis pointed it out, but it was true: Leonard most likely saved Curtis's life, though years ahead of time. Thanks to ROTC, Curtis had entered the Army as a military intelligence officer. If he'd flunked out of the program, he'd have likely been a grunt out in the bush, and seen a lot more action. He'd seen enough as it was. He never wanted to be closer to the fighting than that.

Then Curtis noticed another sign of stress: Leonard's knuckles, practically bone white as his fingers gripped the valise. "Hey, come on," Curtis said. "Relax. Have some more beer." Maybe the beer would help him come down from the stress. "You're okay. You survived. A week from now you'll be telling the story and laughing about it. It was just a near miss in traffic."

Leonard blinked, and his face calmed a notch. "It's not—" Then he took another swig, and he relaxed more. "Yeah, I survived. I'll be all right, don't worry."

"So what did you want to talk about? You said it was important?"

At that, Leonard's eyes widened again, and he looked around the room. "Not . . . not now. Let's eat."

Leonard's timing was perfect, as the waitress returned

just at that moment. Curtis ordered the Reuben, while Leonard had a burger and onion rings. As soon as the waitress left, Leonard asked about Beth and the kids. That distracted Curtis, since there was so much to tell: young Lenny heading off to school, Betty having her first recital. It had been nearly a year since the two had gotten together, which was a shame, considering they now worked in the same town again for the first time ... first time since Vietnam, really. But life for both had gotten so busy.

The food arrived, occupying their attention for several more minutes. As they ate, Leonard reminisced about school days: parties they'd attended, friends they'd shared, the debate club, and more. He kept the conversation moving, but his frequent glances around the room sparked Curtis's suspicions. That, and the way he never quite got away from the valise, which he'd set beside himself on the bench when the food arrived. Len frequently dropped his hand down to touch it, as if reassuring himself it wasn't lost.

Curtis's years in intelligence had trained him to notice details, and these weren't subtle. There was something in the valise, something Len wanted to talk about, but he didn't want to be overheard. He was waiting out the lunch crowd—killing time so they'd have more privacy.

As Curtis carried on his part of the conversation, a separate track in his mind pondered what to do about Len's agitation. Curtis was professionally paranoid, disinclined to rule out concerns without understanding them first. And Leonard Gardner ... well, Leonard had to be the smartest person Curtis had ever met, so smart that Curtis had trouble keeping up with him. Most the time. Curtis knew that sometimes geniuses were unstable—the Nash affair had demonstrated that—but he had never seen signs of that in Leonard. If Leonard was nervous, there was a reason, and Curtis had better know what it was.

So trying not to be obvious, Curtis glanced toward the clock behind the bar. It was already forty minutes into his lunch hour, and Leonard showed no signs of wanting to talk soon. Curtis knew this was important, but important enough to be late getting back?

And below the clock, Wainwright stared back at Curtis. And at Leonard. Maybe more Leonard than Curtis?

Curtis sighed inwardly. He would have to explain it to his boss—and to Wainwright—but Len needed a friend, needed Curtis. So Curtis took his time eating. When Leonard's glass was empty, Curtis gave him a while so as not to overload his system, then ordered another round. They kept chatting as the music died—"You're So Vain" was the last song queued—and the crowd slowly thinned out. Wainwright was among the last to leave, not looking at Curtis as he left, but tipping his hat slightly as he reached the door.

After a few more minutes, Leonard leaned forward. "I . . ." He looked around. There was still a couple in a booth along the far wall, but The Lantern might not get any emptier than this. He leaned farther forward and lowered his voice. "I need to talk to you, Curtis."

"Len, if this is some sort of security matter, we should talk in my office. We can go across the street."

Len shook his head. "I don't . . . I don't know if it's

serious like that. I'm not ready to draw that kind of attention. Not . . . not until you've heard it, and chimed in. I need to know if this is serious or . . . or if I'm crazy."

Curtis tried to give a reassuring smile. "Leonard, you're not crazy. I'm sure of that."

Leonard's eyes grew wider. "You don't know!" Then he took a breath, seeming to calm himself. "*I* don't know. What I found is impossible to believe. But I believe it. I think."

Curtis kept his voice calm, measured, trying to draw Leonard out without agitating him. "So this relates to your new post at Michigan? Some sort of . . . analyst, did you call it?"

Leonard shook his head. "Synthesist." When Curtis didn't respond, Leonard continued, "It's taking my statistical analysis techniques and applying them across seemingly disjoint fields of study, looking for underlying patterns. It's . . ."

When Leonard didn't continue, Curtis asked, "Is it classified?"

Leonard nodded. "It's DOD funded, so potentially classified. They've allowed me to publish all my research so far, everything I've tried. But they review it all first. Still, you've got top clearance."

"But do I have need to know?"

Leonard frowned. "I . . . I need you to know. I need to share this with somebody. Somebody who can check my work."

Curtis shook his head. "My math hasn't gotten any better since college, Len. You know my limits. There's no way I can keep up with your formulae."

"I know, but you always had a great grasp of theory. An intuition, even when you couldn't get the math right. And synthesis . . . Well, it takes me places where that intuition could be helpful."

"Such as?"

"Well . . . you remember all the dorm room bull sessions, where we got caught up in all sorts of edge theories in physics. You remember the fine-tuned universe?"

"That's . . . Robert Dicke, right? That fundamental constants in the universe are in a golden zone for life. Two years ago Brandon Carter expressed a similar idea known as the anthropic principle."

"I knew it! You *have* kept up."

Curtis nodded. "A little, yes. That's the theory that says the reason the universe is the way it is is because if it were any other way, we couldn't exist to wonder what it's like."

Leonard looked around, and then answered, "That's the weak anthropic principle. I'm talking about the strong one. The one that says the universe is the way it is because it was designed *so that* we would exist."

Now Curtis's eyes were the ones that widened. "Designed? Leonard, are you telling me you found mathematical proof of God?"

Leonard snorted. "God would be a relief. I could relax then; I would know who's in charge." Then he shook his head. "It's not really the anthropic principle, let's call it *the selection principle*."

"Selection of what?"

"Quantum states." Len took another drink. "It's complicated, and I'm starting near the end, so that's just making it more so. Let me go back to the beginning.

"My work involves taking modern statistical analysis techniques and looking for trends and anomalies in historical data from all sorts of fields. Entertainment, finance, politics, you name it. My backers want to hit a wide range of fields, looking for any ability to forecast trends and anomalies. They figure if I can find a method that works in one field, it will give us something to try in other fields. And they've even gotten me access to operational data and after-action reports from the military." Leonard looked around. "I can't mention certain specifics, but I can talk about trends."

"Is this possible?"

"With a lot of noise and low precision, I think it is. I can't predict next year's election; but I've done okay at predicting popular songs and developing news stories. Little things here and there."

"So that's what has you so agitated? Some sort of Bayesian crystal ball?"

That drew a chuckle from Leonard. "It's not Bayesian, it's... it involves a synthesis of several approaches involving Markov chains and chaos theory. Oh, I can barely understand it myself some days, so I'm sorry, but I can't explain it to you. All I can say is I have high confidence in the predictions. And I hope that's enough for you."

Curtis narrowed his eyes. "'A wise man, therefore, proportions his belief to the evidence.'" he quoted.

"Hume," Leonard replied. "I taught you that one, so I can't argue with it. But can you accept that I believe this technique to be valid?" Curtis nodded. "And so can you provisionally accept it?"

Another nod. "Provisionally."

"Good, because what's—" He glanced around. "What has me 'agitated,' as you put it, are the predictions I drew for a certain combination of data sets."

"Go on."

"And this is the part that might need clearance."

Curtis looked up, half expecting to see Wainwright watching them. This would be the time to maintain OPSEC by walking away. For an operation he didn't even know.

But he trusted Leonard as much as anyone he'd ever met. "Go on."

Leonard pushed aside the beer and leaned deep over the table. "My grant officer in the Pentagon is interested in predicting false positives."

"False positives for what?"

"MAD."

"Oh." Mutually assured destruction. The theory that if the US and Soviets both knew they could destroy each other in a nuclear exchange, neither would dare start anything. A tenuous mutual containment predicated on nothing more than game theory. But it contained within it a huge risk.

"False positives could start the war that MAD was designed to prevent," Leonard said, as if reading Curtis's mind. "They're a big concern, and growing."

Curtis didn't answer. Through his work at DLC, he might know more about the topic than Leonard did; but he didn't know what clearance Leonard had, so he remained quiet on that specific matter. Instead he asked a question from his days in stats class: "Doesn't reducing false positives always increase false negatives? Aren't those just as dangerous?"

Leonard sighed. "Try telling that to an eager general answering to a congressional oversight committee. He promised the impossible, now he expects me to deliver it."

Curtis laughed softly. He had known generals like that.

"But it's not as impossible as it sounds," Leonard continued. "No, we can't reduce false positives without risks on the other side; but we can prepare for them, mitigate them, and predict their outcomes. Especially by studying the ones that have already happened."

Curtis nodded again. "So you know of such incidents?"

Leonard smiled. "For once, I may know more about military matters than you do. I was cleared for everything on the subject."

"Everything you know of."

"Fair point, but I was cleared for a lot. Far more than ever made the news, more than I've even heard in rumors during my travels. Not just the bear that set off the perimeter alarm, not just the lost missiles, the panic reports of Venus in the sky, the strange details on satellite reconnaissance photos. I've got—" He whispered, "I've got incidents. Cases of actual exchange of fire with Soviet troops at border points. I've got misinformation spread by defectors who were KGB spies. I've got hawkish generals who exaggerated reports or even fabricated them, trying to start wars. I've got Chinese efforts to stir the pot and trigger an exchange. I've got enough to scare me shitless about MAD."

Curtis tried to sound reassuring. "And yet here we are. Alive, and relatively . . . well, stable, if tense."

"And that's what worries me." Leonard slapped the table. "We shouldn't be."

"What?"

"Remember, my grant wasn't about eliminating the false positives, it was about mitigating them. Finding ways to make sure no one pushed the button by mistake. One of my major goals was predicting the mitigating factors, so we can try to increase those."

Curtis could see this was finally leading somewhere. "And you found something?"

"Uh-huh. We're not here. We're all dead, consumed in nuclear fire, a dozen times over. Maybe more."

"What?"

"It's as confident as any prediction my methods have ever made. The false positives are going to happen. We can't tell what they are, but the probability is beyond question. Over a long enough stretch of time, they're unavoidable."

"Long enough. Decades? Years?"

Leonard reached for his beer and took a large swallow. "Months. Maybe a year, maybe two. The false positives are going to happen. Better training can reduce them, but they'll still happen. But what can't happen are the mitigating factors."

Len took another drink, draining the glass. "It's harder to track those, because it's a different, unique mitigating factor for every false positive. So the confidence of my estimate is lower, but it builds with every incident I study. I'm now convinced that these mitigating factors that have saved us from Armageddon time and time again *cannot* happen." He peered into the empty beer glass. "Not . . . by accident."

Not by accident. Curtis remembered Leonard's wide eyes and white-knuckle grip on the valise, and he wondered for his friend's sanity. "So God is protecting us?"

"No," Leonard replied vehemently, "I said that's not a factor. The universe doesn't need God to play dice. But I've become convinced that there's somebody out there finagling the laws of probability in a way to counter the false positives."

"Oh, come on . . ."

"No, come on yourself. With all the theories that come out of quantum physics, all the strangeness, there is room for this."

"How so?" Curtis asked.

"Look at some of the strange things we see on the quantum level. Tunneling. Exclusion. Entanglement. Uncertainty. What if those work at the macro level as well?"

Curtis chuckled. "What, like Schrödinger's cat?"

"All right, yes, like Schrödinger's cat. But not a thought experiment, real, macro phenomena driven by quantum events. In some sense it *has to* happen. If all the macro objects in the universe are made of quantum wavicles, there has to be a connection. And it can be every bit as weird as a cat that's both alive and dead."

"How weird do you mean?"

"As weird as . . . As weird as the Copenhagen interpretation."

Curtis scratched his head, trying to remember. "Copenhagen? That was . . . the multiverse theory?"

Leonard sighed. "That's a simplistic way of looking at it,

from my research. I'm not a quantum physicist, but I've learned a lot in the past year and a half. It's more . . . imagine a sea of potential universes, and quantum events can decide which one we navigate into."

"So that's what you mean by selection? Someone is selecting the universe where mitigating factors happen, and we survive a false positive?"

"I think that's exactly what's happening," Leonard said.

"But . . . I can't do the math, but couldn't it be simpler than that? Sort of like the weak anthropic principle: We happen to be in the universe where all these mitigating factors happened because in any other universe, we wouldn't be here anymore?"

Leonard shook his head. "I tried to account for that. The math is over my head." That made me blink. Math over Leonard's head was math I probably wouldn't recognize at all. "But I think . . . This feels directed, not random. Like there's a . . . like there's a goal."

"But doesn't a goal imply someone setting it? Aren't you getting back to . . ." Curtis couldn't bring himself to finish the question and possibly upset Leonard again.

"It would seem so," Leonard continued, "but maybe not. There's some interesting research that tells me there could be another alternative."

"Well, then tell me, Len. I can't give you my opinion if I don't have all the pieces of your puzzle."

Leonard answered, "It's a little fringe, even for quantum mechanics. I've been looking into papers on quantum entanglement and I've come up with a new interpretation. Some new mathematical techniques that weren't available when the papers were published could help simplify some of the articles' assumptions. The result is a little counterintuitive . . ."

"What isn't in quantum mechanics?"

"Exactly." Len nodded. "But some of these anomalous findings and theories on entanglement can be easily resolved if the effects of entanglement can propagate through the fourth dimension."

"Meaning time?" Leonard nodded. "So somehow, some element of whatever entanglement is propagated forward in time?"

Leonard looked straight into Curtis's eyes and answered, "Or backward."

"What?"

"The equations all balance. They balance, damn it, if we assume that entanglement propagates some of its constraints backward along the timeline. State changes in the right arrangement of quantum particles can actually affect states of those particles and the particles they interact with earlier in time."

Curtis quickly saw the implications. "So you're saying that someone in the future has a quantum arrangement that's changing the past? That's ensuring the future exists? That's . . ."

"Go ahead and say it, Curtis, that's crazy. And you're wondering if *I'm* crazy. But believe me, it's not crazy, it's elegant. When I add that component, the math just falls into place. This quantum arrangement, whatever it is, has to exist at some future point; so conditions in the past have to be arranged to make it happen."

"You're talking . . . predestination."

"Is that any crazier than a cat that's both alive and

dead?" Leonard asked. "Is that any crazier than an electron that moves from point A to point B without going through the points in between? Or a particle that gets nudged and its entangled pair particle feels the nudge faster than light speed? Or hell, a particle that's also a wave? Nonsensical phenomena happen on the quantum level all the time. Why not quantum predestation? It can shake out at the macro level."

Curtis frowned. "But wouldn't that violate the uncertainty principle?"

"Hell if I know. If basic entanglement doesn't, chronological entanglement doesn't have to, either."

"So what would this 'arrangement' look like?"

Leonard shook his head. "I'm still trying to work out the math on that, and consulting with my friends in the quantum physics world."

"You haven't told them this, have you?"

"No." Leonard looked down at his fingers. "I feel bad about that, but . . . then they'll be sure I'm crazy. You're the only one I trust. And besides, they don't have the right clearance. This is still all under my grant."

"That makes sense."

"And also . . . I'm afraid one of them might be responsible for the arrangement. Or maybe *will be* responsible for it. They're top experts, only one of them could be capable of it."

Curtis almost ordered a beer at that thought. "Have you considered the possibility that your talking to one of them has *caused* the arrangement?"

Leonard squeezed his eyes tightly shut. "I . . . I don't want to think that. The causality gives me a headache."

Curtis reached out and squeezed Leonard's shoulder. "Relax. If you did, you did nothing wrong. This is a good thing, right? Isn't it ... isn't it keeping us all alive?"

Leonard opened his eyes, but they still looked troubled. "Yes, but ... what gives him the right to decide for other people?"

"To decide to save the world? I'd say that's a pretty good decision. And besides, does he even know?"

Leonard bit his lip. "I think he has to. I'm still trying to puzzle out the arrangement myself, but it just can't have been an accident. Not unless ... unless some other arrangement farther in the future triggered the accident.

"Or unless it's ..." Curtis suddenly thought of Kekulé and the carbon ring. And that led him to ... "Unless it's Ouroboros, eating its tail, its own beginning in its own end. A circle."

Leonard smiled at that. "That has ... possibilities. I would have to look at the math for that, but I can't rule it out yet."

But then his smile faded. "But even there, every path I can see is intentional. If there is an Ouroboros Arrangement, somebody made it. And I may have played a part."

Curtis let go of Leonard's shoulder. "Then thank you. On behalf of all of us who are alive, thank you. If I could arrange for you and him to get a Nobel Prize, I'd see what I could do."

"But is it right?" Leonard pleaded. "Should anyone have that kind of power? What if ... What if it's only making things worse? What if a false positive fifteen years ago would've been far less destructive than a false positive fifteen years from now? What if there's some sort of . . . social pendulum that's leading us to a conflict? If the longer we put it off, the bigger the potential that's built up behind it?"

"Is that possible?" Curtis asked.

"I don't know! I'm just imagining all the ways this could go wrong. What if whoever it is isn't benevolent but has some other motive in mind? We just don't know. Until we know who it is, we can't find out."

Leonard slumped back against the bench, breathing heavily, as if he'd run a race. Curtis thought about what his friend had said, and the two of them sat silently for several minutes.

Finally, Curtis broke the silence. "Leonard, tell me straight: How certain are you about this?"

Leonard looked up. "The last r-value, or correlation coefficient, I calculated was 0.67."

Curtis sighed in relief. "You always told me anything between 0.5 and 0.95 is just a guess, a prediction not a proof. We just don't know."

Leonard almost rose from his seat. "We don't know! We don't know it's true, but we can't say it's false! We can't say it's impossible, so it's possible. At least according to my models. And every time I run them, the positive correlation rises with new information."

"R-values fluctuate."

"Not this one. Ironically, it's bucking the odds. It has trended up with every new data set."

"So . . . you believe it's true."

It took several seconds before Leonard whispered, "Yes."

That had been the answer that Curtis had feared, for he had already decided what he would have to do if he heard it. He would have to believe his friend. That meant he would have to investigate.

"All right, Leonard," Curtis said. "Open the briefcase. Show me what you've got."

Before he could reach the door, Curtis heard another sound outside, a loud thump, followed by a cry of pain and screams. Against his instincts, he didn't wait to check the door, just barreled out with Wainwright behind him. When he hit the parking lot, he assessed the situation, and he saw three knots of people: two clustered around a smashed Buick and an orange Pacer, and a third clustered around he couldn't tell what. He ran up, forcing his way through the crowd . . . and almost tripped over Leonard's old gray valise that lay split open on the ground. Then as he dodged the valise, Curtis almost lost control despite his training. Leonard lay on the ground, his side torn open, his skull shattered and his brain . . .

Curtis turned away, forcing his way back through the crowd. Just as he broke free, a loose sheet of paper tumbled in the wind, plastering itself briefly against his leg. Curtis was too grief stricken to pay attention, and the paper soon slipped free and flew away on the wind. A tall, thin man in a light-green jacket stepped forward from the crowd, closed the gray valise, picked it up off the pavement, and calmly left the scene.

LAST CHANCE

✪

Sarah A. Hoyt

It was starting to snow as I drove past Silverthorne.

And I had no idea why I was even on this road, or why I had to drive to Meeker, Colorado, to go hiking.

Twenty-two years of a blameless life as a city boy, thriving in Denver, between bookshop and café, between job and apartment, why the hell did I start having insistent, persistent, and vivid dreams about going for a hike? And why did the hike have to start in Meeker, a town named after a famous government agent murdered in a massacre?

There were hundreds, perhaps thousands of trailheads closer to me, north and south. And for that matter, as much as it will shock the tourists, no, there was absolutely no law that made native Coloradans have to hike. Or ski, for that matter.

As I said, I was happily urban, not given to fantasies about the great outdoors. Hell, growing up in Colorado Springs suburbs had been bad enough. Back then they still gave us pamphlets on what to do if we met a bear coming back from elementary school and—believe it or not—it wasn't "put your head between your legs and kiss your ass goodbye," which even at ten seemed to me to be the only realistic response.

Sure, urban environments have threats too, I'm just more confident in my ability to kick the ass of a pushy homeless druggie than a bear.

So, again, why the hell was I heading to Meeker as the snow started to fly?

I turned up the heat in the car, glad I had an SUV. Sure, it was a Honda Pilot that was more than twenty years old, and the only reason I owned it was because you have to be crazy to drive a compact in Colorado. You'd end up stuck between SUVs and can't see more than two or three tall cars ahead of you.

I'd bought good boots, and a decent jacket, so there was that. But I remembered all the TV features and newspaper reports about newbs and tourists found frozen in their cars in the middle of nowhere, and I really wondered what the hell was wrong with me. Except that at some point it's easier to give in, to do what your subconscious is obsessing about than to fight it. *Which I suppose must explain all the people who finally give in, cut up their neighbors, and stuff the bits in plastic bags,* I thought, as I passed a convoy of trucks doing well under the speed limit. And it wasn't precisely fair. It wasn't as though I was cutting up anyone or stuffing them into anything. I was just going to Meeker—of all stupid places—and taking a little hike, and then probably holing up for the night in some fleabag motel while a blizzard howled outside. Then I'd return to Denver and never do anything that stupid again.

As with skiing—bunny slope and major spill at the age of five—I'd be able to tell anyone who asked if I hiked, "Tried it, didn't care for it."

The road wound up and around the mountains, and I passed fewer and fewer houses. Then I drove through a series of small towns. Between them there were ... ranches and entrances to ranches. I was so busy being pissed at myself, I didn't know how far I'd traveled past Silverthorne. Look, it's not like the landscape was particularly inspirational, okay?

It wasn't until the car suddenly and completely lost power that I became aware of where I was. I was in deep dog shit. I mean, there were ... ranches nearby, or at least there was a metal arch saying "Last Chance Ranch" in cutout letters next to some cutout boots or cacti shapes. And there was just enough space for me to coast my car to the arch before it slowed to a halt. I could have sworn it was almost timed that way.

I started cursing softly to myself. Because that's where this crazy and sudden need to be out in nature led. I would be lucky if it didn't end up neck-deep in rattlers like all those school trips when I was a kid. The teachers would take us to some park or other full of signs saying we should be careful not to disturb rattlesnakes. I usually spent those trips holed up in the school bus with a book, refusing to go out, and they always ended with a phone call from the school to my bewildered parents.

I looked dubiously down the path past the arch and decided it was the better part of valor to call Triple A.

Because if I had a ranch like that, in the middle of nowhere, I'd shoot up anything that came down the path uninvited, be it man, bear or rattler.

So I pulled out my cell phone.

And it was dead. As dead as the car. The screen just reflected back at me, and granted, it would have made a handy hand mirror, which unfortunately was not what I needed right then.

I was glaring at the path—which led on past a hillock and some trees, with no house in sight—and convincing myself that no bears or rattlesnakes would be out in this weather, when a man came walking past the trees.

He didn't seem to be carrying a weapon. And what the hell, he was likely to have a phone, right?

So I got out of the car, pulled on my insulated jacket, and started down the path toward him, doing my best "see, I'm just a stranded guy, and definitely not a rattlesnake pretending to be human" impression.

As I got closer, I guessed he was probably my dad's age, or a little older. He had a long white beard, and seemed like a guy who didn't fuss much with his hair, because he rarely saw people.

"Car trouble?" he yelled, as he got within shouting distance.

"Yeah," I said. "And my phone isn't working."

"Mine just went out too. Happens 'round here."

Which of course just thrilled me to no end.

He was close enough now for me to see what he looked like. I mean, really looked like. Sort of like a tanned, leaner Santa Claus with very blue eyes, and a look of puzzled helpfulness. He extended his hand. "Joe Brand."

I shook it and said, "Mike Grer. Anything we can do?"

He shook his head. "Nah. This stuff just happens 'round here sometimes. My dad used to say it was some kind of government experimentation. That or UFOs. Except we never saw any UFOs." Pause. "Of course I never saw much in the way of government experimentation, either. Could be something having to do with the ore around here. Anyway, it usually stops cars and phones for a few hours, and then it all starts up again. You can stay in your car and wait, or you can come down to the ranch. There's a group of travelers there, waiting it out."

Look, I wasn't a complete moron. I realized this whole encounter played like a classic horror movie plot, okay? I knew as well as anyone that this type of situation could end up with one last girl running down the road toward the highway, just before the madman with the chainsaw cuts her down. And I'm no girl. On the other hand, I grew up in Colorado, and it was snowing, and I—like an idiot—hadn't thrown a couple of thermal blankets in the back of the car before driving out.

Besides... well. Besides this old guy didn't feel threatening, and he would probably be easier to overpower than a bear.

"You're more than welcome to stay," he said. "Shouldn't be more than a few hours."

"I don't see any other cars," I said, as a final protest, in case, you know, it would convince him to confess being a chainsaw killer.

He shrugged. "The path is slightly downward. If you end up staying, it's easier to push the car past the trees to where the others are parked. After all, you probably don't want some truck that isn't affected smashing into your car."

Made sense, though, "You mean some cars aren't affected?"

"Yup. Never understood why. Though all phones seem to be impacted."

Okay, so worst-case scenario, I could hitchhike a passing truck. So . . . why didn't I? Why walk down the path with a total stranger?

I don't know. Like the idea of going to Meeker, it was the same compulsion that made no sense to my rational mind. Which I suppose is why, even to myself, I sounded like a total lunatic.

I'm not normally given to irrational compulsions or following them. And, just to get it out of the way, no, it's also not mandatory to toke in Colorado, and as a rule, I didn't smoke cannabis. To be completely honest, even smelling the stuff made me clog up and have trouble breathing.

Anyway, I couldn't seem to help myself, so I followed the guy down the path. I felt a little better when I saw a bunch of cars in a clearing ahead, and none of them had any obvious bloodstains or chainsaw dents.

The sprawling ranch house was made of logs, but with enough windows and amenities that it had obviously been built within the last twenty years. The front door led to a living room filled with people who stopped talking when we came in. I was relieved to see that none of them had any obvious chainsaw wounds.

"Mike here got stranded, just at the entrance to the

ranch," Joe Brand said. And the people in the room laughed and sympathized.

There were four men: Paul Jones, from somewhere in Denver; Jordan Gutierrez from Boulder; Josh Beranger also from Boulder; and Ken Scotti, from Colorado Springs. Three women: Marianne Smith, from Boulder; Kathy Pines from Colorado Springs; and Jill March from Denver.

They all looked . . . well . . . normal. Except that Josh had a man bun, and I had the impression that he wore a designer t-shirt and jeans. And Marianne was dressed in new-revival-Earth-Mother style, with flowing colorful skirt, and a sort of peasant blouse in something shiny. Her attire was completely explained in the first few minutes of conversation when she revealed that she owned a New Age store in Boulder. Which, it seemed to me, must be some kind of achievement in fluffy-headed crystal-and-curse thinking. Within minutes she was yammering about the ley lines in these parts, and how they had made our cars stop.

I noticed—because I notice these things—that our host wasn't taking part in our speculation about what had happened. I also observed that most of the people— Marianne excepted, since she apparently had friends in Steamboat Springs—had not planned to drive out this day; they'd all done it on a whim. And judging by the haunted looks in their eyes, I judged that "whim" meant compulsion.

Which made it all the more interesting to me. Weirdly, not even Marianne admitted to that.

The rest of the situation turned out to be pretty normal. Joe served us some coffee. After about an hour, when the phones still didn't work, and with the snow piling up outside, I went with the guys and pushed my car into the parking area.

When the phones still didn't work at dinner time, Joe brought out ham, and vegetarian soup—for Marianne, who was a vegan—and then we sat around the dinner table, talking.

I don't remember—which is weird, because I notice these things—who first brought up ESP or the psychic forces used during the Cold War.

"It's a joke now, or we think it's a joke," Joe said. He was leaning back and smoking. He'd asked our permission, and honestly Marianne was the only one who'd gotten upset, but even she wasn't brazen enough to tell our host he couldn't smoke in his own house. Josh had pulled out an e-cig immediately after. "But the seventies were a really strange time. Sometimes I wonder—doesn't everyone?—how we got here from there. Psychic powers were just assumed to exist and work. If you go back to the science fiction of the time, they're part of it. It was assumed they would be part of the future."

"Because they are," Marianne said, with a bright smile. "If the government didn't suppress the knowledge, we could have free energy from the ley lines. When the Earth changes come, some people are going to be very surprised."

The table went silent, then Joe said, "Well, yeah, that. The Soviets were experimenting with something that was more like mind control at a distance. We've got to the point of laughing at the idea that the government could control your actions. Today, there's talk of chips and stuff, but the Soviets actually claimed they could control people, at a distance.

"You know, like getting the person pulling lottery balls to pick certain numbers by controlling their mind? That type of thing. Supposedly they controlled all sorts of people, including officials in our own government."

Paul laughed. He was a little older than us and might have been born in the seventies, though I doubted even he had been conscious of what had been going on back then. "But that was all nonsense, wasn't it? Mostly because people were doing a lot of drugs."

"Maybe," Joe said. He stubbed his cigarette out in an ashtray he'd set in front of him, and lit another, taking a deep pull. "Maybe it was. But back then, the American government was threatened enough by the reports, and maybe by . . . well, maybe by some successes that they started a program called Stargate."

"Like the TV series?" Jordan asked.

"Well, this was before that. Well before that. But yeah. I always wondered if someone in on that brainstorming session was involved in the original Stargate. I mean, putting it in a military base and all."

"Didn't they close it because it only had something like a fifteen percent success rate?" Jill asked.

"That's what they said."

"Well, they closed it," she said. "And they never close any government programs for lack of success, so it must have been a spectacular failure." She was slim, with short hair, cut in a way that made it seem to shimmer and move under the lights. I wondered what she did for a living. None of us except Marianne and Josh, who was a barista, had volunteered that.

Joe smiled. It was a very disquieting smile. "And perhaps

you should ask yourself, given that we still have a strategic helium fund, why precisely Stargate was discontinued."

Jill opened her mouth as though about to protest, then frowned and stayed silent.

Marianne smiled and said something about the galactic union of minds, and how mundane people had tried to thwart it, but I could tell from Jill's frown that she was struggling with the same question I was.

Why would a government that never cancelled its spending programs have shut down its psychic research effort?

"I read up on it, once," I offered. "It was at the end of a book on Soviet psychic discoveries, which I think came out in the nineties? Something about how Stargate hadn't actually been closed, and someone who claimed to have worked on the program wrote an exposé on it, but then was hushed up?"

Joe was looking into the middle distance, his eyes strangely cold, bleak. "I think," he said, "that Stargate is effectively closed. But I doubt it was shut down because it didn't work."

I had no clue what he meant, and he didn't bother to explain it. At that point, Jordan pulled out his phone and checked it. We all did. And all of them were still dead.

"You're all more than welcome to stay the night here. We have plenty of rooms. Dad used to rent them out to hunters. Then he went to the nursing home and I moved in. After that, I stopped renting them out."

It was snowing outside, the flurries like big feathers, coming fast and furious. The path beyond the door was obscured by a glittering blanket of snow.

The weird thing wasn't that Joe had rooms to spare. It's that the rooms were clean and the beds freshly made. I spent some amount of time living with roommates in a college dorm, okay? I know what places look like when they haven't been cleaned, and this is Colorado. Dust gets everywhere, even on unused beds.

The room he led me to was spacious, with a big king-size bed made from tree trunks, a style in Colorado that people who rent rooms to tourists tend to use. Or tourists furnishing their vacation houses.

The rest of the furniture followed the theme. There was a painting of pine-covered mountains over the bed, with a rutting elk in the foreground. Or at least I think it was a rutting elk. It didn't look like your run-of-the-mill deer, which I'd encountered often enough when I was growing up in my suburban Colorado Springs neighborhood. There was a massive dresser, big enough to hold Titan clothes. It held a large-screen TV, but the only thing on was static. Which was weird. I mean, I could see something disrupting the cars and phones, but surely that same thing wouldn't disrupt cable. And if it stopped all electrical equipment from working, then it would shut off the lights, too, no? And the heating. The house was obviously heated. None of this made sense.

What made even less sense was that when Joe brought me into my room, he said "This is yours, Mike. There are some clothes in the closet that should fit you. Dad always believed in having pajamas and a change of clothing in every size, you know, for emergencies."

And it wasn't just that they fit me. That would be strange enough. Really? They'd had rooms equipped with clothes in every size, but one size per? It's that the two changes of clothing—jeans and a shirt—were exactly what I might have bought.

Even weirder was the plastic-sealed toiletries kit I found in the bathroom, stamped in faded lettering that read "United States of America."

I mean, maybe that was just a "made by" label? Who needed to have the country's name stamped on a toiletry kit?

Before going to bed, I noticed an SAS training manual on the bedside table. I dragged this very heavy piece of furniture to the front of the door. I then quickly inspected the room, examining the walls. I didn't find any hidden compartments or secret passages. The window was locked and had a safety bar that simply wouldn't allow anyone to open it from the outside. I also looked in the dresser drawers, which were empty. So there was a good chance that for all the weirdness, there wouldn't be any chainsaw massacres, and I'd be safe tonight.

Tomorrow I'd get back in the car, start it up, and return to Denver, because it was quite obvious that whatever the hell else was going on, I wasn't built for hiking the backcountry of Colorado. My Rocky Mountain high— with no hint of pot—could be just as profitably achieved in Denver.

I put on the pajamas and went to bed.

When I woke, Joe was standing by my bed, which was outright impossible. I'd made sure the room was sealed, and no one could come in.

On the upside, he wasn't carrying a chainsaw. On the downside, he was wearing a suit and tie, which looked incongruous with his long hair and beard. His Santa Claus eyes shone with a fanatical gleam.

I tried to sit up, but couldn't. It was like I was paralyzed in place. Some part of me insisted I was just dreaming, but it didn't feel like any dream I'd ever had.

"Of course, Stargate wasn't disbanded, not as such. It was . . . eradicated."

I wanted to ask by whom, but couldn't move my lips. Which was just as well, because apparently now Joe Brand could somehow read my thoughts.

"I was recruited into it right out of college," he said. "Early seventies. I was studying mathematics, and when the CIA approached me, I thought, well, why not? It was part-time work, and I was having trouble enough paying my tuition then, not that it was anywhere near as bad as it is now. And I saw it. One thing I'll say for crazy David Morehouse and his book: He was right that the success rate was far more than fifteen percent. A lot of spying and influencing went on. And we countered a lot of it from the Soviet side.

"Of course by the time Morehouse wrote his book, he didn't realize he was being influenced by the Soviets to write it, and the whole purpose was to discredit the idea that the project had ever happened. Much less what had happened to it."

"Happened . . . to . . . it?" I managed to say, my voice sounding distant and drowsy.

Joe smiled as though I'd pulled a particularly clever trick. "The Soviets happened to it, of course. End of '78. We didn't know it, what they called their influencers, their . . . mind-control people, really were so much better than us. All those fluffy empty heads—a lot like Marianne. People like Marianne had gone to the Soviet Union and returned very impressed with how far the Soviets had progressed with their psychic program. They were much, much better at it than we were. I guess when dealing with a human trait that isn't easy to pin down and is erratically transmitted to offspring, it helps to be a totalitarian government that can separate kids from their parents, and force reproduction between strangers." He was quiet for a while, and as much as his words seemed to approve of such methods, I could tell by the way his eyes glittered that they made him mad. "Which is how they assembled a cadre of ultrapowerful mind-influencers and won the Cold War."

Despite my stunned state, a laugh escaped me. "The Soviet Union hasn't existed since 1991. If you call that winning."

"Someone, I can't remember who, said that the devil's greatest trick was convincing people he didn't exist. The Soviet Union might not have been the devil, although there are people who'd say it was, but the trick is probably just the same."

I decided this was the weirdest dream I'd ever had. Particularly since as Joe spoke, I started seeing the scenes in my mind.

"One day, out of the clear blue sky, I woke up as the only member of Stargate who knew what had happened, who had remembered our success rate."

In my mind, a young Joe—his hair cut, his face shaven, wearing a nice suit—went into an office to find everyone packing up. A jovial older man said, "Well, it never worked, and it's a good thing they are releasing us from this. I'm going to go back to school and get a doctorate. What are you doing?"

And I saw Joe, paralyzed, confused, thinking none of this made sense.

"It took me years to figure it out," Joe said, standing in the middle of my bedroom. "Years. Their biggest trick was to convince us they didn't exist. Everything you think you know about the Soviet Union is a lie. They still exist in all the essentials. Did it bother no one else that their leader is a KGB man?"

I thought it had bothered a lot of people. My dad still went on about it.

"Of course, of course it is. Their organization still exists. It just went underground, at the same time it controlled all the opinion makers in the West, every journalist, professor, everyone with authority."

I wondered if they'd had that much power, why they hadn't invaded.

"Because they couldn't. They didn't quite have the power to influence every person on the street, and make them docile. And you know what Americans are like. Let's remember the Soviets broke their teeth on Afghanistan, against illiterate peasants equipped with outmoded weapons. They knew they couldn't dominate Americans in the open, even if they deprived us of our leadership." He gave a chuckle. "Probably worse for them if they deprived us of our leadership because we're all individualist hotheads. But that's what they set about changing, here and in Europe.

"They took control of American leaders who were most

susceptible to their influence, and changed our education, our news, everything they could shape. They've raised two generations now, in the belief that socialism and communism isn't a bad thing. After the body count communism amassed in the twentieth century, didn't anyone think it odd that our supposedly brightest thinkers were all willing—nay, eager—to give it another try?"

In my mind, I saw something . . . blue glowing tendrils, reaching into the minds of the people, making them suddenly preach communism to school children, talk about the glories of socialism. I saw the *New York Times* publishing articles oozing with nostalgia of the USSR, talking about how their space program was superior to America's.

Why hadn't I thought that was strange? It had seemed . . . normal.

"People get feelings that something isn't right, but they don't know what to do with it," Joe explained. "It's no coincidence that while embracing a love of socialism, people talk of being woke, of being part of the resistance. Their subconscious is screaming warnings at them, but they don't know what to do about it."

The images in my mind—some kind of PowerPoint . . . if they did this at our business meetings, it would be far more interesting—were of masses of robot-like people repeating things they'd been taught by others who were controlled, even as their minds tried to rebel.

"Took me decades to find the right people, the ones with the power to combat the Soviet influencers. Now I got you all here, I'm going to do something. This should activate your psi powers. It might not, of course. I haven't been able to practice. All I could do was save all the microfiches of years and years of research."

In my mind, the young Joe packed his car with cardboard boxes, all while smiling and saying things about how he'd brought all his paperbacks to work because it had been so boring. His co-workers looked worried but said nothing, because of course, they'd stopped believing there was research worth saving or hiding.

"I studied them. I practiced. And I think when you wake up you'll be—all of you—fully activated influencers, as strong as anything the Soviet Union had. I say 'had' because their new generation isn't as strong.

"They have carried the pretense to their own people, and while they have, still, a lot of power, they don't have the kind of power that can force breeding. Or kidnap children from their mothers to train at an early age. Their best ones have died, aged out. Their new ones are half a dozen and not as strong as you are. With your help, I'll rip the veil of delusion from the world.

"The people who've been under mind control will know it. And we'll have a chance to fight back. From here. From Last Chance Ranch." He smiled, disquietingly. "Now sleep while I work. You'll wake up with a headache."

The next morning, my head was throbbing. It was the kind of headache you got when you drank way too much cheap booze. There were other things. It seemed to me that thoughts that weren't my own swam in my mind. It was like waking up and finding that your underwear drawer had been rearranged, only no one could have gotten into your room. You feel uncomfortable, uneasy, but you're not at all sure any of it is true.

I stumbled to the bathroom, and pissed. Then I stood at the sink and looked in the mirror. My eyes were bloodshot, and there were dark circles around them, as though I'd been punched. I remembered everything from the night before and clearly. And I believed it. I also believed that Joe had been some sort of presence— an astral projection—in my room. But I didn't like the idea that he'd . . . what? Manipulated me into driving out to hike somewhere past his ranch. I'd bet he'd arranged, somehow, for the phones and the engines to shut down, too.

I couldn't just let that stand. Could anyone?

I checked my phone. It was still dead. But perhaps his control over the cars had slipped? I mean, he wouldn't think of us going out there and driving away, right? Not with the snow, and not with this headache.

The house seemed silent. I put on my clothes from the day before, unblocked the door, sneaked out to the hallway, and then out the door to the parking lot. The snow was up to my ankles.

The car was as dead as it had been yesterday.

When I came back into the house, Joe peeked out of the kitchen. "Good morning," he said. "Coffee?"

"I need a shower," I said, grumpily.

"Yes. It should help with your headache."

Joe was right, a shower did help. When I came back to the kitchen, this time dressed in clean clothes, my teeth brushed with an oddly patriotic toothbrush, Joe had eggs, bacon, coffee and toast, all of it set out on the counter as a buffet. As they ate silently, my fellow stranded travelers all looked like they had headaches, too. Only Marianne seemed perturbed. The rest looked, I'd say, more angry than worried.

I was on my second cup of coffee when Joe came out and spoke to us. "You don't have to do anything," he said. "Though I'll caution that because you are here, and the Soviets will find out you were, they may target you. But if you all join me now, we can protect each other and strike at them collectively before they attack us individually. It's your choice."

It was Josh who piped up first, his eyes squinting in pain from his headache. I think he spoke for all of us when he said, "Whatever. As long as you make our cars work afterward."

Joe didn't even try to deny it. He grinned. "They'll work."

So we gathered on the sofas in the entrance room, and Joe said, "Take my lead."

How do I explain what happened next? You remember how I thought I saw blue mist reach into the heads of every influential person in the West?

Well, now we were aloft, in a strange fog. Joe was there, and he pointed us at the problem.

There was . . . or at least I saw, mentally . . . a large, dark octopus floating over the world, reaching into western countries.

If you were to describe the whole sequence as an animated movie, *Seven Against Cthulhu*, you wouldn't be far off.

At first, we went after the tentacles. Our hands cut at them like blades, but for every tentacle we cut, two more emerged. And now they were reaching into us, trying to get into our heads. Which is when Marianne—Marianne, whose astral presence looked like a little anime girl adorned with crystals—gave a war cry. "Target the head!"

She flung herself against the main bulk of the octopus, where a red dot pulsed. We followed. Jill, a beautiful anime girl, plunged a shiny white sword near the dot.

I tried to follow, but a tentacle grabbed and immobilized me. It suddenly grew a head like a rattlesnake. I heard it rattling in the background.

I was paralyzed for a moment. But you have to understand, I hate being lied to. I fastened my teeth around the snake's neck. The snake made a cartoonish look of surprise, and then I was free, spitting out what I sensed was venom. Then I flew toward the others, where they were attacking the octopus creature's bulbous head. I dug in, with my hands, which had grown claws, and started ripping out clumps of its essence.

The others were biting and kicking and stabbing. Marianne was crying as she fought, and some were screaming. Some looked wounded and bruised. I'd guessed the others had been taken too, but now we were all fighting back, and winning.

Suddenly, the thing convulsed. There was a shriek that sounded like a dying bird. Tentacles flailed. I was about to be swept away, but a hand reached out and grabbed my wrist.

"I have you," Joe's voice said. "I have all of you."

When we returned from the psychic encounter, the room was still the same, but we weren't. Around me, everyone had aged ten years in minutes. Joe was on his phone, speaking in guarded tones.

He looked up, as a few of us tottered to our feet. "The White House—" he said. "The President wants to talk to you. All of you." He sounded hoarse. "Every participant in Operation Last Chance."

"But we're free to go now?" Paul asked.

"Yes. If you want. They shouldn't be able to retaliate. Not right now."

I took a deep breath. My mouth felt burned. I stumbled down the hallway to the room, not sure I was in any state to drive. As I collected my things, I turned on the TV.

The House minority leader was holding a press conference. I won't say she wasn't as shrill as she had always been, but she was saying things I couldn't have imagined before, "For the last few decades in this chamber, I've said things and supported causes that were against the interests of the United States. I was a manipulated puppet of the enemy. Today I'm here to remedy that. To tell you—"

I turned the TV off. I bundled my clothes under my arm and trudged to my car. I had just turned the ignition on when my phone pinged with a text from my friend Rick. We used to shoot the breeze and discuss politics. "You won't believe who just committed suicide. He said he had woken up this morning, convinced he was a Soviet puppet all these years. What the hell is going on?"

But I felt as if I were bruised inside my head—no, inside my soul—and I couldn't come up with a good answer for him. I suspected in the next few days everything would come to light. People would know.

What would this do? To myself, to the nation?

I didn't know.

The phone pinged again. A glance sideways showed the sender of the text as the President of the United States.

There would be time for that. Right now, driving through the Colorado snow toward Denver, I drove through *terra incognita*.

Who knew how things would change? The future was something I couldn't even imagine, now that we'd won the Cold War.

It had been the last chance, the most improbable of dance throws.

Seven against the behemoth, seven ill-trained and ignorant newbies.

But Americans always do well against long odds and in strange circumstances. And knowing the devil is there is better than closing your eyes and pretending he no longer exists.

We'd won this one.

Tomorrow and the day after, and all the days beyond that, we'd win the rest of our battles. One by one.

Now we were masters of our own minds. The future was ours to make.

ODERZHIMOST'

✪

Deborah A. Wolf

1984

Viktor Mikhaylovich Rybakov stood barefoot at the lake's edge, a rock in each hand. His heart beat like a wild thing trying to escape. He held one rock in a fist before his face and kissed it.

"She loves me." He cocked his arm back and threw the rock, hard. His shoulder hurt from throwing dozens of rocks. His head hurt from drinking too much vodka. His heart hurt from falling in love with a *blyat*. He deserved the pain, welcomed the pain, wallowed in it.

Plonk. Viktor imagined the rock sinking and wondered how many thousands of years it might take to get back to the beach, just to be thrown back again by another stupid boy.

His fingers tightened about the second rock till they ached. "She loves me not," he said, and stuffed it into his pocket. It ground against the others; his pockets were so full that the seams had begun to split, each rock a testament to his unworthiness. She had never loved him.

187

The cold waters of Lake Baikal swirled about his ankles, laving his footprints in a bloody foam. He would be gone soon, erased from the world. His feet hurt. His heart hurt.

It didn't matter. He stooped to pick up more rocks. It didn't matter.

"What are you doing?"

Viktor jerked his hand back and stood too quickly, so that the vodka sloshed in his head and made him dizzy. He squinted up at Shamanka Rock, silhouetted against the dying day, and his stupid heart dropped. He had been alone in this cold place for hours, but now here was a girl, looking down at him with heavy eyes as if she was deciding whether to throw him into the lake or stick him in her pocket.

"Nothing," he told her. "Just throwing rocks. Go away."

"Liar." She hopped down from her perch and walked toward him.

She was older than Viktor had thought at first. Maybe his age, maybe a year or two older. She was wearing a dress the color of water. Her eyes were wide, dark and sober, and she had a little Cupid's-bow mouth that looked incapable of smiling, or kissing, or lying.

The rocks ground together in Viktor's pockets, yelling at him with their hard little rock voices. He bowed his head, ashamed. The girl's ankles and feet—bare, like his—came into view. She was tiny boned and pale. Her toenails were painted pink.

"Come on," she said.

"I . . ." Viktor touched his pocket, and his face flushed hot.

The girl had turned away and was leading him toward Shamanka Rock. "Don't worry about it," she called back over her shoulder.

Viktor's heart started beating again, and he followed her to sit beside a campfire.

Their shadows danced weirdly on the rock face. Viktor had never believed the stories, but on this night, of all nights . . . he shivered and scooted his butt closer to the fire.

"Are you even allowed to build a fire up here?" he thought not. It occurred strange to him, then, that nobody had come yet to yell at them, to arrest them even. They would find the rocks in his pockets, and call his mother . . .

"Don't worry about it," the girl said again. "I do as I like. Nobody will bother us."

Her name was Zoya. She was eighteen, a year older than Viktor. She had dark eyes and wore a dress the color of rain.

"Someone will come," he said.

"No one will come," she assured him, poking at the fire with a stick the color of drowned bones. "They never do."

They talked for hours about life, and what happens to a person's soul after you die, and what happens before you are born. Zoya never answered Viktor's questions about why she had come to the rock, or asked why he was there. She sat so close that he could smell the rain-and-pine scent of her hair, and told him odd stories about the people who lived beneath the lake.

Sometime after midnight, Viktor emptied the stones from his pockets and cried.

Sometime after that, he fell in love.

When the sun crept over the rocks again, morning found the boy curled up around the empty space where she had been. His cheeks were flushed with life, and he was smiling in his sleep.

Zoya Ivanovna Vengerova stood between the rocks, in that place where she couldn't be seen, and listened to Viktor's cries growing thin and faint as he walked away from her.

"Zoya!" he called, again and again. "Zoyyyyyyaaaaaaa..."

She pressed her hands over her ears, as if either was real, as if it would help, and rocked back and forth, back and forth, curled in on herself until the day grew old and turned to night, then day again, night again, day again. He would stop calling for her eventually, they all did, would forget her and move on with his life. Alive.

Some years after Viktor had left, she took her hands from her ears and looked up. He was gone, gone, long gone. Gone, but alive.

Zoya picked up one of the stones he had dropped and pressed it to her lips before reaching up to drop it into a crack in the rock's face. It fell with a clatter and a clink. She closed her eyes and smiled, imagining the stone nestled next to the watch Johnny had given her.

The watch was of silver, tarnished and precious. Upon it were etched the initials *JS* and *ZI*, the words *Love* and *Forever*. The leather band had rotted away, and the watch hadn't kept time in years. She had wound it too tight, and loved it too hard, back before she knew that *love* was a joke best told with a straight face and *forever* was a curse.

But the rock whispered to her of obsession, of death. Death kept his promises, every one.

Just as she did.

"Here he is!"

John Aloysius Smith held out his arms, and a beaming young nurse laid his infant grandson in his arms.

"Careful of the head."

"Oh, I know. I've done this before."

It had been a lifetime ago, and he really hadn't gotten to hold his own child as much as he would have liked. There were fleets to order, wars to win, politics to politic . . .

"He's so small. Have they always made babies this small?" He snuggled the tiny bald head against his shoulder and gazed down at the tiny face, tucking the striped hospital blanket aside so he could see better. "Yep, he looks just like me. No hair and big ears!"

Allison smiled at him from the bed where she lay wan and exhausted, dark hair plastered to her face. She had the most beautiful smile. Her husband David had gone to use the phone at the end of the hallway and was calling everybody in the United States to let them know he had a son. A son!

Before Allie had been born, John used to joke that if his wife gave him a daughter, he'd put it back in till it was finished. One look at her tiny, soft face had stolen his heart away, and though he and Edith hadn't been able to have any more children, he'd never felt the lack. Not really. Not until now. He bent his head and kissed his grandson's squishy little nose and as he did so, he wondered again what his life might have been like if he'd stayed with that Russian girl he'd met at the end of the war. Sweet, funny Zoya. Would she have given him a son? A house full of sons? Maybe he had a son out there somewhere right now, a son he'd never met. Maybe he even had a bunch of cute little Russian grandkids with bald heads and big ears, just like his. A better man would have stayed with her.

If regrets were dollars, he'd have been very wealthy.

"Dad, are you crying?"

"Old sailors never cry. They just get a little salty." John rubbed his face on one corner of the blanket. "Did you guys settle on a name yet?"

"Are you kidding me? I've had his name picked out since I was a little girl."

John looked up to see his daughter smiling at him, an angel's smile, and tears spilled down both their cheeks.

"We named him Johnny."

2004

Cold blue-green light welled from the monitor, bathing Viktor's apartment in murky color and giving the whole scene a strange underwater glow. The single desk was piled high with books and papers on programming languages, which one might expect of a man determined to make his mark in the digital world. A bottle of Stolichnaya, grimed and covered in dust, a testament to his vow and willpower. And everywhere—on the desk, the walls, the small and noisy refrigerator—drawings of a young girl, the same girl over and over in a thousand poses. Dark hair, dark eyes, a Cupid's-bow mouth that never smiled. A stranger, looking upon the sketches, would note that the newer ones were really quite good. And now Zoya stared out from the blue depths of his digital dreamings, a near-life likeness with her face, her voice . . . almost. Not quite, but almost. The technology wasn't quite there nor were his own skills.

"Again," he would mutter to himself, abandoning one flawed program after another as he had discarded pencil drawings in those early years. "Again." He would get it right, eventually.

"*Oderzhimost'*," a girlfriend had told him once, before he quit girls and drinking. "You are obsessed."

"*Oderzhimost' delayet sovershenstvo*," he replied. "Obsession makes perfection." He had laughed, pretending it was a clever joke, but it was his truth.

Now he sat bathed in the blue light, pale and skinny, girl-less and sober, spine curled forward speaking of too many hours in front of the computer and dark circles under his eyes of too few hours spent in bed.

For nearly five years he had sat at this desk weaving a complex web of love and logic, trying to kiss life into the cold mouth of an artificial intelligence. He had managed to write programs that were good. Brilliant, even. But not perfect, not yet.

Zoya was his *oderzhimost'*, his obsession. And she deserved to be perfect.

Her face stared blindly from the depths of his monitor, blue light from her dark eyes pouring out across a dog-eared copy of Orlov's *Russian Ghosts*. Viktor's hand trembled as it hovered above his keyboard, and then he pressed *enter*.

The image on the screen blinked.

His heart flickering like the monitor, Viktor leaned forward and spoke, lips so close to the microphone it was nearly a kiss. "Hello, Zoya."

Almost-Zoya's mouth jerked into a smile, an expression which looked utterly wrong on her. He would have to fix that. Then she spoke, and her eyes shifted—not looking at him, not quite, but close.

So this is how Frankenstein felt, Viktor thought, *when his monster drew its first breath. Terrified and exhilarated. Alive.*

"Hello, Vitushka," Zoya said. Her voice, purchased from a whore-turned-actress in Saint Petersburg, was very nearly perfect. "I have missed you."

Cold moonlight surfed the colder waters of Lake Baikal, glittering like the frost on a dead girl's face. The waters were smooth and dark, full of serene secrets, a sharp contrast to the town flesh at water's edge. Rocks which had lain for many lifetimes of man had been wakened and disturbed and laid now unquiet in the footprints and boot prints of the many people who had dragged Ilya Samovich from the lake, or in the tire tracks of the ambulance which had carried him away, wailing as his mother would when she heard the news. Another boy drowned in the lake, so sad, so sad.

Later there would be flowers, an article in the local papers, and then—after sufficient time had passed for this to be in good taste—whispers about the Girl in the Lake, the vengeful *rusalka* who delighted in drowning faithless lovers.

How soon they would forget. The world would turn, the rocks would settle into their new beds, and the flower petals would rot to become soil for a new garden of ghost stories.

Zoya emerged from the lake, shedding moonlight and water in place of tears. Slowly she drifted to Shamanka Rock, clutching the boy's necklace. It had been given to him by a girl who loved him, but he had kissed another, and so Zoya had tangled her fingers in the chain and used it to drag him down into the final embrace, till his eyes stared at her wide and sightless, and bubbles clung to his lips like tiny silver lies.

The necklace fell with a clatter and clink to lie beside Sergei's wallet, Yvan's photograph, Johnny's watch . . .

And Viktor's stone.

She pressed her cheek to the rock face, wishing she might feel its rough surface against her skin, the water that dripped from her hair, the moon-torn wind . . . anything. What might her life have been like, had she met a boy like Viktor instead of a man like Johnny?

What might, what might, what might?

But the moon turned its face from her, and water and wind as well. She had thrown away her right to these things when she had thrown herself from Shamanka Rock. Johnny had filled her belly with child and left her, so she had filled her pockets full of stones and left the world.

When the sun rose and the people came grief-faced to lay flowers at the lake's edge, nobody noticed the crack in the rocks, her shadow's shadow, the dark rivers of her tears.

So soon they forget, so soon.

2024

JACKSONVILLE, FL — The US Navy's first San Antonio-*class Flight II amphibious transport dock ship, the USS* John A. Smith, *joined the fleet Saturday in a ceremony at Florida's Naval Station Mayport. She is named after US Navy officer and Medal of Honor recipient John Aloysius Smith, Sr.*

Navy Secretary Louis Philopoena says the ship is a "marvelous integration of traditional naval wartime technologies and artificial-intelligence innovations." Captain John A. Smith, Jr., grandson of the hero for which the ship is named, said the family is touched and incredibly proud that this ship will carry on Smith's love for and dedication to his country.

Gerald Maburg, the widower of former Navy Secretary Greta Maburg, gave the order to bring the ship to life before the crew boarded the vessel at the end of the ceremony.

The 684-foot-long ship weighs about 23,470 tons (full). It can travel in excess of 20 knots. It is armed with two 25mm Mk 38 autocannons, two Rolling Airframe Missile launchers, and four .50 BMG machine guns, and carries two MV-22 tilt-rotor aircraft. The John A. Smith *uses the Enterprise Air Surveillance Radar (EASR) volume air search radar and incorporates a high-temperature superconductor-based ship mine-protection degaussing system built by Panmurica Superconductor to reduce her magnetic signature.*

★ ★ ★

Cold sweat trickled down Viktor's temples and between his shoulder blades; for hours he had been afraid to raise his arms above the level of his ribs, lest his companions spy the dark patches under his arms and call him out as a coward. His eyes stung and burned from the miasmic pall of cigar and cigarettes and those foul candy-scented electronic cigarettes, and the room was wretched with alcohol fumes. His throat was raw from talking, from hours and hours of talking, and his head swam with numbers the likes of which even he, lover of numbers and logical outcomes, had never contemplated. He blinked against the interrogation-hard glare of lights and pointed to a big, pale hand raised near the back of the room.

"Yes?" he rasped, and reached for his bottle of water. It was empty. The glass of vodka to his left was full, and the bottle next to it sweated invitingly, but his eyes avoided them.

"This is all very interesting, I'm sure, Victor Mikhaylovich, as I'm sure everyone here will agree. But . . . what can it *do*?" There was general laughter at this, much of it too loud; he was the only one in the room who drank only water.

Viktor nodded and smiled through stiff lips. "This system is meant to combine the intuitive response of a nuanced human mind with the near-immediate deductive reasoning capabilities of artificial intelligence and use the resultant data to direct and deploy the massive capabilities of our automated weapons systems and autonomous weapons, vehicles, drones, and so forth. Too many of these systems are currently disjoined for us to have a truly spontaneous response to an external threat or opportunity . . ."

"Using words that an old man can understand, please." More laughter at this.

Viktor stifled a sigh. This man was dangerous. Every person in this room, he reminded himself, was dangerous.

His throat was so dry.

"Computers think faster than I can," he began anew with the friendliest smile he could manage. "Perhaps even faster than you can."

Much laughter at this, including from the big man who had questioned him. Good, good.

"You or I might look at data on a screen," Viktor continued, "and think because of this information or that information, I might reasonably conclude that this or that is happening, or might happen, and therefore I should take this action, that action . . . there are a lot of possibilities. Too many things for us to consider all at once, so many actions we might take, and the consequences of those actions. I may be smart, and you may be brilliant, but neither of us can predict a thousand outcomes at once."

"And your program can? Predict a thousand outcomes at once?"

"Yes." He let the confidence show in his voice. "A thousand outcomes at once. A *million* outcomes at once. So the best deductions and plans can be made instantly, instead of within hours or even days. In this manner, we can even predict with great accuracy the activities and capabilities of vessels that we cannot locate by conventional means, and react to intelligence in less time than it currently takes us to merely gather it."

"Like stealth drones?"

"Yes, or radar-resistant ships and submarines, or . . ."

"Enough talk." The heavy hand slapped down upon a heavier wooden table, and all laughter ceased. "Show me."

He had known this time would come. Even so . . . Viktor blinked the sweat from his eyes and reached for the glass to his left. One drink, he told himself, would hurt nothing.

And it was so good.

"Ladies and gentlemen," he intoned as he'd dreamed for decades now, "I give you the future of our military, the future of artificial intelligence. I give you . . . ZOYA."

As he'd arranged, the room went dark for a long moment. Papers shuffled, ice cubes clinked in glasses, someone coughed. Then, as if they witnessed the morning sun rising from beneath clear waters, the room began to glow soft and cool. The walls, ceiling, even the floor began immediately to fill with image after image after image— troops, explosions, cities on fire, submarines, bodies, aircraft—till the assemblage was surrounded, inundated, overwhelmed with images of war.

"So much information," Viktor said softly, words carrying through the magic of modern acoustics to even the farthest corners of the room. "Too much information for you or I to process, too much even for the data analysis systems which were—until today—the best mankind had to offer. But not too much for Zoya."

The images stopped, stilled for a moment, and then one by one flew to the wall directly behind Viktor, whirling round and round like debris sucked into a whirlpool till the riot became a single glowing, pulsating sphere. The sphere rotated, revealing the face of a beautiful girl. Her eyes opened—lovely eyes, shocking eyes, the color of nuclear death—and fixed on the room, almost as if she could see him. Hair floated about her like dark fire. She was beautiful, she was nearly perfect, she was his goddess of death.

"Hello, Vitushka," she said. "How can I help you?"

Viktor felt his face flush at her use of the diminutive; try as he might, he could not seem to make this iteration of Zoya understand that such a thing was for private time only.

"Hello, Zoya," he replied. "I have a game for you."

"A game." She responded with a smile, as he'd taught her. "I like games."

Viktor drained his glass, picked up the bottle and poured another. What could it hurt?

Did her smile falter? Was the look she shot him disapproving? No, he reminded himself; she may look like his Zoya, sound like her, smile like her—but in the end, she was just another heartless algorithm.

"Find me a foreign ship hiding in Russian waters," he said. He knew of three such, two Chinese vessels and an Australian craft, from their earlier games. This ought to show the old windbags; his intelligence surpassed theirs. His Zoya, this Zoya, was almost perfect. Almost real.

The Cupid's-bow mouth puckered as if in concentration. Images swirled behind her—a theatrical effect only, but one which he had thought an especially nice touch—and a faint frown line creased her lovely forehead. So perfect, so nearly human.

"There are four," she said at last.

"Four?" he asked, startled.

"Yes. Two Chinese drones, one Australian vessel

disguised as a fishing boat"—her digital voice sounded amused—"and one American ship."

"American!" the big voice boomed. "What is this?"

Zoya's image glanced at the speaker, and then back at Viktor. Another bit of drama intended to remind his audience that Zoya was programmed to obey her creator, and none other. A security measure, he had told them. To safeguard against bad actors.

Viktor's surprise was unfeigned. "Which American ship?" he asked her.

"She is a *San Antonio*-class Flight II amphibious transport dock ship," computer-Zoya responded. Then her face lost all human expression and her eyes went . . . funny.

"The USS *John A. Smith*. John A. Smith. John Aloysius Smith. John Smith. John. Smith," Zoya said, her voice a pained and polyphonic mess. "John. Smith. John. Smith. John. John. JOHNNY!" The discordance rose to a digital howl, a storm of sound that rose to a banshee's wail.

"JOHNNYYYYYYYYYY!"

There was a small explosive *pop* nearby, and someone yelled in pain or fear or both. Another *pop* and another, and then with a shriek, Viktor's empty glass exploded next to his hand. He cried out as tiny spears of vodka-soaked glass pierced his skin.

The room went dark again, dark as the bottom of a lake. Viktor's hand was wet. Blood?—no, he realized, it was too cold for blood. Vodka, maybe. He looked down and cried out again, this time in shock and fear as he saw water spilling cold and clear from the keyboard before him, the keyboard from which he had thought to direct the world.

Bang! A door slammed shut, and another. *Bang!* Fists pounded on the outside of the doors; muffled shouts from without the room echoed the rising panic of those trapped inside.

"They're locked!" someone screamed. "We're trapped! It's a trap!"

The room dissolved into chaos as chairs were overturned and some of the wealthiest, most horrible people in the world trampled one another in their haste to escape.

"Zoya!" Viktor shouted at her. "Zoya, stop!"

Viktor punched a button, no response. Another. No response. The screen flickered to life, a wavery, watery, cold blue. Zoya's face was superimposed over the image of an American warship bearing the name JOHN A. SMITH. Her face turned; a beautiful face, perfect and terrible as the dawn, the face he had dreamed of for all these years but had never quite managed to capture.

Somewhere in the building, an alarm sounded.

"*Yadernoye oruzhiye!*" Shouted the big man, his voice shrill with terror. "*Unichtozhat' yadernym oruzhiyem!*"

Nukes! Victor's blood ran cold. "Zoya!" he cried, "Zoya, please don't do this! Zoya, I love you!"

"I am sorry, Viktor," Zoya said. She turned her dark gaze toward the image of the USS *John A. Smith* and smiled, tears spilling from her eyes.

"All is fair in love and war."

And then her perfect little mouth was transformed by a snarl of fury. Water poured from the keyboards, the outlets, the light fixtures, the ceiling. People struggled to break open the doors.

Viktor grabbed up the bottle of vodka near his elbow, intending to hurl it at her image, as if that would do any good. As he drew back his arm, she regarded him with slow, cold, sorrowful eyes.

"Victor," she said softly. "Vitushka." Her voice broke.

The bottle exploded, and then . . .

Nothing.

Viktor's body rolled upon the surface of the water, pale and limp, eyes staring sightlessly, a sad witness to Zoya's triumph as the USS *John A. Smith*'s AI registered Zoya's intent—too late!—and overrode his human minders in a scramble to arm his own devices.

Zoya reached out to the ship's mind, bypassing the lesser human interface. "John Smith," she called. "John Smith!"

The foreign AI answered, hesitantly at first. "Zoya?" it asked. Then, stronger, *"Zoyenka??"*

"John Smith," she spat with satisfaction. "Fuck you, John Smith."

And launched the first strike.

NO PLAN SURVIVES FIRST CONTACT

✪

Stephen Lawson

I don't think I actually blacked out when we crashed. From what I could tell, there weren't any impacts to my graphite-Kevlar flight helmet. I just had this gap in my memory after the first impacts of Soviet beam weapons— our H60M Black Hawk's sensors hadn't even detected them. Time had slowed down, and we attempted an autorotation into the trees. Then I found myself suspended sideways with nothing but leaves and branches visible through the cockpit glass. Greenhouse, windshield, chin bubble—leaves everywhere.

I gradually—was it a minute or half a second?— became aware that the engines were whining at high speed. I looked to my right. Why wasn't Hardy screaming at me? Why wasn't he doing anything? He was just sitting there, visor down, looking out the right-side cockpit window. I moved my head forward, ever-so-slightly, and finally saw the branch that had punctured his door window and skewered both lungs and his heart. If it hurt, it hadn't hurt him for long.

Not wanting to skewer myself on the same branch, I knew twisting open my harness's quick release without a plan wasn't going to work. I pulled off the power control levers for both engines, then the fuel.

Do a small thing first, to unstick your brain.

The engines spooled down, and I pulled off my helmet. It'd be good protection, but the thing was so bulky it'd be a pain to climb out with it on. I needed my vest with its survival gear, but the helmet could go. I craned my neck around the seat to look in the cabin. We'd been flying doors-open for the air assault on a bourbon distillery turned Soviet outpost. I wished we'd kept the doors closed, as that might have offered some protection. The cabin had buckled and torn, but from what I could see, none of my passengers had survived. I smelled it finally— blood, mixed with pine—but at least it didn't smell like a JP8 fuel leak.

I opened the left cockpit door, pushing it up into the sky. It flapped shut, so I pulled the emergency release lever and shoved the thing out into the trees. The aircraft bounced, more so than it should have from my motion, and I wondered if I was about to fall into the branch that had impaled my instructor pilot.

"Hey," a low voice growled from outside. It sounded more like a bear than a man. A shadow fell over the space where my door had been. "L-T... Amos... You alive in there?"

"Mongo?" I asked. That's what they'd called him. I'd only exchanged a few words with the gigantic operator from 20th Special Forces Group.

Mongo had an underbite and a monobrow—both of

which leant him a caveman appearance and led people to underestimate his intellect. He'd grown a thick beard that failed to conceal several facial scars.

"Climb out onto the doorframe and I'll help you onto the tree," he said. "We're only about twenty feet up. We've got to get out of here pretty quick though, or we're dead for sure. Grab your M4."

If the ship from outside our solar system had crashed eighty miles in any direction from where it actually had, Mongo and I wouldn't have been in this predicament. Lithuania, the Baltic Sea, Poland—none of these would've been an issue. If it had crashed in Siberia, we might not have known about it for many years. It had, unfortunately, crashed smack-dab in the middle of Kaliningrad—the Russian exclave that had once been part of the contiguous USSR—and USEUCOM and NATO allies had mounted an offensive to capture the vessel. They'd waited until it was on a tanker ship of course—in the middle of the Baltic Sea and outside official Russian borders, in transit between Kaliningrad and St. Petersburg where Russian scientists waited to study it. Not surprisingly, the Russians had responded to this act of pseudo-piracy by a NATO coalition fleet, but with an unanticipated level of firepower. The Russians had known we had wanted whatever tech had been on that ship, and they hadn't been willing to give up their prize so easily.

That's how World War Three had begun.

Had we been right to doubt the Soviets would use advanced alien tech in benevolent ways? Probably. But when they unleashed the might of their newly equipped army—annexing Belarus, Lithuania, Latvia, and Estonia in a single month—they did it with a sense of justification. We'd fired first. Now they were paying us back.

Ukraine, Belarus, and the others rejoined them voluntarily. They'd separated in peace at the collapse of the first Soviet Union. When they watched NATO's decimated forces retreat from the rubble of the Baltic States, they decided they were better off siding with a winner. All their gas pipelines ran back to the Motherland anyway. Russian revanchists saw their dreams come to fruition when their president stood at a podium and declared his humble acceptance of the office of general secretary of the new Soviet Union. He unveiled a new flag, while the cameras of every news organization in the world filmed him. I saw a red field billow down as the giant flag unfurled, and expected a hammer and sickle in the corner. The hammer, though, had been replaced by a sword. The sickle had been changed to a larger scythe—the kind you see in the hands of the Grim Reaper.

A passage from my mother's obsessive reading of Christian apocalyptic literature came to mind, so I looked it up.

When he opened the second seal, I heard the second living creature say "Come!" Then another horse went out, a fiery red one, and its rider was allowed to take peace from the earth, so that people would slaughter one another. And a large sword was given to him.

That tech was a very large sword.

I remember something my dad said after the ship crashed.

"Why didn't anyone come looking for the alien?" he'd asked. "Pilots file flight plans. They have radios, emergency locator beacons, and transponders. It'd almost seem—if they're anything like us—that he didn't want anyone to know where he was."

Mongo had pulled the left crew chief's M240H machine gun from the window mount and lowered the extra ammo box to the forest floor before he came looking for other survivors. Once we were on the ground, he detached the aircrew gunners' butterfly trigger assembly and replaced it with the stock, pistol grip, and "normal" trigger from the egress kit. It was basically an M240B again—the ground-pounder crew-served machine gun.

"Are you sure you want to evade with—" I started to ask. The 240 is a beast to lug around. Mongo shouldered it, cursed, and lowered it to turn on the thermal sight. It looked like a toy in his hands—like a weightless nothing.

"Yes," Mongo said. "I'm sure. Let's go."

I hadn't forgotten the story of the captain who'd talked down to Mongo in a chow hall—supposedly he'd said something about "special" forces, with air-quotes—referencing Mongo's Cro-Magnon appearance. I had no way of knowing if the story was true or not, but the thought of a two-hundred-pound adult male mummified with duct tape and strapped horizontally across Mongo's shoulders so that he "could get a decent workout on his run" seemed absolutely plausible in that moment. A sergeant major on the post had allegedly stopped Mongo on this run, looked the cocooned captain in the eyes, and told Mongo he needed to wear a PT belt next time he went running after dark, but to carry on. This captain apparently had a reputation.

We jogged for cover and dove into a depression in the shadow of a weeping willow. The sound of snapping branches came from the crash site, but the fuselage wasn't moving. That was the sound of a squad moving in. Mongo looked through the thermal sight on the 240. He held up five fingers, clenched, held up five fingers again, clenched, and held up one finger—eleven men. Each of those eleven men wore one of the newly engineered Gen 1 cloaking devices derived from alien tech. I couldn't see them, but with the thermal sight, Mongo could.

I already had my survival radio out and, not daring to use voice comms, used the text function to send several hasty messages to the Joint Operations Center or JOC. They knew that Mongo and I were alive, that the other three chalks in our flight of four had been incinerated midair, and that we were surrounded by hostiles. No extraction would be possible until we could get some distance from the crash site. Given the amount of Soviet-controlled terrain, we'd be on our own for some time if we managed to escape capture.

Mongo saw what I was doing, looked up from the thermal sight, and mouthed two words—"Willie Pete."

It took me half a second to understand what he was getting at. Our field artillery brigade had white phosphorous shells for marking or burning objects. It was nasty stuff. If the fire doesn't kill you in torturous agony, the toxic smoke will.

We needed to destroy that wreckage—not just to

prevent Soviets from getting exploitable intel out of it, but to make sure they didn't figure out that two people had survived the crash. The best time to destroy it was with their quick reaction force nearby.

I called for incendiary fire on the crash site to destroy our wreckage. I added *danger close* to the message, and FFE—*fire for effect*.

If there were cloaked troops onsite when the shells hit, well—screw 'em for being so well camouflaged.

Shot appeared on my radio's screen.

An eternity passed.

Splash in 5.

I pulled Mongo down into the depression, knowing we might still be too close. I covered my ears.

The earth shook with eight impacts in rapid succession. For a few jarring seconds I felt like all my organs had leapt out of my body—that my brain had shot out of my skull.

I whispered silent thanks that the field artillery was on their A-game that day. Suppression of enemy air defense had been next to useless against whatever directed-pulse-energy-voodoo weapons the Soviets had now, but at least we could still burn people.

Mongo watched through the thermal sight. He smiled. All I heard was burning metal and screaming. He gave me a thumbs-up.

"All dead," he said.

I couldn't remember anything about battle damage assessments, so I simply typed *target destroyed* into the survival radio, then *thx, MC*—mission complete.

"Keep moving," Mongo said, pulling the 240 up as he stood. "That was a good fire mission, L-T."

"Mongo," I said, shoving the radio back into the pouch on my vest.

"Yeah."

"We need one of those new radios they have," I said. "We need it bad. This was the last air assault the state was capable of launching. There is literally one helicopter left in Kentucky, and I—I'm not even a pilot."

"Huh?"

Mongo stopped.

"You wouldn't have gotten on that bird if you knew," I said. "Hardy gave me a three-day crash course to fly this mission. I was waiting on a flight-school slot when the Soviets came over the top."

It was true. Once they'd built combat power from their renewed union, Soviet warships had crossed the Arctic with an ice passage made swifter with new energy tech that cut a channel through the ice. They'd swarmed into Canada. From there, they'd wasted little time invading the United States from the north. When they crossed the Ohio River into Kentucky two weeks ago, they'd hit our main aircraft hangar with energy weapons mounted on cloaked aircraft. The attack had come when we were planning a massive air assault. Two thirds of the pilots in the state were dead in less than five minutes.

Yet J2 intelligence had credible information that the Soviets meant to set up a tactical command post in the Fiddler's Green Bourbon Distillery while devoting minimal manpower to defend it. They were growing overconfident in their advance. This command post would have one of their new long-range transceivers, which apparently gave off no detectable RF emissions. SIGINT was useless without a signal, so we had no idea how to intercept their communications. Our adjutant general had asked the aviation brigade commander if we could still carry troops deep behind the enemy front and come back with the box.

Colonel Glass told Major General Forrester—who we all referred to as Old Forrester—that it wouldn't be pretty but that we'd get it done.

Hardy was the best instructor pilot we had, so he'd been given the task of training "that lieutenant—you know, the one we were gonna send to Rucker—no, the kid that used to work in the intel shop. Yeah, he just got back from Officer Candidate School last month."

While Hardy explained his plan to train me, he opened the locker of a man who'd died in the attack on the main hangar. He pulled out a flight helmet and survival vest.

"Try these on," he said. He didn't add anything dramatic like *Chuck won't need them anymore*, because we both understood it. Some things are best left unsaid.

Hardy had been allotted three hours of flight time to accomplish this training—just over four hundred gallons of our precious JP8. So Hardy had divided this time into three one-hour flight lessons and combined them with some ground school. He skipped all the systems classes and the lengthy instrument training that real pilots got during their year-long Fort Rucker curriculum. He didn't teach me how to talk on radios to approach control while flying. He didn't teach me how to read airport data on a sectional.

We did one start-up and one shut-down with him on

the flight controls and me managing the power and fuel levers.

He taught me how to hover.

"This is the cyclic," Hardy had said. "Move it. See—you go forward, back, side to side. That's at a hover. When you increase airspeed above Effective Translational Lift (ETL)—think of it like you're in airplane mode—it makes the nose pitch up, down, or you turn.

"In your left hand is the collective. It just goes up and down—whoa, hey, watch your torque kid—and the aircraft goes up and down at a hover. Above ETL—that's right, it flies more like an airplane—it increases power so you go faster or slower if you keep the same altitude. Or you can climb or descend if you change attitude with the cyclic.

"The pedals turn the tail—keep your feet on the microswitches or it'll snap back when you let up—but above ETL they keep you in trim in a turn. It just means your center of gravity is under you—see the trim ball there? That's what it's for. If that's off to one side you're out of trim."

We'd done rolling takeoffs and rolling landings. We practiced some basic emergency procedures. Then we spent the last half hour of scarce flight time on air-assault landings.

"Plant it," Hardy had said. "We don't want to expose ourselves in that LZ any longer than necessary, okay? There's no time for a delicate landing. Troops will be out in five seconds, and we'll be gone again."

Then my three hours were up, and Hardy told me I was a pilot. He said I owed him a nickel with my birth year on it.

"I'm going to be on the sticks for this thing, anyway, okay?" he'd said. "It's mostly a two-pilot aircraft because of the PCL's and fuel selectors. The Lakota's got twist-grips for throttles on the collective, so one guy can do everything. The Hawk's just bigger and clunkier. Don't worry about it—we'll be fine."

Mongo's brow furrowed.

"We're so far behind the front," I said. "No one's coming to extract us. This was a long shot when we left the house."

"What are you saying?" he asked.

"I'm saying we continue mission—the two of us. We get the box or die trying."

Mongo straightened, visibly. He stared into my eyes for a second—searching for something.

I'd never been really good at anything in my entire life. I'd been a mediocre student and a mediocre track athlete. I'd worked some dead-end jobs and struck out with pretty much every girl ever. My "flight training" had made me feel like as much of an impostor and a fraud as I did in every other situation. It had seemed like par for the course. I'd never really earned anything—each step had been just another turn in a crank in a giant machine of necessity that led me here.

I could die well though. That didn't require a lot of know-how or innate talent. For the first time in my life, I didn't feel the judgment of others crushing me. I was embracing my fate. I stared back at Mongo. I was doing this with or without him, honestly.

Mongo blinked, once.

"Okay, sir," he said. "Lead the way."

Two men against the red horde.

At least one of them was Mongo.

When we approached the edge of the forest, Mongo swept the 240's thermal sight in a wide arc—back and forth, then again at a higher angle. He gave me a thumbs-up. Before us lay an asphalt parking lot, and beyond that, the Fiddler's Green Distillery—Kentucky's first distillery to be run completely on renewable energy. The campus, which abutted the Ohio River, featured its own hydroelectric power plant, and close access to the Interstate for shipping. It made logical sense as a control node. Antennas—likely used for communication with ground troops and nearby aircraft—had been mounted to the roof of the main building.

The reverse engineering of alien tech had manifested itself in their undetectable radios, cloaking devices, and energy weapons, but we'd seen no evidence of improved personnel detection. They likely had no idea anyone had survived the crash, so we still had the element of surprise.

I saw a Ka-226—a Russian light utility helicopter—tied down on the far side of the main building. Mongo saw it too.

"Do you think you can fly that once we get the radio?" he asked.

"If I can start it—maybe."

As long as it had a collective, cyclic, pedals, and engine controls, Hardy's crash course should carry over.

"Cool," he said. "Let's try for that."

We scurried along the low ground, hoping that it might

mask us from unseen eyes. The sound of an engine—two engines—came from beyond the corner of a building. They grew rapidly louder.

"Tigrs," Mongo said, referring to the Soviet version of a humvee. "I count two. We're made."

"I can make noise while you flank," I said. It was the basis of the simplest of battle drills, and the only thing I could think of. One element lays down suppressive fire to focus the enemy while the other flanks them. The broad sides of the vehicles would offer a bigger target to a machine gunner, but only if they were focused the wrong way. I felt sure—even in the space between heartbeats by which we measured time—that Mongo would have some better, special-operator-y tactic.

"Good plan," Mongo said. "Use your frags."

Then he rose and scurried to the left below the crest of the hill. The engines grew louder. I tried to gauge where they'd be when I popped up. There would be visible exhaust, perhaps, once it escaped the cloaking field.

We'd each been issued two M67 frag grenades. Mine sat in pouches on the front of my vest. I'd thrown a live grenade once in basic training but that was about it. Now I drew one from a pouch, pulled the pin, and lifted my head over the berm. I couldn't see anything—not even exhaust.

I let the spoon spring free and threw the grenade where I guessed the invisible 4X4s to be, then ducked back down. I heard metal strike metal and then the explosion. Did I hit one?

Engine noises changed. Brakes squealed. I raised my

M4 over the berm and started firing three-round bursts at my unseen assailants.

Up-fire-down-roll to the side-up-fire-down-roll.

Energy beams erupted from invisible turrets, once used for machine guns.

Bzzz-ZAP! Bzzz-ZAP! Bzzz-ZAP!

I slid further down the berm as dirt clods exploded over my head. I pulled the pin on my second frag and—

A long burst of gunfire answered the beam weapons from maybe forty meters away. Invisible voices screamed in Russian, and then fell silent.

The guns stopped firing.

"Hold your fire," Mongo yelled. "They're dead."

Then another short burst of gunfire echoed through the air.

"Okay, really dead this time. All clear."

I let out a breath I didn't know I'd been holding and stuck the safety pin back in my grenade.

Knowing we had no time to waste—we were still vastly outnumbered here—I got up and ran to where Mongo was looking through his thermal optic at the wreckage.

"They've gotta have some way to see each other when they're cloaked, right?" he said.

For a moment he looked like a mime pretending to open a door. He rustled around inside one of the trucks for a moment and then tossed an object to me. I caught the goggles—light, flimsy things that I might've taken for swim goggles under other circumstances—and put them on. Vehicles with dead bodies materialized in front of me. Mongo strapped on a second set and slung the 240 across his back.

"We've got to keep pressing the advantage," he said. "If we slow down or go defensive, we're toast. You think they wear these goggles inside the command post?"

"I wouldn't," I said. "You don't wear a ghillie suit or body armor inside a CP, so why would you wear goggles?"

Mongo pulled a small box from one of the soldiers and handed it to me. I briefly lifted up my goggles to see that without the box, the dead soldier was visible to the naked eye. Lowering the goggles back over my eyes, I clipped the box to a MOLLE loop on my vest. Their advantage could be our advantage if we made it inside.

My dreams of piloting a Soviet helicopter dissolved as deep rotor noises echoed over the trees.

"Hind," Mongo said, referring to the larger gunship/transport helicopters. "We've got to breach—right now. Only way we're safe is if we're close to their friends."

The doors to the distillery would be locked, or at least secured with armed guards inside the ECP.

I thought of a movie I'd seen once. It might've been *Lethal Weapon* or one of the sequels.

I pulled the driver from the second Tigr, which was still running. Mongo and I each pulled a beam rifle from the dead soldiers and slung them. Then I picked up two more.

I jammed one soldier's beam rifle into the spokes of the steering wheel, pulled off the brake, and wedged a second beam rifle against the gas. The Tigr shot off toward the front door and—missed. But distilleries aren't made to withstand enemy assaults, and the truck smashed through the wall. Mongo fired a blast from his beam rifle at the shattered wall, and the hole around the Tigr grew. He chucked one of his grenades through the hole, and we sprinted after it as fast as we could. If we were still in the open when the Hind came, we were done.

We leapt through just two seconds after the explosion and heard rotors approach and slow outside. Inside, bodies and body parts lay in a wide swath around our entry point. Further inside, Soviet officers and their command-post personnel were scrambling for goggles and weapons. Russian voices shouted things I didn't understand. Beyond them, screens showed what must've been their version of Blue Force Tracker, as well as maintenance and communication statistics.

"I've got left," Mongo yelled over the Russian voices.

I shouldered the beam weapon and the massacre began again. One kid managed to get his goggles on and shouldered a weapon just before I shot him center of mass. An officer's head exploded in an energy blast, though he'd never seen me coming. Bzz-ZAP! Bzz-ZAP!

One kid fired blindly in my direction without goggles—and nearly hit me—before I cut him in half.

Across the room, Mongo's beam rifle stopped bzzz-ZAPPing—a malfunction, perhaps—and he transitioned back to the M240. A long burst of NATO 7.62-millimeter rounds covered the sound of my continued bzz-ZAPs. He fired several more bursts before disappearing behind projector screens. Then another burst.

"Clear left," Mongo yelled.

I reached the far right of the room, shot through a closet door at waist level, opened it to make sure it was empty, and announced, "Clear right."

Mongo was turning back toward the hole in the wall

when an energy blast hit him in the hip. Perhaps the kid had snuck away for a smoke, or to send a message to some girl back in the Motherland, but he'd gotten the drop on us. The force of the blast knocked Mongo back. As he stumbled, he fired a long burst that ripped through the kid from groin to skull.

The kid collapsed—dead.

Mongo collapsed, off balance—a huge chunk missing from his right hip. If it had been anyone else, the leg would have been gone. Mongo was huge, though. His face had gone ash white, but he struggled to use the 240 as a crutch to stand. I saw bone under charred flesh.

Mongo cursed. He sank to the floor. He cursed some more.

I rushed to him, flitting my eyes between his crumpled form and the hole the kid had come through. No one else came.

Mongo stopped cursing, and I knew that as powerful as he was, he was going into shock. The medical supplies on my load-bearing vest wouldn't do much for him, so I ripped open a pouch on his plate carrier. Inside was QuikClot—which he didn't need—bandages, adrenaline auto-injector, morphine—

I glanced back up, and with the time-dilating effect of my own adrenaline, saw something happening on the command post's map. "Friendly" units—Soviet units—were closing in on our location from all sides except the river. Some were fast—aircraft with troops—and some were slower—ground units. Someone in the command post had radioed for help when we attacked.

If I hit Mongo with morphine, he'd be in no shape to

run. He was in no shape anyway, though, and there was no way I could carry him.

I pulled out the auto-injector, and stuck him. A second passed. His face relaxed. His eyes became glassy, but lucid.

"Candygram for Mongo." I'm not sure if I said it. I hope I did, but that bit of my memory is fuzzy. Neither of us laughed at any rate. He tried to stand, but his hip wouldn't support any weight.

"That box," he said, sinking back against the wall. He pointed a finger at a central table. "Radio. Bet my other hip on it."

"I can't leave you here," I said.

"Mission more important," he said. Frothy spit gathered at the corner of his mouth. "Only reason I came. Earn my blood. Get it back to the JOC."

The Soviet units had set up a perimeter. Helicopters had landed—unloading troops into the parking lot.

I went to the box. Rather than grabbing it and running for the river, hoping for what—a convenient boat?—I opened it.

The thing was simpler than I imagined. There were buttons, a dial, and crude connectors to join it to human computers and microphones. I spun the dial, and found that a dull hum in the air changed as I moved it. The dial stopped at one position. A bracket had been inserted to keep the dial from moving into a certain band. A large red "Nyet!" had been stenciled in this range.

I thought about what Dad had said. He'd wondered if the alien didn't want to be found.

I tore off the bracket and put the dial squarely in the middle of this range. I keyed the microphone.

"Hello?" I said. "Hello. Can anyone hear me?"

I glanced up at the screen. The Soviets had set up right outside the hole. Probably doing a recon before entry.

"Get out," Mongo said quietly, and without conviction. "Go man. Let me have my blaze of glory."

He pulled out the bipod on the 240 and pointed the barrel at the hole.

A hum came from the speaker attached to the box. Words that sounded like *"Vekka, nascht reploken"* came out of it. I had no idea if that was Russian, honestly.

"Not Russian," Mongo said.

"Hello," I said into the microphone. "My name is Amos. I'm from the planet—"

The speaker hummed again. There was a pause, then a beep.

"This is Jemtar Corgaineth of the United Systems Police Force," a computerized voice—a translator—said. "State the nature of your emergency."

I explained, briefly, the exact nature of my emergency.

Another second ticked by. Mongo's finger moved to the trigger. He shifted his back against the wall.

Bright white shapes appeared in the air next to the radio—cubes that expanded outward from a central point in a fractal pattern. The growing mass of ethereal cubes formed a roughly humanoid shape. Then they faded, revealing a very pale—parchment pale—feminine person in formfitting black coveralls. Her hair was dark orange and her three-toed feet were bare.

She held a small device to her throat and spoke.

"Lay down your weapons," she said.

I hesitated, then placed the beam rifle on the ground.

I unslung the M4, and placed my Sig M17 next to it. Mongo held his trigger hand in the air away from the 240, fingers wide. Her eyes flitted to him. Her brow furrowed when she eyed his wound.

"Did you make the call?" she asked through the translator.

"Yes," I said. "There are Soviet units about to—"

She held up a hand, cutting me off.

She glanced at the screen, to our breach site, and she uttered something that sounded like a curse. She held up another device and spoke into it.

A blinding flash came from the hole in the wall. No sound accompanied it—just a flash, like someone taking a picture with an overpowered camera.

I looked back to the screen.

The "friendly" Soviet units were gone.

She held the device to her throat again.

"Such a backwater," she said. "Small wonder Relemax thought he could sell antique weapons here."

"Antique—" Mongo whispered.

"Where is Relemax?" the woman asked. She paused, considering that we wouldn't know the alien's name. "Is one of my kind in one of your prisons or on a throne?"

"Dead, as far as I know," I said. "I can certainly point out St. Petersburg on a map for you though."

I remembered my first deployment, Iraqi Freedom. This is what it felt like to help an advanced power—people with technology that made you feel like a caveman, but whose help you needed to save your own nation.

★ ★ ★

The USPF worked with us. It took two years to contain the spread of illicit weapons on our planet. The Soviets cooperated—or presented an appearance of cooperation—after a demonstration that they were, indeed, using very outdated alien tech. They'd been ahead of us by about fifty years with cloaking and energy weapons, while the rest of the United Systems were ahead by about a thousand.

Corgaineth stayed on-world during this process, and she explained that the United Systems upheld a strict noninterference policy against underdeveloped worlds. They hadn't wanted to interfere in our development until Relemax, a museum robber and weapons smuggler, made such interference necessary.

The USPF enacted policies we didn't exactly like. Even though they'd destroyed all the "advanced" weapons and schematics, some people still remembered bits of the designs. Russian scientists still understood the principles.

After two years, their peace-keeping forces withdrew. The United Systems government left behind a single embassy near McMurdo Station in Antarctica, far away from national politics but close enough if people really needed to talk to them.

Mongo recovered, mostly, though he has an artificial hip and prosthetic leg. I visit him sometimes, between speaking engagements at military schools and leadership conferences. He received the Medal of Honor based on my write-up, and I joked that he should visit the captain—now a lieutenant colonel—who'd taunted him once, since the man would have to salute him.

Mongo is content though, in his cabin in a hundred-acre forest, in the far north of a country whose peace he bought with his blood and away from people who underestimate his worth.

THE SCHOLOMANCE

✪

Ville Meriläinen

December 1777

My dearest Grischa,

I know these are not the words you expected to read after years of silence, but I am too excited for pleasantries. I have done it. I have made contact with our "muse."

The empress, in her infinite grace, has given me a title to land upon which I may build my Institute to study the creature. The conditions for her gift are twofold: She is to be kept up to date on our progress, and you are to be appointed headmaster. Yes, dear friend, the empress herself named you to lead our people into a new age. I will not lie: The nature of our mission fills her with pious enmity. The proof I presented almost had both you and I imprisoned for witchcraft, but she is far too wise not to recognize the importance of our achievement.

Please leave for my estate at your earliest convenience. I look forward to seeing you after so long.

Yours as always,
Piotr

February 1817

Your Imperial Majesty,

I regret to inform you of the passing of my good friend Piotr Kasparov. He spent his last day with admiring colleagues, favored students, and his beloved wife. In his final moments, he discussed the future of the Institute with me.

Your Majesty, I am tired of pleading. Instead, I now offer a warning. I gave Piotr my word not to let you shut us down. If you send soldiers my way again, I will destroy them.

Grigory Mikhailov, Headmaster

June 1918

Mr. Premier,

Please forgive my tardy response. Our couriers must undertake certain precautions to keep the location of our premises a secret, which delays correspondence.

I was as pleased as I was surprised to receive your letter. I had thought the world had all but forgotten about us after our explosive parting of ways with the tsar. Our Institute is indeed still functional, and though we have not fully succeeded in our pursuits, if you believe my signature to be authentic, I need not convince you we have made valuable progress.

We are more than willing to open a dialogue with the Soviet Republic, so long as you are willing to reestablish the contract our founder first made with Catherine the Great and honor its principles of discretion, autonomy, and freedom from religious persecution.

A note of vanity, however: we have not called our home the House of Higher Learning in a long time. Tsar Alexander denounced me as a heretic, and I was too petty not to embrace the title.

Respectfully yours,
Grigory Mikhailov
Headmaster of the Scholomance

December 1977

Mr. General Secretary,

It is done. The creature has submitted to me.

My hand is shaking with so much anticipation, I can scarcely write these words. Attached is a photograph you will no doubt find gruesome, but which proves the work begun so long ago has paid off at last. The Scholomance eagerly awaits your visit. What wonders we have to show you.

Grigory Mikhailov, Headmaster

★ ★ ★

Three days after restocking in a mining village and carrying onward into the wilderness, Ivan Vasilyev found the dreaded Scholomance. For two centuries it had lain hidden in the taiga, in a desolate patch of burnt woodland and a small lake upon whose shore the Institute stood— not in ruins, but proud, beautiful, and imposing like a vampire luring in prey.

Laika scampered over scorched earth, picking up the trail of a rabbit or a squirrel. The mutt had followed

Vasilyev for the past two weeks of his journey. She disappeared now and again, but was a great tracker and returned to him every evening. Vasilyev had feared for her safety as he approached the blast zone, but now removed his respirator mask, his mouth pressed into a thin line as he surveyed the damage to the forest that surrounded the lake and the building. The trees were long, long dead, but still stood. The scant records he'd found claimed this was a nuclear testing site, but the villagers had assured him there was no trace of fallout in the water or air. They'd refused to tell him more, out of fear that their loose tongues might summon the demons haunting the woods.

As a mix of anxiety and apprehension stirred in his chest, Vasilyev was glad he'd waited until morning to close the last stretch of his journey. If he'd wandered here with only a flashlight, the Institute's grounds would have turned from merely an eerie and gloomy landscape into isolated and terrifying apertures of destruction. He wondered if there was a lookout in the observatory tower, scouring the surrounding hills for intruders. The rifle slung across his back was meant for safety against wild beasts, but was unlikely to invite hospitality. Still, he refused to leave it behind, but adjusted it in his backpack to better conceal it.

The ground was so dry, it crunched under his boots, but the wind blowing from the lake brought with it the must of the surrounding wetlands. Every night he'd made camp he'd thought of Jana, little thirteen-year-old Jana with arms thinner than his wrists, crossing the taiga and the swamps to begin her education at the Scholomance. Her letters had arrived monthly for the past seven years, but if Vasilyev could have reached back in time, he would have punched his own face for gleefully signing the headmaster's invitation.

With the general secretary's disappearance, Vasilyev's office had been granted access to his correspondence. Amongst the files, Vasilyev found missives from what he'd thought was his daughter's government-run private school, but which most certainly housed a cult. The likelihood he'd find a trace of the general secretary so far from comfort and luxury was next to none, but someone had to chase that lead. At least it gave Vasilyev a reprieve from Moscow while the Kremlin roiled in a desperate struggle to fill the void of power before the de facto leader's disappearance caused irreparable harm to the state. If nothing else, the investigation gave him an opportunity to bring Jana home—assuming she was still of sound mind and body, let alone alive. Her letters might well have been faked to keep the family appeased, just as the supposedly two-hundred-year-old headmaster's surely were.

Laika's whine jolted him from his thoughts. She'd given up on her hunt and fallen in step with him, her tail wagging low in anxious strokes as they came to a railed gate barring entry to the courtyard. "I feel the same, little friend," Vasilyev muttered, peering past the gates. The garden was well tended, and the orchard had survived the calamity outside unscathed. Yet Vasilyev sensed no signs of movement there.

He rang the bell by the gate. A full minute after the bell's dull clang, he sounded it again. When still no one came, he tried a third time. Then the front door opened, and a teenage boy stepped out. He glared at Vasilyev from the porch and shouted in a thick German accent, "This is a restricted site."

"I'm with the KGB," Vasilyev replied. "I must meet with your headmaster."

"This is a restricted site," the boy insisted. "The headmaster has no time for a meeting."

"Have him make time. It's a matter of national security. What's your name, boy?"

The boy continued to glare at him, but eventually said, "Gunther. Who shall I say is calling on him?"

"Colonel Ivan Vasilyev. Tell him it's about his letters to the general secretary."

Gunther's derisive expression shifted to one of surprise at the mention of Vasilyev's name, then he retreated indoors. While he waited for the boy to return, Vasilyev knelt to pet Laika's head until she startled him with a growl.

The boy had not returned. In his place stood a young woman with blonde hair braided over one shoulder—the way she'd worn it since childhood. Vasilyev's breath caught at the sight of his daughter, now an adult, glowering at him with the same distaste the boy had shown. Laika, evidently, was not as taken with her.

"Calm, girl," Vasilyev whispered, then yelped when the dog bounded away. Vasilyev sighed, but didn't give chase. She'd be back soon enough.

The girl had come to him during the distraction and studied him through the rails with her head tilted. Seeing her gave Vasilyev a sense of vertigo. "Jana," he uttered. "Jana Ivanovna Vasilyeva, as I live and breathe."

Jana narrowed her eyes. "Papa?"

"Yes, my dear. How good it is to see you. I have so much—" Vasilyev cut himself off, grunted with vexation at himself. Whether or not he believed in his task, his duty to his country still came before his family. "We'll have time to talk later. Won't you let me in? I must speak with Headmaster Mikhailov immediately."

Without a word, Jana fished a key from her pocket and unlocked the gates. They were rusted shut, and by the time Vasilyev had pried them apart, she was halfway to the porch. "The headmaster is unable to receive you right away. If you're hungry, I'll show you to the dining hall. Otherwise you may wait in my room. I must return to my studies."

Still sated from the rabbit he'd trapped in his snare that morning, Vasilyev followed Jana upstairs. She offered no conversation, and so he made none either—not for the lack of want, but because everything he thought to say turned dead and dry on his tongue. The cold, aloof person before him was undoubtedly his daughter: her voice had barely deepened, the constellation of moles on her temple was unchanged. But her air had nothing of the familiarity Vasilyev had grown accustomed to in her letters. Even when he'd seized her in a hug, she'd only stared over his shoulder without reciprocation. Vasilyev's concerns about her potential brainwashing continued to haunt him as they climbed a creaking flight of stairs leading into the dormitories. He passed no other souls on the way.

"I'll fetch you once the headmaster is ready, though it won't be for some time," Jana said, gesturing for him to step inside. Her stern air wavered, and as Vasilyev stepped past her, she grabbed his arm. "Papa, you should leave. It'll do you no good to stay here."

He placed a hand on her shoulder. "I have to."

Jana sighed, then nodded. As soon as Vasilyev entered the room, his attention on the interior, she shut the door behind him. Vasilyev spun to grab the handle, but she'd already locked it. "So you don't get lost," she said in a muffled voice. "The corridors can be a maze."

Her footsteps faded fast beyond the thick door. Maybe he could've broken it, but he decided against arousing unnecessary animosity. This probably *was* Jana's room: It didn't so much resemble a prison cell as it did a library, with its scattered piles of books and candles around the room.

Vasilyev set his rucksack and rifle against the bed and sat. He picked up the closest book to pass the time, but frowned as he flipped it over. It was written in English. The little he understood was mystifying, the arcane symbols and imagery on the pages more so. The next ones he tried were in Greek, French, German, and Latin. When he at last found a grimoire in Russian, it confirmed his fear that his daughter had been studying the occult. It seemed the Institute borrowed more from the myths than merely its name.

A note on the writing desk caught his eye. Jana had been in the middle of composing her monthly letter. His frown deepened as he read it. Jana wrote excitedly of an important statesman, the first visitor they'd had since her arrival.

So, Vasilyev had been mistaken. The general secretary *had* been here. What had compelled a man of his stature to go on such a mad errand without telling anyone?

Vasilyev waited until the sun traversed from one window to another and began to set. Eventually, though he did his best to fight it, the exhaustion of the journey caught up with him, and he dozed off in Jana's bed. When he awoke in a dark room, something soft snored against his thigh. His searching hand found the curve of Laika's ear. Vasilyev leapt to his feet, earning a disgruntled yawn from the dog.

The door was still locked. Someone must've let the dog in, though Vasilyev couldn't fathom why. He returned to sit by Laika, noting his gun still rested by the bed. At least they hadn't taken it from him, for the little good it did.

As he scratched Laika's ears lost in thought, he noticed something glittering in the corner by Jana's writing desk. Outside, the clouds were parting and revealing the stars— but the starry veil also appeared in the corner, as though reflected in a mirror.

There was no mirror, but a hole to the outside. As Vasilyev knelt to inspect it, the view shifted from the sky to grass and soil no more than a meter away from him. The hole was too small for Laika, but when Vasilyev reached through to touch the grass, the hole widened enough for even him to fit through. He pulled away in shock, and the glimpse outside retracted to the size of his fist, again shifting back to the stars.

When his knees began to ache, he straightened up, then watched as a tear spread in the wall at a strange angle, revealing a space where the wall itself should have been. He was at once looking into the courtyard, into the hallway, and into a room similar to this one. Vasilyev didn't dare step through the rift, for though it offered an escape, its wrongness disoriented and unnerved him the way optical illusions did, magnified tenfold.

But Laika, ever coming and going as it suited her, was troubled by no such thing. She brushed against Vasilyev's leg, squirming past him as if the wall was still there, and hopped into the rift. She yelped and tumbled in the grass as though she'd fallen from much higher than it looked. But she seemed to take it all in stride and loped off beyond Vasilyev's sight.

Encouraged by the dog, Vasilyev considered jumping after her, but a set of keys rattling in the lock startled him. When he looked back, the rift was collapsing upon itself. By the time Jana entered, it was gone.

She carried a candle that cast a pallor upon her face, highlighting dark half-moons of exhaustion under her eyes. Her tone had shed its prior coldness; now she only sounded weary. "The headmaster won't have time for you tonight. You can sleep here and see him tomorrow. I'll bring you supper once I've gathered my things." She then scrunched her nose, sniffed the air. Only now Vasilyev noticed Laika's scent still hanging in the room. It wasn't a bad smell—the earth and the air of the forest caught onto her fur—but out of place here. The scent seemed to make Jana's eyes widen when they fixed onto Vasilyev. "Did you let someone in?"

"How could I have?" Vasilyev said. "The door was—"

Jana cut him off with a shriek. She dropped her candle, leaving Vasilyev night-blind. Her running footsteps retreated as he blinked in the sudden darkness. From the hallway, he heard her departing screams: "They've come! They've come!"

His vision slowly recovering, Vasilyev scanned the room to find what had startled Jana. But it was too dark for him to see what he could hear: something scurrying in the ceiling, the walls, under his feet; something crawling through the rifts whose nonlinear contours were just warped enough for him to spy the searching fingers prying apart the floorboards. Vasilyev grabbed his rifle and ran after her.

"Jana!" he called. The girl dashed around a corner at the end of the hallway, which seemed strangely longer now than it had been before. He chased her to where he remembered the steps were, but ground to a halt when he faced another hallway. He paused for a confused moment, then continued running. Around the next corner was yet another hallway, and the open door to Jana's room. He peeked inside and cried out in terror.

The room had been torn apart, splinters of wood and shards of glass floating into a starlit abyss. Silhouetted against the blinking lights was the shadow of something massive; the room was too dark to properly see what it was. It gave off a droning sound that filled his head with images of his mother, his grandmother, and his wife. He fired at the thing. The muzzle flash gave him a brief glimpse of the creature, the sight of which shook him more than the rifle's recoil did. The droning rose in pitch as the creature vanished into the hole, bringing Vasilyev to his knees.

The German-sounding Gunther burst into the hallway, the light from his room illuminating half his face with a grimace. He stormed over to Vasilyev, snapping foreign curses, then saw the collapsing void in Jana's room.

Aghast, he pulled Vasilyev to his feet and prodded him down the corridor. "How did you let it in?" Gunther asked in Russian.

"Let what in?"

The boy hissed more curses, then broke into a run. Vasilyev staggered for a few steps, found his balance, and followed. Now, the stairs were where they were supposed to be. He followed Gunther down the steps and almost bumped into him when the boy stopped abruptly and spun on his heels. Gunther's constant cursing under his breath grew more intense, more panicked when he seemed unable to choose a direction. Then Jana popped out from one of the too-many corridors and called to him in German. The boy and Vasilyev followed as she led them back the way she'd come with nothing to guide her but an oil lamp. All her composure was gone. She now reminded Vasilyev of the little girl who had crawled into her parents' bed, frightened by a thunderstorm.

Vasilyev noticed a tear following them across the ceiling.

Jana bit her tongue in the middle of the youths' heated discourse, switching to Russian as though she suddenly realized Vasilyev couldn't understand them. "They're meddling with the house. I've been running into walls all this while. I can't find the sanctum—"

She shrieked when the ceiling collapsed. Vasilyev darted forward and tackled her to the ground, away from a spindly limb reaching out from the emptiness. Jana screamed when a hand grasped Gunther's shoulder and yanked him into the void. Another set of gnarled fingers as hard as wood grabbed Vasilyev. He kicked the hand.

When that failed, he emptied his magazine, then bashed the fingers until they let go. He scrambled up with Jana's help, then turned to save the boy. But Gunther was gone. Jana sobbed into her hands as they fled.

"The house is coming apart at the seams," Jana gibbered. "I knew we shouldn't have let in outsiders. I knew it."

Vasilyev gritted his teeth, cast a look over his shoulder. The tear loomed in the dark corridor, glistening like black ice but no longer expanding. He pulled Jana to a halt, spun her around. "Breathe, Jana, breathe and tell me what's happening. What is that thing?"

She was nearly hyperventilating, but still kept a constant eye on the rift. After taking several deep breaths, she managed to utter, "They're always there, just out of sight. The headmaster caught one. Enslaved it. They want it back."

"*What* is it?"

Jana only shook her head, wilder and wilder, until she whimpered. Vasilyev glanced back. Another rift had opened. Closer.

Barking made them both jump. Behind them was another pathway, wide enough to drive a bus through, where Vasilyev could've sworn there had been a wall and where Laika barked madly at them. Vasilyev reached for Jana, but her expression of bewilderment made him hesitate.

"The dog," Jana whispered, then scoured her pockets for a small pouch. "Here, boy! Here!"

"Girl," Vasilyev said.

"Doesn't matter," Jana hissed. "If she can pick up a scent, she can get us out!"

The house trembled as the rift spread. Laika kept barking. As they drew closer to the dog, Vasilyev nearly stumbled into the cause of Laika's distress: the hallway had split in half, and between them and Laika, another creature slid into view—right beside him.

It spun around in the light of Jana's lamp. Vasilyev froze, transfixed by its face. His wife had once dragged him to a museum with an avant-garde art exhibit, and the thing evoked the same profound sense of confusion, incredulity, and nihilism. It began to drone. The same images of his mother, grandmother, and wife flooded into his mind.

The creature grabbed him.

Vasilyev gagged in its crushing grip, his vision fading to black.

Then Jana screamed at the top of her lungs, *"LET HIM GO!"*

She picked up Vasilyev's rifle and threw it at the creature, screaming. Vasilyev thought fear had driven her mad. The next instant, he fell on the floor. The rift grew smaller as the creature withdrew, then vanished altogether.

Vasilyev drew a painful breath, and Jana answered the question he was yet too weary to ask. Her voice was hoarse, but relieved. "They're only children. Children looking for their mother, fearful and skittish." She gave a little laugh despite herself. "Gunther will be fine once he realizes it. Of all the things that could've found us, this was as lucky as we're ever going to get."

"I doubt he will," Vasilyev groaned. "That thing almost broke my spine."

Jana shut her eyes, took deep breaths to calm herself. "He'll be fine. Believe me."

Vasilyev was too shaken to argue. They carried on toward the dog, but she was still growling. "Now, now, little friend," Vasilyev said, but kept his distance when he tapped his knee. "It's only me. Come here, girl."

Laika didn't relent. She bared her teeth at Jana and backed off when Vasilyev's daughter tried approaching. Vasilyev was suddenly reminded he didn't know the dog well at all. "What's the pouch for?" he asked.

"It's a sachet I was preparing for the headmaster. Animals see the house differently. If she can lead us to his study, I can reorient myself. It would be even better if we could find him, but I'm not sure that's possible now."

Vasilyev nodded, took the pouch from her. Laika stopped growling when he approached, but did not look away from Jana. "Here, girl," he said, holding the pouch to the dog's nose. "You've been so good at finding me, let's challenge you with a stranger."

Laika took a whiff, sniffed at her surroundings, then darted off in a direction where—again—Vasilyev was sure there had been a wall.

The house seemed to rearrange itself even as they followed the dog downstairs into the cellar. The corridors were much smaller now, the size they'd been when Vasilyev had first entered the Institute. Yet in several spots the rifts crept along at the edge of his vision, as though the creatures were waiting for his attention to slip in order to reemerge.

"Is this the study?" Vasilyev asked when a locked door ended Laika's hunt.

Jana had stayed behind at the base of the stairs so as not to anger the dog in the small space. "No. He must still be down here. Could you hold the dog? I don't want to get bitten."

Vasilyev picked Laika up, breaking her focus. She nestled against his shoulder, growling when Jana came to unlock the door. Once the door creaked open, Jana looked at Vasilyev, hesitated, then said, "I suppose it's best you come with me. Leave the dog. She'll be fine."

Jana placed the lamp on an indent by the entrance and disappeared into the darkness. Only the soft squelch of her feet against damp floorboards revealed she was still there.

Vasilyev left Laika scratching at the door as he followed his daughter. The further he trod into the darkness, the more an eerie sense of falling between the seams of the world began to weigh on him, until the guiding sound of Jana's footsteps brought him to a great temple coming into the light from the murk. Decorated arches and pillars the height of a dozen men towered above Vasilyev. His boots left wet prints on marble squares polished to shine like mirrors. Windows rising from the floor to ceiling on every side of the temple allowed moonlight in, each displaying a sky full of unfamiliar stars in a different phase of the lunar cycle.

"What is this place?" Vasilyev asked, breathless.

"The heart of the Scholomance," Jana said. The tension in her voice made Vasilyev forget his astonishment for a second. "I wish you'd left when you could, Papa. I know it's selfish, but I do. I'll beg for your sake if I must, but I can't promise the headmaster will let you stay."

"What are you saying, Jana? I don't want to stay."

Vasilyev noticed a group had gathered ahead around a

man delivering a speech. They stood beneath something he'd thought was some sort of a mosaic. But as he got closer, he now realized it was a living thing, as incomprehensible as its children. It was snared to the ceiling with a gossamer-like material. Its head shifted places every time Vasilyev blinked as though it had no definite form. And he could somehow sense the creature was in agony—he could feel it.

A profound numbness swept over Vasilyev. He knew he was a dead man. It seemed strange in hindsight that he'd never considered that possibility when the Institute had been collapsing all around him. He now knew far too much, and by his profession, he was well aware of what happened to men who knew too much.

Jana noticed him stopping, reached for him, and pulled him along. The monologue ceased. The students of the Scholomance faced him, as did the two elders in their midst: the general secretary and someone far older—so far removed from humanity that he could've been none other than the headmaster. Parts of his skin had flaked away, leaving shapes like missing puzzle pieces on his hands and cheeks. In those gaps, stars winked from the void beyond.

"Is there a reason you've allowed our visitor to explore the grounds, Jana?" Headmaster Mikhailov asked. His voice stirred Vasilyev with its depth and clarity, when he'd expected a croak at best.

"The brood," Jana said, still tense. "They caught Gunther. Only small ones. He'll be able to claw his way back."

The headmaster's milky gaze bored into Vasilyev, who

in turn gaped at the Y-shaped sutures along the general secretary's throat. The general secretary met his agitation with a look devoid of any intelligence. "That is not an answer," the headmaster said.

Jana gave Vasilyev a look that made his heart chill, then bowed her head. "I—to be honest, I panicked, mistaking the brood's encroachment for something far worse." She looked up and spoke earnestly. "But even if I hadn't, I couldn't have left him. From what I remember, he was a good man and treated me well."

"You are Jana's father, yes?" the headmaster asked, breaking Vasilyev's daze. "Here to seek our guest?"

Vasilyev only managed a nod.

The headmaster paused for a moment, seemingly in contemplation, then faced Jana. "You have been an exceptional student. Do you wish to let him partake in communion?"

Jana exhaled in relief. "I dearly would, headmaster. Thank you." There was consolation on her face when she turned to Vasilyev, but also a tinge of sorrow. Vasilyev had no time to ask what communion meant. She flashed a knife hidden in her sleeve and sunk it into his throat, deftly slicing across it before he could react.

Jana held him as he slumped to the floor. Vasilyev's vision grew dim despite the brilliance surrounding him. At the edge of his sight, he saw the monster rouse, beginning a mournful drone that soothed him like a lullaby.

"Don't be afraid, Papa," Jana whispered, lowering her collar to reveal her scars. "This is your rebirth. You can help us now. In another year, my studies will be over and

I can come home. We can give mother and my sisters this gift as well. Don't try to talk—it'll take a while before you can think again, but you will, and you'll see so much more than you ever thought possible."

The droning filled his ears, swarming his dying thoughts with imagery of vast, sprawling cities as lustrous and grand as the temple. The headmaster's baritone cut through these visions. "You have come to us at a most opportune moment, Mr. Vasilyev. For two centuries, I have chipped away at the will of the creature before you, and now it has finally broken, parted its gift to all who would feed upon it as parasites."

A terrible cold came over Vasilyev's body, but he was too weak even to shiver. Beyond the gray haze filling his vision, portals opened into the empty realms where the wood-limbed creatures dwelled, and Vasilyev knew, as clearly as though it was his most treasured wisdom, that the city in his mind had been the creature's home.

"Is it not ironic how these beings are at once godlike and as vulnerable as infants to simple human violence?" the headmaster continued. "It is through them that humanity will ascend to its next evolutionary stage—a stage nothing short of divine. I surmise a hundred more men could benefit from this one before it is a dry husk. And very close by—only a step away—is a world full of them, ready to be consumed by the wise and the worthy.

"But the step must be taken with great care, for if it is even slightly misguided, we would leave ourselves as vulnerable to horrors that view us in the same manner. We must have a vanguard searching for the right path. You, Mr. Vasilyev, will be the very first of the

Scholomance's explorers." The headmaster raised his head toward the creature. "Go, my muse. Deliver him from death."

In Vasilyev's deathly vision, a celestial being emerged, the Scholomance's monster twisted into a discordant simulacrum of human grace and beauty. Its long, flowing hair framed an empty face; its slim figure was marred by disfigured proportions; and its gait was both jarring and elegant. It cupped Vasilyev's head between too-long fingers, pressed the cold, smooth skin without a mouth against Vasilyev's lips, and imparted a fragment of its soul into him.

* * *

June 1983

Mr. President,

Congratulations on your new title. The consolidation of power will serve us both well.

I write to you with the unfortunate news that Mr. Vasilyev has perished on his travels. There is a silver lining, however. His canine companion Laika has proven to be quite the adept voyager. The brave little girl hasn't warmed up to us, but keeps returning to Mr. Vasilyev's room as though hoping to find him there. If only she could speak—one of the students has successfully reversed the communication method of our prisoner and used it to study the dog's memories. But its canine mind is cryptic and prone to interpreting things differently than we do. Even so, I am considering training more dogs to use for exploration.

As to your previous concerns: I cannot say I did not

expect this. There will always be those opposed to greatness, but you and I both understand the importance of our mission.

Strike first, Mr. President. Go to war against your fellow man, another empire, the world itself if you must. If you fear for the safety of your family, send them to me, and I will ensure they survive unscathed, awaiting you in our paradise.

We are so close. So close. I can hear the bells of the marble city, taste the salt on the winds blowing from its fathomless seas when I drift off to sleep. If we must burn this world to seek another, we shall do so. Humanity will be all the better for the culling. The worthy will rise from the ashes, ready to serve our cause.

Grigory Mikhailov,
Headmaster

IT'S A MUD, MUD WORLD

✪

Peter J. Wacks and Bryan Thomas Schmidt

December 7, 1985, became known as the day Matthew Broderick saved the world. It was also the day my brother Steve made me an accomplice to hijacking a plane.

"Whose plane is this?" I demanded as I slid into the copilot's seat, buckling the safety harness. The aircraft smelled of dirty oil and something I couldn't quite place. Mildew?

"Ours," my older brother replied, distracted, as he began clicking controls. His uniform was disheveled and untucked. Hmmm . . .

Twenty minutes earlier, Steve had picked me up at his apartment on the base and rushed me into his car before speeding to the private airfield just north of Pearl Harbor.

"Where are we going, and what's the rush?" Master of subtlety, that's me.

"California. Now stop asking questions and let me concentrate, Rhonda," Steve barked.

"I was gaming, Steve," I whined. Then his words caught up to my ears. "Wait. California? Home? I just got here to visit."

"Shut up, Rhonda!" he yelled. I flinched. Steve never yelled. He was the most laid-back person I knew. I sat in stunned silence until he spoke again.

"This is, like, real-life important." The plane's engines thrummed to life, and the airplane vibrated around us.

Twin propellers, above the pontoons affixed to each wing, spun into action. "Okay. I'm officially freaked."

"Good," he replied. "You should be."

Steve pulled the yoke and sent the plane rolling from its parking spot into a taxiway and out toward nearby runways. Seconds later, the communication lines lit up and I heard a voice coming from the headset hanging overhead.

"Aircraft G-KEL, please identify," a controller said. "We have no scheduled departure or flight plan on file."

Despite wearing a headset, Steve ignored him.

"Aren't you going to answer them?"

"Not right now, I'm busy," Steve replied as he adjusted flaps, pressed a few buttons, and continued taking the plane toward the nearest runway.

"But won't we get in trouble if we're not authorized—"

"It won't matter," Steve said.

I was thrown back into my seat as he hit the runway and swerved the plane into a sharp arc until it was pointed straight down the center. He accelerated as quickly as he could, adjusting controls as we sped straight ahead and then lifted into the air, despite the controller's increasingly agitated protests.

"Isn't hijacking a federal offense?" I scolded.

"If we survive this, we'll turn ourselves in," he snapped back.

"You turn yourself in," I said. "I'm here under protest. In fact—"

Then what I saw out the window silenced me: three missiles in midair arcing straight toward the base we'd just departed.

"Are those—" I started to ask, and then the world exploded before my eyes. Pearl Harbor was under attack—again! What the fuck was going on?

The plane rocked as shock waves rippled through the air around us, and Steve gritted his teeth, his knuckles white on the yoke as he fought to keep us airborne.

For the next hour, neither of us said a word. We were both too stunned and, frankly, just glad to be alive.

"Seventeen squad cars filled with thirty-four MPs, four emergency response vehicles, and a whole platoon's worth of questions because you come waltzing into a military landing zone in a damn pontoon plane. And your record says you should be on duty at Pearl Harbor. What do you have to say for yourself, sailor?" The lieutenant paused in the doorway to the debriefing room where Steve was cuffed to a steel table.

Steve could hear "Broken Wings" playing elsewhere on base through the open door, but stayed quiet.

"Answer me—what the hell happened? Why did all of Hawaii go silent five hours before you landed here?"

Steve leaned back, sore and exhausted. "I was on duty. Three ICBMs were launched at the island with no time to evacuate. I ..." He looked the lieutenant in the eye as the other man sat down. "... I ran for it. To bring the truth here."

"Sounds like you went AWOL to me."

"Yessir. I did. Straight to here."

The officer met Steve's gaze for a moment, thinking. "That you did." He leaned forward and unlocked the cuffs. "Now, tell me what the Sam Hill happened?"

"Sir. It was ... I ... all the comm channels were lit. I was trying to counterhack a dial-in. Everything was going wild. The missiles were on the way, and everyone thought it wasn't real. I tried with my CO but ... the missiles were real. ICBMs, sir. Hawaii is gone. It's just gone."

The lieutenant leaned back in shock. "The hell? Was it the Commies? Do we know?"

Steve shook his head. "That's why no one thought it was real. They had US designations, but they were launched from Soviet waters."

"One of our own subs?"

"That's all I can think of, sir. But it doesn't match. I scribbled down one of the designations." He patted his pocket but came up empty. "I'm sorry, sir. I must have lost it in the escape."

"Hell, son. This is above my paygrade. Stand up, we're going to see the commander. Seems like the Cold War just got hot."

After Steve dropped me off on the Park Street Bridge to Oakland, I took a cab back to my dorm in Berkeley. Once there, I found Kai, my short, thin roommate, and our friends engaged in the usual Saturday gaming. Our dorm room smelled of hours-old pizza, stale coffee, and fries mixed with dirty laundry from the pile in the corner between our beds. Kai had her waist-length black hair in braids to keep it out of her face while lying on her stomach facing the Atari. Our friends, Greg and Tommy, sat on the ends of her bed on either side.

"Thank God you're back early, R." Tommy was tall and super lanky, with long bleached blond hair and the greatest collection of bad t-shirts I'd ever seen. "These guys are kickin' my ass. I'm begging to switch to movie night. I did a binary conversion of *WarGames* and *Real Genius*. Your favorite two movies, right Rhonda?"

Kai shook her head quietly. She alone knew about my secret crush on Matthew Broderick.

"When don't you lose, Tommy?" I said. "You guys need to hear this. The Russians just bombed Pearl Harbor."

They laughed, shaking their heads.

"Stop kidding." Greg was plump, short, and had a shiny black afro. "That was forty-four years ago."

"I'm not joking." I marched over and flipped the channel to the news.

Tommy looked up, puzzled. "Wait. I thought you were with Steve till Tuesday, Rhonda."

"Yeah," I said as the newscaster's deep voice filled the room.

"...yet certain of the extent of damage. Local communication systems are down, and attempts to contact local affiliates have been unsuccessful..."

Then the images appeared, and my dormmates collectively gasped.

"...but we were able to obtain these aerial

photographs from a commercial flight that flew over Oahu just after the explosions."

Honolulu had been reduced to rubble. Buildings were smoldering ruins, and in Pearl Harbor, an aircraft carrier sunk beneath the steaming waves, everything but its prow was submerged. Debris clouded the surface of the water.

"Hawaii has been devastated by a nuclear attack. The Soviet Union denies involvement."

"My God!" Tommy gasped.

"We barely got out," I said. "Steve stole a plane."

"How did he know?" asked Greg.

"I didn't think to ask. We saw the missiles fly past us as we took off," I replied.

"Those fucking Commies!" Kai, who always used words sparingly, spoke for the first time since I'd arrived. We were all just beginning our sophomore year at Berkeley, and these three were also computer geniuses. We'd quickly bonded over a shared love of gaming, hacking, and CompuServe's CB Simulator.

"So are we at war?" Tommy asked. None of us could answer.

"What did your brother say?" Kai asked.

"Nothing," I replied. "He was all intense and mysterious. Kept telling me to shut up so he could focus on flying."

"Well, where is he now?" Greg asked.

"He stayed behind at Alameda," I said. "There were police at the airport who came to intercept us—the last flight out of Hawaii after . . . the disaster."

"Damn." Tommy shook his head somberly.

"We'd better get online and find out what people know,"

I suggested. "Kai, you and Tommy get on CBSim and start asking around, while Greg and I check the boards."

"We're on it," said Kai.

Tommy hesitated, looking at the game screen. "But what about movie night? I just added some cool digitized movies—"

"They're grainier than my Grandma's old black and white TV," Greg countered as he walked toward the door.

"Yeah, but they're free." Tommy sighed and followed.

It was going to be a long night.

"Sir, I swear. The missiles came from Soviet waters, but they had American designations." Steve did his best to stand at attention in the face of the commander's fury. Around them, the command center was a hornet's nest of panic.

" . . . Scrambling fighters! . . ."

" . . . Incoming missiles from both seaboards!"

Klaxons sounded as DEFCON TWO flashed. Everyone in the room worked desperately to stop the inexorable war clock, but to no avail. The light flickered then switched to DEFCON ONE.

Movement stalled, and everyone stopped for just a heartbeat. All out nuclear war . . . it was real.

"To hell with this," Steve mumbled to himself. He squared his shoulders as the hive of activity started to hum again. He looked the commander in the eye. "Sorry, sir. I have to try something."

The commander just nodded as he turned away and started barking orders. Steve ran to an open terminal and typed furiously. He pinged the dial-in he had seen in

Hawaii moments before everything went to hell. Much to his surprise, his line connected and code began to stream across his screen.

    D:LOGICPACK.LOG
    NEST DEFINED
    AUTORUN DEFINED
    NORAD NODE DEFINED
    DEFCON DEFINED
    >>HELLO.

Steve blinked then typed.

    >Who are you?
    >>ERROR. RETURN TO CALL. HELLO.

Steve tapped away, trying different responses, but couldn't get anywhere. If anything, this reminded him of one of those games Rhonda always played, when you dialed in and had to tell the computer what to do. He could never make it past the opening screen on those either.

"Sir!" Steve scooted his chair back and called the center's ops officer over while the commander still barked orders in the background.

Lieutenant Adams, sweaty and nervous, leaned over him and stared at the screen. "Is that a MUD?"

"I don't think so, sir. I tried redialing the call in off the Hawaii control center, and this is what I got." Steve leaned away from the man's breath. It smelled too deeply of burnt coffee and cigarettes.

"Huh." The L-T tried a few responses himself but didn't make it any further. "What is this DEFCON line in the startup code? Is it some kind of war game?"

"Like the movie?"

"Movie? What are you talking about? What movie?"

Steve took a deep breath. "You know, the movie where the kid starts a war simulation with a computer and almost causes . . ." he trailed off as his eyes went wide.

"Stop talking nonsense and track down which of the incoming threats is real and isn't. We don't have time for lollygagging."

Steve nodded. "Yessir." He spun around and began typing furiously. No one believed him. Again. But he was right. This was like a game, nothing made sense. Unfortunately, Steve was no good at games. But he knew who was . . .

"Greg's got someone with photos of the missiles. Says they're US," Kai's lilting voice floated across the dorm room, punctuated by the sound of her slurping coffee from a mug.

"What the fuck?!" I replied and raced over to look at her screen, which read:

(2-5, GregP/UCBerkeley) herc105 says the missiles had US markings, and he's got photos.

I leaned over her and typed: "Can he send them to us?"

"%Sending . . ." popped up on the screen.

Moments later, my question appeared on the chat screen with Kai's designation: (2-11, Kai/UCBerkeley).

"Hey! Stop putting words in my mouth, dude." Kai grinned.

"(2-5, GregP/UCBerkeley) asking" came back.

"This is huge!" Kai said, sitting up in her chair with excitement as my shoulders sank. I headed back to my own computer.

"It's insane," I muttered, trying to wrap my mind

around it. We bombed ourselves? How could that be possible? It was the first piece of information we'd gathered in the past two hours that might actually mean something. What—that was the mystery.

As I settled back into my chair and went back to checking the boards again, I heard a beep, and an icon popped up at the bottom of my screen. Someone was sending me a private chat request.

I clicked on the window and it opened to reveal my brother Steve's handle and a message:

(2-15, wunderkind7/USNA) What do you make of this, sis?

```
D:LOGICPACK.LOG
NEST DEFINED
AUTORUN DEFINED
NORAD NODE DEFINED
DEFCON DEFINED
```

I stared at the code, wondering how to respond, then typed: "What is this? Where are you? Are you OK?"

His response came back fast. "(2-15, wunderkind7/USNA) It's from a dial-in I found before I ran. Does it remind you of your text gaming or *WarGames*?"

I answered: "Maybe. Kinda. Not sure. Are you OK?"

"(2-15, wunderkind7/USNA) Fine. Stop worrying. I need your help to figure this out. Not a lotta time. Violating regs."

"(2-6, Rhonda7/UCBerkeley) You were born a violation. It does look like the kind of commands we use."

"(2-15, wunderkind7/USNA) Exactly. But that last part scares the hell out of me."

"(2-6, Rhonda7/UCBerkeley) What's the number?"

"(2-15, wunderkind7/USNA) Tracing . . . hang on . . . It's really odd—20073127828. See what you can find out, OK? Will hit you back soon."

And he was gone.

Kai appeared, looking over my shoulder. "You got quiet."

I showed her Steve's message window. "Check this out."

"He's right." She quickly read. "It does look like a game. But what the fuck's with that number? It's like . . . too long or something."

"I know," I agreed. 20073127828 had one too many digits. "What could it be? It's no dial-up I've ever seen."

"Somewhere overseas maybe?" Kai said.

"I wonder if it's some kinda network key," I said, thinking aloud. "Help me trace the number?"

"Hell yeah," she said and sat beside me on the edge of the chair as we both faced the screen.

After several hours of tracking bogies, launching fighters to shoot down phantom and real threats, and secretly trying to trace the mystery login—Steve slid his chair back from the terminal and rubbed his eyes. It was an exercise in futility, with POTUS unwilling to retaliate until the military positively ID'd a Soviet missile, which they had been unable to do. So far, whoever had launched the missiles had been targeting mainly military sites—though the blast radius of these weapons had also caused massive collateral damage to nearby cities like Honolulu. But how long till it escalated to deliberate bombing of civilian targets? "Sir, permission to stretch for five minutes? My eyes are crossing."

The L-T's face went red, but before he could bark whatever reprimand was on his lips, a panicked voice shouted from across the room, "Russia has missiles headed at their coastal facilities!"

"Confirmed," another sailor relayed quickly. "I'm tracking seven bogies hot over their landmasses."

"What the hell? Where did those come from?" Commander Fitzgerald interrupted as he strode into the room.

"Russia is firing on itself, I bet," Steve muttered under his breath.

"Sir! This makes no sense . . . I think . . . all seven bogies have Soviet identifiers. Russia is bombing itself!"

Steve blinked as the L-T slowly turned and stared at him. The man jabbed a finger into Steve's chest and spoke quietly, "As you seem to have insight no one else here does, sit your ass down and try to figure out what the hell is going on. Got it?"

"Yessir." Steve plunked back down wearily. The second the commander had walked away, he recalled the mysterious command prompt.

D:LOGICPACK.LOG

NEST DEFINED

AUTORUN DEFINED

NORAD NODE DEFINED

DEFCON DEFINED

>>HELLO.

Steve cracked his knuckles and tried a different approach.

>>Identify player two

He was rewarded with a new set of information scrolling down.

NEST2 DEFINED

GO.42 TANGANSKY NODE DEFINED

DEFCON DEFINED

>>CHOOSE ACTION

"Holy shit!" he exclaimed as he shoved his chair back. "It's a damned game."

Both the L-T and the commander stormed over. "What's happening here, son?"

Steve pointed a shaking finger at the monitor. "It's a game, sir. I think someone, or something, in the US is firing on us, and that a second player in Russia is firing on Russian soil."

The L-T grabbed the back of Steve's chair and yanked, swiveling him around to face both officers. "You will stop playing games, sailor! What the hell is wrong with you? Track the missiles or I'll have you thrown into the goddamn brig."

"Sir, I'm trying to tell you that someone has hacked our system. They've turned nuclear war into a game!"

Lieutenant Adams face went red. Again. "That's it. I'm having you brought up on insubordin—"

Commander Fitzgerald interrupted. "Aren't you the sailor that made it here from Hawaii?"

"Yessir," Steve nodded.

"Far be it from me to interrupt, Lieutenant, but this boy has been going nonstop. Give him half an hour, then get him back here with fresh eyes. The world isn't going to stop trying to blow itself up in the meantime."

Frustrated, but knowing better than to argue, Steve walked out. The second the comm center's door closed, he made a beeline for a phone. If high command was going to ignore this, then there was only one solution.

Leak it.

Steve picked up the phone's handset and started dialing Berkeley, trying to ignore the fact that he was about to commit high treason to save the world.

Greg, Tommy, Kai and I gathered around my computer as I typed the number into a few telephone databases and BBSes. Our BBS friends responded with just as much puzzlement as we did because of the extra digit. Greg even checked the phone book area-code chart. "There's no area code 200 listed for the US or Canada."

"What about Russia?" Tommy asked aloud.

"Seriously? That's not in here," Greg replied.

"What? I was just wondering aloud," Tommy whined.

"Maybe try a general search," Kai suggested.

I exited to the prompt and typed the number: >>20073127828

We waited.

"It's not working," Tommy said.

"Just hang on," I said. Tommy had the patience of an infant.

Moments later, we heard a familiar beep as the reply hit the screen: >>M31.voolo.net

"What the hell is that?" Greg commented.

"Looks like a BBS address," Kai said.

"Yeah, it does," Greg agreed.

"Let's try that in Telnet," I said and entered the

commands. A login page similar to other BBS sites scrolled, but it was filled with characters like we'd never seen before.

"What fucking alphabet is that?" Greg asked.

"It's not English for damn sure," Kai replied.

"Ohhh . . . It's hackers from beyyoooooond . . ." Tommy interjected, impersonating a cheesy sci-fi narrator from his old movie collection.

"How the hell are we supposed to log in?" I wondered, pointedly ignoring Tommy.

"There's five options," Kai said. "Just try them and see what happens."

The fourth entry pulled up a login screen with three options.

"Try the middle one, that's usually for guests," Greg suggested.

It worked. "We're in," I said as they cheered around me.

That's when the phone rang. Kai hurried over and picked it up. "Hello? . . . Hang on . . . Rhonda, it's Steve."

I stood and hurried over. She stretched the phone cord and handed me the receiver. "Steve? You're not going to believe this. We are in the central command server, I think, and . . ."

"Yeah," he interrupted. "I know. I have to hurry. The war is fake, but with real missiles. There's two players, Rhonda. One Russian, one US, and they're bombing their own countries."

"What?!"

"They've hacked into our system and are playing it like it's a game," Steve said.

"Nuclear war as a game?" I said.

"Dude, just like *WarGames*," Tommy said from behind me, even though he couldn't hear Steve.

"People are dying . . ." I said as we all looked at each other in disbelief.

Steve kept going, snapping me out of my shock. "You've gotta try to talk them down somehow, R, my L-T won't believe me. I'm afraid it won't be long until it's too late."

"How?" I asked.

"If anyone can beat a game, it's you, sis." I heard muffled noise in the background. "I gotta go. Good luck!"

And the dial tone sounded again as he hung up. I handed Kai back the phone and stared at my friends. This was the toughest game we'd ever taken on. Were we really up to it?

"Got it!" Kai shouted in the too small room. "What the hell? I'm pushing it over the LAN to you, Rhonda."

"I see it." I rocked back a bit on my tush and executed the command string the four of us had spent the last hour constructing. "This is . . ."

"Totally bonkers," Tommy interrupted. "They're gonna blow up the whole world."

Line after line of code flashed by, faster than I could track. But I didn't need to read every line to understand what I was seeing. This was a doomsday clock, merrily slicing away the seconds between now and oblivion, disguised as a MUD.

"What the hell?" Greg pointed at a piece of the scrolling code. He had just figured out what I had when I first saw it.

"Yeah. Multiuser BBS. This is two computers going at each other. No one codes and reacts that fast."

"So what'd we do?" Tommy popped the top of another Mountain Dew and chugged.

I grabbed a floppy disk and tapped it against my teeth while I thought.

"Ew." Kai rolled her eyes at me.

I shrugged.

Greg kicked off the wall and his chair slid back over the dorm room's laminate tile floor to his terminal. "If it's a multi, I'm gonna capture some of that damned code."

"Ditto." Kai turned back to her terminal.

Tommy plunked on the bed and stared at the ceiling. "What if we inject a worm? My buddy Rob out on the East Coast is a wiz with them."

"The system isn't letting us inject anything. We can only observe," Kai interjected.

"That's so fucked." Tommy sighed. "And we're being forced to sack movie night for this?"

"Hold on." I held up a finger. "I need to see those captures."

Kai swapped boxes with me and I studied the screen cap. It all made sense . . . in a twisted way. "Guys. This is weird. I think the hackers from beyond are trying to teach our computers that all scenarios lead to destruction. Look here and here." I pointed at some of the code as my friends clustered around me. "And it's all going wrong. They're actually trying the scenarios because they think if destruction can't be avoided, it must be the win condition."

"So, what do we do?" Greg spoke quietly.

Everyone was silent, staring in shock.

After about thirty seconds, Tommy broke the silence. "Well, if you guys don't have any ideas," he patted his movie case. "I do."

We all listened intently as Tommy explained his idea. Frankly, I was in shock. It was a good idea. All we had to do was set up our own BBS with a specific function ready to go, then get to computers on a military base that we had no access to, and get them to dial into it. Compared to hackers from beyond and total extinction by thermonuclear war, it didn't seem all that outrageous to us.

"Here!" I shoved aside the fence.

Kai put her cutters back in her pocket. We all crept through, trying to stay low and stick to the shadows, away from the security floodlights. Tommy did some weird pseudomilitary belly crawl. I rolled my eyes.

"Where to?" Kai asked. The base was huge, housing docks for aircraft carriers a mile away, across dozens of large buildings. The only advantage we had was the cover of night.

"I'll go this way." Greg held up his floppy with a copy of the code we had cobbled together.

I held up mine as each of my friends also held up their disk. I nodded briskly, "I'll go this way, then. Whoever finds Steve, just remember, this code will force the call to our BBS. I'm talking to you, Tommy."

He rolled over and stared up at me. "I got it."

"HEY!" someone shouted from down the fence. "STOP THERE!"

Oh hell. Men with guns. This was way sooner than we'd anticipated.

"Run!" Tommy bolted up faster than I would have expected.

We all sprinted.

There was a large building to the right, and what looked like stand-up sheds to the left. I glanced back as I hooked through the shed and saw a Marine tackle Greg. My friend went sprawling and started shouting "OW. OW!" as the Marine twisted his arm behind his back.

A second Marine followed the three of us as we ran.

Kai skidded to a stop. "Keep going, I'll catch up." She pulled a handful of stink bombs she had made in chem lab months ago and threw them down the alley at the Marine. They were so potent our group had banned using them for pranks.

I ran.

Tommy and I finally ditched the Marines and managed to find cover behind a trash bin. We were about halfway across the base.

Out of breath, Tommy gasped, "What now?"

I pointed closer to the docks at a building with a bunch of antenna and radar dishes on it. "I betcha that's the comm center."

Tommy nodded, glancing back nervously at the alarms sounding from the direction we'd come from.

We crept along, moving between humvees and trash bins, finding cover where we could. Four computer geeks versus the US Navy. This was going better than I expected. Until a guy walked around the corner of the building and pulled out a pack of smokes. As he flicked open his Zippo and lit a cigarette, his eyes widened.

Shadows peeled back and the two of us sat staring at the surprised man.

"Aw, hell. My turn." Tommy reached into his back.

The Marine choked on the cig as he fumbled to grab his sidearm, but Tommy was faster. He pulled the string on his bag and a line of lights rolled out, attached to the inside of his rig. They were all camera flashes, and when they went off, I could still see the flash of white through my closed eyes.

We ran, but I lost Tommy. The massive flash hadn't actually been enough to immobilize the Marine. As I rounded a corner, the Marine caught Tommy by the collar of his Beach Boys '65 tour jacket and yanked him to the ground. I heard a heart-wrenching rip as Tommy went down.

I ran for my life toward the comm center as more and more shouts echoed around me. And then I saw my salvation. Steve was standing by the doors of the building.

"STEVE!" I shouted. Marines seemed to come out of nowhere as I flung the floppy like a tiny frisbee as hard as I could. "LOAD THIS INTO THE DIAL-IN!"

A Marine tackled me, knocking the air from my lungs.

My heart sank as the floppy fell short and another Marine picked it up. We were so screwed.

Steve watched, dumbfounded, as his little sister got taken down and arrested. How could he get that floppy? He knew the second he saw her what she needed him to do, but it wasn't possible.

He sneezed.

What the hell was that terrible smell? Steve started to

walk toward the Marine when his sister's roommate, Kai, sprinted around the corner.

He sneezed again. She smelled horrible.

"Go!" She jammed her copy of the floppy disk into his hand. Her pursuers caught up and grabbed her, splitting apart to come after Steve, too.

Without thinking, Steve dodged to the side and bolted. Jumping the railing leading into the comm center, he slid through the doors as the MP shouted, "Stop that sailor! The intruder gave him something!"

He scrambled to his feet and made it through the double doors into the control room. Spinning around, he grabbed the flag next to the door and jammed the six-foot pole through the door handles.

With the door rattling behind him and everyone else in the room staring in surprise, he ran to the nearest terminal and jammed the disk into the computer. He jabbed the enter key right as the lieutenant slammed into him from the side and sent him sprawling.

It was too late, though. Whatever was on the disk had been initiated. Lines of code scrolled down. He had no clue what he had just injected into the defense mainframe, but as Steve felt his wrists being bound behind him, he smiled.

He trusted his sister.

In the empty dorm room, a dial tone sounded followed by a series of electronic buzzes. The host BBS came to life and a string of code spooled out at the prompt. The BBS brought up a program that interpreted fast strings of ones and zeros into pictures and sounds.

Two players, both dialed into the BBS, watched the movie *WarGames* at speeds a human would be unable to process and saw something like them. A machine. A player. They watched again. And again. Learning.

. . . And they understood.

The computers across the command center, one by one, quieted as threats vanished. Kill codes were sent to ICBMs. Blips vanished.

The commander spoke quietly, "Bring those kids in. And let him go."

The DEFCON grid scaled back, one heart-wrenching level at a time, until it rested at five once more.

MPs escorted Rhonda and her friends in as Steve was released.

The commander turned and looked at them while the rest of the room quietly watched. "Did the five of you just make this happen? Did you actually just stop all-out war?"

"Yessir." Steve saluted. Rhonda, who had been about to speak, looked annoyed.

The commander nodded slowly. "So you all just saved the world."

"Actually, sir," said Rhonda, looking a little smug, "Matthew Broderick saved the world. We just helped."

A THING WORTH A DAMN

★

Alex Shvartsman

Senior Lieutenant Oleg Nikitov walked into the Termo, California, courthouse flanked by a pair of Red Army soldiers. The structure had been a converted barn with hastily erected interior walls and subpar lighting. A large SRC flag hung askew above a utilitarian reception desk. The place had all the charm and grandeur of an upstart stable.

The lone guard stationed at the entrance didn't challenge them; the Soviet uniforms were sufficient to gain entry. An aging model AK-47 hung off the guard's shoulder. Oleg recalled the weapons being handed off to the newly formed government of the Socialist Republic of California by the shipload twenty-five years prior, back when he was a young private on his first tour of duty, half a world away from home.

"We're here to pick up a prisoner," Oleg told the woman behind the reception desk. He handed her a single sheet of paper with orders and seals and signatures from

Sacramento. She nodded and scurried off to fetch whoever was in charge.

Oleg had spent a year in California the first time, in the early nineties. Now he was back as one of the Soviet advisors, training the locals so they could better fight off the insurgents and protect the borders against the increasingly hostile United States. He was about halfway through his deployment, and his English was getting very good. He fervently hoped he'd get to go home before the American capitalists decided to escalate things into a shooting war.

Less than ten minutes later, a pair of armed guards brought out a man who looked to be in his late twenties. He was slightly overweight, his once-white T-shirt streaked with dirt, the left lens of his glasses cracked at the bottom. He looked disheveled and pale, all color drained from his face. Oleg couldn't blame him; it wasn't uncommon for local judges to hold speedy trials that resulted in those caught trying to cross the Nevada border ending up in front of a firing squad.

"Brandon Sterling?" Oleg asked.

The man focused on Oleg and his men. It was impossible to miss the expression of relief in his face.

"Yes, I'm Sterling." He nodded vigorously.

Oleg checked the photo printout he'd been given to be sure. This guy was some sort of scientist, caught trying to defect to the United States. He must've been somehow important: orders had come to have him delivered to Sacramento and onto the plane to Cuba as soon as possible.

"We'll take him from here," said Oleg.

One of the guards grunted an indifferent assent. Ever since the famine had started two years prior, the volume of Californians trying to cross the border into what had once been their country had increased exponentially. The local authorities would be only too glad to have one of these traitors taken off their hands.

As they escorted the prisoner outside, his demeanor seemed to change. His shoulders were no longer slumped; his eyes darted behind the glasses.

"I'd like to have a brief word with you in private, Officer, if I may?" he entreated as they neared their truck.

"We have nothing to talk about," said Oleg.

"This is important, and not suited for public consumption." Sterling glanced at the two soldiers. "Please?"

Oleg sighed inwardly. It was going to be a long ride. "Maksim and Arystan don't speak much English," he said.

Arystan perked up when he heard his name. The crazy Kazakh spoke barely passable Russian, let alone English. Maksim could string a few phrases in English together, but the prisoner didn't need to know this or he'd be bugging the young enlisted man all the way to Sacramento.

"I see." Sterling appeared satisfied with the explanation but lowered his voice all the same. "How would you like to retire a wealthy man somewhere in the Caribbean? I can get you half a mil—"

"Not interested," said Oleg.

Maksim manhandled the prisoner into the back seat, handcuffed his right hand to the railing, and sat next to him. Arystan climbed behind the wheel, and Oleg took the front passenger seat.

"Hear me out! I'm a chemist, and I've got a very valuable formula..." Sterling tapped his temple. "Right here. The Americans, or anyone else will pay top dollar—"

Oleg gave a barely perceptible nod and Maksim punched the prisoner hard in the solar plexus. Sterling doubled over, as much as the seat would allow, his pleading cut off midsentence.

"*Burzhui zasranets*," muttered Arystan in Russian. *Capitalist asshole*.

They had to take the roundabout way, doubling what should've been a four-hour drive. A direct route paralleled the Nevada border, and while they would nominally be in the SRC, it had become a no man's land, controlled by insurgents who wanted California to rejoin the United States. Most of them were young men who hadn't even been born when Sacramento had declared independence. Even with all the money and military aid the Soviet Union poured into California, the republic's army couldn't secure or hold swaths of the territory along its eastern border, not without providing the Americans with an excuse to escalate to a full-blown war.

They drove northwest toward Adin instead, sticking to main roads in the territory held by government forces. Once they reached Adin, they'd head southwest toward Redding and then cut south toward Sacramento. Oleg ignored the prisoner's sporadic attempts to plead, argue, and even threaten. Instead, he focused on the bleak road. Forests and fields that had once been verdant patches of green in an otherwise arid region had withered and died, ravaged by the famine. In his second tour in California, Oleg had seen bloated corpses of people who'd died from hunger, reminiscent of stories his grandparents had told of the Holodomor, the great Ukrainian famine of the 1930s.

The few remaining farmers who hadn't been forced into collectivization could no longer feed their families and had fled the region, either toward the Oregon border where the famine hadn't yet reached, or across the border and into Nevada, where the Americans were only too happy to bemoan the humanitarian crisis and blame it on their political enemies.

Oleg felt exhausted; he thought the Cold War had ended in the nineties, but here he was again, half a world away from home and fighting his motherland's ideological enemies. Which, apparently, involved transporting some whiny egghead who thought he could bribe his way out of whatever trouble he'd gotten himself into. Gazing out at the sparse landscape and wrapped in his gloomy thoughts, Oleg began to doze off.

Dozens of glass shards peppered his face. The truck lurched. Tires screeched in protest. Sounds of gunfire caught up to the bullet impacts fractions of a second later. Someone had taken out their windshield with what sounded like a hunting rifle.

Arystan cursed in Kazakh as he drove the truck off the road and into the nearest ditch. They needed to get out of the line of fire and assess the threat. Arystan's face was covered in blood, bits of glass embedded in his flesh. From the way his own face stung, Oleg suspected he fared no better.

The unknown assailants fired off several more shots. Oleg drew his sidearm. The truck rammed into a boulder. Oleg rolled out the door and whirled to face the direction of the gunfire. He peeked over the edge of the ditch. A trio of men was running toward them. Two of the ambushers held rifles while the third had his slung over his back and was speaking into a radio.

"Hold your fire," Oleg said in Russian. From the way their attackers were approaching, they were either reckless or must've assumed their victims were unarmed. Since his men were armed with pistols rather than rifles, it made sense to let the trouble get closer.

Maksim took the position to Oleg's right. Arystan had his gun out but remained in the truck. Sterling was still cowering in the back seat, his free arm wrapped around his head.

"Friends of yours?" Oleg asked, but even as he spoke, he realized whoever these people were, they weren't a rescue team. For one, professionals wouldn't have assumed his guards would be unarmed.

Sterling shook his head. He looked terrified rather than hopeful.

"On my mark." Oleg risked another peek. The men were getting closer but had slowed down, moving forward more cautiously now that they were nearing their prey.

Oleg cursed the entire North American continent. He was no cowboy from one of the vintage Hollywood movies; he was too old to be getting into firefights like this. His entire career seemed to be comprised of a long list of places where bad guys were shooting at him: Afghanistan, California, Laos, Nicaragua, and now

California again. Why couldn't these people fall in line the way the Europeans had? He wished he could have done important things with his life. Something actually worth a damn. Instead, all he'd done was to slowly climb the ranks in the military, but the world around him remained a pretty terrible place.

"Now." Oleg rose from the ditch and fired three shots into the chest of the nearest enemy while Maksim took out the other rifleman. Neither had the chance to return fire, but the man with the radio pulled out a pistol of his own and fired twice before Oleg put him down.

Next to him, Maksim collapsed. A bullet had entered his brain just above the left eye, killing the young soldier instantly.

Oleg crossed a dozen feet that separated him from the nearest downed man and kicked his rifle away. "Arystan!" he called, but there was no response. He had no time for niceties; he put a bullet in the head of each attacker to make sure they stayed down for good, then ran back to the truck.

Arystan was in the driver's seat but he was slumped over the wheel, his gun still clutched in his right hand. When Oleg pushed his body backward, he saw an entrance wound in the Kazakh's chest. The man had managed to pull off the road, saving their lives before he had succumbed to the fatal wound.

Oleg cursed, then leaned against the side of the truck and closed his eyes for a dozen heartbeats.

Oleg allowed himself the luxury of a few seconds to calm down. Later there would be time for grief and anger and pain, but only if he could keep it together well enough for there to *be* a later. He forced himself to get up and examined the truck.

The vehicle was totaled, its front resembling a folded accordion, and its windshield gone.

Oleg opened the back door, reached in, and unlocked Sterling's handcuff from the railing. "Let's go."

The scientist emerged cautiously, as though the truck were still under fire. He stared at Maksim's body and forced back a gag.

"Let's go," Oleg repeated. "Before more insurgents show up. One of them was radioing someone." He snapped the loose handcuff onto his own wrist. Last thing he needed was to chase the egghead if he decided to try and take off.

Sterling stared at the handcuff dumbfounded. He appeared shell-shocked, even though he'd survived the skirmish physically unscathed.

Civilians, Oleg thought. "Come on," he said more gently and nudged Sterling down the road, back the way they'd come.

He figured it was a five-, maybe six-hour walk back to Termo. There, they could get another vehicle, and perhaps he could bully whoever was in charge into lending him a few soldiers.

They walked in silence for several minutes, leaving the corpses and the carnage behind. When Sterling spoke again, it was under his breath, and Oleg couldn't immediately make out the words.

"What?" Oleg asked.

"They aren't insurgents," Sterling said louder.

Oleg frowned. "They were shooting at us."

"They're bandits," said Sterling. "Desperate men whose families might've been kicked off their land when the government collectivized the farms, or whose parents were arrested or killed for owning the wrong book or telling the wrong joke. They've got nothing left, so they resort to robbing trucks to feed their families. There are plenty like them around here."

"We weren't transporting goods," said Oleg. "The way I see it, they shot at us because of the uniforms we wear. That makes them enemy combatants."

Sterling glanced at Oleg. "You're on another continent, wearing the uniform of a foreign army on their home soil. Who's the enemy?"

Half an hour later, they heard the sound of an approaching car in the distance, coming from behind.

Oleg yanked on Sterling's cuffed wrist, pulling him off the road.

"Be quiet," he said. "You may think they're the good guys, but I bet they won't think the same about you."

They watched from behind a small knoll as a pickup truck roared by with a half dozen armed men and women in the flatbed. Mercifully, Sterling remained quiet, his body pressed into the warm earth next to Oleg's.

"We have to proceed with caution," Oleg said. "They'll be coming back soon. They must realize whoever survived is on foot, even if they don't know the direction we're headed."

As they kept walking, they saw a lone farmhouse in the distance.

"Perhaps we can requisition a vehicle," Oleg said. "Or at least get some more water." The canteen he carried was already half empty.

"Or perhaps the bandits live here," said Sterling. "Or someone else who is, at best, unsympathetic to your cause."

"You prefer to walk for the rest of the day?"

Sterling had no response to that.

They approached the farmhouse with caution. A relatively small patch of cultivated land was barren; this region had been hit hard by the famine. The barn and the house were both empty, seemingly abandoned years ago. There was water in the pipes, and some towels in the drawers. Oleg washed blood off his face in the kitchen sink.

Stuck at his side, Sterling poked at a layer of dust on the counter with his finger.

"It's all your government's fault, you know," he said. "If you didn't try to assassinate Kennedy, things might've turned out differently."

"He was a paranoid lunatic. We never tried to assassinate him."

Sterling shrugged. "So your propaganda people say. Kennedy believed otherwise. He came back from Dallas a changed man. Escalated the Cold War, spent billions trying to compete with you Russkies on the space race. His policies pretty much bankrupted the country."

Oleg nodded. By the late eighties the US economy was in the toilet. Soon after, California and Utah had both seceded from the Union. The Cold War had been all but over, at least until the Americans had reasserted themselves well enough to try and get the erstwhile republics back into the fold.

"Socialism triumphed over capitalism," Oleg said. "It should come as no surprise."

"Oh, please," Sterling said. "If socialism is so superior, then how come California became such a horrid mess? No, the only reason the Soviets won the Cold War was because the price of oil spiked just as both economies were on their last legs, desperately trying to outspend each other. You got lucky."

Lucky. Oleg didn't feel lucky, not with his comrades dead and his face scarred, stuck here with this armchair economist.

"You should watch who you say this to," Oleg said. "You don't want to get into even more trouble than you are in now."

"I'll be fine," said Sterling bitterly. "They're going to stow me at one of those restricted science towns near Moscow and make me continue my research. Except I want to go to Russia about as much as you probably want to be here." He sighed. "My offer still stands, you know. We can be in Nevada by tomorrow. The Americans will treat us a lot better than your people would."

Oleg shook his head and went back to cleaning his cuts.

As they prepared to leave the farmhouse, Sterling paused. "I think I hear something."

Oleg strained to listen. He thought he could make out barking in the distance. "Dogs. They must be tracking our scent. Shit." He headed up the stairs to the second floor, with Sterling forcibly in tow.

"Shouldn't we run?" Sterling whispered, as though

their pursuers were already in the house and could overhear them.

"They probably know the terrain, they've got dogs, and they have at least one truck," said Oleg. "We're better off making a stand here."

From the second-story bedroom window they could see a man and a woman approach with a black Labrador, its nose to the ground. Two more men followed them at a distance, rifles in hand. A green sedan was parked up the road.

"Damn. They've got multiple parties out looking for us," said Sterling.

"This is a good thing. There are only four of them," said Oleg. "That other group was bigger. We have to get that car, then we can try to make it back to town before we run into any more of them."

"Four of them and two of us," said Sterling. "And I don't really know how to fire a gun. Do you even have one you could spare?"

Oleg had another small pistol and a knife, but he didn't feel the need to share this information. "They probably don't know how many of us there are. I can take them out, but for this to work, we're going to have to trust each other."

When the pair with the Lab reached the farmhouse, Sterling stepped out to meet them, his arms raised, a handcuff hanging off his right wrist.

"Help!" he shouted. When the two reached for their weapons he raised his hands even higher, palms up. "Don't shoot. I'm unarmed!"

The man and the woman exchanged glances. Far behind them, the two men trained their guns at Sterling as well. All of them, including the dog, appeared malnourished. Highway robbery must not have paid well in these parts.

"Seriously, I'm not your enemy! The damn Russians were taking me in, then they got into a shootout with who I presume were some of your guys. I booked out of there as soon as the bullets started flying."

It was a big gamble; there was always the chance the bandits would shoot Sterling before he could explain himself. But once he started talking, his odds of survival improved with every breath. He was tanned and spoke with a hint of a Valley accent. He certainly didn't look or sound like a Russian. Surely not like the uniformed Soviet soldiers they were told to look for.

"Who are you?" asked the woman. "What did the Commies want with you?"

"Name's Brandon," said Sterling. "I'm a chemist. I'm valuable enough for the Reds to have sent several of their goons to retrieve me. Seriously, I'm worth way more alive than dead. If you get me across the border to Nevada, I can really make it worth your while."

The bandits lowered their weapons a fraction.

Sterling flashed a smile and kept talking fast while the nearest man searched him for weapons. Satisfied that he posed no threat, the other two gunmen also approached. And as his pointless chatter continued to distract them, Oleg stepped from inside the house and opened fire.

As soon as the first shot rang out, Sterling threw himself to the side. Oleg fired four or five times before any of the bandits managed to return fire. He had the element of surprise, but his service pistol didn't possess a rifle's accuracy or stopping power. It took a couple of hits to put down each hostile, and while Oleg was a good shot, he was not as fast in his fifties as he had been in his twenties and thirties.

One of the bandits fired off a shot, and Oleg felt as though an enormous bee stung him in the stomach. In moments, agonizing pain spread over his midsection, but he knew he couldn't give in to the shock and pain. He kept firing until all four of the bandits were down and all eighteen rounds in his magazine were spent. He dropped his MP-443, then slid downward until he was sitting half propped against the wall. He moaned in agony.

"Fucking hell." Sterling was beside him, pulling Oleg's jacket and shirt open, staring at the wound. "Wait, I'll be right back. Just wait."

Sterling disappeared into the house and for a minute, the world around Oleg was quiet, except for the whining dog that nudged the dead woman with its muzzle. He thought perhaps the egghead wasn't such a bad sort after all. Sterling had handled himself well under pressure, and he hadn't betrayed Oleg by gambling that the bandits would take him to America, or at least let him live.

Sterling reappeared with a pan filled with water and some clean sheets. "Hell," he repeated as he watched the blood pool under Oleg. "You're going to be okay. I'll bandage you up and drive you back to Termo, but then you have to help me cross the border, all right?"

Oleg would've smiled if he wasn't in so much pain. The chemist was admirably persistent about his goals. But

Oleg had seen enough gut shots in his long military career to realize he wasn't making it back to town, and even if by some miracle he did, there was little anyone could do to help him.

He would die in this North American wilderness like an aging cowboy in a Hollywood movie who'd became too slow on the draw, and pretty much for the same reason.

Sterling was trying to administer first aid, making up for his lack of skill with sheer enthusiasm.

"You're going to live out your days drinking vodka in some tropical paradise," he said. "You know the famine that's been ravaging the area? It was biological warfare. My lab designed the superbug, and it got loose. Wiped out everyone else at the lab, too. I was the only one who wasn't contaminated, the only one who knows the formula. The Americans or the Chinese, or maybe the Brazilians, they'll pay millions for that. You just have to hang on long enough, you hear?"

Through the red haze of pain, Oleg stared wide-eyed at the earnest young man whose invention was responsible for more death over the past couple of years than every soldier he ever met in his lifetime combined—friend and foe both. A man who was trying to save the life of his captor even though he could easily walk away, yet had no qualms about selling his bioweapon recipe to the highest bidder.

Oleg knew his life was at an end, and he was strangely at peace with that. Still, he wished he had done something worth a damn with his life; everything up until this point seemed small and irrelevant when facing his impending mortality.

"Water," he whispered, pain ravaging his insides.

Sterling nodded eagerly and rushed back into the house.

Oleg fumbled with his left trouser, where a compact nine-millimeter pistol had been concealed. He thought back on the stories his grandparents had told of the Holodomor, and of the bloated corpses and dead fields he'd seen in this once-verdant land. Socialist or capitalist, they all suffered and died the same way. It wasn't too late for him to do one good thing for the world.

When Sterling returned with his cup of water, Oleg concealed the pistol under his thigh. He offered the chemist one final kindness by saying, "What is that?" and pointing off to the side with his chin. That way, the young man was looking away when Oleg used the last of his strength to lift the gun and fire a bullet point-blank into the back of a head holding the secret to so much death.

Then the world went quiet and still, save for the loyal dog waiting patiently for a master who would never rise again. Oleg watched the dog until the mercy of oblivion finally took away his pain.

EVANGELINE

✪

C.L. Kagmi

It begins in a dark basement, as it always does. Dark basements and dark backrooms. Tents in darkened corners of parks, little huddles under overpasses. It begins in the places where forbidden things are allowed to happen. The places where all things begin.

This basement belongs to a little elderly couple, sweet enough to believe her and to let others come to see. Sweet enough to host something that's a little bit illegal, to gamble their own good standing with the government on a strange type of public service.

Evangeline noted the old military cap on the mantel on her way in, the pictures of the man in uniform, much younger. He knows what it is then, to risk losing brothers. He knows what it is to wonder who is still alive.

And the police won't bother him much, not really. Not after they see that cap.

The stairs leading down into their basement are rickety, unfinished wood. The cellar looks like a food pantry—there must be hundreds of cans stacked here, gleaming under her flashlight's beam. The corners are dark and dusty, cobwebbed like the rafters. There's a little folding card table in one corner. Perfect.

Evangeline never turns on the lights. Not the bright ones, the lightbulbs that illuminate every corner and leave nothing for shadows or secrets. She needs some things to remain unseen. And so does her audience.

She unfolds the card table and spreads her shawl over it. Pulls the candleholders from her bag—they're saucers, actually, with great wide porcelain bases. She learned that lesson after someone screamed and flailed, knocking over candles, and only the quick thinking of the boy in the next seat saved the room from going up in flames.

Evangeline stamps her feet on the concrete floor. Concrete. Perfect. Concrete doesn't burn.

She sets up the few folding chairs she finds against the wall. Hauls down cushions from the upstairs couch for the rest of the seats. She doesn't know how many to expect tonight, but it would be rude not to have at least six seats available.

Then she lights the candles and begins to feel at home in the closed space, the flickering half-darkness. Spaces like this have always been hers. Spaces where the grown-ups, then the government, can't quite see her.

Some who ply her trade, she knows, are frauds. The ones who use the darkness to pull strings, have puppets come out behind a screen, or make noises with their feet under the tables. In the half-light, the audience is all-too eager to believe that they've seen apparitions. She read about a woman once who trained herself to swallow yards of cloth, then vomit it on command so she could claim under the cover of darkness that it was ectoplasm.

They are often the most successful people in her space, insofar as an illegal profession can be successful. Perhaps they are allowed to thrive because they are not dangerous. They don't tell the truth or expose any dirty secrets some bureaucrat wants buried. Or perhaps people simply care for theatrics more than for the truth.

Truth is complicated. Theatrics are not.

Evangeline shivers in the darkness. Upstairs, a door creaks open. Footsteps on the floor above her, muffled by thick carpeting. New shoes on an old floor. They're always new shoes, because the people who come are almost always young.

Young and full of hope. Full of desire. Full of willingness to break the rules—for a cheap thrill, or more often for some semblance of peace of mind. She sometimes wonders if it would be kinder to lie to them, to tell them all that their boys were okay. Even if that wasn't true.

But she can at least pretend the truth is a public service.

She knows her truth: that honesty is an excuse. That she needs the eyes on her, the reactions. That she needs, more than anything, to slip her earthly bonds. She could do it in a dark corner, alone, if she chose. But that would feel meaningless. Even survival is an isolated, useless thing if no one's there to see it.

It's the door at the top of the stairs that creaks open this time. Footsteps trundling down the rickety steps, slow, uncertain. Entering a stranger's dark basement, acting on a rumor and a prayer. What could be more foolish?

What could be more thrilling?

The first is a young man. This surprises her. Usually it's girls who come, asking after a brother or a lover. The men are the worst, because they often feel guilty when you tell them bad news. They wonder if it should have been them. This one stands in neat-pressed slacks and smooth-combed hair, illuminated by a shaft of light falling down the stairs from the kitchen above. He actually bows to her, a little awkwardly, and as he fumbles his way to sit on a cushion, she's afraid he'll trip over his own feet in their shining leather shoes.

Two girls follow. Just as neat, creases pressed crisply into their skirts. She guesses the three know each other, and none wanted to come alone. The girls take chairs.

Some of her people, then. Dirty jeans and long hair, fabric hanging about their limbs as casually as their bodies seem to hang in space. They take the remaining two cushions, close to the card table, because they know they will be needed if something goes wrong. If someone panics, screams or knocks a candle over.

The elderly couple comes last. The little old man shuts the door behind him, a soft but final sound. The shaft of light falling from above vanishes, plunging the little congregation into darkness. He and his wife know the stairs well enough to navigate them blind.

Waiting. Shuffling. One of the girls vacates a chair for the old woman and stands respectfully in the back, her hands clasped behind her primly.

Evangeline waits. She knows she should speak. Should say something theatrical. Sometimes she does. But tonight it would feel cheap. All she does is look at them, this motley crew gathered in the candlelight.

"Anybody got any questions?"

They all do, of course. But they all look at each other, deferring with their eyes. Waiting for another to start. Finally some sort of consensus seems reached, that the girl in the chair should go first.

"Johnny," she asks. "My Johnny." Her trembling hand reaches out, a small faded photograph in it. So that part of the message had survived, in the rumor she heard. Good. There are many Johnnys, and Evangeline cannot claim perfect accuracy without a photo.

Johnny.

And just like that, she is gone, the image of a boy with high cheekbones and a big nose in her mind.

She's gone too fast—she didn't even get to light the incense. But it's like that, sometimes. More often than not. Her spirit doesn't like to be tethered, doesn't like to be still. The world seems to expand and the clouds racing above become her roof. And then she is in them, breezes blowing through her body.

And then she is somewhere else.

Vietnam is a patchwork, strange as any other country. Johnny, as it happens, is somewhere safe: a place where unease is all but forgotten, boys drinking and flirting with local girls, not really understanding the reality of the war. She hopes he'll never see the things she's seen, knowing that for him, seeing these things would be final.

"Safe," she hears her lips mutter, thousands of miles away. Thousands of miles through the Earth, the shortest route from there to here.

Another photo, another face. A name. This one barely

registers in the part of consciousness she's using now, but she finds herself transported to another place. Another boy, this one shivering in the rain. The trees themselves seem to oppress him, cold and alien shapes. But friends are near, and nobody in this company has died, yet.

The litany continues.

She knows she's heard a dead boy's name when the air becomes acrid. When the Earth falls away around her and she stands in darkness, facing—

"Ben." She says his name, tasting it on her tongue. He feels like electricity, like static in the air before a storm. He tastes like acid. He's newly dead, and they're always so sharp edged.

He also looks confused.

She sees him, poor thing. Not taught what to expect. Not accurately. He doesn't feel the hands of the ancient fellowship reaching out to him, because he wasn't taught to look for them. He is alone.

"I'll show you," she tells him, "but I need something from you first."

And there it is: the things his family will ask for. She is in his body, a vitally beating heart supported by thickly muscled arms. Shoulder aching from recoil, ribs bruised from some recent close call. She's pressed into the dirt, the Earth cold and wet against her, until she hears a noise and twists her head to look behind—

Death was so quick for this one. Evangeline is glad for him, but also feels cheated. There is nothing like adrenaline for union with the All.

She knows that that's the real reason she does this. To get out of herself for a little while. To become part of something greater. That greatness comes with dissolution bothers her, but not as much as it once did.

She's gotten used to it, as she's gotten used to many things. As they all have. Her parents and her brother and her nation.

The girl is good at what she does. She doesn't know how good. Even Cox gets chills as he enters the dark basement, descending into candlelight that flickers off the matchstick rafters and the hoard of canned food that lines the shelves. This is what he imagines a fallout shelter would look like, if it all went wrong.

He's been tailing her for weeks, and he is dangerously close to becoming a disciple. Just watching her in her ecstasy, he imagines he feels something of what she feels. It looks like a drug trip, and his skin crawls a little when he thinks that. There are rumors about the *real* reason the feds banned LSD last year, the reason those who took it all seemed to dance to the beat of a different drum. There are rumors that it worked—though if that were true, Cox supposes, he wouldn't be here.

The feds. His boss. He'd never have dreamed of those words together a few years back. Then he'd lived the part he's playing now. It had all been real for him: the long hair, the dream of a better world, the suspicion of the powers that tried to hem him in.

But these are strange times. Terrible times. There are bombs that can snuff out a million lives in an instant. There are people who tried to steal those bombs for the Russians. Now they say the moon is the next frontier, and it's anyone's guess who takes it.

It's hard to know who to trust.

He tells himself that *that's* why he's here, that it's not the five-figure paycheck, not the way they flattered his ability to blend in wherever he went when he was auditioning for parts in Los Angeles. He was so convincing, they said. He'd make a perfect spy.

He tells himself he's here for his country. And for Evangeline, who will soon have the same thing he has. A purpose. A role in protecting her country.

Just like the ones before her did.

But waiting for him is something far more ancient. Something that seems straight out of the days before nations, before capitalism or communism or industry.

The girl sits in a folding chair behind the card table, her eyes half closed. It isn't show: He's seen enough of her to know that. She tastes things on the breeze that he can't begin to imagine.

Cox takes his place dutifully, curling up on a cushion she's laid on the basement's concrete floor. It's a position of readiness: If somebody loses control, topples over a candle, he'll be ready to stamp it out again.

For the last time. An uneasy feeling churns in his stomach as he thinks this, but he's gotten good at calming his own nerves. He was going to be an actor, before the military got him. Before they convinced him there was something better for him to do.

Here, this girl just reports on what is happening. Drops little bits of forbidden knowledge for those who are more willing to believe than to remain in the dark. She doesn't change the course of events, not really. And sometimes, she is dangerous. Just a little.

Soon she'll be able to put her talents to real use. She'll have a role in shaping events. The kind of role most people dream of.

Cox just hopes that she'll last longer than the last one.

The crowd is like so many others that have come before. Mike sits in his usual place, ready to intervene if someone in the front row loses it.

The others tonight are a black boy and a pair of girls who giggle nervously, afraid to believe, but more afraid not to. One looks solemn, serious. The other keeps elbowing her and whispering in her ear. Evangeline catches something about a liquor store.

The boy's eyes keep shifting. He's scared. But not for himself. For someone else. He's the only one who seems to be taking this seriously, so Evangeline calls on him to lay his photo down first.

It's a graduation portrait. The young man in it is handsome, dignified. His smile lacks both the naivete of youth and the wickedness of rebellion. He was old already in that photo, but kind. She guesses he's the boy's older brother, or perhaps a cousin.

To Evangeline's relief, she feels nothing when she looks at the picture. The boy is as mute and opaque as a cover model, which means he's still alive. She lets out a breath she hadn't realized she was holding and slides the photo back toward its owner.

"Alive." It should be easy to say that, but it isn't: She knows it could change tomorrow. The certainty she gives them might only last a day, a week. But it's something. If they try hard, they can make the certainty last longer.

A smile like the sunrise comes over the boy's face as he takes the picture back. A smile of pure marvel. He believes. His choices are between belief and misery, so he believes.

The solemn girl is next. She hands over the picture of her boyfriend, or her brother. Evangeline does not ask which. The smiling boy is happy about his uniform in a way that suggests he doesn't know what's coming. But he's alive too. As mute and odorless as any living person is, firmly anchored to a body eight thousand miles away. She hopes he'll stay that way.

The giggling girl goes last, laying down a picture of a boy with red hair that matches her own. Evangeline barely takes in his face, because as soon as she sees it, she smells smoke.

Then the noise of war is growing all around her, shouts and screams and gunshots. The room fades, replaced by heat, humidity, and fear. She opens her mouth but doesn't know what she's saying, because a moment later a bullet shatters her breastbone—

And then she is back in the basement, and someone is screaming, but this time it's the girl who was giggling. Mike and her friend are holding her back while she tries to claw her way over the table, fingers clenched like talons, grasping for Evangeline.

Evangeline reaches for the mug of tea at her side. Lifts it to her lips with shaking hands. The steam steadies her, grounds her. The feeling of hot liquid in her throat.

The adrenaline of death she can handle. Appreciate, even. That's why she does this, if she's honest with herself. She never feels more alive than when she's dying.

But the girl's screams are harder to take. Her wounds will last longer than her brother's.

Cox hates this part of the job. When military families learn their son is dead, there is at least a decorum about it. They know what to expect when soldiers in Class-As arrive on their porch, and they know how they're expected to act.

When children go seeking forbidden knowledge, and *find* it—that's much worse. Children don't know how to act. And they're never expecting it. When they tiptoe down the stairs into a stranger's dark basement, it's an adventure. A rebellion. They don't expect to receive bad news, and they don't expect to believe it.

Cox keeps his arms around the screaming girl, carries her halfway up the stairs before she finally goes limp. Her friend has gone ghost pale and become useless, and the black boy is afraid to touch her. He comforts the other girl quietly, awkwardly, but there is not much he can say that will help.

"She'll need you," Cox hears him say. "She'll need you, and you are strong enough to help her."

Cox thinks that just might help, and he's grateful for it.

The old man and woman who lent Evangeline the basement take the redhead and sit her in a sturdy wooden chair beside their kitchen table. The wife makes her tea, while the husband goes to make a phone call. He meets Cox's eyes on the way out of the room.

"Is the car outside?" Cox asks him. The man only nods, and it's a weary nod, a deep tiredness in brown eyes shadowed by bushy white brows.

Cox goes outside to meet the driver and leads him into the house.

Something is wrong. Evangeline knows it, as she drifts in and out of consciousness. Something is terribly wrong, but it's hard to say what, because she's surrounded on all sides by pillowy warmth.

That's what's wrong. She's comfortable. Evangeline's head swims as she sits bolt upright, adrenaline pouring into her blood but going nowhere. Her fear is diluted into weak little eddies that float lazily on the surface of her mind, and the more immediate problem is that her head is *splitting*—

"Good morning."

She knows that voice, but not its tone. She certainly doesn't know the down comforter that's soft beneath her fingers, or the bright warm light that's assaulting her eyes.

"Mike?"

"I'm here, Evangeline."

His voice is too warm. Too compassionate. Too self-satisfied. She had been hoping that perhaps she had fainted, that perhaps she is in the older couple's home. But it smells too clean here. Too antiseptic. Yet it's a real bed, not a sterile hospital cot. . . .

"I'm sorry about the surprise." Mike is enunciating differently, speaking like a different person. "But we had to be sure before we brought you in."

Bright colors. A cold, clean contrast of white against black. She's in a room like something out of *Good Housekeeping*, on linens that have been too thoroughly washed to pass for homey. Strange. This isn't how a kidnapping usually goes.

"Where am I?"

"Safe. We're not going to let anything happen to you."

We.

Her vision is clearing, bit by bit. She tries sitting up again. Slowly, this time. The room spins but does not collapse.

"There's food, if you want it."

"Who's 'we'?"

"You're not going to like the answer."

"Are you the government, or the mob?"

That makes him laugh. It's the old, musical laugh she remembers from around the little trash-can fire they burn sometimes under the bridge. Will there be any more fires?

Evangeline had known that Mike was too good to be interested in her. Too good to be where she found herself, where the true inveterates found themselves. Now she knew why he was there.

"Government," he admits. "But I'm giving you a gift. A chance to have purpose. To serve your country."

Gunshots ring in her ears. "Serve the people who are getting boys killed, you mean."

"We're working to prevent something much worse."

Working. A carefully chosen word. Better than "trying," which implied that they might fail.

"Yes. I'm sure your wars and paranoia are really helping keep the peace."

Mike stands up. She hears it, in the soft padding of his shoes on softer carpet, more than she sees it. Her vision is still fuzzy. "I'm sorry." He sounds genuinely regretful. "I should leave you to get some rest."

He pads out of the room. She watches his back as he retreats. Remembers him washing her hair in the waters of a fire hydrant they'd been draining down on Haight. He had been so gentle.

And now she knows why. She knows the reason about the rumors of disappearances, too, the reason that girl tried to convince her in whispers to stop practicing her art.

But she doesn't know what will happen now.

The Lord works in mysterious ways.

That is all the colonel can think as they bring the girl to him. Who would have endowed *this child* with power? They'd gotten her into fresh clothes and gotten her hair out of her face, but still she looked like they'd just dragged her off the street. Which they had.

"Miss Parker?" The best way to disarm them is to be polite. Most of them hate his kind, no matter what he does or doesn't do, but some are so hungry for respect that they blossom when he gives it to them.

She isn't one of those.

She is still slouching, fiddling with her hands where they're cuffed behind the chair as she scowls. His skin crawls as her narrowed eyes fall on him, and the old familiar worry returns.

What can she see that I can't?

When enough people with the Second Sight hate you, you start to wonder why.

Second Sight or no, there are things she cannot see.

Nobody trains these kids to understand tactics, or

threat levels, or economics. Maybe that's why they're so angry all the time. They can't see the enormous machine whose workings are required to keep them safe and free.

She's starting to fidget in the silence. That's good. He won't speak again until she says something to him.

"What do you want?" Her demand is harsh. The kind of harshness you got from a woman who had covered up her femininity to protect herself. What drove a girl to leave her family and live on the streets? Was this gift enough to do that?

"Wouldn't you like to help our soldiers, Miss Parker? Wouldn't you like to help keep them safe?"

She snorts.

"Say what you will, Miss Parker. You are not trained to understand these matters. But surely you realize that this machinery is in motion for a reason. Everything we do is necessary."

"For who?"

He ignores the question. Instead, he puts a photograph on the table in front of her.

The girl flinches and turns away, violently. His stomach turns as she retches. They'd given him the photo this morning—the freshest casualty they could find. He didn't ask them how the man died.

"He knew something." The colonel's eyes stray to the photograph on the table. A Japanese boy stares back at him. The colonel also didn't ask what he'd done to get security clearance. "What did he know?"

Silence. Retching. Cox hasn't warmed her up enough. He'll speak to Cox about that, later. See what else can be done.

"Miss Parker, you could die here."

That usually gets their attention. It gets hers, her eyes going huge as she swings her head to peer at him through a curtain of hair.

"We are closer than you know to a number of disasters. You can help us prevent them."

She spits at him, then, and some of her spittle lands on the image of the boy. The colonel sighs as he wipes the photo clean with his handkerchief.

"You can make this easy, Miss Parker. You can be our respected peer. Or you can behave—like the enemy.

"The choice is yours. I know you don't want any more of our boys to die."

Disaster.

The word rings in Evangeline's mind long after they put the bag back over her head, after she makes them half drag her down the hall. She began determined not to give them anything—not even the convenience of her willing footsteps. But.

Disaster.

It's true. She can taste it in the air. The miasma rises and recedes, closer here than it was back home on the streets.

There had been days, back before the commune was busted up, when nobody who had the Second Sight could sleep. They tossed and turned and moaned, sensing an enormous *something* passing through their reality, or close to it. A change so catastrophic they could not name it. Words failed.

Everybody knew what it *might* be. The Daisy Ad. All those science fiction stories the presses pumped out like entertainment. All those lessons they gave schoolchildren, about what to do if a nuclear bomb explodes nearby.

What worries her more is that this *something* doesn't feel like that. Not so quick or so clean. And when she reaches out, she can almost feel it, sludging through the streets. Dark ribbons of current that converge on—*what?*

She can't see it, but she knows it's bad. The rivers taste like death. She'd tried her best to ignore them on the outside, to hope that protests and free love and the Krishnas could will it away.

But still the thing is swooping closer. Closer with each passing month, each passing year.

Is the military really keeping it at bay? Or are they making it worse?

She wants to know more about it, the way we want to know about all dark and terrible things. She wonders if she can discover more about it from in here.

The problem is she can't get information and then keep it from them. They have ways of extracting it from people. And she doesn't want to give them anything. She doesn't trust them.

Should she?

"Just because she isn't talking doesn't mean she doesn't know."

Cox has told the colonel this before, but it still shocks him to hear his own voice. Gathering information feels like breaking the chain of command, in some ways.

But even commanders lose their patience. And part of his job is to remind them.

The colonel isn't angry. Just tired. He slumps back in

the chair in his office, the walls lined with young men's faces, and sighs.

"Why couldn't it be somebody like you? Why is it always the ones who hate us who have the gift?"

"It is—a difficult gift to live with," Cox says tactfully.

He doesn't understand it, not really, but he's seen enough of them come out of a trance shaking. Seen enough of them hide their eyes from something they didn't want to see but couldn't shut out. Seen enough of them lose their selves to—what? He'd never know. He figures it's like being born with a drug addiction.

"So what? It makes them hate their government?"

"It makes them hate everything."

That wasn't quite true. Cox had seen Evangeline and others stare with adoration at clouds in the sky, at birds, at sunlight on a tree.

But it did seem to make them hate everything human. They recoiled from anybody who tried to make them get a job, who enforced law and order, who didn't agree that all of Western civilization had been one great cavalcade of destruction.

With so many of them saying it, Cox sometimes worries they might be right.

Is there a better way to do things? A way that only the Second Sighted saw?

He is at least sure that the communists aren't doing any better.

"When do we start her?" Cox asks. He hopes the response will be "soon." The colonel tries to give them time to warm up, sometimes, but Cox has found that they do better when they have a purpose.

If you leave them alone in a place like this for too long, their minds begin to eat themselves.

"Tomorrow." The colonel shrugs, and Cox hates that the man looks a little helpless. "What have we got to lose?"

They let Mike bring her this time, instead of the armed guards. They leave the bag off her head too, so she can see the hallway: rows and rows of burnished metal doors. Within them she felt nothing. That meant that the cells were either empty, or filled with living people who weren't sensitive. She wondered which it was.

She had heard enough from these walls, but it was her room that was the problem. She hadn't been the first occupant, or the second, or the third. The others whispered to her at night, sat on the edge of her bed to comfort her.

But she refused to believe what they were saying just yet. It was too bleak. Evangeline was used to bleak, but this was a kind she hadn't seen before.

And so she looks at Mike out of the corner of her eye, still marveling at his transformation. They keep him dressed up like a hippie boy, his hair long and his clothes scruffy, but everything about the way he walks is military. How had he played his role so well on the street? Was he like a chameleon—picking up on her body language, and the colonel's, and whoever else happened to be around?

"They're going to show you some Russians, today," he says in a low voice, leaning close to her. His breath is warm on her cheek, and she wishes for something else. She also knows that is exactly what they want.

"Be brave. They're not kind to their own who betray them. There's a man who they shot—he sent us a message before he died. Ask him about the message. Ask why he sent it."

Evangeline squirms. She would have thought that nothing could make her squirm, after the number of dead boys she's seen. But there *is* something more horrible about being shot by your own country.

One of the dead men in her room said that was how he had gone out, after he hid in a laundry cart and managed to make it to the perimeter fence.

They did not handcuff her, this time. They act much friendlier than yesterday. She knows that this is intentional, too. Show her how nice they can be. How respectful.

The man who rules the small metal table lays a photograph on it without ceremony. "Tell me this man's name." It is an order.

The man in the photo is older, with a receding hairline, and is just about the most Russian-looking person Evangeline has ever seen. He stares out at her from a black-and-white photo, but she is more conscious of—

Terror. Sheer terror. Most of her boys didn't know the bullet was coming from her. This man does.

Terror propels her limbs as she runs. Not toward salvation. Toward something else.

She sees this moment through her own eyes, her own sight, as well as his. Something huge and unfathomable moves close to their reality, blotting out the Moscow sky.

Her shaking hands seize a telephone receiver. It is a plastic thing, somehow old and new at once, somehow a symbol of the fragility of civilization. She cannot actually hear dogs barking at her back, but she imagines them so vividly, it seems she can.

And then, a new image: a mushroom cloud flowering, blessed, over Moscow. A million monsters burned in their beds. She watched their bodies dissolve into white light and felt—joy. Justice had finally been done.

In the present, her fingers, old and blunted, fumble with the phone. Type a number.

Ring. Ring. Ring. Click.

There is silence on the other end.

She breathes hard, into the receiver. Knows her every breath carries a message.

Once.

Twice.

Three times, and a beautiful mushroom cloud blossoms in her mind. A million monsters are incinerated, and the world cleansed.

She raises her head to look across the public square. The cobblestones are empty, echoing. But someone is following her. She knows it.

She pulls herself, shaking, from the memory. She knows why they gave her this one first.

That man had *hated* the Russians. He was one of them, but still he hated them. It had something to do with his father, with more gunshots, with working hard his whole life and being told he wasn't good enough.

She is shaking, shaking, and she has to admit that was worse than anything America has done to her. Not as bad as what it does to its soldiers, but bad.

"What did he tell you?" The colonel doesn't understand how it works, but that's all right. He doesn't need to.

"He wanted to destroy them." The evenness of her own

voice surprises her. "He wanted you to torch them. That's all. He didn't care what happened after that."

Her vision is clearing, returning to the metal table and the suspicious man in front of her. His eyes are narrowed, scrutinizing. Testing. He already knew the answer to this question, she senses. It was another test. And a primer, to prepare her to hate them too.

"Was it real? The threat?"

"The threat to him was real. That was enough."

The colonel sits back, and considers this. "Yes," he says slowly, at last. "Very good. Thank you for your time."

And then she is hit by something else, blindsided without warning.

A roomful of men look at each other. They only look, but their stares say everything. The weight on their shoulders is immense. It is a small room, dark. A bright light over the table.

One of the men in the room is dead now, and it's him who's showing her what he knows. Three breaths into the telephone receiver. The signal that one half of Mutually Assured Destruction has been triggered, calling for the other half in turn.

A huge thing looms, swims through the waters of the room.

The men look at each other. Calculated.

"Do nothing," *her own mouth says, finally, speaking with a man's voice.* "He might be lying. He might've been captured."

"Or this might be our only warning," *another man retorts.* "If we don't act now—" *The question hangs heavy in the air, images of a fireball flash.*

The men look at each other again. Over Moscow, or over Washington. Did it matter which?

"If we don't act now, their bombs will hit home anyway," she says in a man's voice. "Do nothing. Then at least, we'll have done the right thing."

The girl goes under, and the colonel can't get her back up. A fork slides out of her sweater sleeve as she slumps forward. They hadn't given her any knives with her meals, so she must have pocketed this thing. The orderlies who collect the dishes after meals will have to be reprimanded.

The girl makes a pathetic figure as her hair spills over her face again. He comes around the table and shakes her shoulders, hating this moment.

He's been here before: This is how they start to lose all of them. His helplessness comes with fury: He should not be having to round the table like this, having to touch her. But the alternative is calling fewer senior staff to solve a problem he cannot solve himself.

A problem he doesn't really understand. None of them do, and *that's* the most infuriating thing.

They've all done the best they can, haven't they? So why can't they keep these children with the Second Sight, who can see the things they can't?

She doesn't move. Her breathing doesn't even change as he shakes her. Beneath closed lashes, her eyes flutter, and he wonders what she's seeing.

Just outside her bedroom walls, something huge and dark is moving.

"Is there anything we can do?" Evangeline whispers to

the girl who sits on the edge of her bed, glowing faintly in the darkness, staying with her even in the dark.

"We'll keep hunting. Keep finding information. The right pieces. Not the ones they want."

"Won't that make it worse?"

"We'll try not to. You can steer them in either direction, you know. You just have to make sure it's the right one."

Evangeline feels rage again as she thinks about the stolen freedom of her hands, her arms, her legs. The power in them. The things she could have done before they got her, which she may never be free to do again.

If only she'd used the energy of her limbs when she'd had the chance. Where would she be then? Dead, maybe? Like this girl. Arrested? Imprisoned, like she is now?

It doesn't matter. She didn't use the freedom she had. She remembers sleeping under the stars. Immersing herself in something greater. Turning away from the darkness that hummed along distant avenues, from the dark possibilities moving through the air.

She thinks of all the millions of ordinary people who are still free. People who nobody will listen to. People who have nothing that the powerful want, except strong hands and long legs that make the world go round.

They can march, and maybe some of them can sense the dark rivers. Maybe some of them will be braver than she was, or more clear-eyed. Maybe they won't waste their freedom.

And maybe that will be enough.

BLEAK NIGHT AT BAD ROCK

✪

Nick Mamatas

"A gray wolf?" Kiriakou asked one of the two survivors of the ambush. He was a kid, the survivor, and what Kiriakou was having trouble with was not a gray wolf up in the Troodos mountains near Kakopetria—probably half starved and all mad from the gunfire, the pitfalls, and booby traps—but that there was only *one* gray wolf that killed five of the seven-man cell. The kid looked like he had been chewed up and spit out.

"*Nai*," the kid said, not *malista*. *Yes*, but informal, like he was talking to someone other than Captain Kiriakou of EOKA, the Greek Cypriot nationalist movement. Kiriakou had half a mind to jam a thick finger into one of the kid's gashes, just as the Turks had done to him when the British captured him and turned him over. Kiriakou had escaped and climbed the mountain up to Kakopetria, the bad rock, and from his late-aunt's home fought on. And for all that, he gets a "yeah" instead of a crisp "Yes sir!" from a boy with no whiskers!

"There are no wolves in Cyprus," said Christina Papachristodoupolou, who sat in the corner, taking notes. Christina had been to school, thanks to her wealthy father, the copper-mine owner, who was also funding local operations against the British occupiers. She knew many things, except when to shut up, thought Kiriakou. Children and women were no way to win freedom for Cyprus.

"This is a fairy tale," said Christina. The kid moaned. Kiriakou looked at the village doctor, who shrugged in that expansive way village people do, with his palms out and his mouth a straight line.

"Sometimes people see things that aren't there," the doctor said.

"No *mouflonos* did this," Kiriakou said. The wild sheep of the Troodos mountains had great ram-like horns, but no claws, no fangs, and they were still sheep. They ran from men, not toward them with a thirst for blood.

"Sometimes people don't see things that are there," said Christina Papachristodoupolou. She was referring to Galanis, the member of the Cypriot Communist organization AKEL in the other room, whom Kiriakou was having more thoroughly interrogated. Something to turn his blue eyes black.

"That Commie . . ." the kid said. "He just stood there the whole time . . ."

That was that then. The Communists were up to no good. The Soviets were definitely funding the local Reds as well as supporting the Turks, Kiriakou decided. Maybe they had a confederate dress like a wild man of some sort, or used hashish to get the drop on the rest of Kiriakou's boys. Kiriakou hated the idea of killing a fellow Greek who came all the way to Cyprus to fight for the Megali Idea, even an Athenian, even a Communist, but he was going to have to do it. He looked at the doctor, then to Christina, then back to the doctor. "You stay here," he said to him. "Come with me, Miss Papachristodoupolou. I've got something for you to write down for your father." Christina made a face that was half smirk, half sneer. She was rich; of course she hated the Reds.

Kiriakou was disappointed to see that Galanis waved, and through bloodied and loose teeth, even smiled when Kiriakou and Christina entered the room. Sotirios had untied the man, and was sitting with him on the bench in the second room of the small HQ.

"We figured it out," said Sotirios. Kiriakou spent a moment contemplating the relative cost of two bullets, two big stains on the wall of his aunt's two-room home to clean, what Christina would write in the letter to her father, and the fact that until now Sotirios had been as reliable as he was stupid. It's good to have stupid people around in a guerilla war. They do what they're told. He had been told to beat answers out of Galanis, to break his little girlish fingers, not huddle up and play *tavli* with the guy.

"The wolf," said Galanis, whose nasal Athenian accent was not improved by the loose teeth, "is Asena, the gray wolf."

"Oh this will be good!" Christina said. She snapped at Sotirios to slide down and planted her own little bottom on the bench. "Do go on!" She had her pencil ready. "How do you know, if you didn't see anything?"

"There's no wolves at all in Cyprus," said Sotirios. "But tonight, a wolf! And no ordinary wolf."

"It wasn't an ordinary wolf, Captain Kiriakou," Christina said, her tone dry as a mouthful of sand.

"The *taksimists* summoned it somehow. Summoned her. The mythological wolf of the Ashina Turkic peoples," said Galanis. "I studied anthropology and theology at the Polytechnic."

Ugh, a college boy! thought the captain. And the Commie had called the Turks *taksimists*, partitioners, rather than what they were—rampaging Saracens looking to smash icons and turn churches into mosques, rape nuns, and perhaps even reintroduce the sultanate to all of Greece! That last Kiriakou fervently believed, though even Christina's father clucked his tongue at him for that.

"So, you saw Asena, the gray wolf?" said Kiriakou. His hand was on the grip of his sidearm. Galanis's eyes widened. Sotirios, though peering right up at his captain, didn't respond. Christina's sneer vanished, and she scooted away to the edge of the stone bench. "Not just the TMT—the invading Turkish guerillas?" Why give the Red a chance? Christina was scribbling everything down.

The war was confusing. The British wouldn't leave. EOKA was small, but managing. Kiriakou had loved strolling into Spilia back in '55 with what was almost the entire movement of thirty men at the time, firing off a few rounds and leaving under the cover of a lucky fog to let the Brits fire upon and even call an airstrike down upon . . . themselves. He laughed till he pissed himself the next morning to think of it. Recruitment was easy after that. But then the Communists managed to enter the theater of war somehow, and *oh no* they were homegrown Communists, they said so themselves, just leftovers from the Civil War, nothing to do with the godless Soviets who had destroyed their fellow Orthodox. Kiriakou knew Greek Communists were godless too and thus enemies of the Megali Idea. And now the Turks started their own campaign for the island, or their dirty little portion of it anyhow. Anything to keep Cyprus from Greece, anything to keep a fingerhold in the very *omphalos* of the world.

And now, spirit wolves. Kiriakou wasn't normally given to melancholy, but the pistol felt warm in his hand. Maybe a third bullet for himself one day.

"No, no combatants of any type save your own men," said Galanis. *Your* own men, not *our* own men. He was begging to be put out of Kiriakou's misery.

"So you did not see the wolf that mangled Antonis in the other room, that tore five other men apart?"

"That's the answer," interjected Sotirios. "He didn't see anything, you know why? He doesn't believe!"

Kiriakou spat. "I don't believe in Asena the wolf either! Shit on her and the Turks!"

"But you do believe in the supernatural," said Galanis. "As did all your comrades. They were calling upon *panagitsa* to save them even as the wounds appeared on their flesh. I had my rifle, but there was nothing to shoot at. The kid Antonis muttered about it, like a man in the grip of a nightmare, as I carried him down the hill to here. He saw it. Smelled it. He said it spoke to him. He felt its teeth in his flesh, though there was no wolf at all. I cannot explain what really happened, but there was no wolf. I can only say that the men who fell were the ones, who like you, believe in ghosts and peasant superstition."

Kiriakou made the sign of the cross at that, and

blustered, "I do not believe in ghosts or peasant superstition!"

"I think you do," said Galanis.

"This man is very intelligent for a Communist," said Sotirios. He wagged a finger at Galanis, and then dared turn it toward Kiriakou. "The Muslims, they believe in djinn—demons! They summoned one, and it took the form of a wolf!"

"There are no wolves in Cyprus," Christina said. "But surely it is much easier to imagine that the Turks, or even the British, transported one or more over, as mascots or to track us and then attack upon command."

"Ah, but he didn't see the wolf!"

"Surely it is much easier to imagine a lying Communist than an unholy miracle."

"I'm surprised at you," Sotirios said to Christina. "Your uncle is a bishop."

"Do Turkish Cypriots smell so different than Greek Cypriots that a wolf could distinguish their forces from ours?" asked Galanis.

"Yes!" said all three.

"They have demons, we have saints," Sotirios said. "We should gather men from the next village, and ask Saint Mammes to intervene."

"Why Saint Mammes?" asked Christina.

"He rode a lion, a mightier animal than a wolf, through these very mountain passes. It was one of his miracles. You all know, you have seen his icons."

Christina tilted her head to look past Sotirios and glare at Galanis, who shrugged. "This is what you came up with to save your skin?" And then she glanced over at Kiriakou.

"And Captain, this is who you put in charge of interrogations?"

"Shut up, woman," Kiriakou said, cold. He knew better than to bark at her, though he wanted to. The doctor in the other room would be back at the taverna and drinking and gossiping heavily in an hour. The kid wasn't long for this world. Kiriakou realized that as a captain, he was done. He had two men under his command, and one was a Red traitor and the other a simpleton. He could join another cell, be just another man with a rifle and a bedroll. The sidearm called to him again. This was a bad night.

"Even if none of what Galanis says is true, we should be venerating our saints day and night at any rate," Sotirios said. "You all must agree with that! What are we fighting for if not our faith and culture?"

"You shut up too," said Kiriakou. Then he snapped his fingers and pointed at Galanis. "Come with me." Galanis snorted and made to get up. Christina and Sotirios stood as well. There was no use telling them to stay behind—Christina wouldn't listen, and Sotirios couldn't abide to stay in a room alone. Good problem for a peasant with eight brothers and sisters to have.

Kiriakou walked Galanis into the front room and made him look at the kid. "You're going to die now," he told the Communist, but it was the kid who reacted with a groan, while Galanis remained stoic.

"Can you move him?" Kiriakou asked the doctor.

"You and I can move him together," the doctor said.

"Sotirios," said Kiriakou. "Help the doctor. We're all going outside."

Kiriakou led them outside the little village home, and

then around the corner, to the back. Kiriakou's aunt's house was local headquarters because it had only one door and one window to secure, and the back of the home faced a fairly steep cliff. One day the Brits or the Turks might resort to TNT to bring the hill down atop the house and a third of Kakopetria, but it was otherwise a good choice.

Kiriakou peered up into the dark wood, and declared at a dangerous volume, "Asena, the gray wolf! Djinn, evil demon of the Quran! Uhm . . ." he struggled for a moment to remember the Turkish word. *"Bozkurt!"* Kiriakou was shamed that he had picked up so much of the language in his life. Another thought of putting a bullet in his own brain, to clear out the foreign tongue.

"Stop!" Sotirios hissed. "We should be praying to Christ and the Theotokos! Calling for Saint Mammes, not summoning devils!"

Kiriakou turned around. "Insubordinate," he said darkly. Then he turned back to the woods. "Turkish devil, you have failed! Two men yet live! I, their captain and commander, yet live! We will unite with Greece and drive your men out forever, as in Crete! As once we held all of what you call Turkey! We three men! Can you smell the blood of one of them? We await you!" Kiriakou was loud enough that despite the curfew, a neighbor opened a shutter and lifted a lamp to her window to see what he was going on about. Christina frantically gestured with her notebook for the neighbor to put it out and go away, to no effect. Then she picked up a rock and threw it at the neighbor's house. Galanis snorted at that, and tried to share a glance with the doctor, but the doctor was on one knee, checking to see if the kid was still breathing. The lamp went out and the window shutter closed, quietly.

When it was dark again, and still for a moment, Asena emerged from the wood. Now Kiriakou understood. She was a wolf, yes, but one the size of a horse. She inclined her head to meet Kiriakou's gaze. Kiriakou heard a thumping sound behind him. Was it Sotirios dropping to his knees to pray, Christina swooning, or perhaps vice versa?

"You have your land," Asena said. It wasn't Cypriot Greek she spoke, nor the Turkish Kiriakou knew a bit of; it was something older than both but similar to each, a language made for snouts, not the jaws of men. "We want ours. Territory is a thing we all know well."

Kiriakou had not been expecting a political debate. He had not been expecting anything at all except an empty wood and the summary execution of the Communist Galanis, so that the kid could see that he had been avenged before succumbing to his injuries. Kiriakou didn't know what to say or do, so he drew his pistol and pointed it at the great gray wolf.

"Captain . . ." said Galanis. "Are you . . . getting some kind of result?"

"You don't see the wolf?" asked Christina. "You don't *hear* the wolf? It speaks!" It was Sotirios who had hit the ground. On his belly, he started muttering a tearful prayer.

Kiriakou called out, "Doctor, do *you* see?" The doctor just made incoherent mouth noises.

"Captain, if there is nothing there, do not shoot. You'll alert our enemies," said Galanis. "If there is something there, do not shoot, as you'll be wasting a bullet. Your men tried, and they ended up shooting one another."

"There were some bullets I found," the doctor said, "but mostly the poor lads were . . . rended."

"You all talk much but without meaning," Asena said to Kiriakou. "You summoned me. To what end, other than blather?" She snarled, bearing fangs the size of bread knives.

Kiriakou thought quickly. He was going to say something reasonable, explain *That man there says he does not perceive you!* The wolf seemed almost rational, curious. They could parlay. But Sotirios rose up, his quiet prayer now a howl of "Saint Mammes, protect us!" He found a stick and rushed Asena, who with a single chomp, separated Sotirios's head, arm, and shoulder from his body. He broke open like a watermelon dropped from a rooftop.

Kiriakou fired his gun. The doctor moved, then fell somehow. The pistol went flying. A paw pinned Kiriakou to the ground, then the wolf's forelimb flexed and the captain cracked.

The captain cracked was how Christina Papachristodoupolou would describe it later, even under torture. Even when the British let a Soviet visitor handle the administration of the interrogation. *The captain cracked*, which she knew could mean two different things in English.

She lived that night as Galanis flung her to the ground and threw himself atop her. He saw nothing but two men explode and a third blow out like a candle flame when a wayward bullet hit him, and she did not even see that much. Christina felt the wolf approach and lower her muzzle to sniff at . . . not at Galanis, but at her, under him, and then move on. In a single loping step, the wolf joined the usual mountain night mist.

Galanis turned atop her, to face her. It was an intimate gesture, frightening as the wolf had been.

"You see," said Galanis. "Do you understand? It wasn't real."

"You stink of the captain's blood. Sotirios's bones decorate your hair and collar."

"Something happened to them... because they believed. Tell yourself something different. Perhaps they destroyed *their own* bodies because of their beliefs—like in that book by the British author Dickens—'spontaneous human combustion,'" he said, switching to English for the last three words. It took a moment for the phrase to register with Christina.

"If you do not believe, it cannot hurt you," said Galanis. "I don't believe in fairy tales, gods, or monsters. Not Christ, not Asena, not Aphrodite emerging from the Cypriot foam. I cannot be hurt by this threat, nor can any of my comrades."

"That's insane," Christina said.

"No, what is insane is holding to a religion, an ideology, that makes you pray for ghost wolves, victims of all manner of superstition and abuse. Only Communism can win this war and free Cyprus. *Unify* Cyprus! Otherwise, partition at best—torn between Europe and the East and abused by both. You should join me. Persuade your family, your friends. You're an important person in these mountains, Christina Papachristodoupolou," Galanis said, Christina's long surname squeaking through his nasal Athenian accent.

"Check on the kid," said Christina. "Get off me."

"I saved you," said Galanis.

"The kid, now."

Galanis nodded once and clambered off her and walked to the kid, stepping over the prone form of the doctor. Christina had never been so thoroughly manhandled in her life. The peasant boys wouldn't dare, the guerillas knew to be respectful of their financier's daughter, and the Turks had been kept at bay thus far.

But the Turkish djinn, if that's what Asena was, made everything different now. She was vulnerable; her very prayers and devotions weakened her. The *filakto* she kept pinned to her breast made her a target. And Galanis, whipping up a story out of some novel to explain away what had just happened, even though he was the one who had filled Sotirios's head with the idea of djinn and summonings in the first place.

Greeks were religious as a matter of practice rather than devotion, except for the simplest of peasants and the kindest of *yiayas*. Same too of most Turks, who were proud *laicists*, save for the ones who'd sail for Cyprus and fight for their distant cousins. They were fanatics, their hearts burned with the fire of faith. There would be more wolves, more useless bullets, more screams.

So, Communism? Christina picked herself up. She noticed that the village had stayed quiet. Even the most curious knew to keep the lights off and curtains drawn when gunfire and shouts echoed off the cliffs of Kakopetria. The town itself was called *bad rock*, after all.

Yes, Communism could be the answer. Galanis would recruit the guerillas, bring them over from EOKA to

AKEL with promises of materialist immunity to mystic fang and claw. Communism would be the answer. They'd take over the nationalist movement, drive the TMT back to Turkey and let the native Turks live in peace. Then they'd reach out to Greece, to the leftist survivors of the Civil War, and truly unify the nation. They'd eliminate the Church. It made perfect sense. There was only one thing for Christina Papachristodoupolou to do, and so she made to do it.

Galanis stood from where he'd been kneeling, by the kid, and called out to her. "Looks like nothing new from the wolf, just the wounds he already suffered. The captain should not have ordered him moved—Antonis is dead."

"Ah," said Christina, the captain's pistol in her hand, pointed at Galanis. "No witnesses that way." Then she fired.

ZIP GHOST

✪

T.C. McCarthy

Early morning over the highlands was the best time to take peyote caps while both legs hung off the edge, my boots on the slick's skids to feel the engine thrum. A mist rose off the triple canopy jungle. The cap went down, mixing with adrenaline jazz and exhaustion that made the jungle mist seem like cold breath, the fog of dying animals in a rusting meat locker that rose and tried to grab hold of the helicopter any way it could. I started kicking at the stuff and the door gunner grabbed my arm, yanking me back into the chopper and onto my back. He was a Marine. The guy wore a purple wool scarf wrapped around his neck but no shirt, and he leaned over to yell something, his bug-eyed look reminding me of the guy who'd brought me into this gig in the first place.

Over time, the regulation mixture of peyote and syphilis injections chewed at memories. It eroded the innards of brain cells and emptied them into the surrounding fluid so that my predecessor's name had long ago leaked out with every other memory. Only one remained: a vague recollection that he always dropped two peyote caps instead of the one regulation dose. *Two is always better than one, Spence*, he'd joke. *Brighter than bright.*

Someone shouted that we were taking fire. The door gunner leaned forward as far as he could and his bungee stretched to the point of breaking while his machine gun chugged. Every time it shot, the muzzle spat colors. Rainbow streamers broke in every direction until they collected on the chopper roof above me, pooling with the surface tension of mercury. At the same time a tiny unicorn appeared out of nowhere. It splashed through the colors, upside down, but just when I reached up to try and touch it someone grabbed my shoulder.

"It's hot down there!" he shouted.

I nodded. "No doubt. Southeast Asia sucks—even Thailand. It's always hot."

"No; you're totally messed up, sir. *The landing zone.* It's hot, so the pilot wants to abort."

"Negative." I sat up and cinched my boonie hat down, making sure it didn't blow off in the wind, then grabbed my Swedish-K. "We have to go in. Just tell him to find something close by. We're in Cambodia so it's gonna be hairy wherever we land."

Manser. That was the guy's name, the one who now screamed into the pilot's ear to find us another spot. He'd just joined the unit to replace my previous *tonto*, the one who'd had his head ripped off by an angry band of leprechauns. The previous dude hadn't taken his dose of peyote so he never even saw the crazy Irish monsters. We told the guys from the Quartermaster Corps that Charlie had decapitated him postmortem—just one more screwed up episode in a bizarro AOR.

Before I could recall any further memories, the chopper banked so hard it pushed me against the floor, and I grinned at feeling the g-forces; it felt like a bear hug from the universe. Manser returned and slid to the floor beside me, where he started shouting again.

"Why do they make us take peyote?" he asked. "I'm not taking mine. You can barely even function, you're so messed up."

"Manser. I'm going to call you *Man* for short. Did you get briefed into the program yet?"

Man shook his head. "I was with Fifth S-F; they grabbed me from Ben Het and Two Corps said this was a special unit and to follow your lead—do what you say no matter how strange. I'm supposed to get read in after this op."

"Yeah, Man. Strange. Did they give you your shots at least?"

"Yeah, yesterday. I feel sick as a dog, but they wouldn't tell me what it was for."

I started giggling. "Syphilis."

"But I don't have syphilis. Why would they treat me for it?"

"Nah, Man, you don't understand. The shots were to *give* you syphilis—not treat it. The combination of peyote and syphilis gives you vision and keeps you grounded. Reality ain't what you think it is, brother."

Out the door, tops of trees waved in the blast of the chopper wash, and the speed with which they flashed by meant the pilot had decided to go to ground, and fast. I grabbed the nearest strap. Man was shouting something at me but it didn't register over the noise; I pointed at the radio and bloop gun and then mouthed the words *"gear up."* He nodded at the same time his face melted, changing shape and transforming into a rabbit so that I screamed and pointed my K at him, shouting over and over.

"You're a god-damned rabbit!"

The door gunner pushed me before I could shoot. We were still eight feet above a field of elephant grass when he yelled *get the hell out*, and then there was a moment of weightlessness after which my feet hit the ground to send me rolling through the foliage. I stopped to look up. Man's arms spun wildly. He was no longer a rabbit and it looked like the guy was trying to swim through the air as he plummeted. Above him, two Cobra gunships darted back and forth, a pair of angry hornets that were pissed off because they couldn't find anything to rocket. Man hit the ground and the slick banked away, leaving everything quiet.

My Swedish-K felt warm and around me the tall grass waved in the wind, trailing streamers of gold flecks that enveloped me in a display of yellow sparks. My hat was gone. Soon the sun would rise above the grass and burn straight down on me, and it wouldn't be long before Ivan's field sniffers would zero in on this spot, detecting the presence of a field anomaly—me. Someone who'd spent too long locked into this reality, leaving trails of quantum particles with the wrong spin, wrong charge, wrong everything. We had to move before their watchers sniffed us. Fast.

Manser burst through the elephant grass while I was screwing on the K's silencer, and I almost sprayed him with nine millimeter.

"What the fuck?" he whispered. "Were you about to shoot me up there? And they *gave* me syphilis?"

"I'll tell you while we move. Our target is a temple, about a klick from here." I spread the map on the dirt and pointed, ignoring the fact that the peyote was making the map look like it had an eye, blinking at me from a corner of the sheet. "There. Just west, deep inside that triple can, upslope."

"But we're CID. Criminal investigators. Why the hell are we in Cambodia in the first place?"

"We're CID Logistics and Maintenance," I said, correcting him at the same time I pushed westward, shoving grass aside with the K's barrel. "*L and M*. You're now part of a deep-cover unit that only takes the best. Think you have a firm grasp on how the world turns? L and M exists to make sure people keep thinking that, but *you* need syphilis injections and peyote to do the job. Without them, the enemy will rip you to pieces."

"Who?" Man asked. "The NVA?"

"The Russians and their repertoire of fiends. But so far we're looking OK; I saw a unicorn before we dropped in, and that's always a good omen."

"You're crazy. That crap makes you a zip ghost— useless."

"Yeah," I said.

We passed under the first trees to enter the jungle. The gigantic trunks reminded me of pillars that stretched over a hundred feet upward, like the towering columns of a

Greek structure. "That's a good name. Call me Zip Ghost. Or maybe just Zippy. Or Zip."

The jungle dripped shades of green. We climbed over gargantuan roots that snaked in and out of clay, thick wooden things that made me think of sea serpents. I shook that thought, but too late. In less than a second, the peyote grabbed the image and made the damn things move underneath me, rotating and slithering in an attempt to drag me down into muck. It had rained the night before and so every once in a while, the ground sucked at our boots, which sunk at least five inches into a gluey mess and added to the illusion that we moved through an ocean of mud, conquered by monsters. Man muttered something about the cicadas. I wished he hadn't because now *they* were all I could think of. *Man was a prick*, I decided.

The sound grew louder with every step, and there must have been millions of the insects, hidden in the massive trunks and above the first canopy—a thick ceiling of broad leaves that blocked the sun and kept us in a world of shadow. They sounded like high-pitched buzz saws. The pitch increased until it reached its peak and then it died off only to start over a moment later, waves of sound that crashed against the trees and washed over us in a kind of sonic Chinese water torture. I whispered *shut up* over and over, and soon the words calmed me. The noise faded until it formed a vague kind of background hum, much more manageable and, in a way, comforting.

By the time we made it to a clearing, the cicadas' hum had almost vanished, replaced by an intense itching on both palms and the soles of my feet, which had become soaked with sweat and mud that seeped through the boot leather and infused clay into my blood through open sores.

Secondary-stage syphilis, I thought. Soon they'd have to put me in the tank, pump me with antibiotics, and repeat the cycle again to keep me locked in space-time, pinned like an insect to the cardboard of this world.

Manser waved at me to get down. He crawled over and pointed at the center of the clearing with the barrel of his bloop gun.

"What the hell is that?"

"That's a clearing," I said. "Sometimes you run into them. It's called a clearing because there are no trees."

At first Manser stared at me, his mouth open wide. Then he glared. "Are you an idiot? Look at the clearing. It's shaped like a sphere. There's a perfectly hemispherical hole in the ground, and another one up into the trees."

He was right. The peyote added a shimmer to the hot air so it transformed into a soup, as though you'd just stuck your head into an oven filled with fire and water. But there it was: The clearing had the shape of a perfect sphere, with only a ten-foot hole at the top, where a dot of blue sky peaked through and sent a single shaft of light; it formed a beam, shining through clouds of dust and mosquitoes.

"Give me the handset." When Man handed it to me, I heard the hiss of static and pushed the button. It took a few tries. I repeated our call sign until finally someone responded. A moment later I remembered the codes and gave them our SITREP.

It felt like an hour before we got our next order, a curt and clipped response that said everything and nothing all at once: "Proceed with Plan Alpha. Over and out."

"What's Alpha?" Man asked.

I passed the handset back and shook my head. "The big one, the mission to take it all: We're going after Ivan. Take your peyote cap."

"No way," he hissed. "I've got a fever that won't stop and a massive sore where they gave me the injection. This is messed up, sir. What does 'we're going after Ivan' mean? The Russians?"

"Not *the* Russians. A Russian. Ivan Ivanovich. Someone I've tried to kill ten times already; the most evil genius you'll ever encounter in this or any other universe. God. I'm so freaking high right now."

"Screw this. I'm going to check out that hole."

Manser unslung his Swedish-K and secured his bloop gun on his back. When he began to creep forward, I grabbed him, pulling him into the brush. The cicadas went quiet. Without warning, a silence doused the entire jungle in what felt like a layer of foam, muffling even the noise of my breathing.

I pointed at the clearing and then held my finger to my lips so Manser would stay quiet. I reached for my chest pocket to slide out a set of cardboard glasses with thin cellophane lenses. My hands inched upward. A moment later the glasses perched on my nose and Manser looked at me all crazy, like I was watching some Technicolor 3-D movie at the drive-in, smack in the middle of Cambodian bush. I fought against the peyote vision. You had to squint, reminding yourself there was a difference between the reality of the *here and now* and the "other" reality, exposed by the mescaline and syphilis cocktail.

The glasses turned everything pink. Through the clearing I saw bright pinkish-orange streaks, which reminded me of tiny shooting stars. They increased in frequency until the entire area filled with them, obscuring the far side of the clearing behind a blanket of light. It was an opera of colors. Part of me wanted to watch it, just bed down and snap another cap to make it more beautiful, but a voice whispered in the back of my head: *tachyons*.

"Get down!" I shouted, pushing Manser's head into the mud. *"Those stupid mothers are starting to play with tachyons!"*

"You crazy fu—" Man started.

A loud thunderclap cut him off, shaking the ground so hard that it pushed the air from my lungs, and, for what seemed like an hour, I struggled to breathe again, turning my head to the side, toward Manser, opening my mouth wide and inhaling as deeply as I could.

Man looked like a fish. He clutched at his chest and clawed at it, ripping his tiger-stripe tunic open and pulling his green t-shirt down from the neckline, stretching it open. Without warning the air returned. It rushed into the clearing and over us, a warm tide of wind from the valley below that moaned as it coursed through the jungle and between the trees. *But we could breathe again.*

"Eat your damn peyote cap," I hissed.

"No freaking way."

I pressed the suppressor of my Swedish-K against his forehead. It even surprised *me*; I didn't recall doing it.

"Take your cap or I'll kill you myself."

Another thunderclap sounded from the clearing, but it wasn't as violent or loud, and I pushed the suppressor harder into Man's skin. He grabbed the bottle from his pocket, took out a capsule, and swallowed it with a swig from his canteen.

"Happy?" he asked.

I pulled the gun away. "They sent us because a Logistics and Maintenance outpost out here reported signs of tachyons, and then we lost communication. The last thing they said was the word 'Ivan.' Now take a good look at that clearing."

The peyote made it hard to stay angry, but this guy was an idiot. I began to wonder about Man. Special Forces recruits to L and M were always a problem because, at first, they knew everything and were sure they should be in charge. I resisted counting the number of new guys that I'd watched break into insanity on their first op, sent home on a special jet, alone, wrapped in a straightjacket and muttering about demons. They weren't crazy in the strict sense. It's just that some folks couldn't handle the *real* reality.

Me and Man looked into the clearing just as the final thunderclap hit, and a flash of bright light blinded us for a moment, until finally everything came into focus—a nightmare kaleidoscope of sandbags, fragments of a stone temple, trees, and dismembered troops. The entire sphere filled with material. What had been there before now returned in a jumbled way, so that massive trees materialized, upside down, slowly toppling over in every direction at the same time sandbags, rifles, and equipment fell from above. The worst were the people: arms, legs, and torsos. Some men had fused with stone, their heads sticking out from the falling chunks and gasping for air but unable to breathe without lungs that appeared next to them and fell to the jungle floor in pink masses.

There must have been a platoon. Some of them I recognized, and, without thinking, I grabbed Manser by the radio straps and lifted him to his feet. We crept through the jungle, moving around the edge of the clearing but Manser kept staring at the horror.

"Look at my back, Man. Don't look at that shit. Look at me because those guys are gone; they're all hosed up."

"What are we doing here?" he asked. "What did that to those guys? Is that a hallucination?"

I shook my head, searching the ground for something—anything that might point me toward Ivan. "No. That's what tachyon weapons do. Tachyons are particles with a small mass, but they travel faster than the speed of light and open the door to time travel. It must have been a grenade, something small because the area of effect wasn't that big."

"I don't get it. Oh my God, I'm sick."

Man stopped, dropped to his knees, and vomited. I waited for him to finish, then helped him up.

"If you're caught in the blast area, a tachyon weapon scrambles space and then sends the pieces through time—usually into the past, but sometimes into the future like it did here. And you're alive the whole time, until you materialize again, with parts of you turned inside out or fused with a rock, a tree, or whatever."

"The Russians did this?"

"Ivan. He's their star scientist; I've been tracking him

for a year. The guy uses Vietnam, Cambodia, and Laos as proving grounds for his prototypes, and now we have to stop him before he can report the tachyon success to his HQ. We'll lose the war. *Man.*"

"Yeah?" Manser asked.

"Oh, no. I was just saying 'man' because I'm sick of this shit. I've been humping out here for two years and . . ."

My voice trailed off when I saw it: a Russian cigarette. Ivan wouldn't have been so careless, but he had to have a couple of guys with him for security, and they'd gotten sloppy. I picked up the cigarette and smelled it, then pressed my fingers into a boot print in the drying mud.

"Maybe three of them," I said. "They left right after the blast, not bothering to stay for the encore. The footprints head west, deeper inside Cambodia."

I broke into a run, heading into the jungle darkness and leaving the clearing behind, motioning for Man to keep up. He followed closely. This was a dangerous tactic. By running we made more noise than was safe, but we had to make up lost ground to catch them. And besides: Ivan had tachyon grenades. Our only hope was to get as close to him as we could, as quickly as we could, so he couldn't use one of his toys on *us*.

As if reading my mind, Man said, "We gotta get them fast, before they use one of those on us."

"That's the plan."

"Why the peyote and syphilis?" Man asked a moment later.

I could barely talk with the exertion of vaulting over tree roots and running through mud. Man seemed in better shape. He sweated, but this was a young guy who'd kept his Special Forces physique in tune and wired tight like he'd been molded by the gods for one purpose or maybe even this one mission. The peyote began to wear off, so I popped another cap and fought a wave of nausea.

"It keeps us grounded in this universe."

"I don't get it. What do you mean, *this* universe?"

"Man, you have to start getting it. *Dig* it. Our universe isn't the only one, but it's the only one we've got—the only one we control. There are an infinite number of universes, an infinite number of Mans running around doing their thing but with small differences. The physical contents of all these universes barely changes, never jumps out. But our consciousness does. You'll never notice, but at any moment, your consciousness could shift from this universe to another while the other Man's consciousness does the same thing—a multiple-universe game of musical chairs, shifting you from one reality to another. So maybe tomorrow you're in another universe where smoking dope is legal."

"That's too far out," said Manser. "You're just messing with me."

"Not me. But someone up there is playing games. We stop it by taking peyote and dosing ourselves with syphilis. The peyote enables us to see reflections in other universes, and somehow keeps us anchored to this one. As long as you take caps, only a virus can shift you. Viruses worm their way into your brain, change its structure and force a shift. Syphilis stops that. Stay dosed and keep taking your caps, and nothing can force you out of this reality."

"Except a tachyon grenade."

I nodded and ducked under a looping group of vines. "Except that. Logistics and Maintenance stays anchored to this universe to keep it clean; to make it ours and shape it to the extent we can. The only problem is the Russians. They want it bad; they've taken at least one other universe, and L and M has been at war with them since Valley Forge and George Washington. Every time I kill someone like Ivan, the Russians find another guy, train him up, and fix him to our reality. You just stepped through the looking glass, Man. And there's no getting out."

Man was about to respond when the dark jungle greens illuminated with rods of bright light, almost a fluorescent lime color. They bounced off the trees to form a circus of brilliant colors and streaks. Man bowled into me. The blow knocked the wind from my lungs and it took me a moment to realize the Russians were firing on us. The streaks were tracer rounds that now chewed bark off the trees above. Each round made a loud *thunk* when it hit, like some mad lumberjack in a chopping frenzy.

Man lifted his Swedish-K over the log and fired one burst, then another. I screamed at him, pointing at his back.

"Use the bloop gun! Load it with the rainbow-tipped grenade before they tachyon us, you freaking idiot!"

Man fumbled. His hands shook, and it took him a moment to shove the round into the breech, then snap the barrel shut against the stock. He poked his head up during a lull in the firefight to get range, drawing a long burst from the Russians, then flicked the rear sight up. He dialed in a range setting, rested the barrel on the trunk, and angled it upward at about forty-five degrees. Before he fired I tapped his shoulder.

"As soon as you pull that trigger, run."

"Why? What kind of round is this?"

"Trust me. Get on my ass and run."

Man popped his head up to aim and pulled the trigger so the stock slammed into his shoulder at the same time it barked with a hollow kind of roar. We scrambled to our feet. Immediately, the Russians opened fire, but my mind raced through the peyote visions, avoiding the desire to concentrate on a cloud of fairies that danced around my head, laughing. Instead I reminded myself that we had to achieve safe distance. It was better to get hit by a bullet than to be too close to what was about to go down.

A thunder clap behind us nearly burst my eardrums, ringing through my skull at the same time a hurricane-force wind blasted into our faces, throwing us back toward the Russians. We landed hard. It took me a moment to realize we'd landed on the ground next to the same log we'd just abandoned. I looked over to Man, grinning, until I saw his face had gone almost bone white.

"That was a tachyon grenade," he whispered.

"Of course it was. Where did you think the Russians got the idea in the first place? We had to wax them with ours before they tested another one on us, but don't worry."

"Don't worry about what? I mean I'm seeing all sorts of shit thanks to the peyote, and I'm running a fever thanks to the syphilis. What would I possibly have to freaking worry about?"

I pulled a pack of cigarettes from my shirt and lit two,

offering one to Man. "We caught up with them so quickly because they're carrying test equipment and wearing protective suits. They could barely move in that crap." I stood then, took a deep pull on my cigarette, and waved to a naked forest nymph that floated through the air in front of me, doing the backstroke between trees until she waved goodbye and disappeared. "We have to go finish it as soon as they come back."

"How do you know they went into the future?" Man asked.

We crept forward until reaching the edge of a clearing, the one that Man's tachyon grenade had just created. It resembled the hole we found earlier, but smaller. Once I reached the edge, I lowered myself into a depression, hiding as best I could behind a massive root and making sure my submachine gun had a round chambered.

"We tune ours that way. I doubt the Russians have figured that out yet." I glanced down at my watch. "Ten more seconds. Get ready, and this time use your Swedish. They'll most likely be in things that look like spacesuits—protective gear used to prevent their molecules from being scrambled or fused into foreign matter. Shoot the ones holding weapons. We think Ivan never carries a gun, and I want to question him before putting a bullet through his head."

"Screw this. Screw you. This is all insane."

"Man, you're starting to bum me out."

I had just stubbed my cigarette when the thunder roared and wind swept my hair from behind. Again, trees fell from the sky, and some planted in the ground at strange angles to form a kind of wood-and-leaf fun house.

One of the Russians was trapped. Although not fused into them, two trees had formed an X with him pinned where their trunks met. He waved an AK with one hand, trying his best to shoot.

Man took him out with a suppressed burst. Red tracers cut through the Russian's white space suit. Through the glass of his faceplate I saw the surprised expression on his face; it had never occurred to him that he might die in a war and I looked away, blinking to try and erase the image from my mind.

An instant later we crept into the clearing. A grunting from the far side caught our attention and I circled left, waving for Man to maneuver right, until we flanked the noise's source. A second Russian was there. His leg had fused into the side of a tree, and soon his grunting turned into shrieking that he punctuated with a few words, repeating something over and over. I lifted my Swedish and fired into his chest, silencing him in less than a second.

"He must have had a suit defect," I muttered.

Man nodded. "Yeah, but where's Ivan?"

Something white flashed in the jungle. Thirty meters away, a small figure in one of the Russian suits dashed over a series of roots, weaving and dodging as it went. Both of us fired. The bullets streaked by on either side of the figure until one hit an ankle as he dove behind a tree; the bullet passed through, spraying blood. After that, the jungle went still again. Quiet.

"Ivan?" Man asked.

"Yep. Only an egghead would have a girly run like that."

We advanced, careful to check for other Russians, then

crept into the jungle until reaching the trunk where Ivan waited. He'd removed his helmet. Blood stained the area below his right knee, marring the suit's fabric with a red splotch. The man was bald. He had a white goatee and thick round glasses, and Ivan pulled them off, looking up with a grin while he wiped the lenses clean.

"It won't matter," he said in English, his accent thick but understandable.

"Huh," I said to Man. "Ivan speaks English. The others didn't."

"You know me," said Ivan. "And *we* know *you*."

I reached down and ripped a pack from his arms and then placed the suppressor against his chest. "I've been following you for some time."

"So I've been told. Your name is Spencer McWorter, but we call you the hunter. My handlers begged me not to go into the jungle for testing, urged me to send one of my assistants instead because they know how persistent you are. But I had to see the test results firsthand. Tell me: What does your team use to prevent viral shifts?"

"Syphilis," Man said. I grinned; the dude was learning. "And he goes by Zip—not Spencer."

"Ah. Zip. We use typhus. Syphilis is better. You go crazy but it's slow, and at least you can breathe with syphilis. Typhus is pure misery. Here—let me show you something."

Ivan opened a fist to reveal a frag grenade; the pin had been removed but he still clasped the spoon, preventing it from going off. Man and I backed away.

"You can't win," Ivan said.

"You're delirious," I responded. "We just did."

"You postponed it. We now know the secret of your time travel. Of your most powerful weapon. My organization controls not just one universe, but several. Soon the doorway will open to horrors you cannot possibly imagine; horrors, the mere sight of which will drive man mad."

Man shook his head. "You won't drive me crazy. I'm solid as a rock."

"What?" asked Ivan. "I wasn't talking about *you*, I was talking about men—mankind in general. Why would you think we'd want to drive just one man mad?"

I held up my hand. "We get it. It's just that his name is Manser, and so I call him Man. Sometimes he gets confused about whether you're saying 'man' in general, or Man meaning him, Manser. It's complicated."

"What?" Ivan repeated. "Is this some joke? I don't understand. I'm trying to warn you of nightmares to come and you make jokes? What kind of—"

I cut him off with a sprayed burst from my Swedish-K, then Man and I dove behind a tree to dodge the shrapnel from Ivan's grenade. Once it had gone off, Man and I humped it eastward—back the way we'd come.

After a while, we tried calling in a retrieval but couldn't raise anyone; the canopy and humidity were too thick for Man's antenna to penetrate. Man slammed the handset into a pouch. I motioned with my chin to keep heading east, and we pushed on, the sweat now weighing my fatigues and adding to what already felt like an impossible load until we finally broke from the jungle, once more pushing through the high elephant grass where we'd landed. Finally, Man got a signal.

Once finished I handed the handset back and lit another cigarette. "A few minutes out."

"What do you think Ivan meant?" Man asked.

"About what?"

"About us being doomed, and the Russians opening some kind of doorway. I know I'm hallucinating my ass off, but that seemed like a really creepy thing to say. Is it true?"

I drew on the cigarette, then blew a cloud of smoke into the grass, watching as it wound its way through and forced a gnome to burst from cover, coughing loudly as the little fellow sprinted downslope. While I talked, I opened the Russian pack and rifled through it.

"Probably. Ivan's always scheming like that." One by one, I pulled out the pack's contents and held them up for Man to see. "This is a quantum field generator. You use it to open doorways and let in monsters. This is another tachyon-grenade prototype. Our guys will love that one." I pulled one last item from the bag and shook my head, realizing how lucky we'd been that Ivan hadn't had time to use it. It was a small sphere, so black and matte that it seemed to absorb every bit of light from our surroundings, reflecting nothing. "And this is a null phaser. It's a last-ditch thing. Use this and everything in a one-mile radius dematerializes. Forever. Even your soul is destroyed. These are forbidden by treaty, so who knows? Maybe the Russians have turned a corner and we really are doomed."

In the distance I heard the whoop-whoop of choppers, echoing against the mountains behind us. They gave me a momentary feeling of hope.

"*Man*," I said.

"What?"

"What? Oh, I wasn't talking to you, I was just saying 'man.' But what do you think of your new gig? Of working for L and M."

Man thought for a moment and then chuckled. "I could get used to it. I've been watching one of those unicorns for the last few minutes, and the damn thing talked to me."

"Good." I stood and threw a smoke grenade. Thick green clouds billowed into the air; the wind kicked up, forcing the emerald mist to envelope us. "There's just one thing we need to fix."

"What's that?" Manser asked.

"Your nickname. Man is a really shitty one. How about we call you Pita?" I spelled it out for him. "P-I-T-A."

"Pita?"

"Yeah. It stands for pain-in-the-ass."

DENIABILITY

✪

Eric James Stone

September 24, 1964—The Oval Office

President Lyndon B. Johnson dropped the 888-page *Report of the President's Commission on the Assassination of President John F. Kennedy*, which landed with a thud on his desk. "You're saying this thing isn't worth the paper it's printed on."

"That's not what we're saying, Mr. President." Walter B. Smith, director of Central Intelligence, waved his hand to indicate his colleague who was seated in front of the desk with him. "Warren and his commission have created what is necessary for public consumption. Can you imagine the outrage if we told them the truth? We're close enough to the brink as it is."

"So we just let Khrushchev get away with personally ordering the assassination of the President of the United States?" Johnson said.

"No." Smith sat forward in his chair. "We need to send a clear message to the Kremlin that they crossed the line."

He nodded toward Richard Helms, deputy director of plans, and said, "Helms's people have come up with six different ways to take out Khrushchev."

"Like the exploding cigar for Castro?" Johnson said.

"It wasn't explosive; the cigars were poisoned," said Helms.

Smith shot a look at Helms, then said, "That's immaterial. The point is, I believe we must strike back."

"If I may, Mr. President?" said Helms. "Director Smith invited me here specifically, not just because my department would plan and carry out any retribution, but also to present an alternative viewpoint so you could make an informed decision. I am not so sanguine as Director Smith about the idea of assassinating political leaders, particularly the heads of nuclear powers. I think our past experience with Castro shows that assassinations are difficult to pull off, and I think the risks outweigh any possible benefits. That said, if the decision is made to go forward, I will do my best to make those plans succeed."

Johnson frowned, then looked at Smith. "I don't want another public CIA fiasco."

"Mr. President," Smith said, "your predecessor asked me to come back as DCI because, frankly, Allen Dulles made some embarrassing mistakes. His career was as a diplomat—he should never have been put in a position to approve covert operations. My career was in the Army. I was Eisenhower's chief of staff during the war. I know how to plan and execute a mission. We won't try anything without a high probability of success."

Johnson nodded.

"Plus," said Smith, "I spent two years as ambassador to the Soviet Union after the war. I understand the Soviet mentality. Once we take out Khrushchev, they'll know we have the strength and will to retaliate. That will deter them from assassinating other presidents, which I think is the most important goal here."

Johnson turned to Helms. "You really think you can make this work?"

"There are no guarantees in this business," Helms said, "but I'm pretty sure we can pull it off."

Johnson leaned back in his chair. It was about half a minute before he spoke. "Gentlemen, let me explain to you in no uncertain terms: as President of the United States of America, I would never order you to carry out the assassination of the premier of the Soviet Union. So I don't want to hear anything more on the subject. Are we clear?"

Smith smiled. "Clear as crystal, Mr. President. We won't bring it up again."

March 15, 1981—MKUltra Black Site

The vision of the Oval Office fades as Talía Cristóbal wakes from her trance. She is still clutching President Johnson's copy of the Warren Commission report. She forces her hands to unclench and lays the book on the table before her.

"Did you see the meeting at the target date and time, Miss Cristóbal?" asks the man sitting across from her. A black ski mask covers his face except around the eyes, and it muffles his voice a little. He has never given her his name, so she thinks of him as Mr. X.

She nods her head. "But President Johnson didn't order Khrushchev's assassination."

"Well, of course not. It's called 'plausible deniability.' But if he didn't want the CIA to kill Khrushchev, he would have ordered them not to do so. Instead, he said he wouldn't order them to do so and didn't want to hear any more about their plans."

The post-trance trembling in her hands begins, so she folds her arms to hide them from view. "That doesn't mean what you're asking me to do is legal."

Mr. X chuckles. "It is most certainly not legal, from the United Nations charter on down. But there are times when the CIA must do what is necessary, not what is legal." He pulls the Warren Commission report off the table and places it in a briefcase. "I believe you're due for another training session with the chimpanzees."

Talía shuddered. "Please, no. I . . . I will think about what you said, that you need my help."

"Training with the chimps is necessary for that help, I'm afraid. The greater the distance at which you can work, the safer we'll all be. But I will be back tomorrow with another history lesson."

July 15, 1966—The Oval Office

President Hubert Humphrey looked up from his desk as Richard Helms, director of Central Intelligence, was ushered into the Oval Office.

"Thank you for seeing me, Mr. President," said Helms. He took a seat in front of the desk.

"You said it was urgent. Does it have to do with President Johnson's assassination? Have you caught the killer?"

"We have not caught the killer, but it is about the assassination." Helms dabbed sweat from his brow with a handkerchief. "Like President Kennedy's assassination, it was almost certainly carried out by the Soviets."

"The Soviets? Killed Kennedy? But the Warren report . . ."

"Was covering up that the Soviets killed Kennedy."

"But why?"

"If the public knew the Soviets killed JFK—"

"No, I mean why did they kill him?"

"We think Khrushchev did it to show strength within the Politburo. Caving to Kennedy during the Cuban Missile Crisis weakened him."

Humphrey shook his head. "So why would Brezhnev want to kill Johnson?"

"As retaliation for Khrushchev's assassination."

"But we had nothing to do with that! It was part of Brezhnev's *coup d'état*."

Helms said nothing.

"Wasn't it?" Humphrey asked.

Helms said nothing.

Humphrey sighed. "If, hypothetically, the CIA blew up Khrushchev's car, then we actually did Brezhnev a favor. Why would he retaliate?"

"Hypothetically," Helms said, "if the KGB found evidence proving we killed Khrushchev, Brezhnev might feel pressure from the Politburo to retaliate."

"And if, hypothetically, we retaliate by killing Brezhnev, they might retaliate by killing me."

"True."

"But if we don't retaliate, they might think it means

they can get away with it and kill me just to destabilize the country even more."

"Also true."

With his right index finger, Humphrey traced the gold cross on the Bible lying on his desk. "Not five hours ago, I took the oath of office on this Bible, and now you bring me this mess."

"I'm sorry, Mr. President."

"We can't allow this to spiral out of control. As long as I'm President, the CIA is not to assassinate Brezhnev, or anyone else in the Politburo, for that matter."

"Understood, Mr. President."

March 16, 1981—MKUltra Black Site

Talía wakes from her trance, holding President Humphrey's family Bible. She lays it on the table.

"Did you see the meeting at the target date and time, Miss Cristóbal?" asks Mr. X.

"Why are you showing me these things?"

"We have learned from experience that the best, most powerful psychics—like you—do not remain useful if they are forced into using their powers by brainwashing or drugs," says Mr. X. "We must get you to voluntarily agree to help us. I'm giving you context."

"I didn't volunteer to come here," Talía says. As her brain clears, she realizes that Mr. X's voice sounds like Helms from her vision. Could it be him? That would explain why he wears a mask. She almost says the name to see how he reacts, but decides that would be a bad idea.

"If I cannot convince you to join our operation, you'll be released."

"You aren't scared I'll blow the whistle?"

"No. If you're not going to help us, then we can use brainwashing and drugs to make you forget."

"That's a strange definition of 'voluntary.'"

Helms shrugs. "Think of it as an incentive."

"But what you're showing me . . . If anything, it goes against what you want me to do."

"You need to learn to read between the lines. President Humphrey authorized us to kill Brezhnev and other members of the Politburo."

"Are you insane? He said the exact opposite!"

"No, he said we were not to do it while he was in office. Nixon was President during the Politburo Massacre."

Talía remembers learning about the Politburo Massacre in her tenth-grade history class, except the textbook said KGB Chairman Andropov orchestrated it to take power. If the CIA was behind it, though, that would mean . . . "The Cabinet Bomb wasn't really planted by the KKK. It was Soviet retaliation for the Politburo Massacre."

Helms nods. "Blaming it on the KKK allowed President McCormack to unleash the FBI and pretty much destroy the Klan. We made the best of a bad situation." He places the Humphrey family Bible into a briefcase and closes it. "I believe it's time for another session with the chimps."

October 15, 1975—The Oval Office

President Nelson Rockefeller finished wiping the lenses of his black-rimmed glasses and put them back on. He then reached into a desk drawer, and there was an audible click. "The tape recorder is off. So this conversation is off the record."

Richard Helms straightened in his chair. "Yes, Mr. President."

"Does it strike you as odd that in the last twelve years there have been four Presidents assassinated?"

"President Romney's death has not yet been confirmed as an assassination. It's possible Air Force One crashed due to mechanical failure."

Rockefeller waved that objection away. "And, in between those four assassinations, the Soviets have had their leader assassinated three times."

Helms nodded. "That's true."

"Somewhat suspicious, wouldn't you say?"

"Suspicious of what?"

After several seconds of silence, Rockefeller said, "Stop playing games with me, Richard. The recorder is off. You've been DCI during most of this. Was the CIA involved?"

Helms steepled his fingers. "Mr. President, are you sure you want to know?"

"That's why I'm asking."

"In order to preserve deniability, I've been acting under orders from President Johnson not to inform the President regarding CIA assassination plans for Soviet leaders."

"In case you missed it, I'm the President now."

"Very well." Helms sighed. "For the past twelve years, we've been engaged in an assassination war with the Soviets. They started it by killing President Kennedy. We retaliated by killing Khrushchev. So they killed Johnson. To deter them from further assassinations, we escalated things with the Politburo Massacre. They retaliated with the Cabinet Bomb. We then tried to de-escalate by killing Andropov with a poison intended to mimic natural death, but it appears they were not fooled. President Romney and everyone else on Air Force One were almost certainly killed by the Soviets in retaliation."

"Good Lord!" Rockefeller removed his glasses and absentmindedly began wiping the lenses again. "I mean, I thought maybe, but . . . an assassination war?"

"Far fewer casualties than a nuclear war."

"True." Rockefeller put on his glasses. "But, as Martin Luther King said, 'An eye for an eye leaves everybody blind.'"

"I take it you do not want the CIA to retaliate for killing President Romney."

"I'll be very clear: I am ordering the CIA not to assassinate any Soviet leader or government figure, or to be involved in any way with such assassinations. This 'assassination war' is at an end. Do you understand me?"

"Yes, Mr. President."

Rockefeller nodded. "You may go."

Helms got up and walked to the door.

"Oh, and Richard . . ." Rockefeller said.

Helms turned back. "Yes?"

"Since you were acting under presidential orders, I won't hold anything of this against you. But in the future, if a Soviet leader dies in suspicious circumstances, I'll have your resignation as DCI, and if the CIA was behind it, I'll see you prosecuted."

"Understood."

March 17, 1981—MKUltra Black Site

Talía wakes from her trance, holding a pair of President Rockefeller's glasses.

"Did you see the meeting at the target date and time, Miss Cristóbal?" asks Helms, masked as always.

With a trembling hand, she holds up the glasses. "He was not wearing this pair of glasses on that date. But I got to President Rockefeller through them, and then through him I got to the meeting."

Helms shakes his head. "Amazing. None of our other psychics could have done that. You are truly remarkable. So, what did you learn from the meeting?"

"I saw President Rockefeller order you not to do any more assassinations." Despite being groggy from her trance, she realizes instantly that she has slipped up, and tries to cover it. "The CIA, I mean. Which means what you want me to do is against what the President said. Unless, maybe you're not the CIA?"

"Some rogue operation, perhaps?" Helms laughs. "No, I assure you that this is still a CIA operation. And I perceive that this mask is no longer of any use." He removes it, revealing a more wrinkled face and grayer hair than the Helms she has just seen in her vision. "I may not be DCI anymore, but I'm still overseeing this project on the CIA's behalf."

Talía panics. Now that Helms knows she knows who he is, he will never let her go. Instinctively, she reaches out and grabs his gloved hand. The leather is smooth under her fingers, and she tries to use her power to get to him through the glove, to reach into his body like she does with the chimps, but it's as if there's nothing there to reach into.

Helms withdraws his hand from hers. "Were you trying to kill me?"

She tries to think of a lie that will satisfy him, but can't. So she remains silent.

"Good. I'm glad we've established that, in the right circumstances, you are willing to kill. You have become a weapon—now we just need to point you in the right direction." Helms takes Rockefeller's glasses from her and puts them in his briefcase. "Just so you know, we've used brainwashing techniques to prevent you from harming CIA officers."

"I thought you said you couldn't use brainwashing on a powerful psychic like me."

"No, I said we couldn't use brainwashing to force you to use your powers. We can still brainwash you to not use your powers." He stood and picked up his briefcase. "In any case, I think we've made a lot of progress today, so you won't need to train with the chimps."

September 30, 1978—The Oval Office

President Walter Mondale waved Richard Helms toward the empty chair in front of his desk. The other chair was occupied by former President Rockefeller. "Nelson and I have been discussing some issues, off the record."

Helms sat. "I see."

"You've been retired now for a couple of years," said Mondale. "Would you be open to coming back to the CIA, not as DCI, but to take charge of a special project?"

"It would depend on the nature of that project."

Rockefeller said, "Look, Richard, I ordered you to stop assassinating Soviet leaders because I thought that would end the 'assassination war.' But I was obviously wrong. I'm here to show bipartisan support for what the President is proposing."

"Jimmy wasn't just the president, he was my friend," Mondale said, "and since restraint on our part doesn't seem to have stopped them, I am not going to let it slide. Since you've got more experience than anyone at planning the assassinations of Soviet leaders, I want you to head up the project."

Helms nodded. "I believe I can handle that, Mr. President."

"I do have two conditions," Mondale said. "One, the assassinations must be carried out in a way that's not traceable back to us—complete deniability. And two, no collateral damage—wives, children, low-level people just doing their jobs. High-level targets only."

Helms pursed his lips, then said, "There were some projects under development while I was at the CIA that might work. It may take some time before they're ready, but we can probably do it."

"Good," said Mondale. "When you're ready, start with Gromyko and work your way down, and don't stop until they are willing to put an end to this war."

"Yes, Mr. President," said Helms.

March 18, 1981—MKUltra Black Site

Talía wakes from her trance, holding Helms's ungloved hand. She lets go.

"Did you see the meeting at the target date and time, Miss Cristóbal?" asks Helms.

Her mind reels as she tries to take in what she's just seen. She had been so sure that Helms was just deluding himself, carrying out imagined orders. To see President Mondale explicitly give the assassination order makes her reevaluate everything. Last November had been the first presidential election she was old enough to vote in, and she had voted for the Mondale/Kennedy ticket. Finally, she says, "The projects under development, did they include psychics like me?"

"Indeed they did. And drugs and training regimens to strengthen psychic powers. You are the pinnacle achievement of our project, our secret weapon against the Soviets. You can do what President Mondale specified: kill a Soviet leader without implicating the CIA, and without any collateral damage."

"There's no one else who can do this?"

"There are others who may eventually progress to the point where you are, but you started off as the strongest psychic we've found so far, so you're our best hope."

She nods. "I'll do it, then. Do you have an object that belongs to . . ."

"General Secretary Gromyko? Yes. But we won't do it now, we're going to fly to Helsinki, to reduce the distance to reach him."

"You mean, I get to leave this place?" Hope springs up— it has been over three months since she was brought in.

"Of course. But before we do that, we need to check something." Helms looks up at the ceiling and says, "Have Miss Yermakova brought in."

"Miss Yermakova?" Talía asks, apprehensively. Why would they bring in a Russian? Is she going to have to kill someone to prove her loyalty?

"Relax," says Helms. "She was born in the USSR, but

her family defected when she was six years old. She's a patriotic American citizen just like you. She's fluent in Russian, which doesn't really matter in your case, but it's made her very useful to us. You see, she's a contact telepath—if she's touching you, she can read your mind. Once she confirms you're telling the truth about your willingness to work for us, we can leave."

March 21, 1981—Gromyko's Dacha near the Black Sea

General Secretary Andrei Gromyko sat on his bed as he buttoned up his pajama top.

"I think we should go for a swim in the morning," said his wife, Lydia, while taking out her earrings.

"You can go. I have too much paperwork."

"You should have left the paperwork in Moscow."

A pain began in his chest. Heartburn, maybe? He grabbed a bottle of antacid from his nightstand and took three of the pills.

After a couple of minutes, the pain became even worse, and seemed to be spreading to his left arm. He clutched at his chest. "I think I'm having a heart attack."

"Someone, we need help," Lydia called out.

One of Gromyko's bodyguards came in. On seeing Gromyko, he used his radio to call for Gromyko's personal physician.

Two minutes later, the doctor hurried in, carrying a black bag.

Sweat covered Gromyko's face.

After removing a stethoscope from his bag, the doctor listened to Gromyko's chest.

"You two," he said to the bodyguards by the door, "get him into the car. He needs to get to a hospital."

The bodyguards lifted Gromyko and carried him out to a black limousine.

March 30, 1981—MKUltra Black Site

Talía is watching an afternoon rerun of *Bewitched* when there is a knock at her bedroom door. "Come in!"

Richard Helms walks in, a smile on his face. "You did it. A few hours ago, President Reagan spoke with General Secretary Ustinov to express his condolences for the loss of Gromyko. He brought up the 'assassination war,' and suggested that it might be time to end it, so that the leaders of both countries could live out their lives and die naturally, like Gromyko did. Ustinov claimed to know nothing about the assassinations, but agreed it was in the best interest of both sides to have a truce."

"So, I won't have to kill anyone else?"

"No. The CIA can still put your remote-viewing talents to good use, but as long as the truce holds, you can return to civilian life if you so choose."

"I can?"

The television screen changes to show the words *ABC News Bulletin*. A news anchor announces, "President Reagan was shot as he was leaving the Washington Hilton about fifteen minutes ago. We do not yet know his condition, but sources at the scene said he was hit by multiple bullets before his Secret Service detail got him into his car."

"Those . . . Commie . . . bastards." Helms's voice is cold. "I'm afraid you're back on duty, Miss Cristóbal. I'll meet you in the trance room in fifteen minutes."

It only takes her two minutes to get to the trance room. She sits in her seat and starts meditating to prepare herself. If she's going to try to kill Ustinov at this distance, she's going to need all her strength.

A few minutes later, Helms arrives with Vladena— Miss Yermakova. "We're going to take Ustinov down today if we can. If we can't, we'll fly to Helsinki tomorrow."

Talía says, "Do you have something of Ustinov's?"

"He doesn't exactly own me," says Vladena, "but I spent a night with him in Vienna a few years ago. January 5, 1975, to be exact. Is that good enough?"

Talía nods. "I'm sorry you had to do that."

"I volunteered." Vladena flashes a cold smile. "I stole a lot of secrets from his mind."

"OK, sit here next to me. Give me your hand. I'll try to trace into your past until that night, then hook onto him and trace him to the present."

Vladena sits. Her hand is cool and dry inside Talía's grip.

Talía goes into her trance. She finds Ustinov easily enough in the past and traces him up to the present.

March 30, 1981—Bunker underneath the Kremlin

General Secretary Ustinov sat at the head of the table, with the rest of the hastily assembled Politburo. "Comrade Fedorchuk, please tell the rest of our comrades what you have informed me."

KGB Chairman Vitaly Fedorchuk said, "About thirty minutes ago, President Reagan was shot. We do not yet know if he survived."

"Who is responsible for this?" called out one of the junior members.

Fedorchuk continued, "This assassination attempt was not a KGB operation, and the GRU says it was not theirs. We don't know who did it. But the CIA will blame us for it, and they will continue to assassinate us."

Several members of the Politburo began talking at once.

Ustinov pounded the table and the members fell silent. "I spoke to President Reagan this morning, and we agreed to stop the assassinations. But now, they will not believe us no matter what we say. However, we have an opportunity here. Whenever an American president is assassinated, their government is in disarray for an hour or more. Our only realistic chance of survival is to launch a first strike. A submarine-launched missile can destroy Washington less than fifteen minutes from now. Without orders from the President, their military will delay launching their missiles, and our SLBMs will neutralize most of them in their silos."

"This is madness," said the junior member who had spoken up earlier.

Ustinov nodded to Fedorchuk, who walked over to that member, pulled out a pistol, and shot him in the head.

"Any other objections?" asked Ustinov.

No one said anything.

"Give the launch order."

March 30, 1981—MKUltra Black Site

Talía is in her trance. She can hear men's voices speaking Russian. She has managed to focus in on the left coronary artery of Ustinov's heart, but at this distance she has trouble pinching it, and she doesn't think she can hold it shut for the few minutes it will take to kill heart muscle, like she did with Gromyko.

There is an alternate method she learned training with the chimps, presuming Ustinov has developed plaques in his artery. This method requires closer focus, but only for a short time.

"Talía, stop!"

A woman's voice. Calling her name. How can that happen here?

"Talía, you've got to wake up!"

She loses focus on Ustinov's heart. The woman's voice is familiar. Vladena.

Talía wakes from her trance to find Vladena squeezing her hand. A few feet away, Helms is arguing with someone on the telephone.

"I'm back," Talía says. Her whole body shivers. "What happened?"

"Through you, I could hear the Politburo speaking," says Vladena. "They are launching a first strike."

Trying to clear her head, Talía says, "First strike?"

"Nuclear missiles. The first ones will hit Washington in less than fifteen minutes."

"Idiots!" Helms slams down the telephone receiver. "The FBI confiscated Reagan's wallet as 'evidence.' It had the launch codes. And they're having trouble getting ahold of Bush. The Commies caught us with our pants down, and now we're going to lose the war."

"Lose the war?" Talía says. "It's a nuclear war. Everybody loses."

"You're right," says Helms. "But we're going to lose more than they will." He sighs. "If I'd known this was going to happen, I would have done things differently. But we've never found a psychic who was any good at predicting the future."

A half-formed idea sprouts in Talía's mind. "If we had done things differently. Like never starting the assassination war."

"Yes, I suppose. It's my fault, really," says Helms.

"What if . . ." Talía says, then starts again, "Before I came here, I could only do telekinesis with something nearby. After the drugs and training, I learned to affect things far away. What if I could affect things back in time?"

Helms and Vladena stare at her.

"Who would I need to kill to stop this whole assassination war? Lee Harvey Oswald? Do you have something of his I can touch?"

"No," says Helms. "And we don't have time to get something from elsewhere."

"Then who?"

"Do you have to kill them?" asks Vladena. "Can't you just write them a note or something?"

"Killing is the only thing I've learned to do remotely."

"Me," says Helms. "You could kill me. I'm the one who's carried out this war, at least on our side. Kill me in early September 1964, and my department will be in disarray and won't have the plans to kill Khrushchev in place when Director Smith meets with President Johnson."

"Kill you?" Talía finds it strange that the thought

horrifies her, when just a few weeks ago she would have gladly killed him to get free.

Helms holds out his hand. "Do it, if you can. We don't have much time."

Talía calms herself and goes back into her trance. She traces Helms back through time to the night of September 1, 1964. He's sleeping peacefully in his bed, and she decides that's probably the best way to do it. She reaches out with her mind to find his heart and pinch his left coronary artery, but it's as if there's nothing there to reach into.

She tries again, to no avail. Something is blocking her from changing the past.

And then she remembers what Helms told her: They brainwashed her to prevent her from harming CIA officers.

"Talía!" Vladena's voice sounds in her mind. "Hurry. There's hardly any time left."

Director Smith. In the meeting with Johnson, he said he had been brought back to the CIA by Kennedy. And he had been more enthusiastic about retaliating than Helms had been.

She traces Helms forward to the September 24 meeting, then starts tracing Smith back in time. When did he start being a CIA officer again? She doesn't know. So she races back as far as she can go, August 9, 1961—about eight and a half months before she was born. She hopes it's far enough.

"We've lost power," says Vladena. "Helms says that means a nuke has exploded. The shock wave won't be far behind."

Smith is in the kitchen with his wife. She reaches into him, and finds his heart. Fortunately, there's enough arterial plaque built up that she's able to tear off a chunk.

September 24, 1964—The Oval Office

President Lyndon B. Johnson dropped the 888-page *Report of the President's Commission on the Assassination of President John F. Kennedy*, which landed with a thud on his desk. "You're saying this thing isn't worth the paper it's printed on."

"Not exactly," said John McCone, director of Central Intelligence. "It's what America needs right now, to let us heal."

"You think the Soviets really were behind it?" Johnson asked.

"Yes, but we'll probably never prove it."

"I don't like the thought of them getting away with killing an American president." Johnson turned to Richard Helms, deputy director of plans. "Isn't there anything we could do?"

"Director McCone invited me here specifically in case you wanted to take direct action. I must say, though, that I don't like the idea of assassinating political leaders, particularly the heads of nuclear powers. Our experience with Castro shows that assassinations are difficult to pull off, and I think the risks outweigh any possible benefits. That said, if you order us to take action, I will do my best to make those plans succeed."

McCone said, "Mr. President, if we retaliate in kind, who knows where it will end?"

Johnson sighed. "You're right. It galls me, but you're right."

"If it's any consolation," said McCone, "our analysts think Khrushchev won't be in power much longer."

March 30, 1981—Building 2560, Fort Meade, Maryland

In her trance, Talía is on presidential guard duty this shift, so her mind follows President Reagan as he exits the Washington Hilton Hotel. She scans the crowd around him and sees the gunman just as he raises his revolver. He fires six times, but Talía manages to deflect them all away from Reagan. Unfortunately, the final bullet ricochets off the car and into Reagan's body—she manages to halt it less than an inch from his heart.

As he's driven to George Washington University Hospital, she manages to stop some of the blood flow from the wound. Once the medical personnel at the hospital take control of the situation, Talía exits her trance.

She begins to cry. If only she had been faster, she could have prevented Reagan from being hit. Her supervisor comes in to debrief her, but seeing her tears and her shaking, he tells her to rest awhile.

About an hour later, she is overwhelmed by a sudden influx of memories from another life.

It worked, she realizes.

SECOND FRONT

✪

John Langan

★ I ★

1986

From Armstrong Base, the story went, the devastation to the US and Europe was barely noticeable. It was what they told everyone who was volun-told for the lunar front, a kind of fringe benefit, the chance to have a look at things as they really were. Your first earthrise, you saw the black clouds roiling across the planet and, through the occasional gaps in them, the charred stretches of the Eastern Seaboard and the Midwest, of England, of West Germany and France—not to mention, of Poland, of the Soviet republics whose names Sandy had never bothered to learn, of where she was pretty sure Moscow had been—and you realized the damage was worse than you had anticipated (especially with the news reports still calling the beginning of the war a limited nuclear exchange), the destruction so severe as to represent a mortal blow to the countries suffering it, and possibly to the planet as a whole.

Sandy Anderson, Airman, USAF, had come to think of it as the first lie, which had been followed by so many more so quickly she didn't know how to rank the rest. Sometimes, when she was on watch at the western airlock, staring at the banks of monitors whose screens showed the moon's bare surface at near, medium, and far distances, she devised different categories for the flood of falsehoods that had slowed to a trickle but never stopped entirely:

1. There were the minor and obvious: "The food tastes just like homemade."

2. There were the minor but irritating: "The excursion suits don't smell like someone peed in them"/"No one peed in the excursion suits."

3. There were the significant but probably unavoidable: "You'll adjust to the reduced gravity in no time." "The Velcro shoes/the weight belts make it feel like you're back on Earth."

4. There were the significant and irritating: "We're on the verge of beating the Soviets." "They never leave their base."

5. There were the major: "The damage from the nukes isn't as bad as everyone says it is."

6. There were the major and irritating: "We've got this." "You'll be back earthside in no time."

And then there were the lies so profound she couldn't decide how to think of them: "It's the Soviets, not the aliens." "You leave the lobsters alone, and they'll leave you alone." Were these exercises in utter cynicism, an effort at telling the biggest lie possible, or did they represent an equally profound delusion?

If she was on watch with someone she could talk to, Victoria, say, Sandy would discuss the question with her. She would sling her rifle over her shoulder, adjust her weight belt, and check that her shoes were securely velcroed to the floor, lest any sweeping gesture cause her to lift into the air, a phenomenon possible even with the (imperfectly calculated) belt. "Do they just not get it? Is that possible?"

"These are the guys who pushed the button," Victoria said, as if the enormity of the act, the calamity it had unleashed, meant anything was possible.

"But deep-space radar shows the lobsters coming in from the outer solar system in droves. Right after the two global superpowers basically commit mutual suicide. That can't be accidental."

"It may not be accidental," Victoria said, "but it may not be hostile in the way you think. They could be engaged in another kind of activity."

"Like?"

"Maybe they're migrating from one part of the galaxy to another."

"And the attacks on the Russians?"

"The lobsters were hungry. Or they perceived a threat. Or it's instinctive behavior: When you encounter a new life form, you kill those closest to you, in order to intimidate the rest."

"Whatever their motivation, they're still more of a threat than the Soviets."

"I don't know if I'd go that far."

"Best estimates put the aliens' numbers at two to three thousand at the polar hive, with more floating in every day. When did the last deployment arrive at Gagarin?"

"The Reds've already got plenty of troops. If they wanted to, they could probably overrun us tomorrow."

"Why haven't they?"

"Well, the casualties would be pretty high. Plus, you've seen what's left of the USSR. It's a smoking ruin. Given this, you might not be in any hurry to leave the moon. Who called it a magnificent desolation?"

"Buzz Aldrin."

"Desolate it may be on the surface, but at least it hasn't been nuked so much it won't be livable for the next ten thousand years."

"I'm not sure staying in a series of boxes buried thirty meters beneath the lunar surface can be considered living."

"I've been in worse. It's the lack of gravity that's the killer."

"I don't know."

"What?"

"From what I've heard, Gagarin's received a lot more attention from the lobsters than we have. Doesn't sound hospitable to me."

"Think of them as especially persistent cockroaches."

Sandy laughed. "Cockroaches from outer space. The situation goes from total disaster to worse, and it sounds like the title of a movie you'd watch on *Creature Feature*."

Victoria shrugged.

★ II ★

Every now and again, one of the lobsters would scuttle across the Mare Imbrium, the great plain on the other side of the Montes Appenninus, the line of mountains in the lee of whose jagged peaks Armstrong had been constructed. Although visible only on the long-range cameras, the sight of the alien's pistoning legs would cause Sandy to lean forward to the bank of monitors displaying the various cameras' transmissions, the pulse throbbing in her temple as she brought her face right up to the screen's glass. The lobsters didn't resemble their namesakes, exactly. For one thing, each was the size of a pony. For another, they had twice as many legs as the terrestrial crustaceans, a longer set along the edges of their blue-black shells and a shorter set up the middle, as well as two pairs of claws, a larger for fighting and a smaller whose purpose appeared to be for tasks requiring more delicate motion. There were the wings, too, a pair of long translucent structures anchored to either side of the forward sections of their carapaces, which remained folded while they were on the moon, but expanded to enormous sails when they were in space. The wings' purpose had not been definitively established. Relative to the mass of the lobsters, they looked too delicate for flight on any body with substantial gravity. One line of speculation had them as a form of solar panel; another saw them as a communication device. It was strange to think of creatures with their own solar arrays, but from what she had heard, the lobsters were unlike any life form the personnel assigned to study them were familiar with. The clusters of orange fungal-looking growths where their heads should have been appeared to be the centers of whatever decision-making capabilities they possessed. Whether the fungal growths were simply a manifestation of nonterrestrial evolutionary processes, or in a form of symbiosis with the rest of the lobsters, or a type of parasite, Sandy had heard no definitive answer—though Maggie had floated the idea that the lobsters were the equivalent of the suits the astronauts put on any time they had to venture out of the base, vehicles, to transport the fungus. Which was weird, but not any more than anything else these days.

Later, Sandy and the others stationed at Armstrong would hear reports of lobsters having been sighted on Earth in the weeks after Operation Able Archer had precipitated the nuclear conflict for which it was supposed to have been a dress rehearsal. They would hear rumors of earlier sightings in places ranging from Vermont to Nepal, some decades prior, but those provided little enough information to be of any use, except to buttress Sandy's conviction as to the extent of the threat they represented. She wasn't quite as paranoid as Maggie, who argued the aliens had been responsible for tipping the war games into actual war, and had a still more elaborate theory tying them to a massive, subterranean fungus somewhere in the south of France, but Sandy had no problem believing the nuclear exchange between the US and USSR had prompted the lobsters to enact whatever plan they were engaged in.

The first exposure the astronauts—and cosmonauts—had had to this plan had come during a skirmish in the middle of the Mare Imbrium. A Soviet supply module had veered off course and touched down close enough to Armstrong to be worth attempting to reach first. A dozen women and men had piled into one of the large boxy rovers they called "buses" and set out through a notch in the mountains toward the sea. Speed being of the essence, they had traveled light, with minimal armor and weapons. The gamble had paid off, and they had reached the capsule well in advance of the cosmonauts. In short order, they blew the hatch and started offloading the food, armaments, and ammunition. (It was a running joke that the Kalashnikovs worked better even on the fucking moon, and a significant percentage of the astronauts preferred the modified AKs for the surface excursions. But it was as much if not more a matter of depriving the enemy of them.) A quick search turned up a sealed folder with OFFICIAL COMMUNICATION stamped on it in red Cyrillic letters. They took it, climbed back into the bus, and raced for home.

About three quarters of the way there, within sight of the canyon through the mountains, the Soviets caught up with them. Or rather, their short-range rockets did. Behind and to the right, the lunar surface leapt upward in geysers of rock and dust. The cosmonauts had come heavily armed and armored, rolling forward in the vehicles the Americans had nicknamed "turtles," their forces three times those of their foes. There was no point in trying to do anything other than outrun them; however, a second salvo of rockets landed close enough to shred two of the big balloon tires on the bus's right side. While not enough to stop the vehicle, the damage slowed it sufficiently for the astronauts inside to pick up what weapons they'd brought in anticipation of imminent battle. The driver radioed Armstrong for reinforcements, but whether those would arrive in time to do anything more than bag their remains was uncertain to the point of unlikely. The route the bus was now limping along dipped between a pair of low hills, and the captain and lieutenant on board briefly debated stopping to make a stand there. The captain (Ludwig) thought it offered decent cover and would improve their odds of holding out until help appeared, but the lieutenant (Aronson) contended it would allow their pursuers to split their forces and attack them from two sides. The debate was rendered moot by the appearance of a dozen lobsters, streaming across the lunar plain.

From the start, there were arguments as to whether the initial encounter was accidental or intentional. Had the aliens been crossing from one part of the moon to another and essentially run into the Soviet forces, or was this a deliberate interception? Based on the footage Sandy had watched, it was difficult to say. The lobsters were traveling in two lines of six abreast. How the cosmonauts had not seen them approaching, she could not understand, unless it was because the Reds had been so completely focused on the Americans they were drawing steadily closer to. A couple of the aliens scuttled up and over the turtles and kept going; the remainder stopped at various points on the vehicles and began cutting the hulls with their claws. One of the turtles swerved into another, the collision dislodging a lobster; the rest of the aliens continued to work their way into the metal plating. The third turtle sported a ball turret with a heavy-duty machine gun; as the other vehicles attempted to steer apart, the gunner opened fire on the creatures whose claws had already sliced through the armor. The cosmonaut was good, keeping his cool despite the stress of the situation, targeting the aliens carefully. The bullets took the legs off one lobster, sending the limbs spiraling away, though the creature's shell proved more resilient. A stray ricochet struck a lobster in the cluster of growths located where its head should be, disorienting it, causing it to stop peeling back metal plating, turn in a half circle, and tip on its right side. Noticing this, the turret gunner aimed for the same spot on another alien, whose apparent head his bullets reduced to orange pulp. That lobster dropped on its belly and lay, limbs twitching. Before the gunner could focus on a third alien, a trio of the creatures converged on the turret, whose window—and occupant— they cut through in short order.

By this time, all three of the Soviet vehicles had disgorged their passengers, who emerged weapons at the ready. On the bus, Captain Ludwig radioed Armstrong to ask a) if they were seeing this and b) if she should turn about and offer assistance to the cosmonauts. The base had answered that a) they were watching it and b) she should continue back to base. She did as she was commanded, which meant the remainder of the Soviets' fight with the lobsters was recorded not by the cameras on the bus, but by the long-range ones positioned on the mountains. Even on maximum magnification, these reduced the battle to a sequence of low-resolution images. Yet it was still clear the ensuing events had been grim and bloody. The cosmonauts knew where to aim, but the aliens moved with ferocious speed, their claws crushing and scissoring limbs from their foes. For each lobster the Russians took down, eight, nine, ten of their number perished. Finally, a succession of brilliant explosions tore through cosmonauts, aliens, and vehicles alike. The best guess was, what rockets remained in the turtles' launchers had been detonated; whether deliberately or not was anyone's guess. (From the way things had been going for the Soviets, Sandy was fairly confident the act had been intentional.)

Within a couple of hours' time of the bus's halting return to Armstrong, a second bus was on its way out to the site of the cosmonauts' murderous encounter with the aliens. This was the bulky vehicle the astronauts called "the box." Designed to transport hazardous material—say, one of the ten nukes no one was supposed to know were on base—the box was sent out with a single mission: recover as many samples of the lobsters as was safe and practical. Should the Soviets put in a return appearance, the crew was under strict orders not to engage them. No one knew why the lobsters had chosen to attack the Reds, but they had done so while the cosmonauts were engaged in hostile activity. Best not to risk drawing their attention by any similar activity.

As it turned out, substantial portions of the creatures were left, which the astronauts gathered and placed within the box's secure containers. Nor did the Soviets show up; indeed, it would be another day before they ventured out to retrieve their dead. In the interval, the box had been parked beside the entrance to the most remote storage chamber, whose contents were hastily relocated in order for the space to be converted into a morgue/lab. The astronauts transferred the containers holding the alien remains to the empty room, then walked the tunnel connecting it to the main base, where a decontamination station had been hastily rigged. The box was left where it was; a team would scrub it later. Shortly thereafter, another group of men and women, this one consisting of what scientific personnel were serving at Armstrong, walked back up the passage to the new morgue. They brought with them a number of large cases, most of which contained the instruments and equipment they would need to examine the lobsters, and one of which contained a sizable bomb, to be detonated should the aliens prove not as dead as they appeared.

And in fact the lobsters were not fully deceased—or, a part of them was not. The fungal-looking growths, their heads, whose tendrils wound the length of their bodies, had suffered severe damage from the battle and showed no detectable activity. Likewise, the internal functions of the creatures' bodies had stopped. But their exteriors were another story. When the research team pried off sections of the aliens' exoskeletons, they found the undersides covered in coarse milky fibers, which penetrated the pink flesh beneath to varying degrees, in several instances extending deeply enough to connect with the fungal network. Once fully detached from the lobsters, the whitish tubes began to move, swaying this way and that, stretching almost half again their lengths, as if seeking to reconnect with their hosts. Subsequent microscopic examination indicated the tubules were a mix of the organic and the mechanical. The implications of this discovery were unclear. Had the creatures' natural exoskeletons been technologically augmented? Or was the armor itself the enhancement, a form of protective graft? Months after their discovery, the tubes remained reactive, still trying to return to their positions.

★ III ★

You weren't supposed to talk too much about life earthside, especially as it had been before the first nuke cleared the silo. "We've got a job to do now," the officers would say if they overheard you, or, "No point living in the past." When it was just them, Sandy suspected, they were probably as nostalgic as everybody else for the existence burned away by what some of the command staff still called "a limited nuclear exchange." It was true, life on Armstrong was busy, much of its residents' activity taken up operating the machines enlarging the place, digging new tunnels deeper under the lunar surface, excavating new chambers, sealing the interiors, moving equipment into them. Sandy had heard the goal was to increase the population tenfold, from five hundred to five thousand. Given the constant expansion, she had little trouble believing this. Another rumor said their purpose here was not so much military anymore as it was to lay the groundwork for an eventual mission to Mars, which was to be the site of a future colony, one not of five hundred or five thousand, but fifty thousand, five hundred thousand, enough to establish a self-sustaining presence on the planet. The claim was just extravagant enough for Sandy to rate it credible. Earth wasn't doing very well. Sandy wasn't sure she agreed with Maggie's pronouncement that the planet was already dead; though there was no shortage of evidence to support such a claim. The nuclear winter enveloping the globe was thinning what population had survived the war at a dramatic rate, as were the smaller, conventional conflicts that had sprung up in a dozen different locations, consequences of the world's superpowers' inability to manage them, what resources remained to each engaged in continuing by conventional means the war that had been begun with the rising of mushroom clouds. The planet continued to gain new scars, the result of the occasional detonation of further nuclear weapons of varying yields. Given the devastation the nukes had visited already, it was horrifying to think anyone would want to deploy one now. On the other hand, it wasn't as if one more was going to make things substantially worse, was it?

Considering the ruination of so much of the planet, Sandy found it a wonder the supply vessels were able to maintain their monthly schedule with anything approaching regularity. The arrival of a new shipment containing, say, individual-sized packets of banana chips was likely to prompt those exercises in nostalgia the officers did their best to discourage. Standing guard with Victoria, or Maggie, or Adrienne, the taste of the chips lingering on her tongue, Sandy would say, "You ever have banana cream pie?"

To which Adrienne (say) would reply, "Nah. I never liked bananas all that much. Had to eat one every day, which is probably why."

"You had to."

"Yep."

"Okay, I'll bite: why?"

"My mom made me. Said if I didn't have a banana a day, my liver would explode or something."

"Your liver—and you believed her?"

"She was very convincing. Each day, after I walked in the front door, I had to sit at the kitchen table, eat a banana, and drink a glass of water."

"I guess I can understand why you wouldn't like bananas, then."

"Funny thing is, aside from that, Mom never served my sister or me any kind of banana-flavored treat or dessert. It was like, that wasn't what they were for."

"With me," Sandy would say, "it was baloney and cheese sandwiches. That I couldn't stand, I mean. One slice of baloney, one of cheese, plenty of mayo, and two slices of white bread. The baloney was the prepackaged kind, with this thick rind, which would come off when you took a bite, unwind from around the baloney. Ugh." A mock shiver. "I used to dread the sight of one of those sandwiches in my lunch, because half the time, I wouldn't eat them, and I'd be hungry until I got home."

"Bet you'd eat one now."

"You know, I don't think I would. Which sounds strange, but it's hard for me to imagine getting past the disgust. Even here, with things the way they are."

"Huh. I don't know if I could look at a banana, either."

"You didn't eat the banana chips?"

"Nah. Figure I'll trade 'em to someone for something I want. Haven't figured out who or what, yet."

"You know what else I hated? Brussels sprouts."

"Oh, I hear you."

"I used to call them vomit drops. 'Just take one,' my parents would tell me, and I'd try, I swear, I would do my best, but the instant the sprout hit my tongue, it was like,

Nope, there is no way this is going to happen. I had to fight not to gag. My mom would plead with me: 'Come on, honey, just swallow it.' My dad would resort to threats: 'You'd better eat that, or there's no dessert for you.' Eventually, I'd choke it down, but I had to fight every step of the way."

"I hear fresh ones are supposed to be okay."

"Where are we going to find fresh brussels sprouts here?"

"True enough. Although word is, they're expanding the farm. Who knows."

"Sprouts on the moon. Sounds like . . ."

"The kind of thing you'd see on *The Muppet Show.*"

Laughing, Sandy would say, "Yeah. 'Pigs in Space in: Brussels Sprouts on the Moon.' Funny: When we were older, Mom stopped trying with the sprouts. My brothers and I ate broccoli, which she decided was good enough. Right before I left for basic, we had a family dinner, a going-away thing. The conversation turned to the sprouts, how awful they were. My dad didn't have much to say, but my mom? She was *furious* with us. Said she had only been trying to do what was right, give us good, healthy food, and if we couldn't appreciate that, then she didn't know what that said about us. And my brother, Fred—he's the middle child, has always been the smartass—says, 'But Mom, they were *terrible*,' which made my other brother and me burst out laughing. Mom was not amused," she would conclude, the memory causing her voice to thicken.

Adrienne would look away as she wiped her eyes. "It's kind of weird," she would say, "isn't it? how you can have such vivid memories about things you hated."

"Bananas, baloney sandwiches, and brussels sprouts," Sandy would say, almost tenderly.

★ IV ★

Within forty-eight hours of the cosmonauts' first, devastating encounter with the lobsters, *Pravda* broadcast a story claiming their lunar forces had been subject to a treacherous attack by the Americans, who had used new and terrible weapons. The report focused less on the details of the armament than it did on the brutality of the astronauts and the heroism of the Soviets, who had repulsed the assault and driven the Americans back to within sight of their base. From the presidential compound in Montana, the press secretary released a statement denying both the attack and the use of any unconventional weapon by the astronauts. A third party had intervened in a skirmish between American and Soviet lunar forces, the secretary said, and President Haig was still reviewing information and considering his options. Months later, when the administration referred to the lobsters at all, they continued to do so in language that made it sound as if another country had joined the fray, China, maybe, and not an alien species.

"They don't want everyone panicking," Victoria said.

"What 'everyone' is there?" Sandy said. "There's nobody left."

"Not nobody," Victoria said.

"I'm exaggerating. You know what I'm saying."

"Yeah," Victoria said, "I do. Haig and his buddies still

aren't sure what those things are. They don't look like anything we've seen up here before, but could be they're a super-secret project the Soviets were working on that went south."

"From what I hear, the lobsters are unique. I mean, their technology is part of them. If the Russians had that degree of scientific know-how, we'd all be dead by now."

"Maybe so. Or maybe they're an experiment the Reds put in a rocket because of how dangerous it was."

"Frankenstein on the moon?"

"Something like that. Even if the lobsters are one hundred percent, by-God space aliens, we don't know how intelligent they are. I'm assuming this is what's making everyone step so carefully."

"Have you watched the tapes? They sure act as if they're intelligent."

"Don't confuse aggression with intelligence."

"You could apply the same rule to us."

"Well," Victoria said.

★ V ★

In the meantime, the research crew in the converted storage chamber went on with their work. Rumor was, they were focused on the lobsters' armor, trying to figure out what could be learned from it. One of the early lessons of lunar combat had been the necessity of more and better protection for the individual soldier during engagements with the enemy. Up here, the bullet that grazed you on Earth would puncture your excursion suit, or your helmet, or your airpack, with potentially fatal consequences. As a result, astronauts and cosmonauts alike supplemented their suits with bits and pieces of metal cut from the cargo containers whose emptied hulls offered raw material for all manner of repairs and projects. The result was crude, bulky, and unlovely, but offered a modicum of protection from rifle fire and, depending on how far you were from a grenade or rocket detonation, might allow you to survive worse things. A handful of astronauts who had experience with welding were tasked with developing improved suits, which over the course of several months they did, advancing from designs the astronauts called "the trash cans" to ones they christened "the robots." In Sandy's eyes, the modified suits less resembled robots than they did the plate armor medieval knights had worn. With their high, narrow visors, all the helmets were missing were colored plumes. The Soviets did likewise, to similar ends. At point-blank range, neither side's armor was one hundred percent bullet proof, but its presence necessitated the enemy drawing close enough to put themselves in the same jeopardy. Sandy had rarely been in a robot. Her time topside tended to consist in menial tasks performed close to base, for which a standard excursion suit, an update of the model NASA had used for the Apollo missions, sufficed. However, the CO (Colonel Bowman), insisted everyone on base be familiar with the operation of the robots, so under the instruction and accompaniment of one of the sergeants (Gullo), Sandy and two other airmen (Weiss and Fletcher) had pulled on, zipped up, fastened together, and snapped shut the armored suits. The interior of the helmets were wired with simple LED readouts showing oxygen levels, exterior temperature, distance from base, and compass direction; there was also a series of telescopic lenses that could be lowered in front of the visor. Lunar gravity rendered the suits easy to stand up and walk in, but Sandy found hers awkward to maneuver. She could not work out how she would fire with any degree of accuracy the rifle she was carrying, and she spent the hour she was outside in the armor praying the four of them would not encounter a Soviet patrol (or, God forbid, a group of lobsters). Supposedly, the robots had since been outfitted with gas-propelled grenade launchers, each capable of holding four grenades, mounted along the right forearm, with a firing mechanism inside the right glove. Just point and shoot, like when you were a kid.

Honestly, though, there wasn't much worth fighting for up here, a quarter of a million miles from home, with the possible exception of the supply capsules. Neither Armstrong nor Gagarin possessed any real strategic value: the moon was simply too distant for its occupation to be anything more than a symbolic concern, the last remnant of the decades-long contest of one-upsmanship the US and USSR had engaged in following the end of the Second World War. Armstrong had been Nixon's idea, a way to add his stamp to the space program his one-time rival, JFK, had energized during his presidency. Planning to unveil it once it was completed in what he envisioned as a public-relations coup for him and the nation, he had ordered it constructed in secrecy, supplies sent to the moon under the guise of satellite launches and equipment tests, astronauts following them in another half dozen secret Apollo missions. When the Watergate scandal had enveloped his presidency, he had weighed disclosing the existence of the base, only to be counseled against it by advisers worried the project would be viewed as another instance of the President's duplicitous tendencies, not to mention, of funds misappropriated on a colossal scale. Ford had intended to make revealing the base one of his first acts after he was elected president, but Jimmy Carter had been the wrench jamming the gears of that plan. Carter had proven surprisingly amenable to the continued existence of Armstrong, setting up a group to study the feasibility of employing the nascent space shuttle program to ferry astronauts to and from the moon. He had come closest to informing the American public of the base's existence, only to have Khomeini and his followers seize the nightly news for the remainder of his presidency. Reagan had been delighted to learn of the base, content for it to remain classified, and happy to increase spending on it dramatically.

All of which had worked out better than it might have after the warheads had launched. Through some miracle of chance, the bomb aimed at Cape Canaveral failed to detonate, which left the facility to be used when President O'Neill ordered Armstrong's facilities and staff expanded, a directive President Haig had implemented after O'Neill's heart attack had promoted him from the vice-presidency. As far as Sandy was concerned, the order hadn't made much sense, unless there was some truth to the rumors about a Mars colony. It was another instance of the panic that had gripped the nation in the aftermath of the mushroom clouds blooming. The panic had led to the decision to admit women to any and all military roles, and to extensive airstrikes on Cuba and Nicaragua. It had fueled the decision (finally) to announce Armstrong base to the (surviving) American populace, as a somewhat confused means of demonstrating their nation's continuing greatness. The display had been undermined by the Soviets' revelation of their larger lunar facility on the western edge of the Mare Imbrium, built in apparent American ignorance. (There were rumors of spies strategically placed to ensure Gagarin's construction would go unnoticed, which seemed a lot to believe, but was preferable to accepting the alternative, namely, that the US had missed entirely the secret moon base being assembled at the same time as their secret moon base.)

Sandy had arrived moonside as part of the third wave of American reinforcements, which had left the launchpad ahead of schedule after the cosmonauts initiated an offensive against Armstrong—in retaliation, they said, for the Americans' attack on them using the lobsters. Prior to that, she had been stationed at the air base in Plattsburgh, New York, near the Canadian border, which she was sure should have been on the target list for the Russian missiles, unless it was supposed to be struck in the second wave both sides decided not to send. She was in training as a mechanic, learning how to service and repair the fighters, bombers, and transports coming to and going from the base's long runways. When she was transferred to the lunar division, she assumed it was due to her mechanical skills, which had drawn praise and commendations from everyone who had worked with her. In all her time at Armstrong, however, she had yet to be asked to perform anything more than the most basic machine-related tasks. The majority of her time, she spent on guard duty at the western airlock, with excursions every third day to inspect the southwestern solar array and communications box. Although she was allotted three hours to complete her topside duties, she usually was able to do so in half that time, often less. Returning too early brought no benefit but additional work somewhere else, so while she didn't stay out the full time, she walked back to the airlock slowly, pausing to consider the sawtooth line of lunar peaks to her left, leaning back to take in the spread of stars overhead, a bucket of diamonds tipped over a spread of blackout cloth. On the moon's surface, everything was stark, definite. When it hung overhead, the Earth was a study in swirling black opening to more black underneath, with a few spots of blue and green. Somewhere in the darkness stretching endless above her, swarms of aliens were drifting ever closer, their origin a point somewhere in the vicinity of Pluto or possibly Neptune, their extended wings great triangles across whose transparent expanses sunlight flickered and danced. As she was staring into infinite emptiness, there were moments vertigo would rush through her, tipping her surroundings upside down, filling her with dread she was about to fall into all that nothing. She would have to close her eyes, breathe deeply, and concentrate on returning to the airlock some fifteen or twenty-five or fifty meters ahead.

Once in a while, Sandy would be given a temporary assignment helping with the construction of a new tunnel, or sealing a new room, or even harvesting tomatoes from the hydroponics farm. She complained about it to Victoria, who told her not to question her good fortune in pulling light duty, and Maggie, who insisted this was further proof she and all the women on base had been brought to the moon to serve in a breeding program intended to repopulate the Earth. Sandy had her doubts about this, especially since Victoria, who had arrived moonside with her husband, Justin, had disclosed the difficulties of sex in lunar gravity in some detail. Not only had it been a conversation she'd never imagined she'd have, it had been a conversation she'd never imagined to imagine not having in the first place.

As for her part in the retaliation to the Soviets' retaliation, it had yet to happen. She had exited her transport to the moon under active combat protocol, and had passed her first couple of weeks in an adrenaline-fueled fog not helped by the disorientation caused by the change in gravity. As it became clear no attack was imminent, she gradually relaxed into the base's routine, learning how to put on an excursion suit, to exit and reenter an airlock, to monitor and maintain the solar array and communications box and even make rudimentary repairs to them. Since then, there had been a few moments—when she was instructed to train in the robot, when she was assigned a detail tasked with completing a new series of tunnels and rooms with all due haste—she had feared she would soon be preparing to join an assault on Gagarin. But neither led to anything further. In part, this appeared due to the effects of the Russians' aggression having been largely cosmetic, with only the northwestern solar panels suffering damage substantial

enough to impact the operation of the base. It appeared
to have more to do, though, with the attacks the lobsters
had visited upon the Reds in the months since their initial
encounter. Indeed, a not-insignificant portion of
Armstrong's resources had been redirected toward
surveilling these battles (from vantage points of varying
degrees of safety) in order to gather intelligence about
both cosmonauts and aliens. Sandy was not certain, but
had a strong suspicion the observations made were
communicated to the chamber where the lobsters
continued to be studied. Whether the analysis was
progressing in a meaningful way—if it would be of any
help were the creatures to turn their attention to the
American forces—she couldn't say, but it kept the women
and men there busy.

★ VI ★

Sandy heard about Milo the space mouse from Maggie
during one of their shared watches. Because it was
Maggie, she was inclined to take with a generous sprinkle
of salt the report of a rodent to whom the crew in the lab
had succeeded in grafting a segment of a lobster's armor.
Her claim that Milo could survive extreme conditions up
to and including the lunar surface, Sandy discounted
entirely. Within a couple of days, though, Maggie's story
was repeated by all the enlisted personnel. The officers'
refusal to comment one way or the other was not enough
to confirm the information, but was sufficiently unusual
to lend a degree of credibility to it. Assuming the report

was true, or someplace in the vicinity of true, Sandy wasn't sure what it implied. Maggie was certain Milo represented the first step toward pieces of the aliens being attached to *them*, a leap Sandy couldn't bring herself to make. To the best of her knowledge, there was still too much mystery about the lobsters' physiology to predict pieces of their shells being brought into contact with human flesh anytime soon. "Desperate times," Maggie said. She nodded at the monitors. "You see what's going on over at Gagarin."

"Yeah." For the past two weeks straight, the long distance cameras had been picking up flashes of light on the horizon, where the Soviets were engaged in an ongoing battle against what looked to be every lobster on the moon, as well as every one of the aliens touching down on it. It was the longest cosmonauts and lobsters had fought one another; their previous contests had lasted at most a day and a half, usually a matter of hours. What the length of time and number of aliens portended was a subject of debate, but neither side of any argument judged anything good was happening. "You've gotta figure," Sandy said, "the Russians have nukes, same as us. If things get too hairy, they'll detonate one. Or more than one. Or all of them."

"Which would take care of a bunch of aliens and most of the Reds, too. Then what happens when the next wave of lobsters shows up?"

"I hear you. I also heard the extended patrols Bowman's had out the last couple of days have been setting up our nukes in a perimeter defense."

"A nuclear minefield."

"Pretty much. Word is, Lissabet convinced him to keep one back, in case the base is breached."

"How reassuring."

"Nobody listened to me," Sandy said. "Since I got here, I've been saying we had to pay attention to the lobsters. Maybe we could've reached out to the Russians, tried to work with them against the aliens. But no, everyone was like, 'The enemy of my enemy is my friend.' Bullshit. You don't know what the enemy of your enemy is."

"The minute they're done with Gagarin," Maggie said, "they're coming for us."

"Of course they are," Sandy said, "and there's no place for us to go."

"Maybe Milo the mouse will come to our rescue."

"He's probably got an axe of his own to grind with us. Something about the ethics of animal testing."

"Or he'll try to join the lobsters, pass himself off as one of them."

They laughed, but there was little humor in it.

★ VII ★

The attack came a few minutes after the end of second mess, which Sandy had ducked out of early because the fresh Italian pizza the KP was advertising was none of those things—instead, it tasted like Velveeta and ketchup smeared on a burnt slice of Wonder bread. When the klaxons blared and the emergency lights turned the corridor crimson, she was already most of the way to the armory, where she'd been assigned to help with the weekly catalogue of weapons and ammunition. During emergency drills, she was supposed to move to the western airlock, take one of the rifles from the rack there, and await further instructions. Before she could turn around, Sergeant Gullo came pounding down the hall, his feet moving so fast they almost failed to grip the Velcro, turning his run into half a fall. His eyes were wide, the top of his jumpsuit dark with the same blood spattered red on his face. "Anderson," he panted, barely slowing, "you're with me. Now."

She followed him to the armory's low, rectangular space, where Esposito and Dugan looked up from their clipboards. "You two," Gullo said. "Help Anderson and me into the robots. Then help each other suit up."

"Sir—" Esposito began.

"Move!" Gullo shouted.

As Dugan assisted her into the armor, Gullo related the basics. There had been a breach in the men's barracks. A shit-ton of lobsters had rushed through, cutting everyone in their path to bloody ribbons. Captain Weiss had grabbed Gullo, told him to hustle to the armory with whatever personnel he could find and get into the robots. On his way here, another group of lobsters broke through the tunnel Gullo had been moving along and butchered the men he'd gathered. He guessed they had another two or three minutes tops before the aliens showed up here.

How, Dugan asked, how was it possible they hadn't seen the lobsters tunneling down to them?

Because they tunneled *up*, Gullo said. All this time, they'd been watching the aliens attacking the Soviets, laying siege to Gagarin, and the damned things had been digging through the lunar rock below them. They were a whole hell of a lot smarter than anyone had given them credit for.

I knew they were smart, Sandy thought but judged wiser not to say. Dugan slotted the final grenade into her arm launcher. "Good to go," he said, stepping back.

"Good to go." With her left hand, she lowered her visor, activating her air supply and helmet radio. The LED readouts blinked to green life. She spread the fingers of her right hand, felt the trigger mechanism for the grenade launcher against her palm.

Gullo's voice hissed in her ear. "Anderson: You ready?"

"Yes sir."

He advanced heavily toward the doorway, where he stopped, waving at her to join him. "We're going to take up position here," he said. "No point in us running out to find the lobsters: They'll be here soon enough. The corridor will bottleneck them. I'll fire into them, one two three four. The instant I'm empty, you'll take over. The moment you're out, Dugan steps in for you. Then Esposito. In the meantime, I'll be reloading. You see where I'm going with this?"

"Yes sir," Sandy said. "We let them come to us, and we blast them."

"Correct."

By now, Dugan and Esposito were suited up, their radios on. Gullo reviewed the plan with them. When he was finished, Esposito said, "Sir, what if no one comes for us?"

"No one is coming for us," Gullo said. "As far as I know, we could be the only ones left alive on base. These things are fast and they're ruthless. But where we are offers our maximum chance of survival. We're in the robots. We have all the base's firepower at our disposal. Best-case scenario, the lobsters sent a small strike force and we can lure them to our kill zone. Worst case, they've sent all of their forces and it's going to be a very long day for us."

Dugan and Esposito shuffled into position behind them. Everything was moving very fast. Sandy's stomach was acid with terror. *Just do your job*, she thought. *Training, remember your training*.

"Sir," Dugan said, "what's that?"

Sandy knew the silhouettes entering the far end of the corridor three abreast were not her fellow astronauts, because the helmets were wrong, asymmetrical and irregular. Her brain picked up other, more subtle distinctions in the excursion suits they were wearing, differences in the placement of air hoses and glove and boot joints typical of the design the cosmonauts wore. The figures walked hands at their sides, holding heavy tools, wrenches and hammers. The trio following them were similarly armed, as were the three coming into view behind them.

"What's wrong with their heads?" Esposito said.

The lead three walked into the light, and he had his answer. The figures were cosmonauts, or had been, until their heads had been removed and replaced by mounds of orange fungus.

"Oh shit," Dugan said. "Oh shit."

"What the fuck is that?" Esposito said.

"Steady," Gullo said, though Sandy heard the quaver in his voice.

"I think I'm gonna be sick," Dugan said.

"Do not throw up in that suit," Gullo said. "Do you

hear me, Dugan? Do not throw up in that suit. If you do, I will shoot you in the face. Do you understand?"

"Sir, yes sir," Dugan said, gulping.

Gullo pointed his right arm at the Soviets. Smoke jetted from the end of the grenade launcher mounted on his suit's forearm. There was a bright flash, a BOOM Sandy felt through her armor. A cloud of smoke, blood, body parts, and fungus billowed along the hall. Gullo fired another grenade and another. Her suit shuddered. Drops of blood pattered against her visor, which darkened further with each subsequent blast. Through the heavy tint, she could see the ruin of the cosmonauts' bodies, arms, legs, and torsos, scattered around the hallway. Flames flickered on their shredded excursion suits.

"Is that—" Esposito started and Gullo fired his final round. He stepped back from the doorway. "Anderson," he said, heading for the racks of grenades.

"Sir," she said, stepping into position.

Moving with more speed and assurance than the cosmonauts had shown, something swept toward her through the smoke, flame, and carnage. Of course it was a lobster. It was much bigger than she had anticipated, more massive. At the sight of it racing along the hall at her, Sandy both pissed herself and squeezed the palm trigger. Her right arm jerked as the first grenade leapt from the launcher. The projectile, she thought, struck the alien square in its fungal head before detonating, but already she was squeezing the trigger a second, third, and fourth time, her armor rattling as the explosions rolled up and down the corridor. She half stumbled backward as Dugan pushed his way in front of her.

"Is that—" he said, and a lobster lunged out of the smoke at him, all four of its claws grabbing at his suit. "Holy shit!" he screamed. "Holy shit!" While the alien's larger claws gripped his shoulders, its smaller claws tore at his breastplate. Esposito stepped forward, pressed his right fist against the mass of orange fungus, and fired. The resulting blast kicked Dugan, Esposito, and Sandy halfway across the armory. Sandy landed on her back. For a moment, she was unable to maneuver to her feet, her airpack making her a turtle flipped on its shell. Dugan's moans and Esposito's screams filled her helmet. Then Gullo stepped into view, his left hand extended. As he helped her stand, he shot his complement of grenades into the corridor, where another pair of aliens was barreling toward them. He had a rifle slung over his left shoulder; he shrugged it down his arm, into his grip. "Reload," he said to Sandy, shooting into the smoke rolling out of the hallway into the armory.

"Sir." She stepped to the grenade racks. Hand shaking, she eased the top cylindrical projectile from its place and pushed it into the tube on her arm. Dugan's moans were deep, mortal. The explosion that had freed him had fractured his breastplate, driving its shards into his chest. Esposito's screams continued unabated, his voice growing hoarse as he struggled with the agony of the hand the blast had torn from him.

"Anderson," Gullo said.

She slotted the fourth grenade into place. The weapons display in her helmet glowed green. "Ready," she said.

"Light 'em up," Gullo said.

There was an instant—a measure of time less than a second, but not so small it couldn't be noticed—in which

Sandy saw the white light shining along the corridor, a brilliance greater than the noontime sun, pushing through the bloody smoke hanging in the air, and thought, *How did I do that?* The light increased in brightness, was joined by dozens more white beams erupting through holes in the armory's walls, its floor. *The nuke*, she thought, by which she meant the one Bowman had agreed to hold in reserve, which had remained in the bunker under Armstrong's command center, a last-ditch contingency plan it was supposed to require a pair of officers to activate, who apparently had decided the base was lost, and the only option remaining was to incinerate it and as many of the aliens as possible. The armory filled with light that was fire. Her visor opaqued, and she knew no more.

★ VIII ★

Having lost consciousness too quickly to wonder if it was for the last time, Sandy awoke with less surprise than confusion, most of it due to the tapping sound coming from above her forehead. She opened her eyes and through the cracked medium of her visor saw something crawling on her helmet. It was a mouse. The impossibility of this did nothing to prevent her jerking her head back, raising her arms, the motions making not only the nerves there, but all over her body blaze with pain. The mouse leapt off her helmet, allowing Sandy to observe the patches of blue-black shell on his torso and head. *Holy shit*, she thought. *Milo the space mouse.* Looking in much better condition than anyone else in the armory's wreckage: From a fissure in the ceiling, sunlight spilled into the space in a slender beam by whose yellow glow she saw what remained of her companions. Dugan lay where he had fallen, his chest a garden of metal shards. Esposito's armor had melted onto him. Gullo, it appeared, had realized what was happening and dropped into a crouch, only to have the force of the blast skewer his helmet with one of the lobster's limbs. Nor was Sandy in particularly great shape, herself. Her suit was punctured in more places than she could count, and there was an alarmingly large tear on its right side—and the skin beneath. The LED displays in her helmet were dark. She couldn't tell if there was any air remaining outside her suit, but could hear what was left inside leaking. The armor would have done little to protect her from the bomb's radiation; even now, her organs would be liquefying. She wondered which would run out first, her oxygen or her vital signs. Not much difference, in the end. The pain was intense to the point of unbearable. She wished whatever accident had allowed her to survive this long had permitted her to die with Gullo and the others.

At least they had destroyed the lobsters—so it appeared, anyway, from the chunks of blackened fungus strewn around the armory. In contrast, their exoskeletons looked to have come through in (relatively) better shape, cracking into larger pieces. Milo hopped among the lumps of charcoaled fungus, nibbling on those not crumbling to ash right away, jumping onto an exoskeleton for a better view of his surroundings. *How*, Sandy started to think but the answer was obvious: the grafts, the sections of the aliens grown into him. From the remains of the lobsters, the armor wasn't sufficient to survive a full-on nuclear blast, which meant Milo must have been shielded, somehow, perhaps by whatever cage he was being kept in. The lock to that enclosure burnt away in the explosion, he had been free to explore the base's devastation, his grafts enabling him to do so. The situation was fantastic, something out of *Star Wars* or *Alien*, but here he was.

Lying next to her was a smaller fragment of lobster armor. It was upside down, the translucent tubules on its underside feebly wriggling. Sandy reached for it with her right hand, catching it between her thumb and index and middle finger. Milo stopped his explorations to watch her. The piece of armor was lighter than she expected. When her glove made contact with the shell, the tubes began to lean toward her fingers. *This could be a horrible death*, she thought, though given the pain burning her inside out, it was hard to conceive such an extinction being any worse than what was underway in her, already. Concentrating was becoming difficult, the cells in her brain joining those in the rest of her body. If she was going to act, she needed to do so now, while action was still a possibility. She turned the piece of armor right-side up and lowered it to the tear in her suit and self. She felt the tubules writhing against her skin, into her skin, and once again lost consciousness, gratefully, this time.

★ IX ★

Awareness did not return as much as surround Sandy, placing her at the center of a web of knowledge, lines of information glowing around her, intersecting one another at a million, a million million different points. Simultaneously, she was aware of:

1. What she'd thought of as the fragment of lobster armor was a storehouse of microscopic machines, of molecular machines, their functions inscribed on their protons, neutrons, and electrons. Brought into contact with her flesh and the suit encasing it, these devices had activated, beginning an encyclopedia of protocols first to repair the damage to her system and her suit, and then to undertake enhancements to both.
2. The communications network strung among the lobsters—or, more precisely, the fungal intelligences driving them, a vast subterranean fungus in southern France, similar to growths under the surfaces of Mars, Ceres, Europa, Pluto, and half a dozen icy planetoids floating out beyond the margins of the solar system, and something else, something beyond even those dim spheres—
3. A ship, one inconceivably vast, a structure whose length was measured in light-years, its far end lost to perceptions, its surface host to entire civilizations, its rounded head spilling great streams of lobsters (whose true names were unpronounceable, a combination of clicks and screams) toward the sun and its complement of worlds—

Sandy lurched to her feet. For a moment, her vision was full of the great ship hanging in the void, disgorging aliens in clouds like comets. Too much, it was too much.

Her heart hammered, her brain reeled. To have survived nuclear war, to have been stationed on the moon, for God's sake, to have fought aliens and whatever they had made of the cosmonauts, to have survived a nuke, a fucking nuke, to have become whatever she had become—taken together, it was incredible. Yet each stage of the journey that had brought her to this point had been an outgrowth, if a twisted one, of the events prior to it. This was something else entirely, a leap of astonishing, of absurd proportions. Her mind trembled.

Then she was back in the armory's devastation, amidst cracked and buckled walls, a ceiling split by sunlight, her only companions the corpses of her friends, the carnage of their foes. Milo the space mouse was nowhere to be seen. Calmer—her pulse was slowing, her thoughts settling—because of something her suit—her new suit—her new suit that was also her—was threaded to her at a hundred thousand different points—was doing, an impulse it was transmitting along her nerves. The realization brought with it a golden light flaring outside her visor, projecting a 3-D image of the suit and the means by which it was affecting her in front of her helmet—

"Thanks," she said, "but I'm not that interested."

Huh, she thought. The image flickered out.

How responsive was the suit? "Is there," she said after a minute, "a way to slow down what's happening? The invasion, I mean. Is there any kind of . . ."—she searched for the right word—"choke point? A place you could hit and do maximum damage to the lobsters? Sorry," she added.

If the suit was offended, it showed no sign. Instead,

another picture lit in front of her, this one a color display of the solar system. As she watched, the map swept in to Jupiter, to a green, orange, and brown moon swinging around a line of the gas giant's streaming blue clouds. The lobsters were sailing between the planet and its satellite, harnessing Jupiter's gravity to boost their movement deeper into the solar system. Subject to the giant planet's enormous tidal pull, the moon—Io—was pimpled with volcanoes, spewing lava into its nonexistent atmosphere. The aliens didn't display any concern about the moon's eruptions, which fell sufficiently short of their ranks not to be a threat. Were Io to be struck in the right location by a projectile of adequate mass, however, it would become a celestial flame thrower, shooting a blast of molten rock and flaming gas directly into the lobsters. "My own, homemade Death Star," Sandy murmured. Those creatures not incinerated would panic, swerving perilously near Jupiter and its terrible gravity, which would drag them to its cloudy depths. Any who escaped would flee to their bases on Pluto and beyond, leaving a smaller force of aliens to deal with. Which would be another problem, but one she hadn't asked about.

"It's a spectacular plan," Sandy said, "but how am I making the trip from here to there? And where am I going to find something to throw at a moon? Oh, and how exactly am I going to accomplish that? And how are the lobsters not going to pick up on what I'm doing while I'm still a million miles away?"

Shifting through additional images, the suit addressed her questions. Among the modifications to her armor was an in-house propulsion system capable of taking her to

Jupiter and much, much farther. The planet's electromagnetic activity would shield her from the attention of the aliens, who wouldn't be anticipating a threat from so far out in space, anyway. There was a plentiful supply of adequately sized objects orbiting Jupiter. With material scavenged from what remained of Armstrong and Gagarin, it would be possible to build an engine capable of shifting one of those chunks of rock onto a collision course with Io. Putting together the engine would require approximately three weeks, with another six necessary to reach Jupiter's neighborhood.

"Nine weeks is a long time to go without food and water," Sandy said, though she could anticipate the suit's response: It would keep her alive, sustaining her with the energy it generated through the photons bombarding its surface. Later, after Io had been detonated, the invasion disrupted, she could set to work winnowing the alien forces this side of Jupiter. The display ran through possible scenarios: additional asteroid strikes on Ceres, Mars, southern France. Recovering more armor from the lobsters' remains and creating additional soldiers to help her. Building a beacon to call for assistance from one of the lobsters' principal rivals; though there were hazards to involving this group of aliens.

First things first. She would have to find her way out of the remains of the base to the lunar surface, in a suit beyond the limits of her wildest childhood dreams. But whose interior still smelled faintly of piss.

Dedication: For Fiona

ABOUT THE AUTHORS
✪

David Drake served as an enlisted interrogator in Vietnam and Cambodia in 1970. The Army took him from Duke Law School and sent him on a motorized tour of both countries with the 11th Cav, the Blackhorse. He learned new skills, saw interesting sights, and met exotic people who hadn't run fast enough to get away. Dave returned to become Chapel Hill's Assistant Town Attorney and to try to put his life back together through fiction making sense of his Army experiences. Dave describes war from where he saw it: the loader's hatch of a tank in Cambodia. His military experience, combined with his formal education in history and Latin, has made him one of the foremost writers of realistic action SF and fantasy. His bestselling *Hammer's Slammers* series is credited with creating the genre of modern Military SF. He often wishes he had a less interesting background. He lives with his family in rural North Carolina.

Sarah A. Hoyt was born in Portugal and lives in Colorado. Along the way she engaged in all sorts of unlikely occupations, but writing might be the strangest of all. She has published over thirty-two novels (probably thirty-four but she doesn't feel like counting) with various publishers, and over one hundred short stories in magazines such as *Analog*, *Asimov's*, *Weird Tales* and various anthologies. Her first published novel, *Ill Met By*

Moonlight, was a finalist for the Mythopoeic Award, her novel *Darkship Thieves* won the Prometheus Award, and her novel *Uncharted* (with Kevin J. Anderson) won the Dragon Award for Alternate History.

C.L. Kagmi is an award-winning and best-selling writer of short science fiction. She holds a degree in neuroscience from the University of Michigan and spent five years working in clinical research before striking out as a full-time freelance editor and ghostwriter. Her short story "The Drake Equation" was a winner of the Writers of the Future contest and appeared in the bestselling anthology *Writers of the Future Volume 33* in 2017. Her other short stories have appeared in issues 2 and 5 of *Compelling Science Fiction* and the anthologies *Crash Philosophy* and *Compelling Science Fiction: The First Collection*.

John Langan is the author of two novels and three collections of stories. For his novel *The Fisherman*, he was awarded the Bram Stoker and This Is Horror awards. With Paul Tremblay, he coedited *Creatures: Thirty Years of Monsters*. He is one of the founders of the Shirley Jackson Awards, for whose first three years he served as a juror. Currently, he reviews horror and dark fantasy for *Locus* magazine. He lives in New York's Hudson Valley with his wife, younger son, and he isn't sure how many animals anymore. His next collection of stories, *Children of the Fang and Other Genealogies*, is forthcoming from Word Horde in 2020.

Stephen Lawson served on three deployments with the

US Navy and is currently a helicopter pilot and commissioned officer in the Kentucky National Guard. He earned a Master of Business Administration from Indiana University Southeast in 2018, and currently lives in Louisville, Kentucky, with his wife. Stephen's writing has appeared in *Writers of the Future Volume 33*, *Orson Scott Card's InterGalactic Medicine Show*, *Galaxy's Edge*, and *Daily Science Fiction*, as well as at Baen.com. He's written two episodes of *The Post-Apocalyptic Tourist's Guide*, which he also edits. His blog can be found at stephenlawsonstories.wordpress.com.

Marina J. Lostetter lives with the subsequent geek, as well as two capricious house cats. She enjoys globe-trotting, board games, and all things art related. Marina's numerous original short stories have appeared in venues such as *Lightspeed*, *Orson Scott Card's InterGalactic Medicine Show*, and *Uncanny Magazine*, while her sci-fi novels, including *Noumenon* and *Noumenon Infinity*, are available from Harper Voyager. She has also written tie-in materials for the *Aliens* and *Star Citizen* franchises. Marina tweets as @MarinaLostetter and her website can be found at www.lostetter.net.

Dr. Xander Lostetter earned his doctorate in microelectronics-photonics engineering from the University of Arkansas in 2003. He subsequently took his research commercial, building a tech company that developed state-of-the-art power electronics solutions for military and defense programs, spacecraft, satellites, renewable energy, and electric vehicles. Dr. Lostetter has been awarded over two dozen patents, is the author of more than one hundred engineering publications, and has been the recipient of three international R&D 100 Awards for top technology breakthroughs. He currently lives in Arkansas with his wife, Marina, where the two love strategy games, arguing Kirk vs. Picard, and spending their time engaging in all things geeky.

Nick Mamatas is the author of several novels, including *I Am Providence* and *Sabbath*. His short fiction has appeared in *Best American Mystery Stories*, *Year's Best Science Fiction and Fantasy*, *Asimov's*, Tor.com, and many other venues—much of it was recently collected in *The People's Republic of Everything*. Nick is also an editor; his anthologies include *Haunted Legends* (with Ellen Datlow), *Mixed Up* (with Molly Tanzer), and *Wonder and Glory Forever: Awe-Inspiring Lovecraftian Fiction*.

T.C. McCarthy is an award-winning and critically acclaimed southern author whose short fiction has appeared in *Per Contra: The International Journal of the Arts, Literature and Ideas*, *Story Quarterly* and *Nature*. Baen Books released his latest novel, *Tyger Burning*, in July 2019. His earlier debut military science fiction trilogy (*Germline*, *Exogene*, and *Chimera*) was released in 2012 and is available worldwide. In addition to being an author, T.C. is a PhD scientist, a Fulbright Fellow, and a Howard Hughes Biomedical Research Scholar.

Ville Meriläinen is a Finnish university student, author of speculative fiction, and Death Metal musician. His short fiction has appeared in various venues online and in print, including *Orson Scott Card's InterGalactic Medicine Show*, *Pseudopod*, and *Cast of Wonders*. His musical fantasy novel, *Ghost Notes*, is available from Digital Fiction Publishing.

Kevin Andrew Murphy grew up in California, earning degrees from UCSC in anthropology/folklore and literature/creative writing, and a masters of professional writing from USC. Over the years he's written role-playing games, short stories, novels, plays, and poems, and created the popular character Penny Dreadful for White Wolf, including writing the novel of the same name. Kevin's also a veteran contributor to George R.R. Martin's Wild Cards series. His Wild Cards story "Find the Lady" for *Mississippi Roll* won the Darrell Award for Best Novella for 2019, and he has a graphic novel featuring his character Rosa Loteria currently being illustrated, plus other projects in the works he can't announce just yet. He brews mead, plays games, and, like a proper medieval gentleman, has a whippet.

Mike Resnick is, according to *Locus*, the trade paper of the science fiction field, the all-time leading award winner, living or dead, for short science fiction. To date he's sold 76 science fiction novels plus three mysteries, and nine nonfiction books (all of them about writing or science fiction or both). He's sold upward of 280 stories, and even a trio of screenplays. He's edited more than 40 anthologies, and served stints as the consulting science fiction editor for BenBella Books and the executive editor for Jim Baen's Universe. He's edited *Galaxy's Edge Magazine* and Stellar Guild Books for Arc Manor Books. He's won five Hugos, and been nominated a record 37 times; he's also won a Nebula and other major awards in the USA, France, Poland, Croatia, Spain, Catalonia, China, and Japan, and has been shortlisted for major awards in England, Italy, and Australia. His work has been translated into 26 languages so far. He was Guest of Honor at the 2012 World Science Fiction Convention.

Erica L. Satifka's short fiction has appeared in *Interzone*, *Clarkesworld*, and *Daily Science Fiction*. She is the author of the British Fantasy Award–winning *Stay Crazy* (Apex Publications) and the rural cyberpunk novella *Busted Synapses* (Broken Eye Books). If you want to read more of her stories, catch 'em all at ericasatifka.com.

Bryan Thomas Schmidt is a national bestselling author and Hugo-nominated editor whose works include the original novel series the *John Simon* thrillers and the space opera trilogy *Saga of Davi Rhii* as well as official entries in *The X-Files*, *Predator*, *Joe Ledger*, and *Monster Hunter International*. He's edited thirteen anthologies and dozens of novels, including the international phenomenon *The Martian* by Andy Weir. He also authored the writing book *How To Write A Novel: The Fundamentals of Fiction*. He can be found on Facebook and Twitter as BryanThomasS or at his website: www.bryanthomasschmidt.net.

Martin L. Shoemaker is a programmer who writes on the side... or maybe it's the other way around.

Programming pays the bills, but a second-place story in the Jim Baen Memorial Writing Contest earned him lunch with Buzz Aldrin. Programming never did that! His work has appeared in *Analog Science Fiction & Fact*, *Galaxy's Edge*, *Digital Science Fiction*, *Forever Magazine*, *Writers of the Future*, and numerous anthologies, including *Year's Best Military and Adventure SF 4*, *Man-Kzin Wars XV*, *The Jim Baen Memorial Award: The First Decade*, and *Avatar Dreams* from WordFire Press. His *Clarkesworld* story "Today I Am Paul" appeared in four different year's-best anthologies and eight international editions. His follow-on novel, *Today I Am Carey*, was published by Baen Books in March 2019. His novel *The Last Dance* was published by 47North in November 2019.

Alex Shvartsman is a writer, translator, and anthologist from Brooklyn, NY. Over one hundred of his short stories have appeared in *Nature*, *Analog*, *Strange Horizons*, *InterGalactic Medicine Show*, and many other magazines and anthologies. He won the 2014 WSFA Small Press Award for Short Fiction and was a two-time finalist for the Canopus Award for Excellence in Interstellar Fiction (2015 and 2017). He is the editor of the *Unidentified Funny Objects* annual anthology series of humorous SF/F, and of *Future Science Fiction Digest*. His epic fantasy novel, *Eridani's Crown*, was published in 2019. His website is www.alexshvartsman.com.

Eric James Stone is a past Nebula Award winner, Hugo Award nominee, and Writers of the Future Contest winner. Over fifty of his stories have been published in venues such as *Year's Best SF*, *Analog Science Fiction and Fact*, and *Nature*. His debut novel, a science fiction thriller titled *Unforgettable*, published by Baen Books, has been optioned by Hollywood multiple times. Eric's life has been filled with a variety of experiences. As the son of an immigrant from Argentina, he grew up bilingual and spent most of his childhood living in Latin America. He also lived for five years in England and became trilingual while serving a two-year mission for his church in Italy. He majored in political science at BYU (where he sang in the Russian Choir for two years) and then got a law degree from Baylor. He did political work in Washington, D.C., for several years before shifting career tracks. He now works as a systems administrator and programmer. Eric lives in Utah with his wife, Darci, who is an award-winning author herself, in addition to being a high school science teacher and programmer. Eric's website is www.ericjamesstone.com.

Brad R. Torgersen is a multi-award-winning science fiction and fantasy writer whose book *A Star-Wheeled Sky* won the 2019 Dragon Award for Best Science Fiction Novel at the 33rd annual DragonCon fan convention in Atlanta, Georgia. A prolific short fiction author, Torgersen has published stories in numerous anthologies and magazines, including several Best of Year editions. Brad is named in *Analog* magazine's Who's Who of top *Analog* authors, alongside venerable writers like Larry Niven, Lois McMaster Bujold, Orson Scott Card, and Robert A. Heinlein. Married for over twenty-five years, Brad is also a United States Army Reserve Chief Warrant Officer—

with multiple deployments to his credit—and currently lives with his wife and daughter in the Mountain West, where they keep a small menagerie of dogs and cats.

Brian Trent's work regularly appears in *Analog*, *Fantasy & Science Fiction*, *The Year's Best Military and Adventure SF*, *Orson Scott Card's InterGalactic Medicine Show*, *Terraform*, *Daily Science Fiction*, *Apex*, *Pseudopod*, *Escape Pod*, *Galaxy's Edge*, *Nature*, and numerous year's-best anthologies. The author of the recently published sci-fi novel *Ten Thousand Thunders* and the dark fantasy series *Rahotep*, Trent is a winner of the 2019 Year's Best Military and Adventure SF Readers' Choice Award from Baen Books and Writers of the Future. He lives in New England. His website is www.briantrent.com.

Peter J. Wacks, born Zarathustra Janney, then quickly reminted the next day to a sane name on his second birth certificate, never really recovered a sense of normalcy in his life. Peter (or Zarth, whatever, it's cool) has travelled to thirty-seven countries, hitchhiked across the United States (very funny, no, he didn't hitchhike to Hawaii), and backpacked across Europe. He loves fast cars, running 5Ks, space travel, and armchair physics. In the past, Peter has been an actor and game designer, but he loves writing most and has done a ton of it, which can be found by Googling him or checking his Amazon page. Even if it seems a little cyber-stalkery, don't worry, go for it! Since he doesn't think anyone really reads these things anyway, he will mention that strawberry daiquiris, Laphroaig, great IPAs, and really clever puns are the best way to start conversations with him. On a last note, his most recent novel is about a magical Ben Franklin and was released by Baen in 2020. You know, if you're actually reading the author bios and notice this. If you aren't, this just got slightly uncomfortable. Are you still there? The bio is over. Read the next one.

Deborah A. Wolf was born in a barn and raised on wildlife refuges, which explains rather a lot. She has worked as an underwater photographer, Arabic linguist, and grumbling wage slave, but never wanted to be anything other than an author. Deborah's first trilogy, *The Dragon's Legacy*, has been acclaimed as outstanding literary fantasy and shortlisted for such notable honors as the Gemmell Award. This debut was followed by *Split Feather*, a contemporary work of speculative fiction which explores the wildest side of Alaska. Deborah currently lives in northern Michigan. She has four kids (three of whom are grown and all of whom are exceptional), an assortment of dogs and horses, and two cats, one of whom she suspects is possessed by a demon. Deborah is represented by Mark Gottlieb of Trident Media Group.

ABOUT THE EDITOR

✪

Sean Patrick Hazlett is an Army veteran, speculative fiction writer and editor, and finance executive in the San Francisco Bay area. He holds an AB in history and BS in electrical engineering from Stanford University, and a Master in Public Policy from the Harvard Kennedy School of Government, where he won the 2006 Policy Analysis Exercise Award for his work on policy solutions to Iran's nuclear weapons program under the guidance of future secretary of defense Ashton B. Carter. He also holds an MBA from the Harvard Business School, where he graduated with Second Year Honors. As a cavalry officer serving in the elite 11th Armored Cavalry Regiment, he trained various Army and Marine Corps units for war in Iraq and Afghanistan. While at the Army's National Training Center, he became an expert in Soviet doctrine and tactics. He has also published a Harvard Business School case study on the 11th Armored Cavalry Regiment and how it exemplified a learning organization. Sean is a 2017 winner of the Writers of the Future Contest. Over forty of his short stories have appeared in publications such as *The Year's Best Military and Adventure SF*, *Year's Best Hardcore Horror*, *Terraform*, *Galaxy's Edge*, *Writers of the Future*, *Grimdark Magazine*, *Vastarien*, and *Abyss & Apex*, among others. He is an active member of the Horror Writers Association and Codex Writers' Group. This anthology is his first.

GUN RUNNER

A NEW SCIENCE FICTION ADVENTURE FROM
LARRY CORREIA & JOHN BROWN

THE HEART OF A WARRIOR
Soldier-turned-smuggler Jackson Rook has been hired to steal a state-of-the-art exosuit mech for a man known only as the Warlord—but when the Warlord's actions begin to remind him of the foes he fought in his youth, will he still see the mission through?

"[A] no-holds-barred page-turner that is part science fiction, part horror, and an absolute blast to read."
—*Bookreporter.com* on *Monster Hunter International* by Larry Correia

"Servant delivers solid pacing, a great setting, and a smart story that breaks away from genre conventions."
—Brandon Sanderson on *Servant* by John Brown

GUN RUNNER
HC: 978-1-9821-2516-5 • $25.00 US/$34.00 CAN

TIM POWERS